PENGUIN ESSENTIALS
Lucky Jim

Kingsley Amis was born in London in 1922, educated at City of London School and St John's College, Oxford, and worked for a time as a university lecturer. Following the publication of *Lucky Jim* in 1954 he wrote over twenty novels, including *The Alteration* (1976), *The Old Devils* (1986), winner of the Booker Prize and *The Biographer's Moustache* (1995), which was to be his last book. He published a variety of other work, writing about politics, education, language, films, restaurants and drink. Kingsley Amis received a knighthood in 1990 and died in October 1995.

Luke Pearson was born in 1987 and studied illustration at Loughborough University. Since graduating in 2010 he has been working full-time as an illustrator and comics artist. He is the writer and artist of the graphic novella *Everything We Miss* and the all-ages comic *Hilda and the Midnight Giant*, both published by Nobrow Press. He can be found at www.lukepearson.com.

D1237212

Lucky Jim

KINGSLEY AMIS

PENGUIN BOOKS

PENGUIN ESSENTIALS

Published by the Penguin Group
Penguin Books Ltd, 80 Strand, London WC2R ORL, England
Penguin Group (USA) Inc., 375 Hudson Street, New York, New York 10014, USA
Penguin Group (Canada), 90 Eglinton Avenue East, Suite 700, Toronto, Ontario, Canada M4P 2Y3
(a division of Pearson Penguin Canada Inc.)
Penguin Ireland, 25 St Stephen's Green, Dublin 2, Ireland
(a division of Penguin Books Ltd)
Penguin Group (Australia), 250 Camberwell Road,
Camberwell, Victoria 3124, Australia (a division of Pearson Australia Group Pty Ltd)
Penguin Books India Pvt Ltd, 11 Community Centre,
Panchsheel Park, New Delhi – 110 017, India
Penguin Group (NZ), 67 Apollo Drive, Rosedale, Auckland 0632, New Zealand
(a division of Pearson New Zealand Ltd)
Penguin Books (South Africa) (Pty) Ltd, Block D, Rosebank Office Park,
181 Jan Smuts Avenue, Parktown North, Gauteng 2193, South Africa

Penguin Books Ltd, Registered Offices: 80 Strand, London WC2R ORL, England

www.penguin.com

First published by Gollancz 1954
Published in Penguin Books 1961
This Penguin Essentials edition published 2012
001

Printed in England by Clays Ltd, St Ives plc

ISBN: 978-0-241-95684-7

www.greenpenguin.co.uk

Penguin Books is committed to a sustainable
future for our business, our readers and our planet.
This book is made from Forest Stewardship
Council™ certified paper.

ALWAYS LEARNING   **PEARSON**

To Philip Larkin

Oh, lucky Jim,
How I envy him.
Oh, lucky Jim.
How I envy him.

OLD SONG

I

'They made a silly mistake, though,' the Professor of History said, and his smile, as Dixon watched, gradually sank beneath the surface of his features at the memory. 'After the interval we did a little piece by Dowland,' he went on; 'for recorder and keyboard, you know. I played the recorder, of course, and young Johns . . .' He paused, and his trunk grew rigid as he walked; it was as if some entirely different man, some impostor who couldn't copy his voice, had momentarily taken his place; then he went on again: '. . . young Johns played the piano. Versatile lad, that; the oboe's his instrument, really. Well anyway, the reporter chap must have got the story wrong, or not been listening, or something. Anyway, there it was in the *Post* as large as life: Dowland, yes, they'd got him right; Messrs Welch and Johns, yes; but what do you think they said then?'

Dixon shook his head. 'I don't know, Professor,' he said in sober veracity. No other professor in Great Britain, he thought, set such store by being called Professor.

'Flute and piano.'

'Oh?'

'Flute and piano; not recorder and piano.' Welch laughed briefly. 'Now a recorder, you know, isn't like a flute, though it's the flute's immediate ancestor, of course. To begin with, it's played, that's the recorder, what they call *à bec*, that's to say you blow into a shaped mouthpiece like that of an oboe or a clarinet, you see. A present-day flute's played what's known as *traverso*, in other words you blow across a hole instead of . . .'

As Welch again seemed becalmed, even slowing further in his walk, Dixon relaxed at his side. He'd found his professor standing, surprisingly enough, in front of the Recent Additions shelf in the

I

College Library, and they were now moving diagonally across a small lawn towards the front of the main building of the College. To look at, but not only to look at, they resembled some kind of variety act: Welch tall and weedy, with limp whitening hair, Dixon on the short side, fair and round-faced, with an unusual breadth of shoulder that had never been accompanied by any special physical strength or skill. Despite this over-evident contrast between them, Dixon realized that their progress, deliberate and to all appearances thoughtful, must seem rather donnish to passing students. He and Welch might well be talking about history, and in the way history might be talked about in Oxford and Cambridge quadrangles. At moments like this Dixon came near to wishing that they really were. He held on to this thought until animation abruptly gathered again and burst in the older man, so that he began speaking almost in a shout, with a tremolo imparted by unshared laughter:

'There was the most marvellous mix-up in the piece they did just before the interval. The young fellow playing the viola had the misfortune to turn over two pages at once, and the resulting confusion . . . my word . . .'

Quickly deciding on his own word, Dixon said it to himself and then tried to flail his features into some sort of response to humour. Mentally, however, he was making a different face and promising himself he'd make it actually when next alone. He'd draw his lower lip in under his top teeth and by degrees retract his chin as far as possible, all this while dilating his eyes and nostrils. By these means he would, he was confident, cause a deep dangerous flush to suffuse his face.

Welch was talking yet again about his concert. How had he become Professor of History, even at a place like this? By published work? No. By extra good teaching? No in italics. Then how? As usual, Dixon shelved this question, telling himself that what mattered was that this man had decisive power over his future, at any rate until the next four or five weeks were up. Until then he must try to make Welch like him, and one way of doing that was, he supposed, to be present and conscious while Welch talked about concerts. But did Welch notice who else was there while he talked, and if he noticed did he remember, and if he remembered would it affect such thoughts as he had already? Then, abruptly, with no warning, the second of Dixon's two predicaments flapped up into consciousness. Shuddering in his efforts to repress a yawn of nervousness, he asked in his flat northern voice: 'How's Margaret these days?'

The other's clay-like features changed indefinably as his attention, like a squadron of slow old battleships, began wheeling to face this new phenomenon, and in a moment or two he was able to say: 'Margaret.'

'Yes; I've not seen her for a week or two.' Or three, Dixon added uneasily to himself.

'Oh. She's recovering very quickly, I think, all things considered. She took a very nasty knock, of course, over that Catchpole fellow, and all the unfortunate business afterwards. It looks to me . . . It's her mind that's suffering now, you see, not her body; physically she's absolutely fit again, I should say. In fact, the sooner she can get back to some sort of work the better, though it's really too late, of course, for her to start lecturing again this term. I know she'd like to get down to things again, and I must say I agree. It would help to take her mind off . . . off . . .'

Dixon knew all this, and very much better than Welch could hope to, but he felt constrained to say: 'Yes, I see. I think living with you, Professor, and Mrs Welch, must have helped her a lot to get out of the wood.'

'Yes, I think there must be something about the atmosphere of the place, you know, that has some sort of healing effect. We had a friend of Peter Warlock's down once, one Christmas it was, years ago it must be now. He said very much the same thing. I can remember myself last summer, coming back from that examiners' conference in Durham. It was a real scorcher of a day, and the train was . . . well, it . . .'

After no more than a minor swerve the misfiring vehicle of his conversation had been hauled back on to its usual course. Dixon gave up, stiffening his legs as they reached, at last, the steps of the main building. He pretended to himself that he'd pick up his professor round the waist, squeeze the furry grey-blue waistcoat against him to expel the breath, run heavily with him up the steps, along the corridor to the Staff Cloakroom, and plunge the too-small feet in their capless shoes into a lavatory basin, pulling the plug once, twice, and again, stuffing the mouth with toilet-paper.

Thinking of this, he only smiled dreamily when, after a pensive halt in the stone-paved vestibule, Welch said he had to go up and collect his 'bag' from his room, which was on the second floor. While he waited, Dixon considered how, without provoking Welch to a long-lived, wondering frown, he could remind him of his invitation to come and eat tea at the Welches' house outside the city. They'd arranged to leave at four o'clock in Welch's car, and it was now ten past. Dixon felt apprehension lunging at his stomach as he thought of seeing Margaret, whom he was to take out that evening for the first time since she'd cracked up. He forced his attention away on to Welch's habits as a car-driver, and began trying to nourish outrage as a screen for the apprehension, tapping his long brown shoe loudly on the floor and whistling. It worked for five seconds or less.

How would she behave when they were alone together? Would she be gay, pretending she'd forgotten, or had never noticed, the length of time since he last saw her, gaining altitude before she dipped to the attack? Or would she be silent and listless, apparently quite inattentive, forcing him to drag painfully from small-talk through solicitude to craven promises and excuses? However it began, it would go on in the same way: with one of those questions which could be neither answered nor dodged, with some horrifying confession, some statement about herself which, whether 'said for effect' or not, got its effect just the same. He'd been drawn into the Margaret business by a combination of virtues he hadn't known he possessed: politeness, friendly interest, ordinary concern, a good-natured willingness to be imposed upon, a desire for unequivocal friendship. It had seemed only natural for a female lecturer to ask a junior, though older, male colleague up to her place for coffee, and no more than civil to accept. Then suddenly he'd become the man who was 'going round' with Margaret, and somehow competing with this Catchpole, a background figure of fluctuating importance. He'd thought a couple of months earlier that Catchpole was coming along nicely, taking the strain off him, reducing him to the sustainable role of consulting tactician; he'd even rather enjoyed the assumption that he knew something of how these campaigns were conducted. And then Catchpole had thrown her over, right over on to his lap. In that posture his destiny as the only current recipient of these unmanning questions and confessions could hardly be eluded.

Those questions . . . Although he wasn't allowed to smoke another cigarette until five o'clock, Dixon lit one now as he remembered the first series, propounded six months or more ago; about the beginning of last December it had been, seven or eight weeks after he took up his appointment. 'Do you like coming to see me?' was the first he could recall, and it had been easy as well as truthful to answer 'Yes'. Then there'd been ones like 'Do you think we get on well together?' and 'Am I the only girl you know in this place?' and once, when he'd asked her out for the third consecutive evening, 'Are we going to go on seeing so much of each other?' His first qualms had dated from then, but before that and for some time after he'd thought how much simpler this kind of honesty and straightforwardness made the awful business of getting on with women. And the same had seemed true of the confessions: 'I do enjoy being with you', 'I don't get on with men as a rule', 'Don't laugh at me if I say I think the Board did a better job than they knew when they appointed you'. He hadn't wanted to laugh then, nor did he want to now. What would she be wearing this evening? He could just about bring himself to praise anything but the green Paisley frock in combination with the low-heeled, quasi-velvet shoes.

Where was Welch? The old man was well known for an incurable evader. Dixon flung himself up the staircase, past the memorial plaques, and along the deserted corridors, but the familiar low-ceilinged room was empty. He clattered down the back stairs, an escape-route he often used himself, and into the Staff Cloakroom. Welch was in there, stooped secretively over a wash-basin. 'Ah, just caught you,' Dixon said convivially. 'Thought you'd gone without me. Professor,' he added, nearly too late.

The other raised his narrow face, distorted with wonder. 'Gone?' he asked. 'You're . . .'

'You're taking me home for tea,' Dixon enunciated. 'We arranged it on Monday, at coffee-time, in the Common Room.' He caught sight of his own face in the wall-mirror and was surprised to see that it wore an expression of eager friendliness.

Welch had been flicking water from his hands, a movement he now arrested. He looked like an African savage being shown a simple conjuring trick. He said: 'Coffee-time?'

'Yes, on Monday,' Dixon answered him, putting his hands into his pockets and bunching the fists.

'Oh,' Welch said, and looked at Dixon for the first time. 'Oh. Did we say this afternoon?' He turned aside to a streaked roller-towel and began a slow drying of his hands, watching Dixon alertly.

'That's right, Professor. Hope it's still convenient.'

'Oh, it's convenient enough,' Welch said in an unnaturally quiet voice.

'Good,' Dixon said, 'I'm looking forward to it,' and took his dirty old raincoat from a hook in the wall.

Welch's manner was still a little veiled, but he was obviously recovering quickly, and managed quite soon to pick up his 'bag' and put his fawn fishing-hat on his head. 'We'll go down in my car,' he offered.

'That'll be nice.'

Outside the building they turned along a gravel drive and went up to the car where it was parked with a few others. Dixon stared about him while Welch looked thoroughly for his keys. An ill-kept lawn ran down in front of them to a row of amputated railings, beyond which was College Road and the town cemetery, a conjunction responsible for some popular local jokes. Lecturers were fond of lauding to their students the comparative receptivity to facts of 'the Honours class over the road', while the parallel between the occupations of graveyard attendant and custodian of learning was one which often suggested itself to others besides the students.

As Dixon watched, a bus passed slowly up the hill in the mild May sunshine, bound for the small town where the Welches lived. Dixon betted himself it would be there before them. A roaring voice began to sing behind one of the windows above his head; it sounded like, and presumably might even be, Barclay, the Professor of Music.

A minute later Dixon was sitting listening to a sound like the ringing of a cracked door-bell as Welch pulled at the starter. This died away into a treble humming that seemed to involve every component of the car. Welch tried again; this time the effect was of beer-bottles jerkily belaboured. Before Dixon could do more than close his eyes he was pressed firmly back against the seat, and his cigarette, still burning, was cuffed out of his hand into some interstice of the floor. With a tearing of gravel under the wheels the car burst from a standstill towards the grass verge, which Welch ran over briefly before turning down the drive. They moved towards the road at walking pace, the engine maintaining a loud lowing sound which caused a late group of students, most of them wearing the yellow and green College scarf, to stare after them from the small covered-in space beside the lodge where sports notices were posted.

They climbed College Road, holding to the middle of the highway. The unavailing hoots of a lorry behind them made Dixon look furtively at Welch, whose face, he saw with passion, held an expression of calm assurance, like an old quartermaster's in rough weather. Dixon shut his eyes again. He was hoping that when Welch had made the second of the two maladroit gear-changes which lay ahead of him, the conversation would turn in some other direction than the academic. He even thought he'd rather hear some more about music or the doings of Welch's sons, the effeminate writing Michel and the bearded pacifist painting Bertrand whom Margaret had described to him. But whatever the subject for discussion might be, Dixon knew that before the journey ended he'd find his face becoming creased and flabby, like an old bag, with the strain of making it smile and show interest and speak its few permitted words, of steering it between a collapse into helpless fatigue and a tautening with anarchic fury.

'Oh . . . uh . . . Dixon.'

Dixon opened his eyes, doing everything possible with the side of his face away from Welch, everything which might help to relieve his feelings in advance. 'Yes, Professor?'

'I was wondering about that article of yours.'

'Oh yes. I don't . . .'

'Have you heard from Partington yet?'

'Well yes, actually I sent it to him first of all, if you remember, and he said the pressure of other stuff was . . .'

'What?'

Dixon had lowered his voice below the medium shout required by the noise of the car, in an attempt to half-conceal from Welch Welch's own lapse of memory, and so protect himself. Now he had to bawl out: 'I told you he said he couldn't find room for it.'

'Oh, couldn't he? Couldn't he? Well, of course they do get a lot of the most . . . a most terrific volume of stuff sent to them, you know. Still, I suppose if anything really took their eye, then they . . . they . . . Have you sent it off to anyone else?'

'Yes, that Caton chap who advertised in the *T.L.S.* a couple of months ago. Starting up a new historical review with an international bias, or something. I thought I'd get in straight away. After all, a new journal can't very well be bunged up as far ahead as all the ones I've . . .'

'Ah yes, a new journal might be worth trying. There was one advertised in the *Times Literary Supplement* a little while ago. Paton or some such name the editor fellow was called. You might have a go at him, now that it doesn't seem as if any of the more established reviews have got room for your . . . effort. Let's see now; what's the exact title you've given it?'

Dixon looked out of the window at the fields wheeling past, bright green after a wet April. It wasn't the double-exposure effect of the last half-minute's talk that had dumbfounded him, for such incidents formed the staple material of Welch colloquies; it was the prospect of reciting the title of the article he'd written. It was a perfect title, in that it crystallized the article's niggling mindlessness, its funereal parade of yawn-enforcing facts, the pseudo-light it threw upon non-problems. Dixon had read, or begun to read, dozens like it, but his own seemed worse than most in its air of being convinced of its own usefulness and significance. 'In considering this strangely neglected topic,' it began. This what neglected topic? This strangely what topic? This strangely neglected what? His thinking all this without having defiled and set fire to the typescript only made him appear to himself as more of a hypocrite and fool. 'Let's see,' he echoed Welch in a pretended effort of memory: 'oh yes; *The Economic Influence of the Developments in Shipbuilding Techniques, 1450 to 1485.* After all, that's what it's . . .'

Unable to finish his sentence, he looked to his left again to find a man's face staring into his own from about nine inches away. The face, which filled with alarm as he gazed, belonged to the driver of a van which Welch had elected to pass on a sharp bend between two stone walls. A huge bus now swung into view from further round the bend. Welch slowed slightly, thus ensuring that they would still be next to the van when the bus reached them, and said with decision: 'Well, that ought to do it nicely, I should say.'

Before Dixon could roll himself into a ball or even take off his glasses, the van had braked and disappeared, the bus-driver, his mouth opening and shutting vigorously, had somehow squirmed his vehicle against the far wall, and, with an echoing rattle, the car darted forward on to the straight. Dixon, though on the whole glad at this escape, felt at the same time that the conversation would have been appropriately rounded off by Welch's death. He felt this more keenly when Welch went on: 'If I were you, Dixon, I should take all the steps I possibly could to get this article accepted in the next month or so. I mean, I haven't the specialized knowledge to judge . . .' His voice quickened: 'I can't tell, can I? what it's worth. It's no use anybody coming to me and asking ,"What's young Dixon's stuff like?" unless I can give them an expert opinion of what it's worth, is it now? But an acceptance by a learned journal would . . . would . . . You, well you don't know what it's worth yourself, how can you?'

Dixon felt that, on the contrary, he had a good idea of what his article was worth from several points of view. From one of these, the thing's worth could be expressed in one short hyphenated indecency; from another, it was worth the amount of frenzied fact-grubbing and fanatical boredom that had gone into it; from yet another, it was worthy of its aim, the removal of the 'bad impression' he'd so far made in the College and in his Department. But he said: 'No, of course not, Professor.'

'And you see, Faulkner, it's rather important to you that it should turn out to be worth something, if you see what I mean.'

Despite being wrongfully addressed (Faulkner had preceded him in his post), Dixon knew what Welch meant, and said so. How had he made his bad impression? The most likely thing, he always thought, was his having inflicted a superficial wound on the Professor of English in his first week. This man, a youngish ex-Fellow of a Cambridge college, had been standing on the front steps when Dixon, coming round the corner from the library, had kicked violently at a small round stone lying on the macadam. Before reaching the top of its trajectory it had struck the other just below the left kneecap at a distance of fifteen yards or more. Averting his head, Dixon had watched in terrified amazement; it had been useless to run, as the nearest cover was far beyond reach. At the moment of impact he'd turned and begun to walk down the drive, but knew well enough that he was the only visible entity capable of stone-propulsion. He looked back once and saw the Professor of English huddled up on one leg and looking at him. As always on such occasions, he'd wanted to apologize but had found, when it came to it, that he was too frightened to. He'd found the same when, two days later, he'd been passing behind the Registrar's chair at the first Faculty meeting, had stumbled and had knocked the chair aside just as the other man was sitting down. A warning shout from the Registrar's Clerk had averted complete disaster, but he could still remember the look on the face of that figure, stiffened in the shape of a letter S. Then there'd been that essay written for Welch by one of the Honours people, containing, in fact consisting of, abuse of a book on enclosures by, it transpired, one of Welch's own ex-pupils. 'I asked him who could possibly have filled his head with stuff like that, you see, and he said it was all out of one of your lectures, Dixon. Well, I told him as tactfully as I could . . .' Much later Dixon had found out that the book in question had been written at Welch's suggestion and, in part, under his advice. These facts had been there for all to read in the Acknowledgements, but Dixon, whose policy it was to read as little as possible of any given book, never bothered with these, and it had been Margaret who'd told him. That had been, as near as he could remember, on the morning before the evening when Margaret had tried to kill herself with sleeping-pills.

When Welch said in a far-away half-shout, 'Oh, by the way, Dixon,' Dixon turned to him with real avidity. 'Yes, Professor?' How much better to have more of what Welch could provide than thoughts of what Margaret would provide – commodities which he would in any case soon be sampling in their real form.

'I've been wondering if you'd care to come over next week-end for the . . . week-end. I think it should be quite good fun. We're having a few people from London, you know, friends of ours and of my son Bertrand's. Bertrand's going to try and come himself, of course, but he doesn't know yet if he can get away. I expect we shall put on one or two little shows, little bits of music and that. We'll probably call on you to lend a hand with something.'

The car buzzed on along a clear road. 'Thank you very much,

I should love to come,' Dixon said, thinking he must get Margaret to do some intelligence work on the something he'd probably be called upon to lend a hand with.

Welch seemed quite cheered by this ready acceptance. 'That's fine,' he said with apparent feeling. 'Now there's something on the academic side I'd like to discuss with you. I've been talking to the Principal about the College Open Week at the end of term. He wants the History Department to throw something into the pool, you see, and I've been wondering about you.'

'Oh, really?' Surely there were others better qualified to be thrown into the pool?

'Yes, I thought you might care to tackle the evening lecture the Department's going to provide, if you could.'

'Well, I would rather like to have a crack at a public lecture, if you think I'm capable of it,' Dixon managed to say.

'I thought something like "Merrie England" might do as a subject. Not too academic, and not too . . . not too . . . Do you think you could get something together along those sort of lines?'

2

'And then, just before I went under, I suddenly stopped caring. I'd
been clutching the empty bottle like grim death, I remember, as
if I were holding on to life, in a way. But quite soon I didn't in the
least mind going; I felt too tired, somehow. And yet if someone
had shaken me and said, "Come on, you're not going, you're
coming back," I really believe I should have started trying to make
the effort, trying to get back. But nobody did and so I just thought
Oh well, here we go, it doesn't matter all that much. Curious
sensation.' Margaret Peel, small, thin, and bespectacled, with bright
make-up, glanced at Dixon with a half-smile. Around them was
the grumble of half a dozen conversations.

'It's a good sign that you're able to talk about it like this,' he
said. Since she made no reply, he went on: 'What happened afterwards, or can't you remember? Don't tell me if you'd rather not,
of course.'

'No, I don't mind telling you if it won't bore you.' Her smile
broadened a little. 'But didn't Wilson tell you about how he found
me?'

'Wilson? Oh, the chap in the room underneath. Yes, he said
about hearing your wireless booming away and coming up to
complain. What made you leave it on like that?' The feelings
aroused in him by the first part of Margaret's story had almost
subsided now, and he was able to think more clearly.

She looked away across the half-empty bar. 'I don't really know,
James,' she said. 'I think I had some idea about wanting to have
some sort of noise going on while I was . . . going off. It seemed
so horribly quiet in that room.' She gave a little shiver and said
quickly: 'Bit chilly in here, isn't it?'

'We'll move if you like.'

'No, it's all right; just a bit of a draught with that chap coming in . . . Oh yes; afterwards. I think I grasped quite soon what was going on and where I was and all that. And what they were doing to me. I thought, Oh God, hours and hours of feeling ill and wretched, can I bear it? But of course I was passing out all the time, on and off; good thing, really, in the end. By the time I was fully, er, *compos mentis* again the worst was over, as far as feeling awful was concerned. I was terribly weak, naturally; well, you remember . . . But everybody was awfully sweet to me. I should have thought they'd got enough to deal with with people who were ill through no fault of their own. I remember being terrified they'd tell the police and get me carted off to a police hospital – are there such things, James? – but they were just angelic; they couldn't have been nicer. And then you came to see me and the horrible part all began to seem unreal. But you looked so terrible . . .' She leaned sideways on her bar-stool in laughter, her hands clasped round one knee, the quasi-velvet shoe falling away from her heel. 'You looked as if you'd been watching some frightful gruesome operation, white as a sheet and all . . . hollow-eyed . . .' She shook her head, still laughing quietly, and pulled her cardigan up over the shoulders of the green Paisley frock.

'Did I really?' Dixon asked her. He was relieved at this piece of news, to find that he'd looked as bad as he'd felt that morning; then he felt bad again now as he nerved himself to ask the last compulsory question. He half listened for a minute or so while Margaret described how good Mrs Welch had been to her in fetching her from the hospital and installing her at the Welches' home to convalesce. She had undoubtedly been very kind to Margaret, even though at other times, when publicly disagreeing with her husband for example, she was the only living being capable of making Dixon sympathize with him. It was rather annoying to hear how kind she'd been; it entailed putting tiresome qualifications on his dislike for her. Finally, Dixon said in a low voice, having first drunk freely from his glass: 'You needn't say anything if you don't want to, but . . . you are over this business now, aren't you? You wouldn't think of having another shot at it, I mean?'

She glanced up quickly as if she'd been expecting to be asked this, but he couldn't tell whether she was glad or sorry when it came. Then she turned her head away and he could see how thin the flesh was over her jawbone. 'No, I wouldn't have another shot at it,' she said. 'I don't care about him any more; I don't feel anything at all about him, one way or the other. So much so I feel now it was rather silly to have tried at all.'

This made Dixon decide that his apprehensions about the evening had been absurdly out of place. 'Good,' he said heartily. 'Has he tried to get in touch with you or anything?'

'Not a thing, not even so much as a phone message. Vanished without a trace. He might never have existed – as far as we're concerned. I suppose he's too busy with his popsy these days, like he said he'd be.'

'Oh, he said that, did he?'

'Oh yes, our Mr Catchpole was never one to beat about the bush. How did it go? "I'm taking her off to North Wales with me for a couple of weeks. I thought I ought to tell you before I went off." Oh, he was charmingly frank about it, James; quite charming in every way.'

Again she turned away from him, and this time the tendons of her neck were prominent, together with the bones at the base. He felt a pang of alarm, which sharpened when he found he could think of nothing to say. As if searching for a text he examined her face, noting the tufts of brown hair that over-hung the ear-pieces of her glasses, the crease running up the near cheek and approaching closer than before to the eye-socket (or was he imagining that?), and the faint but at this angle unmistakable downward curve of the mouth. There was nothing there of conversational aliment; he felt for his cigarettes, but before he could use the offer of these as a means of breaking into her pose, she switched back to him with a little smile which he recognized, with self-dislike, as consciously brave.

She drained her glass with a quick gay movement. 'Beer,' she said. 'Buy me beer. The night is young.'

While he was securing the barmaid's attention and getting the drinks, Dixon wondered first how many more rounds of blue-label he might be expected to pay for, and then why Margaret, with her full lecturer's salary uninterrupted by her absence from work, so rarely volunteered to stand him a drink. Finally, though this was no more welcome, he thought of the morning before Margaret had taken her overdose of sleeping-pills. He'd had nothing to do at College that day before a two-hour seminar in the afternoon, and she'd been free after a tutorial hour at ten. After coffee at sevenpence a cup in a recently-opened, and now flourishing, restaurant, they'd gone to a chemist's where she'd wanted to buy a few things. One of the things had been a new bottle of the sleeping-pills. He could remember exactly how she'd looked dropping the bottle, in its sealed white wrapper, into her handbag and glancing up to say: 'If you've got nothing better to do tonight I'll be brewing up about ten. What about dropping in for an hour?' He'd said he would, meaning to turn up, but in the event he hadn't been able to get his next day's lecture written up in time, nor, he realized, had the prospect of another conference about Catchpole seemed inviting when ten o'clock came. In the early evening Catchpole had called on Margaret to tell her he was finished with her, and at about ten she'd eaten the whole bottleful of pills. If he'd been there himself, Dixon thought now for the thousandth time, he'd have been able to prevent her, or, if too late for that, to get her to the hospital a good hour and a half earlier than that fellow Wilson had. He shied away from the image of what would have happened if Wilson hadn't bothered to go up to Margaret's room. What had actually happened was much more unpleasant than anything he could have predicted that morning. The next time he'd seen her was in the hospital a week later.

Pocketing the eightpence change from his two florins, Dixon shoved one of the stemmed glasses along to Margaret. They were sitting at the bar of the Oak Lounge in a large roadside hotel not far from Welch's house. From this seat Dixon felt he could recoup himself a little for the expensiveness of the drinks by eating steadily through the potato crisps, gherkins, and red, green, and amber cocktail onions provided by an ambitious management. He began eating the largest surviving gherkin and thought how lucky he was that so much of the emotional business of the evening had been transacted without involving him directly. She'd said nothing about his recent non-appearance at the Welches', nor had any disintegrating question or avowal been let fall.

'By the way, James,' Margaret said, holding the stem of her glass, 'I want to say how awfully grateful I am to you for your tact these last couple of weeks. It has been good of you.'

Dixon alerted all his faculties. Conundrums that sounded innocuous or even pleasant were the most reliable sign of impending attack, the mysterious horseman sighted riding towards the bullion-coach. 'I didn't know I'd been all that tactful,' he said in an uncoloured tone.

'Oh, just the way you've been keeping in the background. You were the only one who took the trouble to work it out, that I might prefer not to be bombarded with kind inquiries, "and how are you feeling, my dear, after your unpleasant experience" et cetera. Do you know, old Mother Welch had people from the village who'd never even heard of me before, dropping in to ask how I was. It was really incredible. You know, James, they couldn't have been kinder, but I'll be awfully glad to get out of that place.'

It seemed genuine. She had been known to interpret some of his laziest or most hurtful actions or inactions in this light, though not, of course, as often as she'd interpreted some gesture of support as lazy or hurtful. Perhaps he could now begin to lead the talk somewhere else. 'Neddy said something about you feeling ready to start work again soon,' he said. 'Of course, the exams'll be on us before very long. Are you going to do anything at College before they start?'

'Well, I shall see each of my classes once to answer any questions they may think worth putting. If the effort of thinking up questions won't turn their poor little brains, that is. But I shan't do any more than that this year, apart from marking the scripts. What'll really bring me back to normality'll be getting away from the Neddies, ungrateful as it may sound.' She crossed her legs spasmodically.

'How much longer are you thinking of staying there?'

'Oh, not more than a fortnight, I hope. I want to get out before the summer vac anyway. It all depends how soon I can find somewhere to live.'

'That's good,' Dixon said, his spirits rising as opportunity for greater honesty seemed to be approaching. 'You'll be there next week-end, then.'

'What, for Neddy's arty get-together? Yes, of course. Why, you don't mean you're coming, do you?'

'Yes, that's just what I do mean. The question was popped on the way down in the car. Why, what's so funny?'

Margaret was laughing in the way Dixon had provisionally named to himself 'the tinkle of tiny silver bells'. He sometimes thought that the whole corpus of her behaviour derived from translating such phrases into action, but before he could feel much irritation with himself or her, she said: 'You know what you're in for, do you?'

'Well, fine talk mostly, I hoped. I can waffle with the best of them. What's been laid on, then?'

She ticked the items off on her fingers. 'Part-songs. A play-reading. Demonstration of some sword-dance steps. Recitations. A chamber concert. There's something else, too, but I've forgotten it. I'll remember in a minute.' She went on laughing.

'Don't bother, that's enough to be going on with. My God, this is really serious; Neddy must be going off his head at last. It's absolutely fantastic. Nobody'll come.'

'You're wrong there, I'm afraid: a chap from the Third Programme's promised to turn up. And a camera team from *Picture Post*. Several of the more prominent local musicians will appear, including your pal Johns with . . .'

Dixon gave a throttled howl. 'This can't be right,' he said, draining his glass chokingly. 'No more fantasy, please. They can't fit a gang like that into the house. Or are they going to sleep on the lawn? And what . . .'

'Most of them are just coming down on the Sunday for the day, according to Mrs Neddy. There will be boarders, though, apart from you. Johns is arriving on the Friday evening, probably driven down with you . . .'

'I'll strangle that little sod before I get into the same . . .'

'Yes yes of course; don't shout. One of the sons is coming too, with his girl. The girl might be rather interesting; a ballet student, I gather.'

'A ballet student? I didn't know there were such things.'

'There are, apparently. This one's called Sonia Loosmore.'

'No, really? How do you know all this?'

'I've heard nothing else from either of the Neddies for the last week.'

'I can imagine that.' Dixon began looking towards the barmaid. 'Then perhaps you can tell me why I've been asked.'

'They weren't very clear about that. Just to join in, I suppose. There'll be plenty of things for you to do, I've no doubt at all.'

'Look, Margaret, you know as well as I do that I can't sing, I can't act, I can hardly read, and thank God I can't read music. No, I know what it is. Good sign in a way. He wants to test my reactions to culture, see whether I'm a fit person to teach in a university, see? Nobody who can't tell a flute from a recorder can be worth hearing on the price of bloody cows under Edward the Third.' He put seven or eight onions into his mouth and began crunching them.

'But he's exposed you to culture before now, surely.'

'Not such a heavy concentration as this looks like being. My God, what the hell does he think he's playing at? What's it all in aid of? I mean it can hardly be all just for my benefit.'

'He's got some idea of an article or a wireless talk on the provincial culture-group. You know, that stuff he came back from Manchester full of at Easter.'

'But he can't really think anyone'll take him up, can he?'

'Who knows what he really thinks? No, it's probably just an excuse for doing it. You know how he loves that sort of thing.'

'None better,' Dixon said, again trying to catch the barmaid's eye. 'You'll have to start finding out what he's got lined up for me. So I can start thinking up reasons for not being able to do it.'

She laid her hand on his. 'You can rely on me,' she said in a soft voice.

Dixon said quickly: 'But how's he got hold of the B.B.C. type and the *Picture Post* people? He must have got someone interested.'

'I gather both lots are contacts of Bertrand's, or perhaps his girl's. But don't let's talk about it any more. Can't we talk about ourselves? We've got so much to say to each other, haven't we?'

'Yes, of course,' he said, trying to stuff comradeliness into his tone. He brought out his cigarettes and, while lighting two of these and getting more drinks, he meditated on Margaret's capacity of talking like this at no notice. He wanted to give an inarticulate shout and run out of the bar, not stopping until he was on board a city bus. Though silenced, he was grateful to notice, by the barmaid's nearness, Margaret was yet managing to keep up the pressure by intimate glances, even touching his knee with hers. He converted his start at this into a glance upwards, to the clock above the counter. The thin red second hand swung smoothly round the dial, giving the illusion of time rapidly passing. The other hands pointed to five past nine.

While he was being given his change, Dixon studied the barmaid, who was large and very dark with a narrow upper lip and rather close-set eyes. He thought how much he liked her and had in common with her, and how much she'd like and have in common with him if she only knew him. With the maximum of deliberation he trousered his change, then picked up and shook a cigarette packet someone had left on the counter. It proved empty. At his side, Margaret heaved the sigh which invariably preluded the worst avowals. She waited until he had to look at her and said: 'How close we seem to be tonight, James.' A fat-faced man on the other side of her turned and stared at her. 'All the barriers are down at last, aren't they?' she asked.

Finding this unanswerable, Dixon gazed at her, slowly nodding his head, half expecting a round of applause from some invisible auditorium. What wouldn't he give for a fierce purging draught of fury or contempt, a really efficient worming from the sense of responsibility?

At last she lowered her eyes and might have fallen to scanning her beer for foreign matter. 'It seemed almost too much to hope for.' After another silence, she went on in a brisker tone: 'But can't we sit somewhere more . . . out of the public eye?'

Dixon said he thought this was a good idea, and they moved across the room, which was starting to fill up, to a vacant corner. Before sitting down, he excused himself and went out to the lavatory.

Out there, he thought how nice it would be if he could give up his dual role of conciliator and go right away from here. Five minutes would be ample for a vituperative phone-call to Welch and a short statement of the facts of the case to Margaret. Then he'd go and pack a few clothes and get on the ten-forty for London. As he stood in the badly-lit jakes, he was visited again, and unbearably, by the visual image that had haunted him ever since he took on this job. He seemed to be looking from a darkened room across a deserted back street to where, against a dimly-glowing evening sky, a line of chimney-pots stood out as if carved from tin. A small double cloud moved slowly from right to left. The image wasn't purely visual, because he had a feeling that some soft unidentifiable noise was in his ears, and he felt with a dreamer's baseless conviction that somebody was going to come into the room where he seemed to be, somebody he knew in the image but not in reality. He was certain it was an image of London, and just as certain that it wasn't of any part of London he'd ever visited. He hadn't spent more than a dozen evenings there in his life. Then why, he pondered, was his ordinary desire to leave the provinces for London sharpened and particularized by this half-glimpsed scene?

He walked thoughtfully out of the lavatory without bothering to close its door, which was fitted with a compressed-air delaying device. The cylinder of this having been unscrewed by some rioter, the door swung to at once behind him, just missing his rear heel. The effect, in that short and narrow passage, was like the discharge of a piece of ordnance. He seemed to catch a hoarse cry of alarm from inside the bar. More than ever it was the moment to dart into the street and fail to return. But economic necessity and the call of pity were a strong combination; topped up by fear, as both were, they were invincible. He went back through the polished door into the Oak Lounge.

3

'Excuse me, Mr Dixon; have you got a minute to spare?'

First making his shot-in-the-back face, Dixon stopped and turned. He was leaving College after a lecture, and so had been hurrying. 'Yes, Mr Michie?'

Michie was a moustachioed ex-service student who'd commanded a tank troop at Anzio while Dixon was an R.A.F. corporal in western Scotland. He now confronted Dixon near the porter's lodge. As always, his manner seemed to be concealing something, though Dixon could never be sure what. He waited for a moment and said: 'Have you got that syllabus together yet, sir?' He was the only student Dixon had ever heard calling a member of the staff 'sir', and apparently reserved the title exclusively for Dixon.

'Oh yes, that syllabus,' Dixon said, playing for time. He hadn't got it together yet.

Michie pretended to think his question needed amplifying. 'You know, sir, the list of stuff for your special subject next year. You said you were going to distribute copies to the Honours people, if you remember.'

'Yes, oddly enough I can remember having said that,' Dixon said, then pulled himself together; he mustn't antagonize Michie. 'I've got the stuff ready in my digs, but I've not given it to the typist yet. I'll try to have it ready for you early next week, if that's all right.'

'That'll do beautifully, sir,' Michie said fulsomely, his moustache writhing a little as he smiled. He began moving away down the drive, keeping his eyes on Dixon, trying, it seemed, to engineer a joint departure from College. A briefcase, swollen with the weekend's reading, swayed in his loose grip. 'If I could come along to your room some time and pick them up?'

Dixon stopped trying to stand his ground, and allowed Michie to draw him away towards the road. 'If you would,' he said. Fury flared up in his mind like forgotten toast under a grill. The getting together of the syllabus had been, of course, Welch's idea; on receipt of it, the candidates for Honours in History were to 'see whether they were interested' in studying this new special subject, in preference to the old special subjects taught by the other members of the Department and examined in one of the eight papers required for B.A. Clearly, the more students, within reason, Dixon could get 'interested' in his subject, the better for him; equally clearly, too large a number of 'interested' students would mean that the number studying Welch's own special subject would fall to a degree that Welch might be expected to resent. With an Honours class of nineteen and a Department of six, three students seemed a safe number to try for. So far, Dixon's efforts on behalf of his special subject, apart from thinking how much he hated it, had been confined to aiming to secure for it the three prettiest girls in the class, one of whom was Michie's girl, while excluding from it Michie himself. Added to Dixon's dislike of thinking about work at all, the necessity of keeping Michie at arm's length went far to explain his present discomfort.

'What are your main ideas so far, sir, if you don't mind my asking?' Michie asked as they turned downhill into College Road.

Dixon did mind, but said only: 'Well, I think the main emphasis of the thing will be social, you know.' He was trying to stop himself from thinking directly about the official title of his subject, which was 'Medieval Life and Culture'. 'I thought I might start with a discussion of the university, for instance, in its social role.' He comforted himself for having said this by the thought that at least he knew it didn't mean anything.

'You don't propose to offer an analysis of scholasticism, then, I take it?'

This question illustrated exactly why Dixon felt he had to keep Michie out of his subject. Michie knew a lot, or seemed to, which was as bad. One of the things he knew, or seemed to, was what scholasticism was. Dixon read, heard, and even used the word a dozen times a day without knowing, though he seemed to. But he saw clearly that he wouldn't be able to go on seeming to know the meaning of this and a hundred such words while Michie was there questioning, discussing, and arguing about them. Michie was, or seemed, able to make a fool of him again and again without warning. Though it would have been easy enough to pick some technical quarrel with him, over an undelivered essay for example, Dixon was reluctant to do so because he felt superstitiously that Michie was capable of insisting on studying Medieval Life and Culture out of sheer spite and desire to do him down. Michie, then, must be kept out, but with smiles and regrets instead of the blows and kicks which were his due. This was why Dixon now said: 'Oh no, I'm afraid there won't be much meat in it from that point of view. I'm not qualified to pronounce on the learned Scotus or Aquinas, I'm afraid.' Or should it have been Augustine?

'It might be rather fascinating to study the effect on men's lives of the various popular debasements and vulgarizations of the schoolmen's doctrines.'

'Oh, agreed, agreed,' Dixon said, his lips beginning to shake, 'but that's a subject for a D.Phil. thesis, wouldn't you say, rather than a fairly elementary course of lectures?'

Michie gave at some length, but luckily without asking any questions, his views of the case for and against such an opinion. After Dixon had voiced his regret that so interesting a discussion must be broken off, they parted at the foot of College Road, Michie to his Hall of Residence, Dixon to his digs.

Hurrying through the sidestreets, deserted at this hour before works and offices closed, Dixon thought of Welch. Would Welch have asked him to get up a special subject if he wasn't going to keep him on as a lecturer? Substitute any human name for Welch's and the answer must be No. But retain the original reading and no certainty was possible. As recently as last week, a month after the special subject had been first mentioned, he'd heard Welch talking to the Professor of Education about 'the sort of new man' he was after. Dixon had felt very ill for five minutes; then Welch had come up to him and begun discussing, in tones of complete honesty, what he wanted Dixon to do with the Pass people next year. At the memory, Dixon rolled his eyes together like marbles and sucked in his cheeks to give a consumptive or wasted appearance to his face, moaning loudly as he crossed the sunlit street to his front door.

On the florid black hallstand were a couple of periodicals and some letters that had come by the second post. There was something in a typed envelope for Alfred Beesley, who was a member of the College's English Department; a buff envelope containing football pool coupons and addressed to W. Atkinson, an insurance salesman some years older than Dixon; and another typed envelope addressed to 'J. Dickinson' with a London postmark. He hesitated, then opened it. Inside was a sheet hastily torn from a pad bearing a few ill-written lines in green ink. Without formality the writer announced that he'd liked the shipbuilding article and proposed to publish it 'in due course'. He'd be writing again 'before very long' and signed himself 'L. S. Caton'.

Dixon took a felt hat of Atkinson's from the hallstand, put it on his head, and did a little dance in the narrow hall. Welch would find it harder to sack him now. It was good news apart from that; it was generally encouraging; perhaps the article had had some merit after all. No, that was going too far; but it did mean it was the right sort of stuff, and a man who'd written one lot of the right sort of stuff could presumably write more. He'd enjoy telling Margaret about it. He replaced the hat, glancing idly at the periodicals, which were destined for Evan Johns, office worker at the College and amateur oboist. The front page of one of them bore a large and well-produced photograph of a contemporary composer Johns might reasonably be supposed to admire. An idea came into Dixon's mind, which was the more ready to receive it in this mood of exultation. He stood still and listened for a moment, then crept into the dining-room where the table was laid for high tea. Working quickly but carefully, he began altering the composer's face with a soft black pencil. The lower lip he turned into a set of discoloured snaggle-teeth, adding another lower lip, thicker and looser than the original, underneath. Duelling-scars appeared on the cheeks, hairs as thick as tooth-picks sprang from the widened nostrils, the eyes, enlarged and converging, spilled out on to the nose. After crenellating the jaw-line and hiding the forehead in a luxuriant fringe, he added a Chinese moustache and pirate's earrings, and had just replaced the papers on the hallstand when somebody began to come in by the front door. He sprang into the dining-room and listened again. After a few seconds he smiled as a voice called out 'Miss Cutler' in an accent northern like his own, but eastern where his own was western. He came out and said: 'Hallo, Alfred.'

'Uh, hallo, Jim.' Beesley was tearing his letter open with some haste. The kitchen door opened behind Dixon and the head of Miss Cutler, their landlady, emerged to see who and how many they were. Satisfied on these points, she smiled and withdrew. Dixon turned back to Beesley, who was now reading his letter, scowling as he did so.

'Coming in to tea?'

Beesley nodded and handed Dixon the cyclostyled sheet. 'Spot of good news to take home with me for the week-end.'

Dixon read that Beesley was thanked for his application, but that Mr P. Oldham had been appointed to the post. 'Oh, bad luck, Alfred. Still, there'll be others to go for, won't there?'

'Doubt it, for October. Time's running pretty short now.'

They took their seats at the tea-table. 'Were you very set on it?' Dixon asked.

'Only in so far as it would have been a way of getting away from Fred Karno.' This was how Beesley was accustomed to refer to his professor.

'I suppose you were quite set on it, then.'

'That's right. Anything new from Neddy about your chances?'

'No, nothing direct, but I've just had a bit of good news. That chap Caton's taken my article, the thing about shipbuilding.'

'That's a comfort, eh? When's it coming out?'

'He didn't say.'

'Oh? Got the letter there?' Dixon passed it to him. 'Mm, not too fussy about stationery and so on, is he? I see . . . Well, you'll be wanting more definite information than that, won't you?'

Dixon's nose twitched his glasses up into position, a habit of his. 'Will I?'

'Well, Christ, Jim, of course you will, old man. A vague acceptance of that kind isn't much use to anyone. Might be a couple of years before it comes out, if then. No, you pin him down to a date, then you'll have got some real evidence to give Neddy. Take my advice.'

Uncertain whether the advice was sound, or whether it arose out of Beesley's disappointment, Dixon was about to temporize when Miss Cutler came into the room with a tray of tea and food. One of the oldest of her many black dresses shone softly at several points of her stout frame. The emphatic quietness of her tread, the quick, trained movements of her large purple hands, the little grimace and puff of breath with which she enjoined silence upon each article she laid on the table, her modestly lowered glance, combined to make it impossible to talk in her presence, except to her. It was many years now since her retirement from domestic service and entry into the lodging-house trade, but although she sometimes showed an impressive set of landlady-characteristics, her deportment when serving meals would still have satisfied the most exacting lady-housekeeper. Dixon and Beesley said something to her, receiving, as usual, no reply beyond a nod until the tray was unloaded; then a conversation followed, only to be abruptly broken off at the entry of the insurance salesman and ex-Army major, Bill Atkinson.

This man, who was tall and very dark, sat weightily down at his place at the foot of the table while Miss Cutler, whom he terrified by his demands for what he called the correct thing, ran out of the room. He studied Dixon closely when the latter said: 'You're early today, Bill,' as if the remark might have carried some challenge to his physical strength or endurance; then, seemingly reassured, nodded twenty or thirty times. His centre-parted black hair and rectangular moustache gave him an air of archaic ferocity.

The meal continued and Atkinson soon partook in it, though remaining aloof from the conversation, which ran for a few minutes on the subject of Dixon's article and its possible date of publication. 'Is it a good article?' Beesley asked finally.

Dixon looked up in surprise. 'Good? How do you mean, good? Good?'

'Well, is it any more than accurate and the sort of thing that gets turned out? Anything beyond the sort of thing that'll help you to keep your job?'

'Good God, no. You don't think I take that sort of stuff seriously, do you?' Dixon noticed that Atkinson's thickly-lashed eyes were fixed on him.

'I just wondered,' Beesley said, bringing out the curved nickel-banded pipe round which he was trying to train his personality, like a creeper up a trellis. 'I thought I was probably right.'

'But look here, Alfred, you don't mean I ought to take it seriously, do you? What are you getting at?'

'I don't mean anything. I've just been wondering what led you to take up this racket in the first place.'

Dixon hesitated. 'But I explained all that to you months ago, about feeling I'd be no use in a school and so on.'

'No, I mean why you're a medievalist.' Beesley struck a match, his small vole-like face set in a frown. 'Don't mind, Bill, do you?' Receiving no reply, he went on between sucks at his pipe: 'You don't seem to any special interest in it, do you?'

Dixon tried to laugh. 'No, I don't, do I? No, the reason why I'm a medievalist, as you call it, is that the medieval papers were a soft option in the Leicester course, so I specialized in them. Then when I applied for the job here, I naturally made a big point of that, because it looked better to seem interested in something specific. It's why I got the job instead of that clever boy from Oxford who mucked himself up at the interview by chewing the fat about modern theories of interpretation. But I never guessed I'd be landed with all the medieval stuff and nothing but medieval stuff.' He repressed a desire to smoke, having finished his five o'clock cigarette at a quarter past three.

'I see,' Beesley said, sniffing. 'I didn't know that before.'

'Haven't you noticed how we all specialize in what we hate most?' Dixon asked, but Beesley, puffing away at his pipe, had already got up. Dixon's views on the Middle Ages themselves would have to wait until another time.

'Oh well, I'm off now,' Beesley said. 'Have a good time with the artists, Jim. Don't get drunk and start telling Neddy what you've just been telling me, will you? Cheero, Bill,' he added unanswered to Atkinson, and went out leaving the door open.

Dixon said good-bye, then waited a moment before saying: 'Oh, Bill, I wonder if you could do me a favour.'

The reply was unexpectedly prompt. 'Depends what it is,' Atkinson said scornfully.

'Could you ring me at this number about eleven on Sunday morning? I'll be there all right and we'll just have a little chat about the weather, but if by any chance I can't be got at . . .' He paused at a small unidentifiable sound from outside the room, but heard nothing further and continued: 'If you can't get hold of me tell whoever answers that my parents have turned up here out of the blue and will I please get back as soon as I can. There, I've written everything down.'

Atkinson raised his dense eyebrows and studied the envelope-back as if it bore the wrong answer to a chess problem. He gave a barbaric laugh and stared into Dixon's face. 'Afraid you won't be able to last out, or what?'

'It's one of my professor's arty week-ends. I've got to turn up, but I can't face the whole of Sunday there.'

There was a long pause while Atkinson looked censoriously round the room, a familiar exercise. Dixon liked and revered him for his air of detesting everything that presented itself to his senses, and of not meaning to let this detestation become staled by custom.

He said finally: 'I see. I'll enjoy doing that.' As he said this, yet another man came into the room. It was Johns, carrying his periodicals, and at the sight of him Dixon felt a twinge of disquiet: Johns was a silent mover, a potential eavesdropper, and a friend of the Welches, especially Mrs Welch. Asking himself whether Johns had in fact overheard enough of the task just assigned to Atkinson, Dixon nodded anxiously at Johns, whose tallow-textured features made no movement. This immobility was prolonged when Atkinson spoke his greeting: 'Hallo, sonny boy.'

Dixon had resolved to travel to the Welches' by bus to avoid Johns's company, so he now got up, thinking he ought to impart some specific warning to Atkinson. Unable to fix on anything, however, he left the room. Behind him he heard Atkinson speaking to Johns again: 'Sit down and tell me about your oboe.'

A few minutes later Dixon, carrying a small suitcase, was hurrying through the streets to his bus stop. At the corner of the main road he had a view downhill to where the last few terraced houses and small provision shops began to give place to office blocks, the more fashionable dress-shops and tailors, the public library, the telephone exchange, and a modern cinema. Beyond these again were the taller buildings of the city centre with its tapering cathedral spire. Trolley-buses and buses hummed or ground their way towards it and away from it, with columns of cars winding, straightening, contracting, and thinning out. The pavements were crowded. As Dixon crossed the road, the sight of all this energy made his spirits lift, and somewhere behind his thoughts an inexplicable excitement stirred. There was no reason to suppose that the week-end would contain anything better than the familiar mixture of predicted boredom with unpredicted boredom, but for the moment he was unable to believe this. The acceptance of his article might be the prelude to a run of badly-needed luck. He was going to meet some people who might well prove interesting and amusing. If not, then he and Margaret could relish talking about them. He must see that she enjoyed herself as far as possible, and doing this would be easier in the presence of others. In his case was a small book of verse, by a contemporary poet he privately thought very nasty, which he'd bought that morning as a completely unprovoked gift to Margaret. The surprise would combine nicely with the evidence of affection and the flattery implied in the choice. A routine qualm gave him trouble at the thought of what he'd written on the fly-leaf, but his mood enabled him to suppress it.

4

'Of course, this sort of music's not intended for an audience, you see,' Welch said as he handed the copies round. 'The fun's all in the singing. Everybody's got a real tune to sing – a real tune,' he repeated violently. 'You could say, really, that polyphony got to its highest point, its peak, at that period, and has been on the decline ever since. You've only got to look at the part-writing in things like, well, *Onward, Christian Soldiers*, the hymn, which is a typical . . . a typical . . .'

'We're all waiting, Ned,' Mrs Welch said from the piano. She played a slow arpeggio, sustaining it with the pedal. 'All right, everybody?'

A soporific droning filled the air round Dixon as the singers hummed their notes to one another. Mrs Welch rejoined them on the low platform that had been built at one end of the music-room, taking up her stand by Margaret, the other soprano. A small bullied-looking woman with unabundant brown hair was the only contralto. Next to Dixon was Cecil Goldsmith, a colleague of his in the College History Department, whose tenor voice held enough savage power, especially above middle C, to obliterate whatever noises Dixon might feel himself impelled to make. Behind him and to one side were three basses, one a local composer, another an amateur violinist occasionally summoned at need by the city orchestra, the third Evan Johns.

Dixon ran his eye along the lines of black dots, which seemed to go up and down a good deal, and was able to assure himself that everyone was going to have to sing all the time. He'd had a bad setback twenty minutes ago in some Brahms rubbish which began with ten seconds or so of unsupported tenor – more accurately, of unsupported Goldsmith, who'd twice dried up in face of a tricky interval and left him opening and shutting his mouth in silence. He now cautiously reproduced the note Goldsmith was humming and found the effect pleasing rather than the reverse. Why hadn't they had the decency to ask him if he'd like to join in, instead of driving him up on to this platform arrangement and forcing sheets of paper into his hand?

The madrigal began at the bidding of Welch's arthritic forefinger. Dixon kept his head down, moved his mouth as little as possible consistent with being unmistakably seen to move it, and looked through the words the others were singing. 'When from my love I looked for love, and kind affections due,' he read, 'too well I found her vows to prove most faithless and untrue. But when I did ask her why . . .' He looked over at Margaret, who was singing away happily enough – she turned out regularly during the winter with the choir of the local Conservative Association – and wondered what changes in their circumstances and temperaments would be necessary to make the words of the madrigal apply, however remotely, to himself and her. She'd made vows to him, or avowals anyway, which was perhaps all the writer had meant. But if he'd meant what he seemed to mean by 'kind affections due', then Dixon had never 'looked for' any of these from Margaret. Perhaps he should: after all, people were doing it all the time. It was a pity she wasn't a bit better-looking. One of these days, though, he would try, and see what happened.

'Yet by, and by, they'll arl, deny, arnd say 'twas *bart* in jast,' Goldsmith sang tremulously and very loudly. It was the last phrase; Dixon kept his mouth open while Welch's finger remained aloft, then shut it with a little flick of the head he'd seen singers use as the finger swept sideways. All seemed pleased with the performance and anxious for another of the same sort. 'Yes, well, this next one's what they called a ballet. Of course, they didn't mean what we mean by the similar . . . Rather a well-known one, this. It's called *Now is the Month of Maying*. Now if you'll all just . . .'

A bursting snuffle of laughter came from Dixon's left rear. He glanced round to see Johns's pallor rent by a grin. The large short-lashed eyes were fixed on him. 'What's the joke?' he asked. If Johns were laughing at Welch, Dixon was prepared to come in on Welch's side.

'You'll see,' Johns said. He went on looking at Dixon. 'You'll see,' he added, grinning.

In less than a minute Dixon did see, and clearly. Instead of the customary four parts, this piece employed five. The third and fourth lines of music from the top had *Tenor I* and *Tenor II* written against them; moreover, there was some infantile fa-la-la-la stuff on the second page with numerous gaps in the individual parts. Even Welch's ear might be expected to record the complete absence of one of the parts in such circumstances. It was much too late now for Dixon to explain that he hadn't really meant it when he'd said, half an hour before, that he could read music 'after a fashion'; much too late to transfer allegiance to the basses. Nothing short of an epileptic fit could get him out of this.

'You'd better take first tenor, Jim,' Goldsmith said; 'the second's a bit tricky.'

Dixon nodded bemusedly, hardly hearing further laughter from Johns. Before he could cry out, they were past the piano-ritual and the droning and into the piece. He flapped his lips to: 'Each with his bonny lass, a-a-seated on the grass: fa-la-la-la, fa-la-la-la-la-la-la-la-la . . .' but Welch had stopped waving his finger, was holding it stationary in the air. The singing died. 'Oh, tenors,' Welch began; 'I didn't seem to hear . . .'

An irregular knocking on the door at the far end of the room was at once followed by the bursting-open of this door and the entry of a tall man wearing a lemon-yellow sports-coat, all three buttons of which were fastened, and displaying a large beard which came down further on one side than on the other, half hiding a vine-patterned tie. Dixon guessed with surging exultation that this must be the pacifist painting Bertrand whose arrival with his girl had been heralded, with typical clangour, by Welch every few minutes since tea-time. It was an arrival which must surely prove an irritant sooner or later, but for the moment it served as the best possible counter-irritant to the disastrous madrigals. Even as Dixon thought this, the senior Welches left their posts and went to greet their son, followed more slowly by the others who, perhaps finding the chance of a break not completely unwelcome, broke into conversation as they moved. Dixon delightedly lit a cigarette, finding himself alone: the amateur violinist had got hold of Margaret; Goldsmith and the local composer were talking to Carol, Goldsmith's wife, who'd refused, with enviable firmness, to do more than sit and listen to the singing from an armchair near the fireplace; Johns was doing something technical at the piano. Dixon moved down the room through the company and leaned against the wall at the end by the door where the bookshelves were. Placed here, savouring his cigarette, he was in a good position to observe Bertrand's girl when she came in, slowly and hesitantly, a few seconds later, and stood unnoticed, except by him, just inside the room.

In a few more seconds Dixon had noticed all he needed to notice about this girl: the combination of fair hair, straight and cut short, with brown eyes and no lipstick, the strict set of the mouth and the square shoulders, the large breasts and the narrow waist, the premeditated simplicity of the wine-coloured corduroy skirt and the unornamented white linen blouse. The sight of her seemed an irresistible attack on his own habits, standards, and ambitions: something designed to put him in his place for good. The notion that women like this were never on view except as the property of men like Bertrand was so familiar to him that it had long since ceased to appear an injustice. The huge class that contained Margaret was destined to provide his own womenfolk: those in whom the intention of being attractive could sometimes be made to get itself confused with performance; those with whom a too-tight skirt, a wrong-coloured, or no, lipstick, even an ill-executed smile could instantly discredit that illusion beyond apparent hope of renewal. But renewal always came: a new sweater would somehow scale down the large feet, generosity revivify the brittle hair, a couple of pints cite positive charm in talk of the London stage or French food.

The girl turned her head and found Dixon staring at her. His diaphragm contracted with fright; she drew herself up with a jerk like a soldier standing easy called to the stand-at-ease position. They looked at each other for a moment, until, just as Dixon's scalp was beginning to tingle, a high, baying voice called, 'Ah, there you are, darling; step this way, if you please, and be introduced to the throng,' and Bertrand strode up the room to meet her, throwing Dixon a brief hostile glance. Dixon didn't like him doing that; the only action he required from Bertrand was an apology, humbly offered, for his personal appearance.

Dixon had been too distressed at the sight of Bertrand's girl to want to be introduced to her, and kept out of the way for a time; then he moved down and started talking to Margaret and the amateur violinist. Bertrand dominated the central group, doing a lot of laughing as he told some lengthy story; his girl watched him intently, as if he might ask her later to summarize its drift. Coffee and cakes, intended to replace an evening meal, were brought in, and getting enough of these for himself and Margaret kept Dixon fully occupied. Then Welch came up to him and said, inexplicably enough: 'Ah, Dixon, come along now. I want you to meet my son Bertrand and his . . . his . . . Come along.'

With Margaret at his side, Dixon was soon confronted by the two people Welch wanted him to meet and by Evan Johns. 'This is Mr Dixon and Miss Peel,' Welch said, and drew the Goldsmiths away.

Before a silence could fall, Margaret said 'Are you down here for long, Mr Welch?' and Dixon felt grateful to her for being there and for always having something to say.

Bertrand's jaws snatched successfully at a piece of food which had been within an ace of eluding them. He went on chewing for a moment, pondering. 'I doubt it,' he said at last. 'Upon consideration I feel it incumbent upon me to doubt it. I have miscellaneous concerns in London that need my guiding hand.' He smiled among his beard, from which he now began brushing crumbs. 'But it's very pleasant to come down here and to know that the torch of culture is still in a state of combustion in the provinces. Profoundly reassuring, too.'

'And how's your work going?' Margaret asked.

Bertrand laughed at this, turning towards his girl, who also laughed, a clear, musical sound not unlike Margaret's tiny silver bells. 'My work?' Bertrand echoed. 'You make it sound like missionary activity. Not that some of our friends would dissent from that description of their labours. Fred, for instance,' he said to his girl.

'Yes, or Otto possibly,' she replied.

'Most assuredly Otto. He certainly looks like a missionary, even if he doesn't behave like one.' He laughed again. So did his girl.

'What work do you do?' Dixon asked flatly.

'I am a painter. Not, alas, a painter of houses, or I should have been able to make my pile and retire by now. No no; I paint pictures. Not, alas again, pictures of trade unionists or town halls or naked women, or I should now be squatting on an even larger pile. No no; just pictures, mere pictures, pictures *tout court*, or, as our American cousins would say, pictures period. And what work do you do? always provided, of course, that I have permission to ask.'

Dixon hesitated; Bertrand's speech, which, except for its peroration, had clearly been delivered before, had annoyed him in more ways than he'd have believed possible. Bertrand's girl was looking at him interrogatively; her eyebrows, which were darker than her hair, were raised, and she now said, in her rather deep voice: 'Do gratify our curiosity.' Bertrand's eyes, which seemed to lack the convexity of the normal eyeball, were also fixed on him.

'I'm one of your father's underlings,' Dixon said to Bertrand, deciding he mustn't be offensive; 'I cover the medieval angle for the History Department here.'

'Charming, charming,' Bertrand said, and his girl said: 'You enjoy doing that, do you?'

Welch, Dixon noticed, had rejoined the group and was looking from face to face, obviously in quest of a point of entry into the conversation. Dixon resolved to deny him this at all costs. He said, quietly but quickly: 'Well, of course, it has its own appeal. I can quite see that it hasn't the sort of glamour of', he turned to the girl, 'your line of country.' He must show Bertrand that he wasn't below including her in the conversation.

She looked perplexedly up at Bertrand. 'But I haven't noticed much glamour knocking about in . . .'

'But surely,' Dixon said, 'I know there must be a lot of hard work and exercise attached to it, but the ballet, well,' he disregarded a nudge from Margaret, 'there must be plenty of glamour there. So I've always understood, anyway.' As he spoke, he gave Bertrand a smile of polite, comradely envy, and stirred his coffee with civilized fingers, splaying them a good deal on the handle of the spoon.

Bertrand was going red in the face and was leaning towards him, struggling to swallow half a bridge roll and speak. The girl repeated with genuine bewilderment: 'The ballet? But I work in a bookshop. Whatever made you think I . . . ?' Johns was grinning. Even Welch had obviously taken in what he'd said. What had he done? He was attacked simultaneously by a pang of fear and the speculation that 'ballet' might be a private Welch synonym for 'sexual intercourse'.

'Look here, Dickinson or whatever your name is,' Bertrand began, 'perhaps you think you're being funny, but I'd as soon you cut it out, if you don't mind. Don't want to make a thing of it, do we?'

The baying quality of his voice, especially in the final query, together with a blurring of certain consonants, made Dixon want to call attention to its defects; also, perhaps, to the peculiarity of his eyes. This might make Bertrand assail him physically – splendid: he was confident of winning any such encounter with an artist – or would Bertrand's pacifism stop him? But in the ensuing silence Dixon swiftly decided to back down. He'd made some mistake about the girl: he mustn't make things any worse. 'I'm terribly sorry if I've made a mistake, but I was under the impression that Miss Loosmore here had something to do with . . .'

He turned to Margaret for aid, but before she could speak Welch, of all people, had come in loudly with: 'Poor old Dixon, ma-ha-ha, must have been confusing this . . . this young lady with Sonia Loosmore, a friend of Bertrand's who let us all down rather badly some time ago. I think Bertrand must have thought you were . . . twitting him or something, Dixon; ba-ha-ha.'

'Well, if he'd taken the trouble to be introduced, this wouldn't have happened,' Bertrand said, still flushed. 'Instead of which, he . . .'

'Don't worry about it, Mr Dixon,' the girl cut in. 'It was only a silly little misunderstanding. I can quite see how it happened. My name's Christine Callaghan. Altogether different, you see.'

'Well, I'm . . . thanks very much for taking it like that. I'm very sorry about it, really I am.'

'No no, don't let it get you down, Dixon,' Bertrand said, with a glance at his girl. 'If you'll excuse us, I think we might circulate round the company.'

They moved off, followed at a distance by Johns, towards the Goldsmith group, and Dixon was left alone with Margaret.

'Here, have a cigarette,' she said. 'You must be needing one. God, what a swine Bertrand is. He might have realized . . .'

'It was my fault, really,' Dixon said, grateful for nicotine and support. 'I should have been there to be introduced.'

'Yes, why weren't you? But he needn't have made it worse. But that's typical of him, as far as I can gather.'

'I sort of couldn't face meeting him. How often have you met him?'

'He came down once before, with the Loosmore girl. I say, it is rather queer, isn't it? He was going to marry the Loosmore then, and now here he is with a new piece. Yes, of course; Neddy gave me a long harangue about when the Loosmore wedding was coming off, and so on, only a couple of days ago. So as far as he knew . . .'

40

'Look, Margaret, can't we go out for a drink? I need one, and we shan't get one here. It's only just eight; we could be back . . .'

Margaret laughed, so that he could see a large number of her teeth, one canine flecked with lipstick. She always made up just a little too heavily. 'Oh, James, you're incorrigible,' she said. 'Whatever next? Of course we can't go out; what do you suppose the Neddies would think? Just as their brilliant son's arrived? You'd get a week's notice like a shot.'

'Yes, you're right, I admit. But I'd give anything for three quick pints. I've had nothing since the one I had down the road yesterday evening, before I showed up here.'

'Much better for your pocket not to have them.' She began to laugh again. 'You were wonderful in the madrigals. Your best performance yet.'

'Don't remind me, please.'

'Even better than your rendering of the Anouilh tough. Your accent made it sound so frightfully sinister. What was it? *"La rigolade, c'est autre chose"*? Very powerful, I thought.'

Dixon screamed softly from a tightened throat. 'Stop it. I can't bear it. Why couldn't they have chosen an English play? All right, I know. Don't explain to me. Look, what's going to happen now?'

'Recorders, I think.'

'Well, that lets me out, anyway. No disgrace in not playing them. I'm only a lay brother, after all. Oh, but isn't it horrible, Margaret? Isn't it horrible? How many of the bloody things do you have going at once?'

She laughed again, glancing quickly round the room. This was a reliable sign that she was enjoying herself. 'Oh, any number can play, as far as I know.'

Dixon laughed too, trying to forget about beer. It was true that he had only three pounds left in his tin box to last until pay-day, which was nine days off. In the bank he had twenty-eight pounds, but this was a fund he'd started against the chance of being sacked.

'Pretty girl, that Christine Whatshername,' Margaret said.

'Yes, isn't she?'

'Wonderful figure she's got, hasn't she?'

'Yes.'

'Not often you get a figure as good as that with a good-looking face.'

'No.' Dixon tensed himself for the inevitable qualification.

'Pity she's so refained, though.' Margaret hesitated, then decided to gloss this epithet. 'I don't like women of that age who try to act the gracious lady. Bit of a prig, too.'

Dixon, who'd arrived at similar conclusions already, found he didn't much want to have them confirmed in this way. 'Oh, I don't know,' he said. 'Can't really tell at this stage.'

This was greeted with the tinkle of tiny bells. 'Ah, you always were one for a pretty face, weren't you? Covers a multitude is what I always say.'

He thought this profoundly true and, debarred from saying so, was at a loss what to reply. They looked anxiously at each other, as if whatever either might say next must be an insult. Finally Dixon said: 'She does seem rather as if she's tarred with the same brush as Bertrand.'

She gave him a curious sardonic smile. 'I should say they've got a lot in common.'

'I imagine so.'

A maidservant was now collecting the used crockery, and the company was moving about. The next stage of the evening was clearly imminent. Bertrand and his girl had disappeared, possibly to unpack. At Welch's summons, Dixon left Margaret to help arrange some chairs. 'What's the next item on the programme, Professor?' he asked.

Welch's heavy features had settled into their depressive look after the manic phase of the last hour and a half. He gave Dixon a mutinous glare. 'Just one or two instrumental items.'

'Oh, that'll be nice. Who's first on the list?'

The other brooded, his slab-like hands on the back of a ludicrously low chair that resembled an inefficiently converted hassock. In a moment he disclosed that the local composer and the amateur violinist were going to 'tackle' a violin sonata by some Teutonic bore, that an unstated number of recorders would then perform some suitable item, and that at some later time Johns might be expected to produce music from his oboe. Dixon nodded as if pleased.

He returned to Margaret to find her in conversation with Carol Goldsmith. This woman, aged about forty, thin, with long straight brown hair, Dixon regarded as one of his allies, though sometimes she overawed him a little with her mature air.

'Hallo, Jim, how's it going?' she asked in her abnormally clear voice.

'Badly. There's at least an hour of scraping and blowing in front of us.'

'Yes, that's badly all right, isn't it? Why do we come to this sort of thing? Well, I know why you come, Jim, and poor Margaret's living here. I suppose what I mean is why the hell do I come.'

'Oh, wifely support for your spouse, I take it,' Margaret said.

'Something in that, I suppose. But why does he come? There aren't even any drinks.'

'James has already noticed that.'

'It would hardly be worth coming just to meet the great painter, would it?' Dixon said, meaning to start a conversation that might diminish his retrospective embarrassment over the recent Loosmore–Callaghan *imbroglio*.

For a reason he didn't then understand, the reception of this remark was perceptibly unfavourable. Margaret looked at him with lifted chin as if ready to reprove some indiscretion, but to her any sort of adverse remark about anybody was, unless they were alone, indiscreet enough. Carol half closed her eyes and smoothed her straight hair. 'What makes you say that?' she said.

'Well, nothing really,' Dixon said in alarm. 'I had a little brush with him just now, that's all. I got into some mix-up over his girl's name, and he was a bit offensive, I thought. Nothing drastic.'

'Oh, that's quite typical,' Carol said. 'He always thinks he's being got at. He often is, too.'

43

'Oh, you know him, do you?' Dixon said. 'I'm sorry, Carol; is he a great pal of yours?'

'Hardly that. We saw a bit of him last summer, you know, Cecil and I, before you got your job. He can be quite entertaining at times, actually, though you're quite right about the great-painter stuff; it does get you down occasionally. You've met him once or twice, haven't you, Margaret? What did you think of him?'

'Yes, I met him when he came down before. I thought he was all right when you got him on his own. I think he feels that when he's got an audience he's got to play up to it and impress everyone.'

A great baying laugh made all three turn round. Bertrand, leading Goldsmith by the arm, was approaching. With the remnants of his laughter still trickling from his face, he said to Carol: 'Ah, there you are, dear girl. And how are things with you?'

'Well enough, thank you, dear man. I can see how things are with you. A bit out of your usual run, isn't she?'

'Christine? Ah, now there's a grand girl for you, a grand girl. One of the best, she is.'

'Any plans for her?' Carol pursued, smiling slightly.

'Plans? Plans? No no, no plans at all. Unquestionably none.'

'Not like you, old boy,' said Goldsmith's furry monotone, so different from his bawling tenor in song.

'At the moment, quite frankly, she's made me more than a little piqued,' Bertrand said, making a circle of thumb and forefinger to emphasize the last word.

'How's that, Bertrand?' Goldsmith asked solicitously.

'Well, as you may imagine, despite my passionate interest in this kind of sport,' he nodded towards the piano, where the amateur violinist was tuning his violin with the cooperation of the local composer, 'it isn't quite enough to draw me down here unaided, glad as I am to see you all. No no; I had been promised a meeting with one Julius Gore-Urquhart, of whom you may have heard.'

Dixon had indeed heard of Gore-Urquhart, a rich devotee of the arts who made occasional contributions to the arts sections of the weekly reviews, who had a house in the neighbourhood where persons of distinction sometimes came to stay, and who was a fish that Welch had more than once vainly tried to land. Dixon looked again at Bertrand's eyes. They really were extraordinary: it seemed as if a sheet of some patterned material were tacked to the inside of his face, showing only at two arbitrary loopholes. What could a man with such eyes, such a beard, and (he noticed them for the first time) such dissimilar ears have to do with a man like Gore-Urquhart?

He learned what they had to do with each other in the next minute or two. As yet, the connexion was tenuous: the Callaghan girl, who knew Gore-Urquhart's family, or was even perhaps his niece, had arranged to introduce Bertrand to him during the current week-end. At some late stage it had been found that Gore-Urquhart was at present in Paris, so that a further visit to this part of the world would have to be undertaken to meet him. There was some reason, which Dixon at once forgot, why a meeting in London would be less satisfactory. And what was Gore-Urquhart going to do for Bertrand when they did meet?

When Margaret had asked for this information in her circumlocutory way, Bertrand raised his great head and looked down his cheeks from face to face before replying. 'I have it on more than ordinarily good authority,' he said in measured tones, 'that our influential friend will shortly be declaring his private secretaryship vacant. I doubt whether the post will be publicly competed for, and so I'm at the moment busily engaged in grooming myself for the part. Patronage, you see, patronage: that's what it'll be. I'll answer his letters with one hand and paint with the other.' He gave a laugh in which Goldsmith and Margaret joined. 'So I'm naturally anxious to strike while the iron's hot, if you'll pardon the expression.'

Why shouldn't they pardon the expression? Dixon thought. Why?

'When do you think you'll be down again then, old boy?' Goldsmith asked. 'We'll have to fix something up. Haven't had a chance this time.'

'Oh, in a fortnight or so, I expect,' Bertrand said, then added significantly: 'Miss Callaghan and I have another engagement for next week-end. You'll understand I don't want to miss that.'

'The week-end after's the Summer Ball at the College.' Margaret cut in quickly, in an attempt, Dixon supposed, to smother the overtones of this last declaration. How could Bertrand possibly bring himself to say things like that in front of one woman he hardly knew and one man he must guess hadn't liked him all that much at a first meeting?

'Oh, is it really?' Bertrand asked with apparent interest.

'Yes; will you be coming again this year, Mr Welch?'

'I might manage it, I suppose. I remember being not unentertained last time. Ah, I see cigarettes are being produced. I like cigarettes. May I detach one from your store, Cecil? Good. Well, what about this Ball, then? They won't be able to keep you away, I suppose?'

'Afraid they will this time,' Goldsmith said. 'There's a conference of teachers of history then at Leeds. Your father wants me to go to it.'

'Dear, dear,' Bertrand said. 'That's most unfortunate, most unfortunate. Isn't there anyone else he could send?' He looked over at Dixon.

'Afraid not. We went into all that,' Goldsmith said.

'Pity, pity. Ah well. Will any other members of the company be attending, I wonder?'

Margaret glanced at Dixon, and Carol said: 'What about you, Jim?'

Dixon shook his head firmly. 'No, I've never been much of a dancing man, I'm afraid. As far as I'm concerned it would be just money thrown away.' It would be terrible if Margaret blackmailed him into taking her.

'Oh well, we don't want that, do we?' Bertrand said. 'That wouldn't do at all. I wonder where young Callaghan has got to. Her nose must be fairly thickly encrusted with powder by now, I should hazard. And why the delay among the musicians?'

Dixon looked over and saw that the two performers, tuning evidently completed, music set up, and bow resined were hanging about smoking and chatting. Welch was nowhere to be seen; he must be displaying his rather terrifying expertise as an evader. At the other end of the long, low, softly-lit room the door opened and the Callaghan woman came in. For so well-built a girl Dixon thought she moved awkwardly.

'Ah, my dear,' Bertrand said with a gallant bow, 'we were wondering what had become of you.'

She seemed disconcerted. 'Oh, I've only been . . .'

'We've been discussing Mr Gore-Urquhart, and wondering whether he'll be available the week-end after next, there being a species of dancing festivity at the College during that time. Can you enlighten us, I wonder?'

'Well, his secretary said he'd probably be in Paris till the middle of next month, which would be too late for that, wouldn't it?'

'Yes, I think it would. Yes, it would. Oh well, it'll have to be another time, won't it?' He didn't appear at all put out by this news.

'I've written to Uncle asking him to let me know when he's coming back.'

Dixon wanted to laugh at this. It always amused him to hear girls (men never did it) refer to 'Uncle', 'Daddy', and so on, as if there were only one uncle or daddy in the world, or as if this particular uncle or daddy were the uncle or daddy of all those present.

'What's the joke, Jim?' Carol asked. Bertrand stared at him.

'Oh, nothing.' He returned Bertrand's stare. He wished there were some issue on which he could defeat Bertrand, even at the risk of alienating his father. Any measure short of, or not necessitating too much, violence would be justified. But there seemed to be no field of endeavour where he could employ a measure of that sort. For a moment he felt like devoting the next ten years to working his way to a position as art critic on purpose to review Bertrand's work unfavourably. He thought of a sentence in a book he'd once read: 'And with that he picked up the bloody old towser by the scruff of the neck, and, by Jesus, he near throttled him.' This too made him smile, and Bertrand's beard twitched, but he said nothing to break the pause.

As ever, Margaret had thought of something to say: 'I was reading about your uncle only recently, Miss Callaghan. There was a piece about him in the local paper. He was presenting some water-colours to our Gallery here. I don't know what we should do without someone like him to keep things going.'

This remark, in itself virtually unanswerable, had the effect, familiar to Margaret's acquaintances, of dumbfounding its audience by the obviousness of its intention – namely, the intention of forcing them to talk. Some feet away the amateur violinist could be heard laughing huskily at something the local composer was telling him. Where was Welch?

'Yes, he is very generous,' the Callaghan girl said.

'It's a good job there are some people still about who can afford to be, in that way,' Margaret said. Dixon looked up to catch Carol's eye, but she was exchanging a glance with her husband.

'Well, there won't be much longer, I fear, if the lads at Transport House go on running our lives for us,' Bertrand said.

'Oh, I don't think this crowd have done too badly,' Goldsmith put in. 'After all, you can't . . .'

'Their foreign policy might, I agree, have been a good deal worse, with the exception of their spectacular inability to pour water on troubled oil.' Bertrand looked quickly round the group, then went on: 'But their home policy . . . soak the rich . . . I mean . . .' He seemed to be hesitating. 'Well, it is that, pure and simple, isn't it? I'm just asking for information, that's all. I mean that's what it seems to be, don't we all agree? I take it that it is just that and no more, isn't it? Or am I wrong?'

Pretending not to notice Margaret's warning frown and Carol's expectant grin, Dixon said quietly: 'Well, what's wrong with it, even if it is that and no more? If one man's got ten buns and another's got two, and a bun has got to be given up by one of them, then surely you take it from the man with ten buns.'

Bertrand and his girl were looking at each other with identical expressions, shaking their heads, smiling, raising their eyebrows, sighing. It was as if Dixon had just said that he didn't know anything about art, but he did know what he liked. 'But we don't think anybody need give up a bun, Mr Dixon,' the girl said. 'That's the whole point.'

'Hardly the whole point, I should have thought,' Dixon said at the moment when Margaret said, 'Don't let's get involved in a set-to about . . .' and Bertrand said, 'The whole point of this is that the rich . . .'

It was Bertrand who won the little contest. 'The point is that the rich play an essential role in modern society,' he said, his voice baying a little more noticeably. 'More than ever in days like these. That's all; I'm not going to bore you with the stock platitudes about their having kept the arts going, and so on. The very fact that they are stock platitudes proves my case. And I happen to like the arts, you sam.'

The last word, a version of 'see', was Bertrand's own coinage. It arose as follows: the vowel sound became distorted into a short 'a', as if he were going to say 'sat'. This brought his lips some way apart, and the effect of their rapid closure was to end the syllable with a light but audible 'm'. After working this out, Dixon could think of little to say, and contented himself with 'You do', which he tried to make knowing and sceptical.

It seemed to encourage Bertrand. 'Yes, I do,' he said even more loudly, so that all his listeners looked quickly at him. 'And shall I tell you what else I happen to like? Rich people. I take pride in the contemporary unpopularity of that statement. And why do I like them? Because they're charming, because they're generous, because they've learnt to appreciate the things I happen to like myself, because their houses are full of beautiful things. That's why I like them and that's why I don't want them soaked. All right?'

'Come along, dear,' Mrs Welch called from behind them. 'If we wait for Father we'll be here all night. Shall we make a start? If you'll come over here we can all sit down.'

'All right, Mother,' Bertrand said over his shoulder, and the group began to dissolve, but before he moved himself he said, his eyes on Dixon: 'That's quite clear, is it?'

Margaret pulled at Dixon's sleeve and he, not wanting to go on fighting after the end of the round, said amicably: 'Oh yes. You seem to have been luckier in the rich people you've come into contact with than I have, that's all.'

'That wouldn't surprise me in the least,' Bertrand said with some contempt, standing aside so that Margaret could pass him.

Dixon said angrily: 'Well, you'd better make the most of them while you've got them, then, because you won't have them much longer, you know.'

He began to push past after Margaret, but the Callaghan girl halted him by saying: 'I'd rather you didn't talk in that strain, if you don't mind.'

Dixon looked about him; the rest of the company were seated, and the amateur violinist was snuggling his instrument in under his chin. Dropping into the nearest chair, Dixon said in a lowered voice: 'You say you'd rather I didn't talk in that strain?'

'Yes, if you don't mind.' She and Bertrand also sat down. 'I always get a bit irritated by that sort of thing. I'm sorry, I can't do anything about it; it's just a thing about me, I'm afraid.'

If Dixon hadn't learnt to dislike this argument when offered by Margaret, he probably wouldn't have answered as he did. 'Seen anybody about it yet?'

The amateur violinist nodded the top half of his body and, supported by the local composer, burst into some scurrying tune-lessness or other. Bertrand leaned over towards Dixon. 'What the hell do you mean?' he asked in a loud undertone.

'Who's your alienist?' Dixon said, broadening his field of fire.

'Look here, Dixon, you're talking as if you want a bloody good punch on the nose, aren't you?'

Dixon, when moved, was bad at ordering his thoughts. 'If I did; you don't think you're the one to give me one, do you?'

Bertrand screwed up his face at this enigma. 'What?'

'Do you know what you look like in that beard?' Dixon's heart began to race as he switched to simplicity.

'All right; coming outside for a bit?'

The latest of this string of questions was drowned by a long rumbling shake in the bass of the piano. 'What?' Dixon asked.

Mrs Welch, Margaret, Johns, the Goldsmiths, and the contralto woman all seemed to turn round simultaneously. 'Ssshh,' they all said. It was like a railway engine blowing out steam under a glass roof. Dixon got up and tiptoed to the door. Bertrand half rose to follow, but his girl stopped him.

Before Dixon could reach the door, it opened and Welch entered. 'Oh, you've started, have you?' he asked without dropping his voice at all.

'Yes,' Dixon whispered. 'I think I'll just . . .'

'Pity you couldn't have waited a little longer. I've been on the phone, you see. It was that chap from the . . . from the . . .'

'See you later.' Dixon began edging past to the doorway.

'Aren't you going to stay for the P. Racine Fricker?'

'Shan't be long, Professor. I just think I'll . . .' Dixon made some gestures meant to be indecipherable. 'I'll be back.'

He shut the door on Welch's long-lived, wondering frown.

5

'He was going down-grade making ninety miles an hour, when his whistle began to scream,' Dixon sang. 'He was found in the wreck with his hand on the throttle . . .' He broke off, panting; it was hard work walking up the dry sandy track to the Welches' house, especially with so much beer distributed about his frame. A dreamy smile stretched his face in the darkness as he savoured again in retrospect that wonderful moment at ten o'clock. It had been like a first authentic experience of art or human goodness, a stern, rapt, almost devotional exaltation. Gulping down what he'd assumed must be his last pint of the evening, he'd noticed that drinks were still being ordered and served, that people were still coming in and that their expressions were confident, not anxious, that a new sixpence had tinkled into the works of the bar-billiard table. Illumination had come when the white-coated barman struggled in with two fresh crates of Guinness. The little town and the city were in different counties; the local pubs, unlike the city pubs and the hotel he went to with Margaret, stayed open till ten-thirty during the summer, and the summer had now officially begun. His gratitude had been inexpressible in words; only further calls at the bar could pay that happy debt. As a result he'd spent more than he could afford and drunk more than he ought, and yet he felt nothing but satisfaction and peace. Rebounding painfully from the gatepost, he began creeping round the cobbled environs of the house.

The large, long room at the back, where the music had been going on, was in darkness. That was good. Further round, however, where the drawing-room was, there were lights and, he soon found, voices in conversation. Peering through a chink in the curtains, he saw Welch, in his crimson-striped blue raincoat and fishing-hat, just going out of the door, followed by the local composer and Cecil Goldsmith, both of them also dressed in raincoats. People were evidently about to be driven home; Dixon grinned as he imagined the sort of drive Welch would give them. Carol, in a light tweed coat, stayed for a moment to exchange a last remark with Bertrand. Nobody else was in the room.

A nearby window was open, but Dixon couldn't catch the words now spoken by Bertrand. He could tell from their intonation, however, that they formed a question, to which Carol said: 'Yes, all right.' At this, Bertrand stepped forward and put his arms round her. Dixon couldn't see what followed, because Bertrand had his back to the window, but if there was a kiss it lasted only a moment; Carol freed herself and hurried out. Bertrand went too.

Dixon went back to the music-room and got in through the french window. What he'd seen had disturbed him in some way he couldn't tie down. Though theoretically inured to that kind of activity, he found its close proximity disagreeable rather than anything else. To have seen and talked to Cecil Goldsmith several times a week for some months didn't make the fellow any less a nonentity, but it gave him a claim on one, a claim which was somehow invoked by the sight of his wife being handled by a third party, especially that third party. Dixon wished he hadn't found that gap in the curtains, then thrust the matter from his mind. All his attention would be needed for the operation of getting up to his bedroom undetected.

Deciding that the small risk of someone coming into the music-room had got to be faced anyway, Dixon groped through the darkness to an armchair, lay back in it, closed his eyes, and heard with satisfaction the sound of Welch's car being started up and driven away. After a moment, he felt as if he were heeling over backwards, and the pit of his stomach seemed to swell so as to start enclosing his head within it. He opened his eyes again, making his tragic-mask face; yes, it had after all been a bad idea to take that last pint. He got up and began a skipping-with-arms-raising exercise he'd learnt all about in the R.A.F. Five hundred skips and raising

53

of the arms had helped to clear his head before. After a hundred and eighty an unclear head seemed much preferable to more skips. It was time to move.

Half-way across the hall he heard the sound of Bertrand's laugh, but well muffled by an intervening door. He creaked up the stairs and across the landing. Through some architectural vagary, his bedroom could only be approached by way of a large bathroom, the outer door of which he now tried to open. Nothing happened. The bathroom was evidently occupied; perhaps Johns had decided to blockade the bedroom allotted to the defacer of his periodical. Dixon stood well back, straddling, and raised his hands like a conductor on the brink of some thunderous overture or tone-poem; then, half-conductor, half-boxer, went into a brief manic flurry of obscene gestures. Just then somebody opened a door on the other side of the landing. There was no time to do anything at all except adopt the attitude of one waiting outside a bathroom, a stratagem vitiated to some extent by the raincoat he still wore.

'James! What on earth are you doing?'

Never had Dixon been so glad to see Margaret rather than anyone else. 'Ssshh,' he said. 'Get me away from here.'

He liked her even more when she beckoned to him and led him, without more words, into her bedroom. Just as he closed the door of this, whoever it was came out of the bathroom. Dixon realized his heart had been pounding. 'Thank God for that,' he said.

'Well, where have you been all the evening, James?'

While he told her he commented adversely to himself on her resentful expression and manner, which soon overrode his feelings of relief. What would this sort of thing be like if they ever got married? At the same time he had to admit she looked at her best in the blue dressing-gown, her brown hair, tawny in places, loosed from its pins and rolls. He took off his raincoat and lit a cigarette, beginning to feel better. He finished what he had to say without mentioning what he'd seen through the drawing-room window.

After hearing him out in silence she smiled slightly. 'Well, I can't really blame you, I suppose. It was rather rude, all the same. I could see Mrs Neddy thought it was a bit off.'

'Oh, she thought that it was a bit that, did she? Where did you say I'd gone?'

'I didn't get a chance to say anything: Evan told her he thought you'd probably gone to the pub.'

'I'll wring that little bastard's neck one of these days. My God, that's good, isn't it? Nice friendly spirit. This ought to put me nicely in bad with the Neddies. And don't call him Evan.'

'Don't worry too much. Neddy didn't seem to mind.'

Dixon snorted. 'How can you possibly be sure of that? There's no way of telling what goes on inside that head of his, if anything. Just hang on here a minute, will you? There's something I want to do in the bathroom. Don't go away.'

When he came back she was still sitting on the bed, but had evidently put on some lipstick for him. This pleased him, more from the implied compliment than from the actual effect; indeed, he was beginning to feel really good again, and stayed like that, even leaning back in his chair, while for a few minutes they discussed the early part of the evening. Then Margaret said: 'I say, don't you think you ought to be going? It's getting late.'

'I know, I will in a minute. I'm enjoying this.'

'So am I. It's the first time we've been really alone for . . . how long?'

One of the effects of this query was to make Dixon feel very drunk, and afterwards he could never quite work out why he did what he did next, which was sitting down beside Margaret on the bed, putting his arm round her shoulders and kissing her firmly on the mouth. Whatever his motives – the blue dressing-gown, the uncoiled hair, the specially-put-on lipstick, the pints of local bitter, his wish to bring their relations to some crisis, his wish to avoid a further salvo of intimate questions and avowals, and his worry about his job all came into it – the effects were unequivocal: she put her arms round his neck and kissed him back with zeal, with more zeal, in fact, than she'd shown in any of their previous, rather half-hearted and altogether inconclusive, sexual encounters in her flat. Dixon twitched off his, then her, spectacles and put them down somewhere. He kissed her again, harder; he felt his head spin, faster. After a minute or two there seemed no reason why he shouldn't put his hand in under the lapel of her dressing-gown. She murmured some endearment and tightened her arms round his neck.

Why shouldn't he go on? It seemed he'd be able to, though he couldn't tell how far. Did he want to? Yes, in a way, but was it fair to her? He remembered dimly how he'd advised her not to get into even the mildest sexual entanglement for a good long time, say a year, after the Catchpole one. Was it fair to her? Was it fair to him? He could only just handle her as a female friend; as her 'lover' he'd be a cowboy facing his first, and notoriously formidable, steer. No, it wouldn't be fair to him. And it certainly wouldn't be fair to her, confronting her with something that could hardly fail to disturb and upset her in the short run, let alone what might happen later. No, she oughtn't to have it. On the other hand – Dixon battled for clear, or any, thought – she certainly seemed to want it. He felt her breath, soft and warm, on his cheek, and his desire, which had been failing, suddenly strengthened. Of course, all that had been worrying him was fear of a rebuff. He withdrew his hand, then put it back, this time under her nightdress. This, and the shudder she gave, made his head reel the furthest yet; too far, indeed, for him to do any more thinking. The silence roared in his ears.

Some short time later, as they lay on the bed, he made a movement not only quite unambiguous, but even, perhaps, rather insolently frank. Margaret's response to it, though violent, was hard to interpret. Without hesitation Dixon advanced further. There was a brief rolling struggle, then he found himself flung sideways with enough vigour to bring his head, with a brisk report, into contact with the bed's foot-board. Margaret got up, adjusting her dressing-gown, and picked up his raincoat. 'Go on,' she said. 'Out you go, James.'

He struggled to his feet and managed to catch his coat when she flung it. 'I'm sorry; what's the matter?'

'Out.' Her small figure was trembling with anger.

'All right, but I don't see . . .'

She opened the door and gestured with her head. Feet were mounting the stairs to the landing.

'Look, there's somebody . . .'

He found himself bundled out, his coat over his arm, his head spinning in a new direction. Half-way to the bathroom he found himself confronted by the Callaghan woman. 'Good evening,' he said politely. She looked away and went past him to her room. He tried to open the bathroom door; it was again locked. Without thinking he threw back his head, filled his lungs, and let loose a loud and prolonged bray of rage which recalled, in volume and timbre, Goldsmith's performance in the madrigals. Then he clumped down the stairs, hung his coat on a hook, went into the dining-room, and genuflected in front of the fake, or possibly genuine, eighteenth-century sideboard.

In a moment he'd taken a bottle of port from among the sherry, beer, and cider which filled half a shelf inside. It was from this very bottle that Welch had, the previous evening, poured Dixon the smallest drink he'd ever been seriously offered. Some of the writing on the label was in a Romance language, but not all. Just right: not too British, and not too foreign either. The cork came out with a festive, Yule-tide pop which made him wish he had some nuts and raisins; he drank deeply. Some of the liquor coursed refreshingly down his chin and under his shirt-collar. The bottle had been about three-quarters full when he started, and was about three-quarters empty when he stopped. He thumped and clinked it back into position, wiped his mouth on the sideboard-runner, and, feeling really splendid, gained his bedroom without opposition.

Here he wandered about for a few minutes, undressing slowly, thinking as best he could about the encounter with Margaret. Had he really wanted what his actions had implied? As before, the only answer was Yes, in a way. But he wouldn't have tried, would he?

or not so hard, anyway, if she hadn't seemed so keen. And why had she decided to seem so keen, after so many weeks of seeming so not keen? Most likely because of some new novelist she'd been reading. But of course she ought to be keen anyway. It's what she really wants, he thought, scowling with the emphasis with which he put this to himself. She doesn't know it, but it's what she really wants, what her nature really demands. And, God, it was his due, wasn't it? After all he'd put up with. But was it fair to her to implicate her in this sort of situation after all she'd had to put up with? As soon as Dixon recognized the mental envelope containing this question he thrust it away from him unopened, and went into the bathroom tying his pyjama-cord.

It wasn't as nice in the bathroom as it had been in the bedroom. Though it was a cool night for early summer, he found he felt hot and was sweating. He stood for some time in front of the washbasin, trying to discover more about how he felt. His body seemed swollen below the chest and uneven in density. The stuff coming from the light seemed less like light than a very thin but cloudy phosphorescent gas; it gave a creamy hum. He turned on the cold tap and bent over the basin. When he did this, he had to correct an impulse to go on leaning forward until his head lay between the taps. He wetted his face, took a bakelite mug from the glass shelf above the basin, and drank a very great deal of water, which momentarily refreshed him, though it had some other effect as well which he couldn't at once identify. He cleaned his teeth with a lot of toothpaste, wetted his face again, refilled the mug, and ate some more toothpaste.

He stood brooding by his bed. His face was heavy, as if little bags of sand had been painlessly sewn into various parts of it, dragging the features away from the bones, if he still had bones in his face. Suddenly feeling worse, he heaved a shuddering sigh. Someone seemed to have leapt nimbly up behind him and encased him in a kind of diving-suit made of invisible cotton-wool. He gave a quiet groan; he didn't want to feel any worse than this.

He began getting into bed. His four surviving cigarettes – had he really smoked twelve that evening? – lay in their packet on a polished table at the bed-head, accompanied by matches, the bakelite mug of water, and an ashtray from the mantelpiece. A temporary inability to raise his second foot on to the bed let him know what had been the secondary effect of drinking all that water: it had made him drunk. This became a primary effect when he lay in bed. On the fluttering mantelpiece was a small china effigy, the representation, in a squatting position, of a well-known Oriental religious figure. Had Welch put it there as a silent sermon to him on the merits of the contemplative life? If so, the message had come too late. He reached up and turned off the light by the hanging switch above his head. The room began to rise upwards from the right-hand bottom corner of the bed, and yet seemed to keep in the same position. He threw back the covers and sat on the edge of the bed, his legs hanging. The room composed itself to rest. After a few moments he swung his legs back and lay down. The room lifted. He put his feet to the floor. The room stayed still. He put his legs on the bed but didn't lie down. The room moved. He sat on the edge of the bed. Nothing. He put one leg up on the bed. Something. In fact a great deal. He was evidently in a highly critical condition. Swearing hoarsely, he heaped up the pillows, half-lay, half-sat against them, and dangled his legs half-over the edge of the bed. In this position he was able to lower himself gingerly into sleep.

6

Dixon was alive again. Consciousness was upon him before he could get out of the way; not for him the slow, gracious wandering from the halls of sleep, but a summary, forcible ejection. He lay sprawled, too wicked to move, spewed up like a broken spider-crab on the tarry shingle of the morning. The light did him harm, but not as much as looking at things did; he resolved, having done it once, never to move his eyeballs again. A dusty thudding in his head made the scene before him beat like a pulse. His mouth had been used as a latrine by some small creature of the night, and then as its mausoleum. During the night, too, he'd somehow been on a cross-country run and then been expertly beaten up by secret police. He felt bad.

He reached out for and put on his glasses. At once he saw that something was wrong with the bedclothes immediately before his face. Endangering his chance of survival, he sat up a little, and what met his bursting eyes roused to a frenzy the timpanist in his head. A large, irregular area of the turned-back part of the sheet was missing; a smaller but still considerable area of the turned-back part of the blanket was missing; an area about the size of the palm of his hand in the main part of the top blanket was missing. Through the three holes, which, appropriately enough, had black borders, he could see a dark brown mark on the second blanket. He ran a finger round a bit of the hole in the sheet, and when he looked at his finger it bore a dark-grey stain. That meant ash; ash meant burning; burning must mean cigarettes. Had this cigarette burnt itself out on the blanket? If not, where was it now? Nowhere on the bed; nor in it. He leaned over the side, gritting his teeth; a sunken brown channel, ending in a fragment of discoloured paper, lay across a light patch in the pattern of a valuable-looking rug.

This made him feel very unhappy, a feeling sensibly increased when he looked at the bedside table. This was marked by two black, charred grooves, greyish and shiny in parts, lying at right angles and stopping well short of the ashtray, which held a single used match. On the table were two unused matches; the remainder lay with the empty cigarette packet on the floor. The bakelite mug was nowhere to be seen.

Had he done all this himself? Or had a wayfarer, a burglar, camped out in his room? Or was he the victim of some Horla fond of tobacco? He thought that on the whole he must have done it himself, and wished he hadn't. Surely this would mean the loss of his job, especially if he failed to go to Mrs Welch and confess what he'd done, and he knew already that he wouldn't be able to do that. There was no excuse which didn't consist of the inexcusable: an incendiary was no more pardonable when revealed as a drunkard as well – so much of a drunkard, moreover, that obligations to hosts and fellow-guests and the counter-attraction of a chamber-concert were as nothing compared with the lure of the drink. The only hope was that Welch wouldn't notice what his wife would presumably tell him about the burning of the bedclothes. But Welch had been known to notice things, the attack on his pupil's book in that essay, for example. But that had really been an attack on Welch himself; he couldn't much care what happened to sheets and blankets which he wasn't actually using at the time. Dixon remembered thinking on an earlier occasion that to yaw drunkenly round the Common Room in Welch's presence screeching obscenities, punching out the window-panes, fouling the periodicals, would escape Welch's notice altogether, provided his own person remained inviolate. The memory in turn reminded him of a sentence in a book of Alfred Beesley's he'd once glanced at: 'A stimulus cannot be received by the mind unless it serves some need of the organism.' He began laughing, an action he soon modified to a wince.

He got out of bed and went into the bathroom. After a minute or two he returned, eating toothpaste and carrying a safety-razor-

61

blade. He started carefully cutting round the edges of the burnt areas of the bedclothes with the blade. He didn't know why he did this, but the operation did seem to improve the look of things: the cause of the disaster wasn't so immediately apparent. When all the edges were smooth and regular, he knelt down slowly, as if he'd all at once become a very old man, and shaved the appropriate part of the rug. The debris from these modifications he stuffed into his jacket pocket, thinking that he'd have a bath and then go downstairs and phone Bill Atkinson and ask him to come through with his message about the senior Dixons a good deal earlier than had been arranged. He sat on the bed for a moment to recover from his vertiginous exertions with the rug, then, before he could rise, somebody, soon identifiable as male, came into the bathroom next door. He heard the clinking of a plug-chain, then the swishing of tap-water. Welch, or his son, or Johns was about to take a bath. Which one it was was soon settled by the upsurge of a deep, untrained voice into song. The piece was recognizable to Dixon as some skein of untiring facetiousness by filthy Mozart. Bertrand was surely unlikely to sing anything at all, and Johns made no secret of his indifference to anything earlier than Richard Strauss. Very slowly, like a forest giant under the axe, Dixon heeled over sideways and came to rest with his hot face on the pillow.

This, of course, would give him time to collect his thoughts, and that, of course, was just what he didn't want to do with his thoughts; the longer he could keep them apart from one another, especially the ones about Margaret, the better. For the first time he couldn't avoid imagining what she'd say to him, if indeed she'd say anything, when he next saw her. He pushed his tongue down in front of his lower teeth, screwed up his nose as tightly as he could, and made gibbering motions with his mouth. How long would it be before he could persuade her first to open, then to empty, her locker of reproaches, as preliminary to the huge struggle of getting her to listen to his apologies? Desperately he tried to listen to Welch's song, to marvel at its matchless predictability, its austere, unswerving devotion to tedium; but it didn't work.

Then he tried to feel pleased about the acceptance of his article, but all he could remember was Welch's seeming indifference on hearing the news and his injunction, so exasperatingly like Beesley's, to 'get a definite date from him, Dixon, otherwise it's not much . . . not much . . .' He sat up and by degrees worked his feet to the floor.

There was an alternative to the Atkinson plan; the simpler, nicer one of clearing out at once without a word to anybody. That wouldn't really do, though, unless he cleared out as far as London. What was going on in London now? He began to take off his pyjamas, deciding to omit his bath. Those wide streets and squares would be deserted at this time, except for a few lonely, hurrying figures; he could revisualize it all from remembering a week-end leave during the war. He sighed; he might as well be thinking of Monte Carlo or Chinese Turkestan; then, jigging on the rug with one foot out of, the other still in, his pyjamas, thought of nothing but the pain that slopped through his head like water into a sand-castle. He clung to the mantelpiece, nearly displacing the squatting Oriental, crumpling like a shot film-gunman. Had Chinese Turkestan its Margarets and Welches?

Some minutes later he was in the bathroom. Welch had left grime round the bath and steam on the mirror. After a little thought, Dixon stretched out a finger and wrote 'Ned Welch is a Soppy Fool with a Fase like A Pigs qum' in the steam; then he rubbed the glass with a towel and looked at himself. He didn't look too bad, really; anyway, better than he felt. His hair, however, despite energetic brushing helped out by the use of a water-soaked nail-brush, was already springing away from his scalp. He considered using soap as a pomatum, but decided against it, having in the past several times converted the short hairs at the sides and back of his head into the semblance of duck-plumage by this expedient. His glasses seemed more goggle-like than usual. As always, though, he looked healthy and, he hoped, honest and kindly. He'd have to be content with that.

He was all ready to slink down to the phone when, returning

to the bedroom, he again surveyed the mutilated bedclothes. They looked in some way unsatisfactory; he couldn't have said how. He went and locked the outer bathroom door, picked up the razor-blade, and began again on the circumferences of the holes. This time he made jagged cuts into the material, little inlets from the great missing areas. Some pieces he almost severed. Finally he held the blade at right angles and ran it quickly round the holes, rough-ening them up. He stood back from his work and decided the effect was perceptibly better. The disaster now seemed much less obvi-ously the work of man and might, for a few seconds, be put down to some fulminant dry-rot or the ravages of a colony of moths. He turned the rug round so that the shaven burn, without being actu-ally hidden by a nearby chair, was none the less not far from it. He was considering taking the bedside table downstairs and later throwing it out of the bus on his journey back when a familiar voice came into aural range singing in a way that suggested head-wagging jollity. It grew in volume, like the apprehension of something harmful or awful, until the locked bathroom door began to be shaken and its handle to be rattled. The singing stopped, but the rattling went on, was joined by kicking, even momentarily replaced by the thudding of what must be a shoulder. Welch hadn't thought in advance that the bathroom might bear signs of occupa-tion by another when he wanted to get back into it himself (why, in any case, did he want to get back into it?), nor did he soon real-ize it now. After trying several manoeuvres to replace his first vain rattling of the handle, he returned his attention to a vain rattling of the handle. There was a final orgasm of shakings, knockings, thuddings, and rattlings, then footsteps retreated and a door closed.

With tears of rage in his eyes, Dixon left the bedroom, first unin-tentionally treading on and shattering the bakelite mug, which must have rolled out from under something into his path. Downstairs, he looked at the hall clock – twenty past eight – and went into the drawing-room, where the phone was. It was a good job that Atkin-son got up early on Sundays to go out for the papers. He'd be able to catch him easily before he went. He picked up the phone.

What gave him most trouble during the next twenty-five minutes was giving vent to his feelings without hurting his head too much. Nothing whatever came out of the receiver during that time except the faint sea-shell whispering. As he sat on the arm of a leather-covered armchair, putting his face through all its permutations of loathing, the whole household seemed to spring into activity around him. Footsteps walked the floor above his head; others descended the stairs and entered the breakfast-room; still others came from the back of the house and also entered the breakfast-room; far off a vacuum-cleaner whined; a cistern flushed; a door banged; a voice called. When it sounded as if a posse was being assembled immediately outside the drawing-room door, he hung up and left, his bottom aching from its narrow seat, his arm aching from rattling the receiver-rest.

Breakfast technics at the Welches', like many of their ways of thought, recalled an earlier epoch. The food was kept hot on the sideboard in what Dixon conjectured were chafing-dishes. The quantity and variety of this food recalled in turn the fact that Mrs Welch supplemented Welch's professorial salary with a good-sized income of her own. Dixon had often wondered how Welch had contrived to marry money; it could hardly have been due to any personal merit, real or supposed, and the vagaries of Welch's mind could leave no room there for avarice. Perhaps the old fellow had had when younger what he now so demonstrably lacked: a way with him. In spite of the ravages wrought by his headache and his fury, Dixon felt happier as he wondered what foods would this morning afford visible proof of the Welches' prosperity. He went into the breakfast-room with the bedclothes and Margaret a long way from the foreground of his mind.

The only person in the room was the Callaghan girl, sitting behind a well-filled plate. Dixon said good morning to her.

'Oh, good morning.' Her tone was neutral, not hostile.

He quickly decided on a bluff, speak-my-mind approach as the best cloak for rudeness, past or to come. One of his father's friends, a jeweller, had got away with conversing almost entirely in insults for the fifteen years Dixon had known him, merely by using this simple device. Deliberately intensifying his northern accent, Dixon said: 'Afraid I got off on the wrong foot with you last night.'

She looked up quickly, and he saw with bitterness how pretty her neck was. 'Oh . . . that. I shouldn't worry too much about it if I were you. I didn't show up too well myself.'

'Nice of you to take it like that,' he said, remembering that he'd already had one occasion to use this phrase to her. 'Very bad manners it was on my part, anyway.'

'Well, let's forget it, shall we?'

'Glad to; thanks very much.'

There was a pause, while he noted with mild surprise how much and how quickly she was eating. The remains of a large pool of sauce were to be seen on her plate beside a diminishing mound of fried egg, bacon, and tomatoes. Even as he watched she replenished her stock of sauce with a fat scarlet gout from the bottle. She glanced up and caught his look of interest, raised her eyebrows, and said, 'I'm sorry, I like sauce; I hope you don't mind,' but not convincingly, and he fancied she blushed.

'That's all right,' he said heartily; 'I'm fond of the stuff myself.' He pushed aside his bowl of cornflakes. They were of a kind he didn't like: malt had been used in their preparation. A study of the egg and bacon and tomatoes opposite him made him decide to postpone eating any himself. His gullet and stomach felt as if they were being deftly sewn up as he sat. He poured and drank a cup of black coffee, then refilled his cup.

'Aren't you going to have any of this stuff?' the girl asked.

'Well, not yet, I don't think.'

'What's the matter? Aren't you feeling so good?'

'No, not really, I must admit. Bit of a headache, you know.'

'Oh, then you did go to the pub, like that little man said – what was his name?'

'Johns,' Dixon said, trying to suggest by his articulation of the name the correct opinion of its bearer. 'Yes, I did go to the pub.'

'You had a lot, did you?' In her interest she stopped eating, but still gripped her knife and fork, her fists resting on the cloth. He noticed that her fingers were square-tipped, with the nails cut quite close.

'I suppose I must have done, yes,' he replied.

'How much did you have?'

'Oh, I never count them. It's a bad habit, is counting them.'

'Yes, I dare say, but how many do you think it was? Roughly.'

'Ooh . . . seven or eight, possibly.'

'Beers, that is, is it?'

'Good Lord, yes. Do I look as if I can afford spirits?'

'Pints of beer?'

'Yes.' He smiled slightly, thinking she didn't seem such a bad sort after all, and that the slight blueness of the whites of her eyes helped to give her her look of health. He changed his mind abruptly about the first of these observations, and lost interest in the second, when she replied:

'Well, if you drink as much as that you must expect to feel a bit off colour the next day, mustn't you?' She drew herself upright in her seat in a schoolmarmy attitude.

He remembered his father, who until the war had always worn stiff white collars, being reproved by the objurgatory jeweller as excessively 'dignant' in demeanour. This etymological sport expressed for Dixon exactly what he objected to in Christine. He said rather coldly: 'Yes, I must, mustn't I?' It was an idiom he'd caught from Carol Goldsmith. Thinking of her made him think, for the first time that morning, of the embrace he'd witnessed the night before, and he realized that it had its bearing on this girl as well as on Goldsmith. Well, she could obviously take care of herself.

'Everybody was wondering where you'd got to,' she said.

'I've no doubt they were. Tell me: how did Mr Welch react?'

'What, to finding out you'd probably gone to the pub?'

'Yes. Did he seem irritated at all?'

'I really have no idea.' Conscious, possibly, that this must sound rather bald, she added: 'I don't know him at all, you see, and so I couldn't really tell. He didn't seem to notice much, if you see what I mean.'

Dixon saw. He felt too that he could tackle the eggs and bacon and tomatoes now, so went to get some and said: 'Well, that's a relief, I must say. I shall have to apologize to him, I suppose.'

'It might be a good idea.'

She said this in a tone that made him turn his back for a moment at the sideboard and make his Chinese mandarin's face, hunching his shoulders a little. He disliked this girl and her boy-friend so much that he couldn't understand why they didn't dislike each other. Suddenly he remembered the bedclothes; how could he have been such a fool? He couldn't possibly leave them like that. He must do something else to them. He must get up to his room quickly and look at them and see what ideas their physical presence suggested. 'God,' he said absently; 'oh my God,' then, pulling himself together: 'I'm afraid I shall have to dash off now.'

'Have you got to get back?'

'No, I'm not actually going until . . . No, I mean there's . . . I've got to go upstairs.' Realizing that this was a poor exit-line, he said wildly, still holding a dish-cover: 'There's something wrong with my room, something I must alter.' He looked at her and saw her eyes were dilated. 'I had a fire last night.'

'You lit a fire in your bedroom?'

'No, I didn't light it purposely, I lit it with a cigarette. It caught fire on its own.'

Her expression changed again. 'Your bedroom caught fire?'

'No, only the bed. I lit it with a cigarette.'

'You mean you set fire to your bed?'

'That's right.'

'With a cigarette? Not meaning to? Why didn't you put it out?'

'I was asleep. I didn't know about it till I woke up.'

'But you must have . . . Didn't it burn you?'

He put the dish-cover down. 'It doesn't seem to have done.'

'Oh, that's something, anyway.' She looked at him with her lips pressed firmly together, then laughed in a way quite different from the way she'd laughed the previous evening; in fact, Dixon thought, rather unmusically. A blonde lock came away from the devotedly-brushed hair and she smoothed it back. 'Well, what are you going to do about it?'

'I don't know yet. I must do something, though.'

'Yes, I quite agree. You'd better start on it quickly, hadn't you, before the maid goes round?'

'I know. But what can I do?'

'How bad is it?'

'Bad enough. There are great pieces gone altogether, you see.'

'Oh. Well, I don't really know what to suggest without seeing it. Unless you . . . no; that wouldn't help.'

'Look, I suppose you wouldn't come up and . . . ?'

'Have a look at it?'

'Yes. Do you think you could?'

She sat up again and thought. 'Yes, all right. I don't guarantee anything, of course.'

'No, of course not.' He remembered with joy that he still had some cigarettes left after last night's holocaust. 'Thanks very much.'

They were moving to the door when she said: 'What about your breakfast?'

'Oh, I shall have to miss that. There's not time.'

'I shouldn't if I were you. They don't give you much for lunch here, you know.'

'But I'm not going to wait till . . . I mean there isn't much time to . . . Wait a minute.' He darted back to the sideboard, picked up a slippery fried egg and slid it into his mouth whole. She watched him with folded arms and a blank expression. Chewing violently, he doubled up a piece of bacon and crammed it between his teeth, then signalled he was ready to move. Intimations of nausea circled round his digestive system.

They went in file through the hall and up the stairs. The ocarina-like notes of a recorder playing a meagre air were distantly audible; perhaps Welch had breakfasted in his room. Dixon found, with a pang of relief, that he could open the bathroom door.

The girl looked sternly at him. 'What are we going in here for?'

'My bedroom's on the far side of this.'

'Oh, I see. What a curious arrangement.'

'I imagine old Welch had this part of the house built on. It's better like this than having the bathroom on the far side of a bedroom.'

'I suppose so. My goodness, you certainly have gone to town, haven't you?' She went forward and fingered the sheet and blankets like one shown material in a shop. 'But this doesn't look like a burn; it looks as if it's been cut with something.'

'Yes, I . . . cut the burnt bits off with a razor-blade. I thought it would look better than just leaving it burnt.'

'Why on earth did you do that?'

'I can't really explain. I just thought it would look better.'

'Mm. And did all this come from one cigarette?'

'That I don't know. Probably.'

'Well, you must have been pretty far gone not to . . . And the table too. And the rug. You know, I don't know that I ought to be a party to all this.' She grinned, which made her look almost ludicrously healthy, and revealed at the same time that her front teeth were slightly irregular. For some reason this was more disturbing to his equanimity than regularity could possibly have been. He began to think he'd noticed quite enough things about her now, thank you. Then she drew herself up and pressed her lips together, seeming to consider. 'I think the best thing would be to remake the bed with all this mess at the bottom, out of sight. We can put the blanket that's only scorched – this one – on top; it'll probably be almost all right on the side that's underneath now. What about that? It's a pity there isn't an eiderdown.'

'Yes. Sounds all right to me, that. They're bound to find it when they strip the bed, though, aren't they?'

'Yes, but they probably won't connect it with smoking, especially after what you did with your razor-blade. And after all, you wouldn't have put your head right down the bottom of the bed to smoke, would you?'

'That's a point, of course. We'd better get on with it, then.'

He heaved the bed away from the wall, while she watched with arms folded, then they both set about the unmaking and remaking. The vacuum-cleaner could now be heard quite close at hand, drowning Welch's recorder. As they worked, Dixon studied the Callaghan girl, despite his determination to notice nothing more about her, and saw with fury that she was prettier than he'd thought. He found himself wanting to make the kind of face or noise he was accustomed to make when entrusted with a fresh ability-testing task by Welch, or seeing Michie in the distance, or thinking about Mrs Welch, or being told by Beesley something Johns had said. He wanted to implode his features, to crush air from his mouth, in a way and to a degree that might be set against the mess of feelings she aroused in him: indignation, grief, resentment, peevishness, spite, and sterile anger, all the allotropes of pain. The girl was doubly guilty, first of looking like that, secondly of appearing in front of him looking like that. Run-of-the-mill queens of love – Italian film-actresses, millionaires' wives, girls on calendars – he could put up with; more than that, he positively liked looking at them. But this sort of thing he'd as soon not look at at all. He remembered seeing in a book once that some man who claimed to have love well weighed up – someone like Plato or Rilke – had said that it was an emotion quite different in kind, not just degree, from ordinary sexual feelings. Was it love, then, that he felt for girls like this one? No emotion he'd experienced or could imagine came anything like so close, to his way of thinking; but apart from the dubious support of Plato or Rilke he had all the research on the subject against him there. Well, what was it if it wasn't love? It didn't seem like desire; when the last corner was tucked in and he joined her on her side of the bed, he was strongly tempted to put his hand out and lay it on one of those full breasts; but this action, if performed, would have appeared as natural to him, as unimportant and unobjectionable, as reaching out to take a large ripe peach from a fruit-dish. No, all this, whatever it was or was called, was something nothing could be done about.

'There, I think that looks very nice,' the girl said. 'You couldn't guess what was underneath it all if you didn't know, could you?'

'No, and thanks very much for the idea and the help.'

'Oh, that's all right. What are you going to do with the table?'

'I've been thinking about that. There's a little junk-room at the end of the passage, full of broken furniture and rotting books and things; they sent me up there yesterday to fetch a music-stand or whatever they call the things. That room's the place for this table, behind an old screen with French courtiers painted on it – you know, floppy hats and banjos. If you'll go and see whether the coast's clear, I'll rush along there with it now.'

'Agreed. I must say that's an inspiration. With the table out of the way nobody'll connect the sheets with smoking. They'll think you tore them with your feet, in a nightmare or something.'

'Some nightmare, to get through two blankets as well.'

She looked at him open-mouthed, then began to laugh. She sat down on the bed but immediately jumped up again as if it were once more on fire. Dixon began laughing too, not because he was much amused but because he felt grateful to her for her laughter. They were still laughing a minute later when she beckoned to him from outside the bathroom door, when he ran out on to the landing with the table, and when Margaret suddenly flung open the door of her bedroom and saw them.

'What do you imagine you're up to, James?' she asked.

7

'We're just . . . I'm just . . . I was just getting rid of this table, as a matter of fact,' Dixon said, looking from one woman to the other.

The Callaghan girl made an extraordinarily loud snorting noise of incompetently-suppressed laughter. Margaret said: 'Just what is all this nonsense?'

'It isn't nonsense, Margaret, I assure you. I've . . .'

'If anybody minds me saying so,' the girl interrupted him, 'I think we'd better get rid of the table first and explain the whys and wherefores afterwards, don't you?'

'That's right,' Dixon said, put his head down, and ran up the passage. In the junk-room he nudged aside an archery target, making his crazy-peasant face at it – what flaring imbecilities must it have witnessed? – and dumped the table behind the screen. Next, he unrolled a handy length of mouldering silk and spread it over the table-top; then arranged upon the cloth thus provided two fencing foils, a book called *The Lesson of Spain*, and a Lilliputian chest-of-drawers no doubt containing sea-shells and locks of children's hair; finally propped up against this display a tripod meant for some sort of telescopic or photographic tomfoolery. The effect, when he stepped back to look, was excellent; no observer could doubt that these objects had lived together for years in just this way. He smiled, shutting his eyes for a moment before slopping back into the world of reality.

Margaret was waiting for him at the threshold of her room. One corner of her mouth was drawn in in a way he knew well. The Callaghan girl had gone.

'Well, what was all that about, James?'

He shut the door and began to explain. As he talked, his

73

incendiarism and the counter-measures adopted struck him for the first time as funny. Surely Margaret, especially since she wasn't personally implicated, must find them funny too; they formed the sort of story she liked. He said as much at the end of his account.

Without changing her expression, she dissented. 'I could see you and that girl were finding it all pretty funny, though.'

'Well, why shouldn't we have found it funny?'

'No reason at all; it's nothing to do with me. The whole thing just strikes me as rather silly and childish, that's all.'

He said effortfully: 'Now look, Margaret: I can quite see why it looked like that to you. But don't you see? The whole point is that naturally I didn't mean to burn that bloody sheet and so on. Once I'd done it, though, I'd obviously got to do something about it, hadn't I?'

'You couldn't have gone to Mrs Welch and explained, of course.'

'No, "of course" is right, I couldn't have. I'd have been out of my job in five minutes.' He produced and lit cigarettes for the two of them, trying to remember whether Bertrand's girl had said anything about owning up to Mrs Welch. He didn't think she had, which was odd in a way.

'You'll be out in less time than that if she ever finds that table.'

'She won't find it,' he said irritably, beginning to pace up and down the room.

'What about that sheet? You say it was Christine Callaghan's idea to remake the bed?'

'Well, what about it? And what about the sheet?'

'You seem to have got on a good deal better with her than you did last night.'

'Yes, that's good, isn't it?'

'Incidentally I thought she was abominably rude just now.'

'How do you mean?'

'Barging in and sending you off with that table like that.'

Stung with this reflection on his dignity, Dixon said: 'You've got this "rude" business on the winkle, Margaret. She was absolutely right: one of the Welches might have turned up at any moment. And if anyone barged in, it was you, not her.' He began regretting this speech well before it was over.

She stared at him with her mouth a little open, then whipped abruptly round away from him. 'I'm sorry, I won't barge in again.'

'Now, Margaret, you know I didn't mean it like that; don't be ridiculous. I was only . . .'

In a high voice, kept steady only by obvious effort, she said: 'Please go.'

Dixon fought hard to drive away the opinion that, both as actress and as script-writer, she was doing rather well, and hated himself for failing. Trying to haul urgency into his tone, he began: 'You mustn't take it like that. It was a bloody stupid thing to say, on my part, I admit. I didn't mean you actually barged in, in that way, of course I didn't. You must see . . .'

'Oh, I see all right, James. I see perfectly.' This time her voice was flat. She wore a sort of arty get-up of multicoloured shirt, skirt with fringed hem and pocket, low-heeled shoes, and wooden beads. The smoke from her cigarette curled up, blue and ashy in a sunbeam, round her bare forearm. Dixon moved closer and saw that her hair had been recently washed; it lay in dry lustreless wisps on the back of her neck. In that condition it struck him as quint-essentially feminine, much more feminine than the Callaghan girl's shining fair crop. Poor old Margaret, he thought, and rested his hand, in a gesture he hoped was solicitous, on her nearer shoulder.

Before he could speak she'd shaken his hand off, moved over to the window, and begun to talk in a strain that marked the opening, he soon realized, of a totally new phase of the scene they were evidently having. 'Get away. How dare you. Stop pushing and pulling me about. Who do you think you are? You haven't even had the grace to apologize for last night. You behaved disgracefully. I hope you realize you absolutely stank of beer. I've never given you the least impression . . . Whatever made you think you could get away with that sort of thing? What the hell do you take me for? It isn't as if you didn't know what I've had to put up with, all these last weeks. It's intolerable, absolutely intolerable. I won't stand for it. You must have known how I've been feeling.'

She went on like this while Dixon looked her in the eyes. His panic mounted in sincerity and volume. Her body moved jerkily about; her head bobbed from side to side on its rather long neck, shaking the wooden beads about on the multicoloured shirt. He found himself thinking that the whole arty get-up seemed oddly at variance with the way she was acting. People who wore clothes of that sort oughtn't to mind things of this sort, certainly not as much as Margaret clearly minded this thing. It was surely wrong to dress, and to behave most of the time, in a way that was so un-prim when you were really so proper all of the time. But then, with Catchpole at any rate, she hadn't been proper all of the time, had she? But of course it was all wrong to think like this, very bad, in fact, to allow his irritation with some of the things about her to do what it always did, to obscure what was most important: she was a neurotic who'd recently taken a bad beating. Yes, she was right really, though not in the way she meant. He had behaved badly, he had been inconsiderate. He'd better devote all his energy to apologizing. He booted out of his mind the reflection, derived apparently from nowhere, that in spite of her emotion she seemed well able to keep her voice down.

'I was thinking only yesterday afternoon about the relationship we'd been building up, how valuable it was, something really good. But that was silly, wasn't it? I was dead wrong, I . . .'

'No, you're dead wrong now, you were right then,' he broke in. 'These things don't stop just like that, you know; human beings aren't as simple as that, they're not like machines.'

He went on like this while she looked him in the eyes. The rotten triteness of his words seemed, if anything, to help him to meet her gaze. She stood with one leg partly crossed over the other in her favourite attitude, no doubt designed to show off her legs, for they were good, her best feature. At one point she moved slightly so that her spectacles caught the light and prevented him seeing where she was looking. The eeriness of this disconcerted him a good deal, but he soldiered pluckily on to his objective, the promise or avowal, not yet in sight, which would end this encounter, bring some respite from the trek away from honesty. Boots, boots, boots, boots, marching up and down again.

After a while she was no more than implacably annoyed; then annoyed; then sullen and monosyllabic. 'Oh James,' she said at last, smoothing her hair with a convex palm; 'do let's stop this for now. I'm tired, I'm terribly tired, I can't go on any more. I'm going back to bed; I couldn't manage to sleep much last night. I just want to be left alone. Try to understand.'

'What about your breakfast?'

'I don't want any. It'll be over by now, anyway. And I don't want to have to talk to anybody.' She sank on to the bed and closed her eyes. 'Just leave me alone.'

'Are you sure you'll be all right?'

She said 'Oh yes' on a great sigh. 'Please.'

'Don't forget what I said.'

When no reply came, he went quietly out and into his bedroom, where he lay on the bed smoking a cigarette and reflecting, to small purpose, on the events of the last hour. Margaret he succeeded in putting from his mind almost at once; it was all very complicated, but then it had always been that, and he'd hated what she'd said to him and what he'd said to her, but then he'd been bound to do that. How well, really, the Callaghan girl had behaved, in spite of her standoffishness at times, and how sound her suggestion had been. That, and her laughing fit, proved that she wasn't as 'dignant' as she looked. He remembered uneasily the awful glow of her skin, the distressing clarity of her eyes, the immoderate whiteness of those slightly irregular teeth. Then he cheered up a little as he put it to himself that her attachment to Bertrand was a fair guarantee of her being really very nasty. Yes, Bertrand; he must either make peace with him or keep out of his way. Keeping out of his way would almost certainly be better; he could combine it with keeping out of Margaret's way. If Atkinson phoned punctually he'd be out of the house in well under the hour.

He put out his cigarette in the ashtray, taking twenty or thirty seconds over the job, then went and had a shave. Some time later a loud baying bawl of 'Dixon' brought him to the stairhead. 'Somebody want me?' he roared.

'Telephone. Dixon. Dixon. Telephone.'

In the drawing-room, Bertrand was sitting with his parents and his girl. He pointed to the phone with his big head, then went on listening to his father, who, canted over in his chair like a broken robot, was saying splenetically: 'In children's art, you see, you get what you might call a clarity of vision, a sort of thinking in terms of the world as it appears, you see, not as the adult knows it to be. Well, this . . . this . . .'

'That you, Jim?' said Atkinson's cruel voice. 'How are things at Barnum and Bailey's?'

'All the better for hearing your voice, Bill.'

While Atkinson, unexpectedly garrulous, described a case he'd been reading about in the *News of the World*, asked Dixon's opinion on a clue in its prize crossword, and made an impracticable suggestion for the entertainment of the company at the Welches', Dixon watched the Callaghan girl listening to something Bertrand was explaining about art. She was sitting bolt upright in her chair, her lips compressed, wearing, he noticed for the first time, exactly what she'd been wearing the previous evening. Everything about her looked severe, and yet she didn't mind sheets and charred table-tops, and Margaret did. This girl hadn't minded fried eggs eaten with the fingers, either. It was a puzzle.

Raising his voice a little, Dixon said: 'Well, thanks very much for ringing, Bill. Apologize to my parents, will you, and tell them I'll be back as soon as I can.'

'Tell Johns from me where to put his oboe before you go.'

'I'll do my best. Good-bye.'

'That's the real point about Mexican art, Christine,' Bertrand was saying. 'Primitive technique can't have any virtue in itself, obviouslam.'

'No of course not; I see,' she said.

'I'm afraid I shall have to leave right away, Mrs Welch,' Dixon said. 'That phone call . . .'

They all looked round at him, Bertrand impatiently, Mrs Welch censoriously, Welch with incomprehension, Bertrand's girl without curiosity. Before Dixon could begin to explain, Margaret walked in through the open door, followed by Johns. Her recovery from prostrating fatigue had been rapid; had Johns somehow assisted it?

'A-ah,' Margaret said. It was her usual greeting to a roomful of people: a long, exhaled, downward glissando. 'Hallo, everybody.'

Those already in the room began moving uneasily about in response to this. Welch and Bertrand began talking simultaneously, Mrs Welch looked rapidly to and fro between Dixon and Margaret, Johns hung whey-faced at the threshold. When Welch, still talking, sprang ataxically from his chair towards Johns, Dixon, finding his own chance to talk about to lapse, moved forward. He heard Welch use the phrase 'figured bass'. He coughed, then said loudly and with unforeseen hoarseness: 'I'm afraid I've got to be off now. My parents have come to see me unexpectedly.' He paused, to give room for any cries of protest and regret. When none came, he hurried on: 'Thank you very much for putting me up, Mrs Welch; I've enjoyed myself very much. And now I'm afraid I really must be off. Good-bye, all.'

Avoiding Margaret's eye, he walked through the silence and out of the door. Apart from making him feel he might die or go mad at any moment, his hangover had vanished. Johns grinned at him as he passed.

8

'Oh, Dixon, can I have a word with you?'

To its recipient, this was the most dreadful of all summonses. It had been a favourite of his Flight-Sergeant's, a Regular with old-fashioned ideas about the propriety of getting an N.C.O. out of the men's hearing before subjecting him, not to a word, but to an uproar of abuse and threats about some harmless oversight. Welch had revived it as a short *maestoso* introduction to the *allegro con fuoco* of his displeasure over each new item in the 'bad impression' Dixon had been building up, and it heralded at best the imposition of some fresh academic task designed, conceivably, to probe his value to the Department. Michie, too, had more than once used it to signal a desire to talk, and ask questions, about Medieval Life and Culture. It was Welch who delivered the summons now, swaying about in the doorway of the little teaching room which Dixon shared with Goldsmith. Intellectually, Dixon could conceive of such a request leading to praise for work done on indexing Welch's notes for his book, to the offer of a staff post on *Medium Aevum*, to an invitation to an indecent house-party, but emotionally and physically he was half-throttled by the certainty of nastiness.

'Of course, Professor.' While he followed Welch next door, wondering whether the subject for debate was the sheet, or his dismissal, or the sheet and his dismissal, Dixon reeled off a long string of swear-words in a mumbling undertone, so that he'd be in credit, as it were, for the first few minutes of the interview. He stamped his feet hard as he walked, partly to keep his courage up, partly to drown his own mutterings, partly because he hadn't yet smoked that morning.

Welch sat down at his misleadingly littered desk. 'Oh . . . uh . . . Dixon.'

'Yes, Professor?'

'I've . . . about this article of yours.'

With all his incoherences, Welch was always straightforward when reproofs were to be delivered, so that this remark was comparatively encouraging. Dixon said guardedly: 'Oh yes?'

'I was having a chat the other day with an old friend of mine from South Wales. The Professor at the University College of Abertawe, he is now. Athro Haines; I expect you know his book on medieval Cwmrhydyceirw.'

Dixon said 'Oh yes' in a different tone, but still guardedly. He wanted to indicate eager and devout recognition that should not at the same time imply first-hand knowledge of the work in question, in case Welch should demand an epitome of its argument.

'Of course, their problems down there are very different from . . . from . . . The Pass classes in particular. He was telling me . . . It seems that in the first year everybody, doesn't matter whether they're going to go on with History or not, they all have to get through a certain amount of . . .'

Dixon switched off most of his attention, just keeping enough of it going to enable him to nod at proper intervals. He felt relieved; nothing really bad was going to happen, whatever might prove to be the bridge over the fast-widening gap between his article and this Haines character. A resolve began to form in his mind, frightening him before he could properly identify it. Now that he was alone with Welch, he'd have a show-down with him, force him to reveal what had been decided about his future, or, if nothing was definite yet, when it would be definite and what issue was going to make it definite. He was tired of being blackmailed, by the hope of improving his chances, into grubbing about in the public library for material that 'might come in handy' for Welch's book on local history, into 'just glancing through' (*i.e.* correcting) the proofs of a long article Welch was having printed in a local journal of antiquities, into holding himself in readiness to attend a folk-dancing conference (thank God he hadn't had to go after all), into attending that terrible arty week-end last month, into agreeing to lecture on Merrie England – especially that. And it was getting very late in the term: less than a month to go. Somehow he must mortar or bayonet Welch out of his prepared positions of reticence, irrelevance, and the long-lived, wondering frown.

Welch suddenly made him switch everything on again by saying: 'Apparently this Caton fellow was in for the chair at Abertawe at the same time as Haines, three or four years ago it must be now. Well, naturally Haines couldn't tell me much, but he gave me the impression that Caton might well have got the chair instead of him, only there was something rather shady about him, you see. Don't let this out, will you, Dixon? but there was something like a forged testimonial or something of the sort, I gathered. Something rather shady, anyway. Now, of course, this journal of his may be quite above-board and so on, I'm not saying it isn't; it may be quite . . . above-board. But I thought I ought to let you know about this, Dixon, so that you can take any action you think . . . you think you . . . you think fit, you . . .'

'Well, thank you very much, Professor, it's very good of you to warn me. Perhaps I'd better write to him again and ask . . .'

'You haven't had a reply to your letter asking for something definite about when he's publishing your thing?'

'No, not a word.'

'Well then, you must certainly write to him again, Dixon, and say you must have a definite date of publication. Say you've had an inquiry from another journal about what you're writing. Say you must know definitely within a week.' Such fluency, like the keen glance which accompanied it, Welch seemed to reserve specially for telling people what to do.

'I'll certainly do that, yes.'

'Do it today, will you, Dixon?'

'Yes, I will.'

'After all, it's important to you, isn't it?'

This was the cue he'd been hoping for. 'Yes, sir. Actually I've been meaning to ask you about that.'

Welch's shaggy eyebrows descended a little. 'About what?'

'Well, I'm sure you appreciate, Professor, that I've been worrying rather about my position here, in the last few months.'

'Oh yes?' Welch said cheerfully, his eyebrows restored.

'I've been wondering just how I stand, you know.'

'How you stand?'

'Yes, I . . . I mean, I'm afraid I got off on the wrong foot here rather, when I first came. I did some rather silly things. Well, now that my first year's nearly over, naturally I can't help feeling a bit anxious.'

'Yes, I know a lot of young chaps find some difficulty in settling down to their first job. It's only to be expected, after a war, after all. I don't know if you've ever met young Faulkner, at Nottingham he is now; he got a job here in nineteen hundred', here he paused, 'and forty-five. Well, he'd had rather a rough time in the war, what with one thing and another; he'd been out East for a time, you know, in the Fleet Air Arm he was, and then they switched him back to the Mediterranean. I remember him telling me how difficult he found it to adapt his way of thinking, when he had to settle down here and . . .'

Stop himself from dashing his fist into your face, Dixon thought. He waited for a time, then, when Welch produced another of his pauses, said: 'Yes, and of course it's doubly difficult when one doesn't feel very secure in one's – I'd work much better, I know, if I could feel settled about . . .'

'Well, insecurity is the great enemy of concentration, I know. And, of course, one does tend to lose the habit of concentration as one grows older. It's amazing how distractions one wouldn't have noticed in one's early days become absolutely shattering when one . . . grows older. I remember when they were putting up the new chemistry labs here, well, I say new, you could hardly call them new now, I suppose. At the time I'm speaking of, some years before the war, they were laying the foundations about Easter time it must have been, and the concrete-mixer or whatever it was . . .'

Dixon wondered if Welch could hear him grinding his teeth. If he did, he gave no sign of it. Like a boxer still incredibly on his feet after ten rounds of punishment, Dixon got in with: 'I could feel quite happy about everything, if only my big worry were out of the way.'

Welch's head lifted slowly, like the muzzle of some obsolete howitzer. The wondering frown quickly began to form. 'I don't quite see . . .'

'My probation,' Dixon said loudly.

The frown cleared. 'Oh. That. You're on two years' probation here, Dixon, not one year. It's all there in your contract, you know. Two years.'

'Yes, I know, but that just means that I can't be taken on to the permanent staff until two years are up. It doesn't mean that I can't be . . . asked to leave at the end of the first year.'

'Oh no,' Welch said warmly; 'no.' He left it open whether he was reinforcing Dixon's negative or dissenting from it.

'I can be asked to leave at the end of the first year, can't I, Professor?' Dixon said quickly, pressing himself against the back of his chair.

'Yes, I suppose so,' Welch said, coldly this time, as if he were being asked to make some concession which, though theoretically due, no decent man would claim.

'Well I'm just wondering what's happening about it, that's all.'

'Yes, I've no doubt you are,' Welch said in the same tone.

Dixon waited, planning faces. He looked round the small, cosy room with its fitted carpet, its rows of superseded books, its filing cabinets full of antique examination papers and of dossiers relating to past generations of students, its view from closed windows on to the sunlit wall of the Physics Laboratory. Behind Welch's head hung the departmental timetable, drawn up by Welch himself in five different-coloured inks corresponding to the five teaching members of the Department. The sight of this seemed to undam Dixon's mind; for the first time since arriving at the College he thought he felt real, over-mastering, orgiastic boredom, and its companion, real hatred. If Welch didn't speak in the next five seconds, he'd do something which would get himself flung out without possible question – not the things he'd often dreamed of when sitting next door pretending to work. He no longer wanted, for example, to inscribe on the departmental timetable a short account, well tricked-out with obscenities, of his views on the Professor of History, the Department of History, medieval history, history, and Margaret and hang it out of the window for the information of passing students and lecturers, nor did he, on the whole, now intend to tie Welch up in his chair and beat him about the head and shoulders with a bottle until he disclosed why, without being French himself, he'd given his sons French names, nor . . . No, he'd just say, quite quietly and very slowly and distinctly, to give Welch a good chance of catching his general drift: Look here, you old cockchafer, what makes you think you can run a history department, even at a place like this, eh, you old cockchafer? I know what you'd be good at, you old cockchafer . . .

'Well, these things aren't as easy as you might imagine, you know,' Welch said suddenly. 'This is a very difficult matter, Dixon, you see. There's a great deal, a lot of things you've got to keep in mind.'

'I see that, of course, Professor. I just wanted to ask when the decision will be taken, that's all. If I'm to go, it's only fair I should be told soon.' He felt his head trembling slightly with rage as he said this.

Welch's glance, which had flicked two or three times at Dixon's face, now dropped to a half-curled-up letter on the desk. He muttered: 'Yes . . . well . . . I . . .'

Dixon said in a still louder voice: 'Because I shall have to start looking for another job, you see. And most of the schools will have made their appointments for September before they break up in July. So I shall want to know in good time.'

An expression of unhappiness was beginning to settle on Welch's small-eyed face. Dixon was at first pleased to see this evidence that Welch's mind could still be reached from the outside; next he felt a momentary compunction at the spectacle of one man disliking to reveal something that would cause pain to another; finally panic engulfed him. What was Welch's reluctance concealing? He, Dixon, was done for. If so, he would at any rate be able to deliver the cockchafer speech, though he wished his audience were larger.

'Let you know as soon as anything's decided,' Welch said with incredible speed. 'Nothing is yet.'

Left with nothing to say, Dixon realized how wild a notion the cockchafer speech had been. He'd never be able to tell Welch what he wanted to tell him, any more than he'd ever be able to do the same with Margaret. All the time he'd thought he was bringing the matter of his probation to a head he'd merely been a winkle on the pin of Welch's evasion-technique; verbal this time instead of the more familiar physical form, but a technique adapted to meet stronger pressure than he himself could hope to bring to bear on it.

Now, as Dixon had been half expecting all along, Welch produced his handkerchief. It was clear that he was about to blow his nose. This was usually horrible, if only because it drew unwilling attention to Welch's nose itself, a large, open-pored tetrahedron. But when the familiar miraculously-sustained blares beat against the walls and windows, Dixon hardly minded at all; the noise had the effect of changing his mood. Any statement that could be battered out of Welch was invariably trustworthy, so that Dixon was back where he started. But how lovely to be back where he started, instead of out in front where he didn't want to be. How wrong people always were when they said: 'It's better to know the worst than go on not knowing either way.' No; they had it exactly the wrong way round. Tell me the truth, doctor, I'd sooner know. But only if the truth is what I want to hear.

When he was sure that Welch had finished blowing his nose, Dixon got up and thanked him for their chat almost with sincerity, and the sight of Welch's 'bag' and fishing-hat on a nearby chair, normally a certain infuriant, only made him hum his Welch tune as he went out. This tune featured in the 'rondo' of some boring piano concerto Welch had once insisted on playing him on his complicated exponential-horned gramophone. It had come after about four of the huge double-sided red-labelled records, and Dixon had fitted words to it. Going down the stairs towards the Common Room, where coffee would now be available, he articulated these words behind closed lips: 'You *i*gnorant clod, you *stu*pid old sod, you *h*avering *sla*vering get . . .' Here intervened a string of unmentionables, corresponding with an oom-pah sort of effect in the orchestra. 'You *wor*dy old *tur*dy old scum, you *gri*ping old *pi*ping old bum . . .' Dixon didn't mind the obscurity of the reference, in 'piping', to Welch's recorder; he knew what he meant.

The examinations were now in progress, and Dixon had nothing to do that morning but turn up at the Assembly Hall at twelve-thirty to collect some scripts. They would contain answers to questions he'd set about the Middle Ages. As he approached the Common Room he thought briefly about the Middle Ages. Those who professed themselves unable to believe in the reality of human progress ought to cheer themselves up, as the students under examination had conceivably been cheered up, by a short study of the Middle Ages. The hydrogen bomb, the South African Government, Chiang Kai-shek, Senator McCarthy himself, would then seem a light price to pay for no longer being in the Middle Ages. Had people ever been as nasty, as self-indulgent, as dull, as miserable, as cocksure, as bad at art, as dismally ludicrous, or as wrong as they'd been in the Middle Age – Margaret's way of referring to the Middle Ages? He grinned at this last thought, then stopped doing that on entering the Common Room and catching sight of her, pale and heavy-eyed, on her own near the empty fireplace.

Their relations hadn't altered materially during the ten days or so since the arty week-end. It had taken him the whole of an evening in the Oak Lounge and a great deal of expense and hypocrisy to get her to admit that she still had a grievance against him, and more of the same sort of commodity to persuade her to define, amplify, discuss, moderate, and finally abandon it. For some reason, periodically operative but impossible to name, the sight of her now filled him with affection and remorse. Rejecting coffee in favour of lemon squash, for it was a hot day, he got some from the overalled woman at the serving-table and went through the chatting groups over to Margaret.

She was wearing her arty get-up, but had discarded the wooden beads in favour of a brooch consisting of a wooden letter M. A large envelope full of examination scripts was on the floor beside her chair. A falsetto explosion from the coffee-urn across the room made him start slightly; then he said: 'Hallo, dear, how are you today?'

'All right, thanks.'

He smiled tentatively. 'You don't sound as though you mean that.'

'Don't I? I'm sorry. I'm perfectly all right really.' She spoke with extraordinary sharpness. Her jaw-muscles looked tight, as if she was suffering from toothache.

Glancing about him, he moved closer, bent forward, and said as gently as he could: 'Now, Margaret, please don't talk like that. It's quite unnecessary. If you don't feel too good, tell me about it and I'll sympathize. If you feel all right, that's fine. Either way we'll have a cigarette on it. But for God's sake don't try to pick a fight with me. I don't feel like one.'

She moved abruptly on the chair-arm she was sitting on so that her back was to everybody in the room except Dixon, who saw that her eyes were filling with tears. As he hesitated, she gave a loud sob, still looking at him.

'Margaret, you musn't,' he said in horror. 'Don't cry. I didn't mean it.'

She gave a furious downward wave of her hand. 'You were quite right,' she said shudderingly. 'It was my fault. I'm sorry.'

'Margaret . . .'

'No, I'm the one in the wrong. I bit your head off. I didn't want to, I didn't mean to. Everything's so bloody this morning.'

'Well, tell me about it, then. Dry your eyes.'

'You're the only one that's nice to me and then I treat you like

88

that.' However, she took off her glasses and started blotting her eyes.

'Never mind about that. Tell me what's wrong.'

'Oh, nothing. Everything and nothing.'

'Did you have another bad night?'

'Yes, darling, I did, and it's made me terribly sorry for myself, as usual. I keep thinking to myself, Oh hell, what's the use of anything, especially me?'

'Have a cigarette.'

'Oh thank you, James, it's just what I want. Do I look all right?'

'Yes, of course. Just a little tired, that's all.'

'I didn't get off till gone four. I must go and see the doc and get him to give me something. I can't go on like this.'

'But didn't he say you'd got to adjust yourself to doing without anything?'

She looked up at him in something like triumph. 'Yes, he did. But he didn't say how I'm going to adjust myself to doing without sleep.'

'Doesn't anything seem to help?'

'Oh, God, you know all about the baths and the hot milks and the, er, aspirins and the window shut and the window open . . .'

They talked like this for a few minutes, while the other occupants of the room began to disperse to their various tasks. These, since it was the one time of the academic year when everybody was simultaneously not lecturing, must have been largely self-imposed. Dixon sweated quietly as the talk went on, trying to repel the persistent half-recollection or half-illusion of having casually told Margaret a couple of days previously that he'd ring her up at the Welches' the next night – which was now last night. Some invitation or promise was obviously required, if only to smother the problem. At the first opportunity he said: 'What about lunch today? Are you free?'

For some reason, these queries provoked a partial return to her earlier manner. 'Free? Who do you imagine would have asked me out to lunch?'

'I thought you might have told Mrs Neddy you'd be back.'

'As it happens, she's having a little luncheon-party and asked me to turn up.'

'Oh well, somebody has asked you to lunch, then.'

She said 'Yes, that's right' in a puzzled, lost way that, by suggesting she'd forgotten what she'd just said or even what they were talking about, succeeded in alarming him more than her recent tears. He said quickly:

'What sort of a lunch-party is it?'

'Oh, I don't know,' she said with fatigue. 'Nothing startling, I imagine.' She looked at him as if her spectacles were becoming opaque. 'I must go now.' Slowly and inefficiently, she started looking for her handbag.

'Margaret, when shall I see you again?'

'I don't know.'

'I'm a bit short of cash until . . . Shall I get Neddy to ask me down for tea at the week-end?'

'If you like. Bertrand'll be there, though.' She still spoke in an odd, expressionless voice.

'Bertrand? Oh well, we'd better leave it, then.'

With an almost imperceptible increase in emphasis, she said: 'Yes. He's coming down for the Summer Ball.'

Dixon felt like a man who knows he won't be able to jump on to the moving train if he stops to think about it. 'Are we going to that?' he said.

Ten minutes later, it having been established that they were going to that, Margaret was on her way out, all smiles, to lock up her exam scripts, to powder her nose, and to phone Mrs Welch with the news that she wouldn't, after all, be attending the luncheon-party, which had turned out to be of much less importance than had at first appeared; Margaret would, instead, be lunching off beer and cheese rolls in a pub with Dixon. He was glad that his trump card had had such a spectacular effect, but, as is the way with trump cards, it had seemed valuable enough to deserve to win ten tricks, not just the one, and had looked better in his hand than it did on the table.

He had in his possession, however, two pieces of information of which Margaret was ignorant. One was the connexion, whatever it was, between Bertrand Welch and Carol Goldsmith, which had suddenly leapt up again in his thoughts at the news, from Margaret, that Bertrand was taking Carol to the Summer Ball, her husband being committed to go to Leeds as Welch's legate for the week-end. Presumably Bertrand's blonde and busty Callaghan piece had now, to her credit, been discarded. The interest of this situation compensated, in large part, for the likelihood that Carol, Bertrand, Margaret, and himself would be going to the Ball together; 'as a little party', Margaret had put it. The second thing Dixon knew and Margaret didn't was that Bill Atkinson had previously agreed to meet him in the very pub he and Margaret were now about to go to. Atkinson's presence would be a valuable stand-by in case of renewed difficulty with Margaret (though God knew there shouldn't be any of that so soon after the playing of the trump card), and his taciturnity would rule out any risk of their arrangement to meet being suddenly and untowardly revealed. But, more important than any of that, Atkinson and Margaret had not yet met. Trying to imagine what each would say to him about the other afterwards made Dixon grin to himself as he sat down to wait (God only knew how long) for Margaret. To fill in some of the time he found some College stationery and began to write:

'Dear Dr Caton: I hope you will not mind my troubling you, but I wonder if you could let me know when my article . . .'

9

'Professor Welch. Professor Welch, please.'

Dixon huddled himself further into the periodical he was reading and unobtrusively made his Martian-invader face. To him, it was a serious offence to pronounce that name in public, even when there was no chance of its bearer being thereby conjured up; Welch was known to be taking the whole day off, as distinct from days like yesterday (the day of their conversation about Dixon's job) when Welch merely took the early and late morning and the after-noon off. Dixon wished that the porter, a very bad man, would stop bawling that particular name and go away before his eye fell on Dixon and marked him down as a Welch-surrogate. But it was no use; in a moment he felt the approach of the porter down the length of the Common Room towards his chair, and had to look up.

The porter wore an olive-green uniform of military cut, and a peaked cap which didn't suit him. He was a long-faced, high-shouldered man with hairs growing out of his nose, and his age was hard to estimate. His expression, which rarely altered, couldn't be expected to at the sight of Dixon. Still approaching, he said huskily: 'Oh, Mr Jackson.'

Dixon wished he had the courage to twist energetically about in his chair in search of this quite new and unknown character. 'Yes, Maconochie?' he said helpfully.

'Oh, Mr Jackson, there's someone on the telephone for Profes-sor Welch, but I can't seem to find him. Would you take the call for him, please? You're the only person in the History Department I can find,' he explained.

'Yes, all right,' Dixon said. 'Can I take it in here?'

'Thank you, Mr Jackson. No, the telephone in here goes on to the public exchange. The lady wanting the Professor's on the

College switchboard. I'll switch her through to the Registrar's Clerk's room. He won't mind you taking it in there.'

A lady? It must be either Mrs Welch or some poor half-crazed creature connected with the arts. Mrs Welch would be better, in that her message would be comprehensible, but worse in that she might have found out about the sheet, or even the table. Why couldn't they leave him alone? Why couldn't every single one of them without any exception whatsoever just go right away from where he was and leave him alone?

Luckily, the Registrar's Clerk, another very bad man, wasn't in his room. Dixon picked up the phone and said: 'Dixon here.'

'Intermediate Geology, that's right, yes,' a voice said comfortably. 'Who's that?' another said. A buzzing followed, terminated by an eardrum-cracking click. When Dixon had got hold of the receiver again and put it to his other ear, he heard the second voice say: 'Is that Mr Jackson?'

'Dixon here.'

'Who?' It was a vaguely familiar voice, but not Mrs Welch's; it sounded like an adolescent girl's.

'Dixon. I'm taking the message for Professor Welch.'

'Oh, Mr Dixon, of course.' There was a noise which might have been a smothered snort of laughter. 'I might have guessed it'd be you. This is Christine Callaghan.'

'Oh, hallo, er, how are you?' The apparent deliquescence of the bowel that recognition brought on was only momentary; he knew he could deal with her voice creditably enough while the rest of her remained, presumably, in London.

'I'm fine, thanks. How are you? I hope you've had no more trouble with your bedclothes?'

Dixon laughed. 'No, I'm glad to say that's all blown over; touch wood.'

'Oh, good . . . Look, is there any way of getting hold of Professor Welch, do you know? Isn't he anywhere in the University?'

'He hasn't been in all the morning, I'm afraid. He's almost certain to be at home now. Or have you tried there?'

'Oh, how annoying. Perhaps you can tell me, though: do you know if he's expecting Bertrand down?'

'Well, yes, as it happens I do know that Bertrand's coming down at the week-end. Margaret Peel told me.' Dixon's equanimity had departed; evidently this girl didn't know she'd been junked by Bertrand, at least as far as the Summer Ball was concerned. Answering her questions about Bertrand was going to be tricky.

'Who told you?' Her voice had sharpened a little.

'You know, Margaret Peel. The girl who was staying with the Welches when you came down that time.'

'Oh yes, I see . . . Did she happen to mention whether Bertrand will be going to your Summer Ball affair?'

Dixon thought quickly; no questions about Bertrand's possible partner must be asked. 'No, I'm afraid not. But everybody else'll be going, anyway.' Why didn't she get hold of Bertrand and ask him?

'I see . . . But he is definitely coming down?'

'Apparently.'

She must have sensed his puzzlement, because she now said: 'I expect you're wondering why I don't ask Bertrand himself. Well, you see, he's often rather a difficult chap to get hold of. At the moment he's just sort of gone off, nobody knows where. He likes to come and go when he feels like it, hates being tied down and all that. Do you see?'

'Yes, of course.' Dixon bunched his free hand and waggled its first two fingers.

'So I thought I'd see if his father knew where he was or anything. The whole point is, what I really wanted to know is this. My uncle, Mr Gore-Urquhart, got back from Paris sooner than he expected, and he's got an invitation from your Principal to the Summer Ball thing. He doesn't really know whether to come or not. Well, I could persuade him to come if Bertrand and I were going, and then Bertrand and he could get to know each other, and Bertrand wants that. But I must know soon, because it's the day after tomorrow and Uncle would want to know in good time, where he's to spend the week-end, I mean. So . . . well, it's rather a mix-up, I'm afraid.'

'Can't Mrs Welch throw any light on the matter?'

There was a pause. 'I've not actually been on to her.'

'Well, she's bound to know more about it than I do, isn't she? . . . Hallo?'

'I'm still here . . . Listen, keep this quiet, won't you? but I'd like not to get on to her if I can find out any other way. I . . . we didn't hit it off too well when I stayed. I don't want to have to, well, discuss Bertrand with her over the phone. I think she thinks I'm . . . Never mind; but you see what I mean?'

'I do indeed. I don't hit it off too well with the lady either, as a matter of fact. Now I've got a suggestion. I'll ring up the Welches for you now and get the Professor to ring you. If he's not there I'll leave a message or something. Anyway I'll see to it, somehow or other, that Mrs Welch doesn't get involved. If it's no good I'll ring you back myself and tell you. Will that do, now?'

'Oh, that'd be lovely, thanks so much. What a marvellous idea. Here's my number; it's the place I work at, so I shan't be there after five-thirty. Ready?'

While he took it down, Dixon assured himself several times that Mrs Welch couldn't have found out about the sheet or the table, or Margaret would surely have warned him. How nice this girl was being to him, he thought. 'Right, I've got that,' he said finally.

'It's damn good of you to do this for me,' the girl said with animation. 'But doesn't it make me out a bit of a fool, you taking all this trouble just to save me . . . ?'

'Not in the least. I know exactly what these things are like.' None better, he told himself.

'Well, I am grateful, really. I just couldn't face . . .'

A sort of Morse signal fell between these sentences, and then a rushing noise supervened. A woman's voice said: 'Your second three minutes are up, caller. Do you require a further three minutes?'

Before Dixon could speak, Christine Callaghan had said: 'Yes, please, leave me through, will you?'

The rushing noise stopped. 'Hallo?' Dixon said.

'I'm still here.'

'Look, isn't this costing you a packet?'

'Not me; only the shop.' She gave one of her laughs, the non-silver-bells sort. Over the phone its cacophony was more noticeable.

Dixon laughed too. 'Well, I hope this business comes off all right; it would be an awful shame if it didn't, after all these preparations.'

'Yes, wouldn't it? Will you be going to the Ball thing?'

'Yes, I'm afraid so.'

'Afraid so?'

'Well, I'm not really much of a dancing man, you know. It'll be a bit of an ordeal for me, I'm afraid.'

'Why on earth are you going, then?'

'It's too late to get out of it.'

'What?'

'I said I may get some fun out of it.'

'Oh, I expect you will. I'm not much good as a dancer myself, really. I've never learnt properly.'

'You must have had plenty of practice, surely.'

'Not much, as a matter of fact. I haven't been to many dances.'

'We'll be able to sit out together, then.' That's a bit forward, he thought; shouldn't have said that.

'If I come.'

'Yes, if you come.'

The pre-leavetaking pause fell upon them. Dixon felt sad: he realized for the first time that it was really very unlikely that she would come to the Ball, a good deal more unlikely than she had any reason to think, and that it was correspondingly unlikely that he'd ever see her again. It was nasty to think that the deciding factors would be the strength and nature of Bertrand's ambitions, sexual and financial-social.

'Well, thank you again for your help.'

'Not at all. I hope very much you will be coming on Saturday.'

'I hope so too. Well, good-bye. I may be hearing from you later, then.'

'That's right. Good-bye.'

He sat back and puffed out his cheeks, trying to picture her at the other end of the line. She'd be sitting up straight in her office chair, of course, like an airman-clerk told to 'carry on' during an inspection by the Air Vice-Marshal. Or would she? She hadn't sounded like that over the phone; she'd talked in the relaxed style he'd had glimpses of during the sheet and table campaign. But her apparent friendliness over the phone might be an illusion based on her physical absence. On the other hand, how much of her severity at other times was an illusion based on the way she looked? He was feeling for his cigarettes when Johns came in at the door, carrying a sheaf of papers. Had he been listening?

'Can I help you?' Dixon said with caricatured graciousness.

Johns saw that he'd have to speak. 'Where is he?'

Dixon peered searchingly under the desk, into its top drawer, into the wastepaper-basket. 'Not here.'

The other's junket-coloured features stayed where they were. 'I'll wait.'

'I won't.'

Dixon went away with the intention of ringing up the Welches from the Common Room phone. As he was passing the porter's office he heard Maconochie say: 'Ah, there he is now, Mr Michie,' and made his Eskimo face, which entailed, as well as an attempt to shorten and broaden his face by about half, the feat of abolishing his neck by sucking it down between his shoulders. This done, and the final effect held for a few seconds, he turned and saw Michie approaching.

'Ah, Mr Dixon, I hope you're not busy.'

Dixon knew exactly how well Michie knew exactly how and why he, Dixon, couldn't be busy. He said: 'No, not just at the moment. What can I do for you?'

'About your special subject for next year, sir.'

'Yes, what about it?' Until now, the intrigue had been mostly in Dixon's favour; the three pretty girls whom he was plotting to secure for his class had all seemed more 'interested' at their last discussion, while Michie's 'interest', though it hadn't declined, had shown no signs of increasing.

'Shall we go for a stroll on the lawn, sir? It seems a pity to be indoors on such a glorious day, doesn't it? About the syllabus, sir: Miss O'Shaughnessy, Miss McCorquodale, Miss ap Rhys Williams, and I have all been into it very carefully together, and I think the feeling of the ladies is that the reading is a good deal on the heavy side. I don't myself think it is: as I said to them, a subject like this requires considerable background knowledge if it isn't to be quite meaningless. But I'm afraid they weren't convinced. Being women, they're of rather more conservative temperament than ourselves. With Mr Goldsmith's Documents, for instance, they feel on safer ground. They're sure of what they're getting there.'

Dixon was fairly sure too, but he allowed Michie's voice to go on dinning in his ears while they emerged into the heavy, dizzying sunlight and crossed the tacky asphalt to the lawn in front of the main building. Was Michie breaking to him the news that the three pretty girls were crying off and he himself was crying on? He would prevent that, if necessary by unlawful wounding. In a moment he said, without quite succeeding in keeping the plangency out of his voice: 'What am I supposed to do about it, then?'

Michie looked at him. His moustache seemed a size larger than usual; his Windsor-knotted silk tie toned unimprovably with his biscuit-coloured shirt; his lavender barathea trousers swayed gracefully with his walk. 'That's up to you, sir, of course,' he said, with a courtly minimum of surprise.

'I wonder if the thing could be cut down at all,' Dixon said, almost at random.

'I don't think there's much that could easily be sacrificed, Mr Dixon. As far as I'm concerned, the broad basis is the chief attraction.'

This, at any rate, was worth knowing. A basis consisting of a single point – the geometrical entity having position, but no magnitude – was clearly the thing to work for. 'Well, I'll have another look at it, anyway, and see if anything can be cut out.'

'Very well, sir,' Michie said, his demeanour that of a chief of staff about to put into action his general's unworkable plan. 'Will you get in touch with me, then, or shall I . . . ?'

'I'll look through it tonight and see you about it in the morning, if that's convenient.'

'Certainly. Would you care to come to the Second-Year Common Room at about eleven? I'll ask the ladies to come, and we could all have a cup of coffee.'

'That'll be splendid, Mr Michie.'

'Thank you, Mr Dixon.'

After this Victorian, or variety-team, salutation, Dixon went back to the Common Room, which was now empty, and sat down at the phone. Everything that might conceivably interest Michie must be slashed from the syllabus, even, or rather especially, what was indispensable. What did it matter? He'd probably never have to take the course. In that case why was he worrying about the 'interest' shown by Michie and the three pretty girls? He sighed, and picked up the phone.

Things at once happened very quickly. While, as he had reason to know, outgoing calls from the Welches' were liable to take some time, incoming-ones were horrifyingly swift. In less than a quarter of a minute Mrs Welch had said to him: 'Celia Welch speaking.'

He felt as if he'd crunched a cracknel biscuit; in his preoccupation he'd forgotten about Mrs Welch. Still, why worry? In an almost normal tone he said: 'Can I speak to Professor Welch, please?'

'That's Mr Dixon, isn't it? Before I get my husband, I'd just like you to tell me, if you don't mind, what you did to the sheet and blankets on your bed when you . . .'

He wanted to scream. His dilated eyes fell on a copy of the local paper that lay nearby. Without stopping to think, he said, distorting his voice by protruding his lips into an O: 'No, Mrs Welch,

99

there must be some mistake. This is the *Evening Post* speaking. There's no Mr Dixon with us, I'm quite sure.'

'Oh, I'm most awfully sorry; you sounded at first just like . . . How ridiculous of me.'

'Quite all right, Mrs Welch, quite all right.'

'I'll get my husband for you straight away.'

'Well, actually it was Mr Bertrand Welch I wanted to speak to really,' Dixon said, smiling at his own cunning as best he could with a distorted mouth; in a few seconds this horror would be over.

'I'm not sure whether he's . . . Just a minute.' She put the phone down.

Better hang on, Dixon thought, and the information, which Mrs Welch had obviously gone to get, about where Bertrand could be reached was just what he wanted for the Callaghan girl. He'd be able to ring her up and tell her, too. Yes, hang on at all costs.

One of the costs was immediately presented in the form of a well-remembered voice baying directly into his ear 'This is Bertrand Welch', so directly, indeed, that Dixon could have fancied that Bertrand was actually in the room with him and had by some sorcery substituted for the receiver those rosy, bearded lips.

'*Evening Post* here,' he managed to quaver through his snout.

'And what can I do for you, sir?'

Dixon recovered slightly. 'Er . . . we'd like to do a little paragraph about you for our, for our Saturday page,' he said, beginning to plan. 'That's if you've no objection.'

'Objection? Objection? What objection could a humble painter have to a little harmless publicity? At least, I take it it's harmless?'

Dixon got out a laugh, the Dickensian 'Ho ho ho' which was all his mouth could manage. 'Oh, quite harmless, I assure you, sir. We have a few facts about you already, naturally. But we would just like to know what you're engaged on at the moment, you see.'

'Of course, of course, most reasonable. Well, I've got two or three things in hand just now. There's a rather splendid nude, actually, though I don't know whether your readers would want to know about that, would they?'

'Oh, very much so, Mr Welch, I assure you, as long as we tell them in the proper way. I take it there'd be no objection to calling it "an undraped female figure", would there, sir? I imagine it is a female?'

Bertrand laughed like a leading hound announcing the end of a check. 'Oh, she's female all right, you can bet your bottom dollar on that. And "bottom" is the exact word.'

Dixon joined in this with his own laughter. What a story for Beesley and Atkinson this was going to make. 'Anything about what I believe's called the treatment, sir?' he asked when he might have been supposed to be calm again.

'Pretty bold, you know. Fairly modern, but not too much so. These modern chaps jigger up the detail so much, and we don't want that, do wam?'

'Indeed we don't, sir, as you say. I suppose this would be an oil painting, sir?'

'Oh God, yes; no expense spared. She's about eight feet by six, by the way, or will be when she's framed. A real smasher.'

'Any particular title for it, sir?'

'Well, yes, I thought of calling her *Amateur Model*. The girl who sat for it's certainly an amateur of a sort, and she acts as a model, at least while she's being painted, so there you are. I shouldn't put in that little explanation of the title if I were you.'

'Wouldn't dream of it,' Dixon said in something like his ordinary voice; his mouth had tightened involuntarily during the last few seconds and had temporarily abandoned its O. What a lad this Bertrand was, eh? He remembered the insinuations about the week-end with the Callaghan girl that Bertrand had made at their first meeting. God, if it ever came to a fight, he'd . . .

'What did you say?' Bertrand asked, a little tinge of suspicion in his tone.

'I was talking to someone in the office here, Mr Welch,' Dixon said, through the O this time. 'I've got all that, sir, thank you. Now what about the other things you're working on?'

'Well, there's a self-portrait, an outdoor one against a brick wall.

More wall than Welch, as a matter of fact. The real idea is the pallor and sort of crumpledness of the clothing against the great, red, smooth wall. A painter's picture, more or less.'

'Ah, just so, sir; thank you. Anything else?'

'There's a little one of three workmen looking at a newspaper in a pub, but that's hardly started yet.'

'I see; well, that'll do us nicely, Mr Welch,' Dixon said. Now was the moment for a daring switch. 'The young lady said something about an exhibition, sir; would that be right?'

'Yes, I am having a little show locally in the autumn; but what young lady is this?'

Dixon laughed silently with relief through his O. 'A Miss Callaghan, sir,' he said. 'I gather you know her.'

'Yes, I know her,' Bertrand said in a slightly hardened voice. 'Why, where does she fit into this?'

'Why, I thought you must know,' Dixon said with feigned surprise. 'This was really her idea. She knows one of our staff here, and I gather she put the notion of this little paragraph, like, to him, you see, sir.'

'Really? Well, it's the first I've heard of any of it. Are you quite sure?'

Dixon gave a quite professional laugh. 'Oh, we don't make mistakes about things like that, sir; more than our position's worth, if you take my meaning, Mr Welch.'

'Yes, I suppose it is, but it all sounds most . . .'

'Well, I should check with her then, sir, if you're in any doubt. As a matter of fact, when your Miss Callaghan was on the blower to Atkinson . . .'

'Who's this Atkinson character? I've never heard of him.'

'Our Mr Atkinson in the London office, sir. She was on to him just now, sir, and asked us to ask you to ring her, if we could get hold of you. Seems she couldn't get through to your house, or something. Something pretty urgent seems to have come up, and she'd like you to ring her up this afternoon, before five-thirty, if you would.'

'All right, I'll do that, then. What's your name, by the way, in case I . . . ?'

'Beesley, sir,' Dixon said without hesitation. 'Alfred R. Beesley.'

'Right, thank you, Mr Beesley.' (That's the tone, Dixon thought to himself.) 'Oh, by the way, when will the paragraph be appearing?'

'Ah, there you have me, sir. One just can't tell, I'm afraid. But it'll certainly be within the next four weeks. We like to have the material by us in plenty of time, just on the off-chance, you see, Mr Welch.'

'Quite so, quite so. Well, have you got everything you want?'

'Yes, thank you very much indeed, sir.'

'No no, thanks to you, old boy,' Bertrand said, with a welcome return to his earlier comradeliness. 'Very fine body of men, the gentlemen of the Press.'

'Nice of you to say so, sir,' Dixon said, making his Edith Sitwell face into the phone. 'Well, good-bye and thanks, Mr Welch. Much obliged to you.'

'So long, Beesley, old boy.'

Dixon sat back, mopped his face, though he'd have liked to mop his entire frame, and lit a cigarette. Panic had made him fearfully rash, but not, he thought, irretrievably so. The key to the situation lay in dismantling the hoax at once, before Bertrand could get round to blowing it up himself. The Callaghan girl must be carefully coached in the following story: Some unknown calling himself Atkinson had rung her up that morning and, posing as a journalist, discussed Bertrand. He'd talked vaguely about the *Evening Post*, obtained the Welches' phone number, and rung off. When Bertrand came through on the phone, she must greet him at once with the Atkinson story, saying it had all sounded very fishy to her and that the voice of 'Atkinson' had reminded her strongly of whichever of their London acquaintances was most likely, or least unlikely, to play a meaningless practical joke on the pair of them. Without being suspiciously emphatic, she must make it clear that 'Atkinson' had phoned her from a London number, that is, not by a trunk line. Provided she held to her story, both she and Dixon were completely safe, even if Bertrand was already ringing the *Post* in quest of 'Beesley'. The danger obviously was that she wouldn't come in with the conspiracy. There were solid grounds, however, for thinking that she would: her gratitude at his offer of help, his success in his mission against heavy odds, her demeanour over the sheet and table affair, finally, if necessary, his extreme vulnerability if the truth got out. If Bertrand were still suspicious, he might worm the story out of her by emotional pressure, but why should he be suspicious? He could hardly think that she'd go to the lengths of suborning some unknown provincial in order to get hold of some information about the Summer Ball, which in fact was almost exactly what she had done.

The thing now was, obviously, to get hold of her and coach her in her story. He must hurry, because he had to get lunch and be back to invigilate at an examination by two o'clock. Before making any move, however, he threw back his head and gave a long trombone-blast of anarchistic laughter. It was all so wonderful, even if it did go wrong, and it wouldn't. The campaign against Bertrand he'd fantasied about at the Welches' had begun, and with a dazzling tactical success. A warning voice told him that this campaign, even so far, was too dangerous for a man in his precarious position, that the joy of battle was submerging his prudence, but he drowned it in more laughter of the same sort.

Yet again he picked up the phone, got Trunks and then Christine Callaghan's number. Better not tell her anything like the full story of his conversation with Bertrand, he thought. After a moment he leaned forward and said: 'Miss Callaghan? Good. It's Dixon here. Now listen carefully.'

'Honestly, James, she couldn't have been more livid,' Margaret said. 'She kept it well under control, of course, but her mouth went tight and her eyes absolutely flashed fire; you know the way they do. I can't say I blame her, having it thrown at her across the tea-table like that, in front of me and the Neddies.'

'What was actually said?' Dixon asked, executing a turn at the corner of the dance-floor and beginning to lead her up towards the band.

'Well, he just said: "Oh, by the way, Carol, I've been meaning to tell you that Christine's coming to the dance after all, and she's bringing her uncle with her." Then he went all facetious on her: "So as not to have uncle partnering niece, which wouldn't be according to the best usages" or some rubbish like that, "I thought the best thing would be to switch her on to my ticket, if you've no objection" – as if she could object, with all the rest of us there listening – "and Gore-Urquhart would be only too pleased to escort you, I'm sure," and that was that.'

'Mm,' Dixon said. The strain of dancing, always considerable, and of keeping his eyes on Margaret's face as it bobbed and advanced and receded, made elaborate speech difficult for him. In addition, he had to keep straining his ears to catch the beat of the music above the swishing of many pairs of feet and the clamour of many conversations. 'A bit thick, that.'

'I've never seen anything so abominably rude in my life. The man's quite impossible, James, socially and, er, in every other way. I say, though – it struck me at the time – do you think there's anything, well, going on between Bertrand and Carol?'

'I've no idea. What makes you say that?'

'Haven't you ever noticed anything?'

'I don't think so; why?'

'Oh, I don't know. It's really rather odd that he should ever have been taking her to the Ball, and then her looking so furious . . .'

'Ah, but Bertrand's always been pretty thick with both of them – I remember you were there when she told us – and it's only natural she should feel she was being pushed around a bit. Sorry,' he added to a girl whose bottom had come into collision with his hip. He wished this set of dances would end; he was hot, his socks seemed to have been sprayed with fine adhesive sand, and his arms ached like those of a boxer keeping his guard up after fourteen rounds. He wondered why he didn't tell Margaret about the embrace he'd seen during the arty week-end; she always kept her mouth shut when told to. Perhaps it was that the news, as well as shocking her, would make her mildly exultant, and he didn't want that. Why didn't he want that?

Margaret was talking again, animatedly; her face was a little flushed and her lipstick had been more carefully applied than usual. She looked as if she was enjoying herself; her sort of minimal prettiness was in evidence. 'Well, anyway, I think she's done a good deal better for herself with Mr Gore-Urquhart. I must say he seems most charming, something quite exceptional these days. He's got the most beautiful manners, hasn't he? Quite the real thing. Bit of a change after the bearded monster.'

Dixon gargled inaudibly in his throat at this mixture of styles, but before he had time to reply the dance wheeled to an end. In a moment an uneasy thundering, followed by a clashing thump, signalled the end of the set. Dixon heaved a sigh and wiped his palms on his handkerchief. 'What about a drink?' he said.

Margaret was darting her eyes this way and that. 'Wait a minute; I just want to see if I can see the others.'

The dancers were trickling away on to the touchlines of the long dance-floor. The walls were decorated with scenes from the remoter past, portrayed in what was no doubt an advanced style, so that in the one nearest Dixon, for example, some lack of

perspective or similar commodity made a phalanx of dwarf infan-
trymen (Spartan? Macedonian? Roman?) seem to be falling from
the skies upon their much larger barbarian adversaries (Persian?
Iranian? Carthaginian?) who, unaware of this danger overhead,
gazed threateningly into the empty middle distance. At intervals
stood large pillars of some pallid material. Dixon gave a sad,
nostalgic smile; it all reminded him so clearly of those large eating-
establishments at Marble Arch, Charing Cross, Coventry Street,
where he'd enjoyed himself so much. Lowering his eyes from
these memorials, he caught sight of Michie in the crowd, talking
and laughing vigorously with Miss O'Shaughnessy, the prettiest
of the three pretty girls and, in fact, Michie's girl. She had the kind
of water-gipsy face, dusky but rosy, that affected him uncomfortably. The same was true of the low-cut dress she wore. Though
he was fifteen yards away from him, Dixon knew all about the
perfection of Michie's evening clothes, the efficiency of his chat-
ter, and the attentiveness of his audience. Michie now caught his
eye, at once became grave, and made him a shallow but courteous
bow. Miss O'Shaughnessy managed a quick smile before turning
away, beyond all question so as to laugh. 'What about a drink?'
Dixon asked Margaret again.

'Ah, here they are,' she said by way of reply.

Bertrand and Christine were approaching. Bertrand, Dixon had
to admit, was quite presentable in evening clothes, and to say of
him now that he looked like an artist of some sort would have
been true without being too offensive. It was on him that Dixon
fixed his eye, less from interest than to avoid fixing it on Christine.
Her manner to him so far that evening had been not even cold; it
had been simply non-existent, had made him feel that, contrary to
the evidence of his senses, he wasn't really there at all. But, worse
than this, she was looking her best this evening. She wore a yellow
dress that left her shoulders bare. It was perfectly plain, managing,
as if it had been intended just for that, to reveal as decidedly ill-
judged Margaret's royal-blue taffeta, with its bow and what he
supposed were gatherings or something, and with the quadruple

row of pearls above it. Christine's aim, he imagined, had been to show off the emphasis of her natural colouring and skin-texture. The result was painfully successful, making everybody else look like an assemblage of granulated half-tones. For a moment, as she and Bertrand came up, Dixon caught her eye, and although it held nothing for him he wanted to cast himself down behind the protective wall of skirts and trousers, or, better, pull the collar of his dinner-jacket over his head and run out into the street. He'd read somewhere, or been told, that somebody like Aristotle or I. A. Richards had said that the sight of beauty makes us want to move towards it. Aristotle or I. A. Richards had been wrong about that, hadn't he?

'Well, what goes forward, people?' Bertrand asked. He was holding Christine's wrist between finger and thumb, perhaps taking her pulse. He glanced at Dixon, to whom he'd so far been fairly amiable.

'Well, I thought we might go and have a drink,' Dixon said.

'Oh, do be quiet, James; anybody'd think you'd die if you went an hour without one.'

'He probably would,' Bertrand said. 'Anyway, it's sensible of him not to want to take the risk. What about it, darling? I'm afraid there's only beer and cider, unless you want to fare forth to an adjacent hostelram.'

'Yes, all right, but where's Uncle Julius and Mrs Goldsmith? We can't go off and leave them.'

While it was being agreed that these two were probably already in the bar, Dixon grinned to himself at 'Uncle Julius'. How marvellous it was that there should be somebody called that and somebody else to call him that, and that he himself should be present to hear one calling the other that. As he drifted off at Margaret's side between the talking groups on one side and the mutes lining the walls on the other, he caught sight of Alfred Beesley standing rather miserably among the last-named. Beesley, notorious for his inability to get to know women, always came to functions of this sort, but since every woman here tonight had come with a partner (except for women like the sexagenarian Professor of Philosophy or the fifteen-stone Senior Lecturer in Economics) he must know he was wasting his time. Dixon exchanged greetings with him, and fancied he caught a gleam of envy in Beesley's eye. Dixon reflected firstly how inefficient a bar to wasting one's time was the knowledge that one was wasting it (and especially in what Welch called 'matters of the heart'); secondly how narrow a gap there really was between Beesley's status and his own in such matters; and thirdly how little there was to envy in what established him as on the far side of the gap from Beesley – the privileges of being able to speak to one woman and of being in the same party as another. But, fourthly, the possession of the signs of sexual privilege is the important thing, not the quality nor the enjoyment of them. Dixon felt he ought to feel calmed and liberated at reaching this conclusion, but he didn't, any more than unease in the stomach is alleviated by discovery of its technical name.

They reached the bar, a small room not designed for the purpose. The still recent tradition of a 'wet' Summer Ball had been instituted, though few could of course bring themselves to believe it, by the College authorities, on the argument that the amount of drunkenness among student patrons, alarming at one time, could be reduced by providing cheap non-spirituous liquors on the premises, and by thus rendering less acutely attractive the costly and injurious gulping of horses' necks or of inferior gin and synthetic lime-juice in the city's pubs. More oddly still, perhaps, this argument had shown itself to be sound, so that in the room now visited by Dixon and the rest three minor College employees were toiling at barrels of beer and cider under panels representing, similarly to the larger ones in the Ballroom, swarthy potentates about to be danced upon by troupes of midget Circassians, or caravans of Chinese merchants being sucked up into the air by whirlwinds. The pallid pillars were here replaced by potted and tubbed palms of an almost macabre luxuriance. Among these last lurked Maconochie, the titular supervisor of the three barmen, adding to the effect in some indefinable way by wearing a starched white coat over his olive-green trousers.

Gore-Urquhart and Carol were sitting in one of the further palm-groves, talking fairly hard. When he saw the others coming towards them, Gore-Urquhart rose to his feet. This formality was so unfamiliar in the circles Dixon normally moved in that for a moment he wondered whether the other meant to oppose their approach by physical force. He was younger than Dixon had expected any distinguished man, and an uncle of Christine's, to be: somewhere in the middle forties. His evening suit, too, was not nearly as spectacularly 'faultless' as might have been predicted. His large smooth face, surmounting a short thin body, was the least symmetrical, short of actual deformity, that Dixon had ever seen, giving him the look of a drunken sage trying to collect his wits, a look intensified by slightly protruding lips and a single black eyebrow running from temple to temple. Before the party was finally seated Maconochie, no doubt well tipped already, loped forward to see what drinks were wanted. Dixon watched his servility with enjoyment.

'I've managed to keep out of your Principal's way so far,' Gore-Urquhart said with his strong Lowland-Scottish accent.

'That's no mean achievement, Mr Gore-Urquhart,' Margaret said with a laugh. 'I'm sure he's got all his spies out for you.'

'Do you think so, now? Will I be able to get away again if he catches me?'

'Most unlikely, sir,' Bertrand said. 'You know what they're like in this part of the world. Throw them a celebrity and they'll fight over him like dogs over a bone. Why, even in my small way I've had a good deal of that sort of thing to endure, especially from academic so-called society. Just because my father happens to be a professor, they think I must want to talk to the Vice-Chancellor's wife about the difficulties her wretched grandson's having at his school. But, of course, it must be a thousand times worse for you, sir, am I right?'

Gore-Urquhart, who'd been listening to this with attention, said briskly 'In some ways,' and drank from his glass.

'Anyway, Mr Gore-Urquhart,' Margaret said, 'you're quite safe for the moment. The Principal holds court on these occasions in a room at the other end of the dance-floor – he doesn't mix with the rabble in here.'

'So while I'm with the rabble I'm fairly safe, you mean, Miss Peel? Good, I'll stay with the rabble.'

Dixon had been expecting a silver-bells laugh from Margaret to follow this remark, but it was still hard to bear when it came. At that moment Maconochie arrived with the drinks Gore-Urquhart had ordered. To Dixon's surprise and delight, the beer was in pint glasses and, after waiting for Gore-Urquhart's 'Find me some cigarettes, laddie,' to Maconochie, he leaned forward and said: 'How on earth did you manage to get pints? I haven't seen anything but halves in here the whole evening. I thought it must be a rule of the place. They wouldn't give me pints when I asked for them. How on earth did you get round it?' While he said this he saw irritably that Margaret was looking from him to Gore-Urquhart and back again and smiling deprecatingly, as if to assure Gore-Urquhart that, despite all evidence to the contrary, this speech betokened no real mental derangement. Bertrand, too, was watching and grinning.

Gore-Urquhart, who didn't seem to have noticed Margaret's smiles, jerked a short, nicotined thumb towards the departing Maconochie. 'A fellow Scottish Nationalist,' he said.

All the people facing Dixon and to his left – Gore-Urquhart himself, Bertrand, and Margaret – laughed at this, and so did Dixon, who looked to his right and saw Christine, seated next to him with her elbows on the table, smiling in a controlled fashion, and beyond her Carol, at Gore-Urquhart's left, staring rather grimly at Bertrand. Before the laughter cleared, Dixon noticed Bertrand becoming aware of this scrutiny and looking away. Perturbed by the small tension in the company, and finding now that Gore-Urquhart's eyes were fixed on him from under the black eyebrow, Dixon twitched his glasses on to the right part of his nose and said at a venture: 'Well, it's an unexpected pleasure to be drinking pints at a do like this.'

'You're in luck, Dixon,' Gore-Urquhart said sharply, handing round cigarettes.

Dixon felt himself blushing slightly, and resolved to say no more for a time. None the less he was pleased that Gore-Urquhart had caught his name. With a braying flourish of trumpets, the music started up in the Ballroom, and people began to move out of the bar. Bertrand, who'd settled himself next to Gore-Urquhart, began talking to him in a low voice, and almost at once Christine addressed some remark to Carol. Margaret said to Dixon: 'It is sweet of you to have brought me here, James.'

'Glad you're enjoying yourself.'

'You don't sound as if you are very much.'

'Oh, I am, really.'

'I'm sure you're enjoying this part of it, anyway, better than the actual dancing part.'

'Oh, I'm enjoying both parts, honestly. Drink that up and we'll go back on the floor. I can do quick-steps.'

She looked earnestly at him and rested a hand on his arm. 'Dear James, do you think it's wise for us to go round together like this?' she asked him.

'Why ever not?' he said in alarm.

'Because you're so sweet to me and I'm getting much too fond of you.' She said this in a tone that combined the vibrant with the flat, like a great actress demonstrating the economical conveyance of strong emotion. This was her habit when making her avowals.

In the midst of his panic, Dixon managed to find the thought that this, if true, would indeed be grounds for their seeing less of each other; then he hit on a remark both honest and acceptable: 'You mustn't say things like that.'

She laughed lightly. 'Poor James,' she said. 'Keep my seat for me, will you, darling? I shan't be long.' She went out.

Poor James? Poor James? It was, in fact, a very just characterization, but hardly one for her to make, surely, her of all people. Then a sense of guilt sent him diving for his glass; guilt not only for this latest reflection, but for the unintentional irony of 'you're so sweet to me'. It was doubtful, he considered, whether he was capable of being at all sweet, much less 'so' sweet, to anybody at all. Whatever passably decent treatment Margaret had had from him was the result of a temporary victory of fear over irritation and/or pity over boredom. That behaviour of such origin could seem 'so sweet' to her might be taken as a reflection on her sensitivity, but it was also a terrible commentary on her frustration and loneliness. Poor old Margaret, he thought with a shudder. He must try harder. But what would be the consequences to her of treatment more consistently sweet, or of a higher level of sweetness? What would be the consequences to him? To drive away these speculations, he began listening to the conversation on his left.

'. . . I've the utmost respect for his opinion,' Bertrand was saying. The bay in his voice was well throttled back; perhaps someone had upbraided him about it. 'I always say he's the last of the old-fashioned professional critics, and so he knows what he's talking about, which is more than you can say for most of the fraternity nowadays. Well, we kept running into each other at the same exhibitions, and funnily enough in front of the same pictures.' Here he laughed, momentarily raising one shoulder. 'One day he said to me: "I want to see your work. People tell me it's good." So I packed up an assortment of small stuff and took it round to his house – it's a lovely place, isn't it? You must know it, of course; one might really be back in the *dix-huitième*. Wonder how long before the Rubber Goods Workers' Union takes it over – and I must say that one or two pastels seemed to fetch him . . .'

Fetch him a vomiting-basin, Dixon thought; then horror overcame him at the thought of a man who 'knows what he's talking about' not only not talking about how nasty Bertrand's pictures were, not only not putting his boot through them, but actually seeming to be fetched by one or two of them. Bertrand must not be a good painter; he, Dixon, would not permit it. And yet here was the Gore-Itchbag fellow, not on the face of it a moron, listening to this frenzy of self-advertisement without overt protest, even with some attention. Yes, Dixon saw, with very close attention.

Gore-Urquhart had tilted his large dark head over towards Bertrand; his face, half averted, eyes on the ground, wore a small intent frown, as if he were hard of hearing and couldn't bear to miss a word. Dixon couldn't bear not missing any more of it – Bertrand was now using the phrase 'contrapuntal tone-values' – and switched to his right, where for some moments he'd been half-conscious of a silence.

As he did so, Christine turned towards him. 'Look, do join in this, will you?' she said in an undertone. 'I can't get her to say anything.'

He looked over at Carol, whose eye met his without apparent recognition, but before he could start working on what to say Margaret returned.

'What, still hanging over the drink?' she said vivaciously to the whole party. 'I thought you'd all be on the floor by now. Now, Mr Gore-Urquhart, I'm not going to permit any more of this sulking about in here, Principal or no Principal. It's the light fantastic for you; come along.'

Gore-Urquhart, smiling politely, had risen to his feet and, with a word to the others, let himself be led away out of the bar. Bertrand looked across at Carol. 'Don't let's waste the band, my dear,' he said. 'I've paid twenty-five shillings for them, after all.'

'So you have, my dear,' Carol said, stressing the appellation, and for a moment Dixon was afraid she meant to refuse and so bring the situation, whatever it was, to a crisis; but after that moment she got to her feet and began to move towards the dance-floor.

'Look after Christine for me, Dixon,' Bertrand bayed. 'Don't drop her; she's fragile. Good-bye for a little, my sweet,' he fluted to Christine; 'I'll be back soon. Blow your whistle if the man gets rough.'

'Care for a dance?' Dixon said to Christine. 'I'm not much good, as I told you, but I don't mind having a crack if you don't.'

She smiled. 'Nor do I, if you don't.'

11

As he left the bar with Christine at his side, Dixon felt like a special agent, a picaroon, a Chicago war-lord, a hidalgo, an oil baron, a mohock. He kept careful control over his features to stop them doing what they wanted to do and breaking out into an imbecile smirk of excitement and pride. When she turned and faced him at the edge of the floor, he found it hard to believe that she was really going to let him touch her, or that the men near them wouldn't spontaneously intervene to prevent him. But in a moment there they were in the conventional pseudo-embrace, actually dancing together, not very skilfully, but without doubt dancing. Dixon looked past her face in silence, afraid of any distraction from the task of not leading her into a collision, for the floor was a good deal more thickly populated than a quarter of an hour earlier. Among the dancers he recognized Barclay, the Professor of Music, dancing with his wife. She permanently resembled a horse, he only when he laughed, which he did suddenly and seldom, but was momentarily to be seen doing now.

'What was the matter with Mrs Goldsmith, do you know?' Christine asked.

This inquisitiveness surprised him. 'She did look rather fed-up, didn't she?' he fenced.

'Was it because she was expecting Bertrand to bring her here tonight instead of me?'

Did that mean she knew about the switch of partners? It needn't, but it might. 'I don't know,' he said in a muffled voice.

'I think you do know.' She sounded quite angry. 'I wish you'd tell me.'

'I know nothing at all about it, I'm afraid. And in any case it's nothing to do with me.'

'If that's your attitude, then there's nothing more to be said.'

Dixon felt himself flushing for the second time in the last few minutes. Obviously she'd been at her most typical when helping Bertrand to bait him at their first encounter, when reproving him for drinking too much, when treating him this evening as non-existent. Her formal, not her relaxed, pose was the true one. Her cooperation over the sheet had been given in return for anecdote-material likely to amuse her London friends, her amiability over the phone had been to get something out of him. No doubt she was disturbed by the Bertrand–Carol business, but the feminine manoeuvre of using an innocent bystander as whipping-boy was one he'd learnt to recognize and dislike.

They danced on in silence for some time. She'd not been modest in declaring herself an indifferent dancer, but Dixon's enforced avoidance of anything ambitious kept them fairly well together. The other couples moved round them, wheeling when a space momentarily presented itself, huddling and marking time in the crushes. Everybody else seemed to be talking, and eventually a female voice of Christine's pitch, heard close at hand, deceived Dixon. 'What did you say?' he asked.

'Nothing.'

Something would have to be said by him now, so he said what he'd been waiting to say all the evening: 'I never got a chance to thank you for playing up so well over that phone business.'

'What phone business?'

'You know, me pretending to Bertrand that I was a reporter.'

'Oh, that. I'd sooner not discuss that, if you don't mind.'

She couldn't be allowed to get away with that. 'Supposing I do mind?'

'How do you mean?'

'You seem to forget that, but for me, and but for my little imper-sonation, you probably wouldn't be here at all tonight.'

'Well, that wouldn't have mattered very much, would it?'

The dance came to an end, but neither of them thought of leav-ing the floor. Through the applause he said: 'No, perhaps it wouldn't, but you seemed to want to come at the time, didn't you?'

'Look, can't you shut up about it?'

'All right, but don't you try to queen it over me. You've no call to do that.'

She shrugged clumsily, then dropped her eyes. 'I'm sorry; that was silly of me. I didn't mean to be like that.'

As she spoke, an inaudible piano introduction led into the last of the set. 'O.K., then,' Dixon said. 'Dance?'

'Yes, of course.'

They moved off again. 'I think we're getting the hang of this quite well,' he said in a moment.

'I wish I hadn't said what I did say. I was a fool. I acted like a perfect fool.'

He saw that when, as now, she abandoned her set expression, her lips were full, and protruded like her uncle's. 'It's all right, really; it was nothing,' he said.

'No it wasn't nothing; it was ridiculous. I thought the whole of the *Evening Post* business was brilliantly funny.'

'Oh come, there's no need to go to the opposite extreme.'

'But you see I didn't feel like discussing it with you because that would have been like laughing at Bertrand behind his back, and that would have been wrong. I'm afraid I must have sounded a bit unfriendly over the phone the second time, but that was only because I couldn't have let myself go like I wanted to without seeming as if I was getting mixed up in a conspiracy to get the better of Bertrand. That's all it was.'

The whole thing sounded rather childish, but better that than peevish. All the same, what messes these women got themselves into over nothing. Men got themselves into messes too, and ones that weren't so easily got out of, but their messes arose from attempts to satisfy real and simple needs. He was saved from having to reply by the intervention of an enormous, half-incoherent voice, like that of an ogre at the onset of aphasia, which now began to sing through loudspeakers with an intonation rather resembling Cecil Goldsmith's:

Ah'll be parp tar gat you in a taxi, honny,
Ya'd batter be raddy 'bout a parp-parp eight;
Ahr, baby, dawn't be late,
Ah'm gonna parp parp parp whan the band starts playeeng . . .

In trying to pull Christine out of the path of a short red-faced
man dancing with a tall pale-faced woman, Dixon got badly out
of time. 'Start again,' he mumbled, but they seemed unable to
move together as before.

'Here, you'll never do any good while you stand right over
there,' Christine said. 'I'm not close enough to you to feel what
you're doing. Get hold of me properly.'

Gingerly, Dixon moved forward until they were standing up
against each other. He again took her warm right hand, and steered
her off. This time things were much better, though Dixon was a
little shorter of breath than he thought he should be. Her body felt
rounded, and rather bulky, against his. They moved down the
floor away from the band, through the sound of which Dixon
faintly caught a baying laugh. Bertrand, his big head flung back,
was just disappearing into a gap some yards away. Though Dixon
couldn't see Carol's face, this seemed to indicate that she'd been
at least partly mollified. What the hell was Bertrand up to? This
was a problem deserving as urgent attention as the problem of
why he wore a beard. Was he trying to have two mistresses at
once, or was he trying to discard one in favour of the other? If the
latter, which one was he trying to acquire and which one was he
trying to reconcile to being discarded? Would he bother, though,
about reconciling people to what he wanted to do with them?
Probably not, in which case it was presumably Carol who was in
the ascendant, because that was the only way of explaining her
presence here tonight. Christine must be functioning merely as
Gore-Urquhart's niece, but would have to be somehow retained
on Bertrand's establishment until the Gore-Urquhart deal was
safely concluded. Dixon found his head beginning to sing slightly
as he realized that the third round in his campaign against Bertrand

was about to begin, though he didn't yet see how battle was going to be joined.

'How are you getting on with Professor Welch these days?' Christine asked suddenly.

Dixon stiffened. 'Oh, not too badly,' he said mechanically.

'He hasn't been on to you about that phone call?'

He couldn't stifle a howl, but hoped the music would drown it. 'You mean Bertrand did find out it was me after all?'

'Find out it was you? How do you mean?'

'That I was pretending to be the reporter that time.'

'No, I wasn't talking about that business. I meant the phone call from that man in your digs, that Sunday.'

As the body of a decapitated hen is said to go running about the farmyard, Dixon's legs continued to perform the requisite dance-steps. 'He knows that I arranged for Atkinson to tell me my parents had come down?'

'Oh, is that who Atkinson is? He seems to have done a lot of phoning since we met. Yes, Mr Welch knows you asked him to ring you up about your parents.'

'Who told him? Who told him?'

'Please don't dig your nails into my back . . . It was that little man who played the oboe – you did tell me his name . . .'

'Yes, I did. Johns is his name. Johns.'

'That's right. It was the only thing I remember him saying the whole time I was there. Except for when he said you must have gone to the pub the previous evening, that is. He seems to have got it in for you rather.'

'Yes, he does, doesn't he? Tell me: was Mrs Welch there when he blew the gaff about the phone call?'

'No, I'm sure she wasn't. Just the three of us were chatting together after lunch.'

'That's good.' There was a fair chance that Welch hadn't noticed what Johns had told him, since he'd presumably only told him once; Mrs Welch, on the other hand, would have been likely to go on telling Welch until he did notice. But perhaps Johns had told her separately, out of Christine's hearing. Then a fresh aspect of the situation struck him: 'How did Johns say he got to know about this? I didn't tell him, as you can imagine.'

'He said he was there when you were arranging it.'

'That's pretty rich, isn't it?' he said, scowling. 'As if I'd have said a word in front of that little ponce . . . Sorry. No, he was listening outside the door. Must have been. I remember thinking I heard something.'

'What a filthy trick,' she said with unexpected venom. 'What had you done to him?'

'Only mucked about with a photograph of a chap on the front of a paper of his with a pencil.'

This utterance, enigmatic enough in itself, was half blotted out by the disturbance which now arose to mark the end of the set. After Dixon had explained, Christine, who was just starting to move off at his side, turned and looked at him, laughing with her mouth closed. When he smiled sourly, she began laughing with her tongue between those slightly irregular teeth. Dixon felt desire abruptly flooding his entire frame with an immense fatigue, as if he'd been struck by a bullet in some vital spot. All his facial muscles relaxed involuntarily. She caught his eye and stopped laughing.

'Thank you for the dance,' he said in a normal tone.

'I enjoyed it very much,' she replied, compressing her lips after she spoke.

Dixon realized with wonderment that he didn't really care about Johns's latest piece of gaff-blowing, for the moment anyway. It must be because he was having such a good time at the dance.

In the bar again, they found Gore-Urquhart in his former seat, already being talked to by Bertrand, as if their conversation had never been interrupted. Margaret was in even closer attendance, if possible; she broke off from laughing at a retort of Gore-Urquhart's to look up casually at Dixon with an air that suggested she was wondering idly who he might happen to be. More drinks arrived, proving inexplicably to be double gins. They were brought, of course, by Maconochie, one of whose jobs at these functions was to prevent the importation of spirits. Dixon, who was beginning to do what he'd have described as 'feeling his age', sat down in a chair and began drinking his drink and smoking a cigarette. How hot it was; and how his legs ached; and how much longer was all this going to go on? After a moment he roused himself to talk to Christine, but she was sitting next to Bertrand and, though unheeded, evidently listening to what he was saying to her uncle, who was keeping his eyes on the floor in the way that Dixon had noticed earlier. Margaret was laughing again, swaying towards Gore-Urquhart so that their shoulders kept touching. Oh well, Dixon thought, each must enjoy himself as and when he can. But where was Carol?

Just then she reappeared, walking up to them with a kind of deliberate carelessness that made Dixon suspect her of having a bottle of something, now no doubt much depleted, hidden in the ladies' cloakroom. The expression on her face boded ill for somebody, or perhaps everybody. When she reached the group, Dixon saw Gore-Urquhart look up at her and try to flash some facial signal; 'You see how I'm placed' was possibly its nearest equivalent. Then, alone among the men present, he stood up.

Carol turned to Dixon. 'Come on, Jim,' she said rather loudly, 'I want you to dance with me. I take it that nobody here will object.'

12

'What's going on, Carol?'

'That's what I'd like to know.'

'How do you mean?'

'You know how I mean, Jim, unless you go about with your eyes shut. And you don't do that, do you? No, I'm sick and tired of being pushed around. I don't mind telling you this, because I know. I do know you, don't I? In fact, I've got to tell someone, so I pick you. You don't mind?'

It was having to dance again, and so soon, that Dixon minded, not hearing what Carol wanted to say, which promised to be at least interesting. 'You go ahead,' he said encouragingly, looking round to see who was dancing near them. The floor seemed fuller than ever of jigging, lurching couples, who every few seconds lurched all one way together, bearing one another along like a crowd that knows a baton-charge is imminent. The noise was enormous; every time it rose to a maximum Dixon felt sweat start out on his chest as if it were being physically squeezed out of him. Above eye-level, the painted Pharaohs and Caesars seemed themselves to be twisting and toppling.

'He thinks he's only got to crook his bloody finger and I'll come running,' Carol announced in a shout. 'Well, he's mistaken.'

It was on the tip of Dixon's tongue to tell Carol not to think she was fooling anyone by talking and behaving so much more drunkenly than she was in fact feeling, but he didn't, guessing that she needed some sort of mask and knowing by experience that this was a much more efficient one than drunkenness itself. He only said: 'Bertrand?'

'That's the fellow; the painter, you know. The great painter. Of course, he knows he isn't great really, and that's what makes him behave like this. Great artists always have a lot of women, so if he can have a lot of women that makes him a great artist, never mind what his pictures are like. You're familiar with the argument. And with the fallacy too, no doubt. Undistributed how-d'you-call. Well, you can guess who the women are in this case. Me and the girl you've got your eye on.'

Dixon started insincerely; the charge was quite unfounded, but at the same time it managed in some unscrupulous way to be well-founded too. 'What the hell are you talking about?'

'Don't waste time like this, Jim. What are you going to do about it, anyway?'

'About what?'

She dug her nails into the back of his hand. 'Stop doing that. What are you doing about Christine Callaghan?'

'Nothing, of course. What can I do?'

'If you don't know what to do I can't show you, as the actress said to the bishop. Worried about what dear Margaret would do?'

'Look, do cut it out, Carol. You're supposed to be telling me something, not cross-questioning me.'

'I thought so. And don't worry; it's all connected, all connected. No, you let dear Margaret stew in her own juice. I've met people like that before, old boy, and believe me, it's the only way, only thing to do. Throw her a lifebelt and she'll pull you under. Take it from me.' She nodded, her eyes half-closed.

'What do you want to tell me, Carol? If anything.'

'Oh, I've got plenty to tell, plenty. You knew he was bringing me to this hop originally?'

'Yes, I had gathered that.'

'Dear Margaret again, no doubt. Well, then he ditches me so that he can bring his new piece and her uncle, and pairs me off with the uncle. Not that I minded that after a bit, because I think old Julius and I have got a lot in common. We started to, anyway, until dear Margaret decided she could make sweeter music with old Julius than I could. I'm using her vocabulary, you understand; not mine.'

'Yes, I understand very well, thanks.'

At this point they both heeled over sharply in the crowd, but he heard her say: 'None of your Galsworthy dialogue here, please, Jim. Can't we go and sit down for a bit? This is a bit too much like a C. and A. sale for me.'

'All right.'

They made their way effortlessly towards the Carthaginians, under whom they found two vacant chairs against the wall. As soon as they were seated, Carol leaned vivaciously over to Dixon, so that their knees were touching. Her face was in shadow, and seen so it had a romantic bloom. 'I suppose you've guessed I've been sleeping with our friend the painter, haven't you?'

'No, I hadn't.' He began to feel frightened.

'That's good; I shouldn't like it to be generally known.'

'I won't tell anybody.'

'That's the spirit. Especially not dear Margaret, eh?'

'Of course not.'

'Good. Rather a surprise, isn't it?'

'Yes, it is.'

'You're a bit shocked, aren't you?'

'Well, no, not that exactly. Not in the ordinary way, that is. It's just that he seems such a queer fish for you to have . . . gone for in that way.'

'Not so queer as all that. His determination's rather a good thing about him, you know. And he's very attractive in his way.'

'Is he?' Dixon's mouth tightened.

'And, well, old Cecil isn't much of a boy for that kind of business, as you can imagine. We've more or less packed it in, that side of things. The trouble is that I still quite like it.'

'And so does Bertrand, eh?'

'Of course, the thing's been dragging on for some time now. We'd been getting rather fed-up. Bertrand was always in London hopping into bed with people, the Loosmore girl chiefly, and I'd been getting sick of his line about being a great artist and so on. Then it flared up again the last time he was down. I think perhaps

Christine wasn't coming up to scratch, or not quickly enough, possibly.'

'Oh, then you don't think they've . . . ?'

'Hard to say. I should think not, on the whole. She doesn't seem the type, really; at least, she doesn't talk or behave like it, though she does look it in a way. It depends how deep that prim, prissy look of hers goes. Still, the point is that he gets me all lined up for the Ball, with a hint of other things to follow, and then tells me he's not taking me after all in front of that mother of his, and in front of dear Margaret too. That's what annoyed me in the first place. Then he starts trying to conciliate me in front of Christine this evening. That got me down again. Then he takes me in here for a dance and tries to laugh the whole thing off by treating me man-to-man and telling me I know what little girls like Christine are like and how I'm not the sort of person he's always taken me for if I let that sort of thing interfere in a friendship – note that – between two adults – note that too. Oh, I know I oughtn't to be taking it like this, but . . . Honestly, Jim, it does get you down, the whole thing. I feel so fed-up with it all. I don't even want to bash his brains out any more.'

Dixon had been studying her face during this speech. The movements of her mouth were beautifully decisive, and her voice, abandoning its synthetic fuzziness, had returned to its usual clarity. These things helped to give her presence a solidity and emphasis that impressed him; he felt not so much her sexual attraction as the power of her femaleness. It was just as well that her married status put her beyond his ambition, since even their friendship demanded reserves of an attention, of a sort of mental and emotional integrity he wasn't sure he really possessed. After a short pause he said hurriedly: 'How have you managed to keep all this out of Cecil's way?'

'You don't think I haven't told him all about it, do you? I wouldn't dream of doing anything behind his back.'

Dixon fell silent again, reflecting, not for the first time, that he knew absolutely nothing whatsoever about other people or their lives. Then Carol's face moved out of the shadow. Though quick to detect a change in expression, he wasn't usually observant of the actual lineaments of people's faces, but this time he saw clearly that the outline of her lips was slightly blurred and there were two well-marked lines in her cheeks. When she spoke again he noticed something else: that the whiteness and regularity of her top teeth gave place to a black gap beyond the canines. He felt uncomfortable again.

'The only thing to settle now is what you're going to do about Christine, Jim.'

'I've told you: nothing.'

'Put dear Margaret out of your mind for once.'

'Nothing to do with her. It's just that I . . . well, I don't want to try anything on with Christine, that's all.'

'I've heard that one before, but it's a good one. I always laugh at that one.'

'No, honestly, Carol. I'd much rather see her once or twice and not do anything about it – what could I do about it anyway? She's a bit out of my class, don't you think? If I did try to do anything I'd only get sent off with a flea in my ear. We're both tied up with other . . .'

'You sound as if you're in love with her.'

'Do you think so?' he said almost eagerly; he couldn't help regarding her remark as a compliment – one that he'd been needing for a long time, too.

'Yes. Your attitude measures up to the two requirements of love. You want to go to bed with her and can't, and you don't know her very well. Ignorance of the other person topped up with deprivation, Jim. You fit the formula all right, and what's more you want to go on fitting it. The old hopeless passion, isn't it? There are no two doubts about that, as Cecil used to say before I broke him of it.'

'That's rather adolescent, isn't it? If you don't mind me saying so.'

'Yes, it is, isn't it? Have you got a cigarette, Jim? . . . Thanks. Yes, I was quite sure when I was about fifteen that that was the way things worked, only nobody could afford to admit it.'

'Well, there you are, then.'

'Yes, here I am now. I don't mind telling you, since I've been rather letting my hair down, that after the maturity of my twenties was over I began going back to that way of explaining things with a good deal of relief. And justification, I'd like to think, too. I'm rather keen on that formula these days, as a matter of fact.'

'Are you?'

'I certainly am, Jim. You'll find that marriage is a good short cut to the truth. No, not quite that. A way of doubling back to the truth. Another thing you'll find is that the years of illusion aren't those of adolescence, as the grown-ups try to tell us; they're the ones immediately after it, say the middle twenties, the false maturity if you like, when you first get thoroughly embroiled in things and lose your head. Your age, by the way, Jim. That's when you first realize that sex is important to other people besides yourself. A discovery like that can't help knocking you off balance for a time.'

'Carol . . . perhaps if you hadn't got married . . .'

'I couldn't have done anything else, could I?'

'Couldn't you? Why not?'

'Christ, haven't you been listening? I was in love. Let's go back to the bar now, shall we? It's so noisy in here.' Her voice trembled a little, for the first time since they'd begun talking.

'Carol, I'm terribly sorry. I shouldn't have said that.'

'Now, don't be silly, Jim, there's nothing to apologize for. It was a perfectly natural thing to say. Don't forget, though; you've got a moral duty to perform. Get that girl away from Bertrand; she wouldn't enjoy an affair with him. It wouldn't be her kind of thing at all. Mind you remember that.'

Dixon found, when they got up, that he'd forgotten about the dancers and the band; he remembered them now, however, very vividly. A tune was being played, sparing of melodic invention, free too of any marked variation in volume, rhythm, harmony, expression, tempo, or tone-colour, and, more or less in time with it, groups of dancers were wheeling, plunging, and gesticulating while the ogre, more aphasic than before, mumbled at full strength:

Ya parp the Hawky-Cawky arnd ya tarn parp-parp,
Parp what it's parp parp-parp.

They re-entered the bar. Dixon felt that he'd been doing this for weeks. The sight of their party still, or again, just where they'd been before made him want very much to pitch forward on to the floor and go to sleep. Bertrand was talking; Gore-Urquhart was listening; Margaret was laughing, only now she had a hand on Gore-Urquhart's nearest shoulder; Christine was also probably listening to somebody, only now she had her head in her hands. Beesley was standing at the counter, morosely and tremulously raising a full half-pint glass to his mouth. Dixon went over to him, in search of a break from routine, but Carol looked back and converged on him. Greetings were exchanged again.

'What's this, Alfred?' Dixon asked. 'A bender?'

Beesley nodded without stopping drinking; then, lowering his glass at last, wiping his mouth on his sleeve, making a face, and referring to the quality of the beer by a monosyllable not in decent use, he said: 'I wasn't getting anywhere in there, so I came in here and came over here.'

'And you're getting somewhere over here, are you, Alfred?' Carol asked.

'On the tenth half, just about,' Beesley said.

'Bloody but unbowed, eh? That's the spirit. Well, Jim, this is obviously the place for us two – agreed? Nobody wants either of us. What's the matter? What are you looking at?' To Dixon's slight irritation, the pseudo-drunken quality had again taken possession of her voice and demeanour.

Beesley leaned forward; 'Come on, Jim: beer or beer?'

'Here we are and here we stay till they throw us out,' Carol said with synthetic defiance.

'Yes, I'll just have one, thanks, but I mustn't stay,' Dixon said.

'Because you've got to go and see how dear Margaret's getting on, is that right?'

'Well, yes, I . . .'

'I thought I told you to let dear Margaret stew in her own juice. And how about just using your eyes? She's enjoying herself ever so much, thank you, Mr Dixon, and thank you, Mrs Goldsmith. And thank you, too. Now's your chance, Jim; remember your moral duty? Thank you, Alfred; here's to you, my boy.'

'What moral duty's this, Carol?'

'Jim knows, don't you, Jim?'

Dixon looked over at the group in the corner. Margaret had taken off her glasses, a certain sign of abandonment. Christine, her back to Dixon, was sitting as immobile as if she'd been mummified. Bertrand, still talking, was smoking a black cigar. Why was he doing that? A sudden douche of terror then squirted itself all over Dixon. After a moment he realized that this was because he had a plan and was about to carry it out. He panted a little with the enormity of it, then drained his glass and said quaveringly: 'Here goes, then. Good-bye for now.'

He went over and sat down in a vacant chair next to Christine, who turned to him with a smile; rather a rueful smile, he thought. 'Oh, hallo,' she said; 'I thought you must have gone home.'

'Not quite yet. You look as if you're being rather left out of things here.'

'Yes, Bertrand's always the same when he gets talking like this. But I mean, of course he did really come here to meet Uncle.'

'I can see that.' Just at that moment Bertrand got up from his seat and, without looking in Christine's direction, walked across to where Carol was standing with Beesley; a faint bay of salutation could be heard. Glancing at Christine, Dixon was favoured with the rare sight of somebody engaged in the act of flushing. He said quickly: 'Now, listen to me, Christine. I'm going to go out and order a taxi now. It should be here in about a quarter of an hour. You come outside then and I'll take you back to the Welches' in it. There'll be no funny business; I can guarantee that. Straight home to the Welches'.'

Her immediate reaction looked like anger. 'Why? Why should I?'

'Because you're fed-up, and no wonder either, that's why.'

'That's not the point. It's a ridiculous idea. Absolutely mad.'

'Will you come? I'm ordering the taxi in any case.'

'Don't ask me that. I don't want to be asked that.'

'But I am asking you. What about it? I'll give you twenty minutes.' He looked her in the eyes and laid his hand on her elbow. He must be out of his mind to be talking to a girl like this like this. 'Please come,' he said.

She snatched her arm away. 'Oh don't,' she said, as if he'd been telling her that she had the dentist to go to in the morning.

'I'll wait for you,' he said in an urgent undertone. 'In the porch. Twenty minutes. Don't forget.'

He turned and left by a route that gave a view of part of the dance-floor and band. She wouldn't come, of course, but at any rate he'd made his gesture. In other words, he'd thought of a way of hurting himself more severely than usual, and in public. He stopped for a moment to wave good-bye to the band, then, receiving no response, went off to find a phone.

13

Dixon paused in the portico to light the cigarette which, according to his schedule, he ought to be lighting after breakfast on the next day but one. The taxi he'd ordered was due any minute. If by the time he'd finished his cigarette Christine had still not appeared, he'd just ask the taximan to take him to his digs, so whatever happened he'd be in a car soon. That was good, because total inability to move was almost upon him. Ten minutes to go; he tried not to think about it.

The darkness of the street was uneven. The daylight lamps above a nearby main road were glowing pallidly; the cars parked along the kerb had their sidelights burning; the windows of the building behind him were full of light. A train moved slowly and with great steadiness up the incline from the station. Feeling less hot, Dixon heard the band break into a tune he knew and liked; he had the notion that the tune was going to help out this scene and fix it permanently in his memory; he felt romantically excited. But he'd got no business to feel that, had he? What was he doing here, after all? Where was it all going to lead? Whatever it was leading towards, it was certainly leading away from the course his life had been pursuing for the last eight months, and this thought justified his excitement and filled him with reassurance and hope. All positive change was good; standing still, growing to the spot, was always bad. He remembered somebody once showing him a poèm which ended something like 'Accepting dearth, the shadow of death'. That was right; not 'experiencing dearth', which happened to everybody. The one indispensable answer to an environment bristling with people and things one thought were bad was to go on finding out new ways in which one could think they were bad. The reason why Prometheus couldn't get away from his vulture was that he was keen on it, and not the other way round.

Dixon abruptly made his head vibrate; without tilting it, he moved his lower jaw as far over to one side as he could. His cigarette was smoked right down, so that, after about twenty-five minutes, he not only had no Christine, but no taxi. At that moment a car rounded the corner from the main road and stopped near him where he stood at a lower corner by a side-street. It was a taxi. A voice from the driver's seat said: 'Barker?'

'How do you mean, barker?'

'Taxi for Barker?'

'What?'

'Taxi for name of Barker?'

'Barker? Oh, you must mean Barclay, don't you?'

'Ah, that's it: Barclay.'

'Good. We're nearly ready now. Just back into that side turning, will you? and I'll be back in a couple of minutes. I may be taking a friend back with me. Don't let anyone else hire you, mind. I'll be back.'

'That'll be all right, Mr Barclay.'

Dixon walked briskly back to the portico and looked up the lighted corridor, nerving himself to contemplate going back and trying Christine again. A bend hid all but the first couple of yards of the corridor from his view. Without delay Professor Barclay appeared round this bend, squirming into his overcoat and followed by his wife. Dixon had the sense of having heard him referred to recently in some connexion. Then he glanced up the street; the taxi, in mid-road, was just beginning to reverse cautiously into the side turning, where it would be hidden by an office block. As Barclay came up, it still had several yards to go.

Dixon barred his path. 'Oh, good evening, Professor Barclay,' he said in measured tones, as if dealing with a hypnotic subject.

'Hallo, Dixon. Haven't seen a taxi waiting for me, have you?'

'Good evening, Mrs Barclay . . . No, I'm afraid I haven't, Professor.'

'Oh dear,' he said pleasantly. 'Well, we shall just have to wait, then.' As he spoke, a loud brassy chord rang down the corridor, almost obscuring the sound of a handbrake ratchet from the side-street. 'Was that a car I heard then?' he asked, raising his head like an old cob disturbed at grass.

Dixon put on a listening attitude. 'I can't hear anything,' he said regretfully.

'I must have been mistaken.'

'All the same, Simon, I think I should walk along a bit, just in case he arrived and parked before Mr Dixon came out.'

'Yes, dear, that is a possibility.'

'He couldn't have done that, Mrs Barclay. I've been out here for nearly half an hour, and I can assure you quite certainly that no taxi has driven up here.'

'Well, it's most odd,' she said with a glandered movement of her jaws. 'My husband ordered the taxi half an hour ago at least, and City Taxis are usually so punctual.'

'Half an hour; oh well, he couldn't have made it before I came out,' Dixon said, as one making calculations. 'The City Taxis garage is over the other side of town, behind the bus station.'

'Are you waiting for a taxi too, Mr Dixon?' Mrs Barclay asked.

'No, I . . . I just came out to get a breath of fresh air.'

'You've had time for several lungfuls,' the Professor said, smiling.

His amiability made Dixon a good deal ashamed of having stolen the taxi, but it was too late to withdraw. 'Yes, I have,' he said, trying to sound casual. 'I'm waiting for a friend as well, actually.'

'Oh, really? We might as well walk along a little way, Simon; it's getting rather chilly, standing here.'

'Yes, dear, we could do that.'

'I'll stroll along with you,' Dixon said. He hated leaving his post, but not to leave it seemed the worse alternative. But what was he going to do to prevent the Barclays finding their taxi?

When the three were within ten yards of the relevant corner, a car swept round the corner above it. Dixon knew at once it wasn't his proper taxi, because all City Taxis taxis had a little illuminated sign over the windscreen, and this one hadn't. Nevertheless, a diversion was now possible. When they were right at the corner, Dixon stepped into the road and raised his hand, shouting urgently: 'Taxi. Taxi.'

'Taxi yourself,' a shrill voice called from the back seat.

'Ah, taxi off, Jack,' the driver snarled, accelerating past him.

He went back to the Barclays, who'd had their backs to the corner to watch. 'No good, I'm afraid,' he said. But it was good for him; the incident made it seem natural to turn back towards the portico. What would happen at the next outward journey? A regular service of private cars past that corner was too much to hope for. He hoped fervently that his own taxi, the one he'd ordered, wouldn't take it into its head to turn up; he'd have to go away in it and leave the Barclays to find the one he'd taken from them. Or could he persuade them to have his?

They stood about for a minute or two at the portico, while nobody came and nobody went. Another walk to the corner became imminent. Dixon glanced desperately up the corridor. Two people appeared round the bend in it almost together. The first one wasn't Christine, but a drunken man clicking frenziedly at a cigarette lighter. The second one, on the other hand, was.

The manner of her appearance was so ordinary that Dixon was almost shocked. He didn't know what he'd expected, but it wasn't this look of recognition on her face, this purposeful walk towards him, this matter-of-fact sound of her shoes on cloth, on wood, on stone. Glancing over at the line of cars, she said abruptly: 'Did you manage to get one?'

Dixon knew that the Barclays, or Mrs Barclay at any rate, would be listening. He hesitated a second, then said 'Yes' and patted his pocket. 'I've got it here.'

He tried to get her to walk off with him, but she stayed where she was in the doorway, the lights from the corridor throwing her face into shadow. 'I meant a taxi.'

'A taxi? a taxi? Just for three or four hundred yards?' He gave a shuddering laugh. 'I'll have you back with Mum in less time than it'd take to phone. Good-night, Professor; good-night, Mrs Barclay. Well, it's a good thing we haven't far to go; rather chilly. Did you say good-bye to the others for me?' They were far enough away by now for him to be able to add: 'Good. That's fine. Well done.' Nearby a car started up. Behind him he heard Mrs Barclay say something to her husband.

'What's going on?' Christine asked with undisguised curiosity. 'What's all this about?'

'We've pinched their taxi, that's one of the things that's going on. It's parked just round this corner.'

As if answering its name, the taxi, tired of waiting, emerged from the side-street and turned up towards the main road. He ran furiously off in pursuit, calling loudly: 'Taxi. Taxi.'

It drew to a stop and he went up to the driver's window. After a brief conversation, the taxi moved off again and disappeared into the main road. Dixon ran back to Christine, whom the Barclays had now rejoined. 'Sorry I couldn't get him for you,' he said to them. 'He'd got someone to pick up at the station in five minutes. What a nuisance.'

'Well, thank you very much, Dixon, for trying,' Barclay said.

'Yes, thank you all the same,' his wife said.

He took Christine's arm and walked her round into the side-street, calling good-night. They started to cross over.

'Does that mean we've lost the taxi? It was ours, was it?'

'Ours after it was theirs. No, I told the driver to drive round the corner and wait for us a hundred yards along the road. We can cut up through this alley, be there in a couple of minutes.'

'What would you have done if he hadn't driven out just then? We couldn't have driven off under the noses of those people.'

'I'd already worked out we'd have to do something like that. We'd got to establish that we and the taxi were leaving separately. That's why I was quick off the mark.'

'You were, very.'

With no more said they reached the taxi, parked outside the

lighted windows of a dress-shop. Dixon opened a rear door for Christine, then said to the driver: 'Our friend isn't coming. We'll make a start, if you're ready.'

'Right, sir. Just by the Corn Exchange, isn't it?'

'No, it's further than the Corn Exchange.' He named the small town where the Welches lived.

'Oh, can't make it there, I'm sorry, sir.'

'It's all right, I know the way.'

'So do I, but they told me at the garage the Corn Exchange.'

'Did they really? Well, they told you wrong, then. We're not going to the Corn Exchange.'

'Not enough petrol.'

'Bateson's at the foot of College Road doesn't shut till twelve.' He peered at the dashboard. 'Ten to. We'll do it on our heads.'

'Not allowed to draw petrol except at our own garage.'

'We are tonight. I'll write to the company explaining. It's their fault for telling you you were only going to the Corn Exchange. Now let's go, or you'll find yourself eight miles out without any petrol to get you back.'

He got in beside Christine and the car started.

14

'That was all very efficient,' Christine said. 'You're getting good at this sort of thing, aren't you? First the table, then the *Evening Post* thing, and now this.'

'I didn't use to be. By the way, I hope you don't object too much to the way I got hold of this taxi.'

'I've got into it, haven't I?'

'Yes, I know, but I should have thought the method would strike you as unethical.'

'It does, at least it would in the ordinary way, but it was more important for us to get a taxi than for them, wasn't it?'

'I'm glad you look at it like that.' He brooded on her use of the word 'important' for a moment, then realized that he didn't much care for her easy acquiescence in his piratical treatment of the Barclays' taxi. Even he now felt it had been a bit thick, and she presumably hadn't his excuse for wanting a taxi very badly. Like both the pretty women he'd known, and many that he'd only read about, she thought it was no more than fair that one man should cheat and another be cheated to serve her convenience. She ought to have objected, refused to go with him, insisted on returning and handing the taxi over to the Barclays, walked back, revolted by his unscrupulousness, into the dance. Yes, he'd have liked that, wouldn't he? Ay, proper champion that would have been, lad. His hand flew to his mouth in the darkness to stifle his laughter; to sidetrack it, he began distilling alarm from the thought that he'd have to find something to talk to this girl about all the way back to the Welches'. The only thing he felt at all clear about was the fact that this abduction of her was a blow struck against Bertrand, but it seemed less than prudent to begin there. Why had she consented to ditch her boy-friend in this emphatic way? There were several possible answers. Perhaps he could start with that. 'Did you manage to get away all right?' he asked.

'Oh yes; nobody seemed to object very much.'

'What did you say to them?'

'I just explained things to Uncle Julius – he never minds what I do – and then I just told Bertrand I was going.'

'How did he react to that?'

'He said, "Oh, don't do that, I'll be with you in a minute." Then he went on talking to Mrs Goldsmith and Uncle. So I came away then.'

'I see. It all sounds very easy and quick.'

'Oh, it was.'

'Well, I'm very glad you decided to come with me after all.'

'Good. I couldn't help feeling guilty rather, at first, about walking out on them all, but that's worn off now.'

'Good. What finally made you make up your mind?'

After a silence, she said: 'I wasn't enjoying it much in there, as you know, and I started feeling awfully tired, and it didn't look as if Bertrand could leave for some time, so I thought I'd come along with you.'

She said this in her best schoolmistressy way, elocution-mistressy in fact, so Dixon repeated as stiffly: 'I see.' In the light of a street-lamp he could see her sitting, as he'd expected, on the very edge of the seat. That was that, then.

She suddenly broke in again in her other manner, the one he associated with their phone conversation: 'No, I'm not going to try and get away with that. That's only a part of it. I don't see why I shouldn't tell you a bit more. I left because I was feeling absolutely fed-up with everything.'

'That's a bit sweeping. What had fed you up in particular?'

'Everything. I was absolutely fed-up. I don't see why I shouldn't tell you this. I've been feeling very depressed recently, and it all seemed to get too much for me tonight.'

'A girl like you's got no call to be depressed about anything, Christine,' Dixon said warmly, then at once fell against the window and banged his elbow smartly on the door as the taxi lurched aside in front of a row of petrol pumps. Behind these was an unlit building with a painted sign, faintly visible, reading *Car's for hire – Batesons – Repair's*. Dixon got out, ran to a large wooden door, and began to pound irregularly upon it, wondering whether, or how soon, to add shouts to his summons. While he waited, he ran over in his mind some handy all-purpose phrases of abusive or menacing tendency against the appearance of a garage-man unwilling to serve him. A minute passed; he went on thumping while the taxi-driver slowly joined him, his very presence a self-righteously pessimistic comment. Dixon laid down for himself the general lines of an appropriate face, involving free and unusual use of the lips and tongue, and endorsed by manual gestures. Just then a light sprang up inside and very quickly the door was opened. A man appeared and declared himself able and willing to serve petrol. During the next couple of minutes Dixon was thinking not about this man but about Christine. He was filled with awe at the thought that she seemed, not only not to dislike him to any significant extent, but to trust him as well. And how wonderful she was, and how lucky he was to have her there. The admissions, the implied confessions about his feelings for her he'd made to Carol, had seemed outlandish at the time; now they seemed perfectly natural and just. The next half-hour or so formed the only chance he'd ever have of doing anything whatever about those feelings. For once in his life Dixon resolved to bet on his luck. What luck had come his way in the past he'd distrusted, stingily held on to until the chance of losing his initial gain was safely past. It was time to stop doing that.

Dixon paid the garage-man and the taxi moved off. 'You haven't any reason to be depressed, I was saying,' he said.

'I don't see how you can know that,' she said, severely again.

'No, of course I can't know it, but I shouldn't think you have too bad a time on the whole,' he said with an ease that surprised him. He could see that she needed time and encouragement to work back to her more open manner, and reflected that this sort of perception was as unfamiliar in him as all the other things he was feeling. 'I'd have put you down as somebody reasonably successful in most things.'

'I didn't mean to sound like a martyr. You're right, of course, I do have a good time and I've been very lucky in all sorts of ways. But, you know, I do find some things awfully difficult. I don't really know my way around, you know.'

Dixon wanted to laugh. He couldn't imagine any woman of her age less in need of such lore. He said as much.

'No, it's perfectly true,' she insisted. 'I haven't had a chance to find out yet.'

'You mustn't mind me saying this, but I should have thought there'd be plenty of people only too willing to show you.'

'I know, I see what you mean exactly, but they don't try to. They assume I know already, you see.' She was talking animatedly now.

'Oh, they do, do they? How's that, would you say?'

'I think it must just be because I look as if I'm full of poise and that sort of thing. I look as if I know all about how to behave, and all that. Two or three people have told me that, so it must be right. But it's only the way I look.'

'Well, it is true you look fairly sophisticated, if that's the right word. Even a bit upstage sometimes. But it . . .'

'How old would you say I am?'

Dixon thought an honest answer would, for once, be appropriate. 'About twenty-four, I should say.'

'There you are, then,' she said triumphantly. 'Just what I thought. I'm twenty next month. The eighteenth.'

'I didn't mean of course you didn't look very young as far as just your actual face goes, I just . . .'

'No, I know; but it's the age I seem, isn't it? It's the way I look, isn't it?'

'Yes, I suppose it is. But it isn't just that on its own, is it?'

'Sorry: what isn't what on its own?'

'I mean it's not just your appearance that makes you seem older and more experienced and all that. It's the way you behave and talk, a lot of the time, too. Don't you think so?'

'Well, it's awfully hard for me to tell, isn't it?'

'Must be, naturally. It's . . . you seem to . . . keep getting on to your high horse all the time; hard to describe it exactly. But you have got a habit, every now and then, of talking and behaving like a governess, though I don't know much about them, I must admit.'

'Oh, have I?'

Though the tone of this question illustrated just what he was talking about, Dixon, feeling it couldn't matter what he said, said: 'There, you're doing it now. When you don't know what to do or say, you fall back on being starchy. And that all fits in with your face; that's probably what gave you the idea of being starchy in the first place, your face, I mean. And that makes a total effect of a prim kind of self-assurance, and you don't want to be prim but you do want to be self-assured. Yes . . . But that's quite enough of Uncle Jim's Corner. We're getting off the point. How does all this tie up with being depressed? There's still nothing to be depressed about.'

She hesitated while Dixon sweated slightly, repenting of his burst of old-trouper confidence, then she said with a rush: 'It's all to do with men, you see. I hadn't had much to do with men till I got my job in London last year . . . Look, you don't mind talking about me all the time, do you? It seems so self-centred. You don't think . . . ?'

'You can forget all that. I want to hear about this.'

'All right, then. Well . . . I hadn't been working in the bookshop very long, when a man got talking to me and asked me to come to a party. So I went, of course, and there were a lot of artist kind of people there, and one or two ones from the B.B.C. You know the sort of thing?'

'I can imagine.'

'So . . . then it all started. I kept being asked out by men, and of course I kept going, it was such marvellous fun. And I still do enjoy it a great deal. But they kept . . . trying to seduce me the whole time. And I didn't want to be seduced, you see, and as soon as I'd convinced them of that, they were off. Well, I didn't mind that much, because there always seemed to be another one ready to . . .'

'I'll bet there did. Go on.'

'I'm afraid this sounds terribly . . .'

'Go on.'

'Well, if you're quite sure . . . Anyway, after a few months of that I met Bertrand, that was in March. He didn't seem quite like the others, chiefly because he didn't start trying to make me be his mistress the entire time. And he can be very nice, you know, though I don't suppose you . . . After a bit the thing was, I was starting to get rather fond of him, and at the same time – this is the funny part – I was getting a bit fed-up with him in other ways while I was still getting more fond of him. He's such a queer mixture, you see.'

Naming to himself the two substances of which he personally thought Bertrand a mixture, Dixon said: 'In what way?'

'He can be extremely understanding and kind one minute, and completely unreasonable and childish the next. I feel I never know where I am with him, or what he really wants. Sometimes I think it's all to do with how he's getting on with his painting. Anyhow, what with one thing and another we started having rows. And I can't bear rows, especially because he was always putting me in the wrong by them.'

'How do you mean?'

'You know, he'd start one with me when he could put me in the wrong by starting one, and force me to start one when starting one would put whoever started one in the wrong. There'll be one over tonight, of course, and he'll put me in the wrong, as usual. But he's in the wrong, he's the one who's wrong. All this business with Mrs Goldsmith – it's all right, I'm not going to ask you about it – but I know there's something going on there, but he won't tell me what it is. I don't suppose it's anything much; he just gets a bit excited when . . . But he won't tell me what's happening. He'll pretend there isn't anything, and he'll ask me if I really think he'd get up to anything behind my back, and I'll have to say No, otherwise . . .'

'This is none of my business, Christine, but in my opinion friend Bertrand's letting himself in for you giving him the air.'

'No, I can't do that, unless . . . I can't do that. I'm in too deep now to back out like that. It'll have to go on as it is. You've got to take people as you find them.'

Not wanting to speculate what 'it' was, and how it was going on, Dixon asked hurriedly: 'Have you and he got anything planned for the future?'

'Well, I haven't, but I think he may. I've got an idea he wants us to get married, though he's never actually mentioned it.'

'And what do you feel about that?'

'I haven't decided yet.'

This seemed all for the moment. It crossed Dixon's mind that apart from her voice he'd no evidence that she was beside him at all. When he turned to his right he saw only the darkest and most anonymous shape; she held herself so still that there was no sound of movement from clothing or upholstery, she seemed to use no scent, or anyway he couldn't smell any, and he was a long way from being able to think of touching her. The shoulders and hatted head of the taxi-driver, outlined against the glow of the car's lights, and whose movements controlled their course, were in a way much more real to him. Dixon looked out of the side window, and his spirits rose at once at the sight of the darkened countryside moving past him. This ride, unlike most of the things that happened to him, was something he'd rather have than not have. He'd got something he wanted, and whatever the cost in future embarrassment he was ready to meet it. He reflected that the Arab proverb urging this kind of policy was incomplete: to 'take what you want and pay for it' it should add 'which is better than being forced to take what you don't want and paying for that'. It was one more argument to support his theory that nice things are nicer than nasty ones. Christine's unshared presence was a very nice thing, so nice that his feelings seemed overloaded by it like a glutton's stomach. How splendid her voice was; to hear more of it he asked: 'What are Bertrand's pictures like?'

'Oh, he hasn't shown me any of them. He says he doesn't want me to think of him as a painter until he can think of himself as one. But people have told me they think they're pretty good. They were all friends of his, though, I suppose.'

Whatever aureole of choking nonsense surrounded this view of Bertrand's, Dixon thought the view itself worthy of some respect, or at least of some surprise. What a temptation it must be to produce proofs of one's status as an artist, to flatter people and at the same time show one was rather a good chap by asking for and seeming to act on criticism, above all to let people know how much more there was in one than met the eye. Dixon himself had sometimes wished he wrote poetry or something as a claim to developed character.

Christine had continued: 'I must say it's something to meet a man who's got some sort of ambition. I don't mean an ambition like wanting to have a date with a film-star or something like that. It sounds a funny thing to say, but I look up to Bertrand because he's got something to arrange his life around, something that isn't just material, or self-interested. So it doesn't really matter from that point of view what his work's like. It doesn't matter if what he paints doesn't give any pleasure to a soul apart from himself.'

'But if a man spends his life doing work that only appeals to him, isn't that being self-interested just as much?'

'Well, in a way everyone's self-interested, aren't they? But you must admit there are degrees of it.'

'I suppose I must. But doesn't this ambition of his rather leave you out?'

'What?'

'I mean, don't you find he's painting and so on when you want him to take you out?'

'Sometimes, but I try not to mind that.'

'Why?'

'And of course I wouldn't dream of letting him see it. It's not an easy situation. Having a relationship with an artist's a very different kettle of fish to having a relationship with an ordinary man.'

Dixon, feeling as he now seemed to have begun to feel about Christine, was bound to think this last remark unwelcome, but he found it objectively nasty as well. Had it been a line from a film he'd have reacted much as he did now, namely by making his lemon-sucking face in the darkness. But in a way it was a relief to find a loophole of adolescent vulgarity somewhere in that impressively mature and refined façade. 'I don't quite see that,' he had to say.

'Well, perhaps I didn't put it too well, but I should have thought that the work an artist does takes so much out of him, in the way of feeling and emotion and so on, that he hasn't got much left over for other people, not if he's any good as an artist, that is. I think he's sort of got special needs, you know, and it's up to others to supply them when they can, without too many questions asked.'

Dixon didn't trust himself to speak. Quite apart from his own convictions in the matter, his experience of Margaret had been more than enough to render repugnant to him any notion of anyone having any special needs for anything at any time, except for such needs as could be readily gratified with a tattoo of kicks on the bottom. Then he realized that Christine must, perhaps unconsciously, be quoting her boy-friend, or some horrible book lent by her boy-friend, whose desire to range himself with children, neurotics, and invalids by thus specializing his needs was not, at the moment, worth attacking. Dixon frowned. Until a minute ago she'd been behaving and talking so reasonably that it was hard to believe she was the same girl as had helped Bertrand to bait him at Welch's arty week-end. It was queer how much colour women seemed to absorb from their men-friends, or even from the man they were with for the time being. That was only bad when the man in question was bad; it was good when the man was good. It should be possible for the right man to stop, or at least hinder, her from being a refined gracious-liver and arty-rubbish-talker. Did he think he was the right man for that task? Ha, ha, ha, if he did.

'Jim,' Christine said.

Dixon's scalp pricked sharply at this, the first, use of his Christian name. 'Yes?' he said warily. He shrugged his bottom along the seat a little way.

'You've been very decent to me tonight, letting me ramble on about myself. And you seem to have your head screwed on the right way. Would you mind if I asked your advice on something?'

'No, not at all.'

'You must realize, though, that I'm asking you just because I want to hear your advice, not for any other reason.' She paused, then added: 'Have you got that?'

'Yes, of course.'

'Well, it's this. From what you've seen of us both, do you think it would be a good thing if I got married to Bertrand?'

Dixon felt a slight twinge of distaste he couldn't quite account for. 'Isn't that rather up to you?'

'Of course it's up to me; I'm the one who's going to marry him or not marry him. I want to know what you think. I'm not asking to be told what to do. Now, what do you think?'

This was clearly the moment for a burst of accurate shelling from Dixon in his Bertrand-war, but he found himself reluctant to fire. A reasoned denunciation of the foe, followed up by a short account of his recent conversation with Carol, would stand a good chance of bringing total victory in this phase, or at least inflicting heavy losses. He felt, however, that he didn't want to do it like that, and only said slowly: 'I don't think I know either of you well enough.'

'Ah, to hell, man' – had she picked that up from Uncle Julius? Dixon wondered – 'you're not being asked to do a thesis on it for your doctorate.' As Carol might have done, she pinched his arm too hard, making him cry out, saying to him in vocal italics: 'What do you think?'

'Well, it's . . . I must say what I think, you know.'

'Yes, yes, of course, that's what I asked for, isn't it? Do get on with it.'

'Well, then, I should say No.'

'I see. Why not?'

'Because I like you and I don't like him.'

'Is that all?'

'It's quite enough. It means each of you belongs to the two great classes of mankind, people I like and people I don't.'

'It sounds a bit thin to me.'

'All right, if you want reasons, remember they're my reasons, though that doesn't mean to say they oughtn't to be yours as well. Bertrand's a bore, he's like his dad, the only thing that interests him is him. On any issue you care to mention he can't do otherwise than ignore your side of things, just can't do otherwise, see? It's not just him first and you second, he's the only bloody runner. My God, what you said about him putting you in the wrong by starting rows shows you've got his number. I don't see why you have to have someone else to say it for you.'

She said nothing for a moment, then spoke rather in her censorious manner: 'Even if that were true, it needn't prevent me from marrying him.'

'Yes, I know women are all dead keen on marrying men they don't much like. But I'm saying why you oughtn't to marry him, not whether you want to or are going to or not. I think that once the things that are supposed to wear off wear off, you'll have a hell of a time. You couldn't trust the fellow with your best . . . I mean, he'd always be having rows, and you say you don't like rows. Are you in love with him?'

'I don't much care for that word,' she said, as if rebuking a foul-mouthed tradesman.

'Why not?'

'Because I don't know what it means.'

He gave a quiet yell. 'Oh, don't say that; no, don't say that. It's a word you must often have come across in conversation and literature. Are you going to tell me it sends you flying to the dictionary each time? Of course you're not. I suppose you mean it's purely personal – sorry, got to get the jargon right – purely subjective.'

'Well, it is, isn't it?'

'Yes, that's right. You talk as if it's the only thing that is. If you can tell me whether you like greengages or not, you can tell me whether you're in love with Bertrand or not, if you want to tell me, that is.'

'You're still making it much too simple. All I can really say is that I'm pretty sure I was in love with Bertrand a little while ago, and now I'm rather less sure. That up-and-down business doesn't happen with greengages; that's the difference.'

'Not with greengages, agreed. But what about rhubarb, eh? What about rhubarb? Ever since my mother stopped forcing me to eat it, rhubarb and I have been conducting a relationship that can swing between love and hatred every time we meet.'

'That's all very well, Jim. The trouble with love is it gets you in such a state you can't look at your own feelings dispassionately.'

'That would be a good thing if you could do it, would it?'

'Why, of course.'

He gave another quiet yell, this time some distance above middle C. 'You've got a long way to go, if you don't mind me saying so, even though you are nice. By all means view your own feelings dispassionately, if you feel you ought to, but that's nothing to do with deciding whether (Christ) you're in love. Deciding that's no more difficult than the greengages business. What is difficult, and the time you really need this dispassionate rubbish, is deciding what to do about being in love if you are, whether you can stick the person you love enough to marry them, and so on.'

'Why, that's exactly what I've been saying, in different words.'

'Words change the thing, and anyway the whole procedure's different. People get themselves all steamed up about whether they're in love or not, and can't work it out, and their decisions go all to pot. It's happening every day. They ought to realize that the love part's perfectly easy; the hard part is the working-out, not about love, but about what they're going to do. The difference is that they can get their brains going on that, instead of taking the sound of the word "love" as a signal for switching them off. They can get somewhere, instead of indulging in a sort of orgy of emotional self-catechizing about how you know you're in love, and what love is anyway, and all the rest of it. You don't ask yourself what greengages are, or how you know whether you like them or not, do you? Right?'

Outside his lectures, this was the longest speech Dixon had made for what seemed to him years, and, not excluding his lectures, by far the most fluent. How had he managed it? Drink? No: he was dangerously sober. Sexual excitement? No in italic capitals: visitations of that feeling reduced him punctually to silence and, as a rule, petrifaction. Then how? It was a mystery, but one he felt too contented to bother about solving. He looked idly at the ribbon of road ahead of them, unsteadily unreeling itself beneath the wheels. Hedges, bleached to a sandy pallor by the headlights, swung past, dipping and mounting. The isolation of the car's interior seemed comforting and natural.

A movement of Christine's, the first he'd noticed since the journey began, made him glance in her direction. He could see that she was leaning forward and looking out of the window. She said in a muffled voice: 'And the same applies to not liking greengages, of course.'

'Eh? Yes, I suppose so.'

He heard her yawn. 'Where are we now, do you know?'

'Oh, just over half-way, I should think.'

'I feel awfully sleepy. It is wretched; I don't want to be.'

'Have a cigarette, that'll do you a power of good.'

'No thanks. Look, would you mind if I had a nap for a few minutes? It'll make me feel much less tired, I know.'

'Of course, by all means.'

While she snuggled herself together in her corner, Dixon fought his disappointment at this device of hers for quitting his company.

He'd thought he was getting on so well; his usual policy of not talking at length was the right one after all. Just then she laid her head on his shoulder and all his senses grew alert. 'You don't mind, do you?' she asked. 'The back of this seat's like iron.'

'You go ahead.' Forcing himself to act before he could think, he slid his arm beneath her shoulders. She moved her head experimentally to and fro against him, then settled herself and seemed to go to sleep at once.

Dixon's heart began to pound a little. He now had all the evidence he wanted that she was there; he could sense her breathing, her temple against his jaw and her shoulder under his hand were warm, her hair smelt of well-brushed hair, he could feel the presence of her body. It was a pity it wasn't set off by the presence of her mind. It occurred to him that she'd done this merely as a manoeuvre to arouse his desire, and arouse it for no purpose beyond that of somehow feeding her vanity. Then he rejected so familiar and contemptible a notion: she was too trustworthy for that, she'd just been tired. That was all. The taxi swung round a bend and he braced himself with his foot to maintain his position and hers. He couldn't go to sleep himself, but he could see to it that she stayed asleep.

Cautiously and contortedly he got hold of matches and cigarettes and lit one of each in succession. More than ever he felt secure: here he was, quite able to fulfil his role, and, as with other roles, the longer you played it the better chance you had of playing it again. Doing what you wanted to do was the only training, and the only preliminary, needed for doing more of what you wanted to do. Next time he saw Michie he'd be much less respectful to him; next time he saw Atkinson he'd talk to him more; he'd get some sense out of that Caton fellow about his article. Gingerly, he moved a little closer to Christine.

Presently the driver slid the glass aside and asked in a servile tone for more instructions, which Dixon gave. At last the taxi stopped at the end of the track that led up to the Welch house. Christine woke up and said after a moment: 'Are you coming up?

I wish you would, because I'm not quite sure how I'm going to get in. The maid lives out, I think.'

'Of course I'll come up,' Dixon said. He settled a brief exchange with the taxi-driver by refusing to discuss the question of payment until the taxi should be standing outside his, Dixon's, digs, then went off into the darkness with Christine holding on to his arm like a staff.

15

'I think we'd better look for a window first,' Dixon said as they stood in front of the darkened house. 'We don't want to ring the bell, just in case the Welches have got back before us. I don't suppose they'd want to be home very late.'

'Wouldn't they have to wait for Bertrand, because of the car?'

'They might have got a taxi; anyway, I'm not ringing that bell.'

They went off carefully into the yard at the left side of the building. In the darkness Dixon blundered into something which struck him dextrously on the shin and made him swear in a whisper. Christine laughed in a muffled way, as if her hands were over her mouth. By touch, and the sight which the minutes in the dark had given him, Dixon identified the hazard as a water-tap encased in planking which was split and half-shattered by some recent blow, as of an ill-driven car. He hummed a couple of bars of his Welch tune, then said to Christine: 'That'll do, that'll do. This looks like the french window; we'll just try that in case.'

He led the way, tiptoeing crunchingly, and found almost with foreboding that the window was not even latched. He hesitated before entering the room; the senior Welches might well be home already, and how was it possible for Welch not to have some imbecile hobby, watching phosphorescent mould, say, or Yogi meditation, which involved the use of a darkened room? He imagined with horror the dimensions and duration of Welch's wondering frown at the furtive entry of Christine and himself out of the darkness.

'Is it open?' Christine asked at his elbow. In whisper her voice had the same juvenile quality as he'd noticed over the phone.

'Yes, it seems to be.'

'Well, why not go in, then?'

'All right, here goes.' He pulled the window slowly open and stepped into the room past the floor-length curtain. All the others were apparently drawn and the room was like a sealed tank. He moved slowly forward, arms outstretched, until some piece of furniture dealt him the twin of the blow he'd just received. There was a weird moment when he and Christine reacted exactly as before. His hands hissed their way round two walls until he found the light-switch. 'I'm going to put the light on,' he said. 'All right?'

'Yes.'

'Right.' He snapped the switch down and instinctively turned away from it as the room sprang into light about them. His movement brought him very close to Christine. They looked at each other, both blinking and smiling; their faces were about on a level. Then the smile left her face and was replaced by a look as of anxiety. Her eyes were narrowed, her mouth moved silently, she seemed to raise her arms. Dixon took the step that separated them, and then, very slowly at first to give her all the time she might need to step back and away, put his arms round her. She was breathing in when he finally secured his grasp and so at this she caught her breath. He kissed her for some seconds, not holding her too close; her lips were dry, and hard rather than soft; she felt very warm. At length she did step back. She looked an unlikely figure under the bright light; she might have been an effect of trick photography. Dixon felt as if he'd been running for a bus and had in addition been nearly knocked down by a car at the moment of boarding. He could only say: 'Well, that was very nice,' in a sort of wooden vivacity.

'Yes, wasn't it?'

'Worth coming back from the dance for.'

'Yes.' She turned away. 'Oh look, we're in luck. I wonder who thought of this.'

A tray with cups, a flask, and biscuits stood on a small round table. Dixon, who'd been showing a disposition to tremble and stagger, found his spirits abruptly kicking upwards at the sight; it meant he wouldn't have to leave for at least a quarter of an hour. 'I take that very kindly,' he said.

In a minute they were sitting side by side on the couch. 'I think you'd better drink out of my cup,' Christine said. 'We don't want anyone to know you've been here, do we?' She poured out some coffee and drank a little, then passed the cup to him.

Dixon felt that this intimacy somehow symbolized and crowned the whole evening. He remembered some Greek or Latin tag about not even God being able to abolish historical fact, and was glad to think that this must apply equally to the historical fact of his drinking out of Christine's coffee-cup. She took two biscuits when he offered them, which reminded him of how Margaret would never eat on this sort of occasion, as if making an easy claim to individuality, and in the same way always drank black coffee. Why? She wasn't trying to keep herself awake all the time, was she? It was nice, though, to be able to think of her without fear; he half-promised himself to send Gore-Urquhart a box of twenty-five Balkan Sobranie (Imperial Russian blend) for involuntarily engaging Margaret's attention at the dance and so making the taxi-stratagem conceivable. Then he abandoned these fancies, recognizing their origin as a desire to escape from the thought that he'd have to go on with this Christine business, he'd have to press his advantage if he wanted to retain what he already held. His sitting with her like this seemed to distil a domestic calm, but his heart beat uncomfortably. And yet he felt an undefined hope: he had no charts for these waters, but experience proved that it was often those without charts who got the furthest. 'I'm very fond of you,' he said.

He caught a glimpse of the starchier manner as she replied: 'How can you be? You hardly know me.'

'I know enough to be sure of that, thanks.'

'It's nice of you to say that, but the trouble is, there isn't much more to know than you know already. I'm the sort of person you soon get to the end of.'

'I don't believe you. But even if it were true I shouldn't care.

There's more than enough to keep me going in what I've seen up to now.'

'I warn you it wouldn't do you any good.'

'Why not?'

'To start with, I can't get on with men.'

'What awful rubbish, Christine. Don't you go trying to spin me a hard-luck story like that. A girl like you could have any man she wanted.'

'The ones that want me don't stay about very long, as I told you. And it isn't easy to find one I want.'

'Ah, don't give me that. There are dozens of sensible men about. I can even think of a few in our Common Room. Well, one or two. Well, anyway . . .'

'There you are, you see.'

'Let's leave that,' Dixon said. 'Tell me: how long are you staying here this time?'

'For a few days. It's part of my holiday.'

'Grand. When can you come out with me?'

'Oh don't be such a fool, Jim. How can I possibly come out with you?'

'No trouble at all, Christine. You can make out you're out with Uncle Julius. From what I've seen of him he'd back up your story.'

'Don't say any more, it's no good. We're both tied up.'

'We can start worrying about that, if we've got to, when we've seen a little more of each other.'

'Do you realize what you're asking me to do? I'm a guest at this place, Bertrand asked me down here, and I'm his . . . I'm tied up with him. Can't you see yourself how mean it would be?'

'No, because I don't like Bertrand.'

'That doesn't make any difference.'

'Yes it does. I don't say "After you, old boy" to chaps like him.'

'Well, what about Margaret, then?'

'You've got a point there, Christine, there's no question about that. But she's got no real claim on me, you know.'

'Hasn't she? She seems to think she has.'

When Dixon hesitated, he was aware of the utter silence. He turned in his seat, so that he was directly facing her, and said in a less harsh tone: 'Look, Christine. Put it like this. Would you like to come out with me? Forgetting about Bertrand and Margaret for the moment.'

'You know I would,' she said at once. 'Why do you think I let you take me away from the dance?'

'So you did . . .' He looked at her, and she looked back with her chin lifted and her mouth not quite closed. He put an arm round her shoulders and bent towards the neat blonde head. They kissed more earnestly than before. Dixon felt as if he were being drawn downwards into some dark, vaporous region where the air was too heavy to breathe with comfort and the blood became thin and slack. Her body, half against his, was tense; one breast lay heavily against his chest; he raised his hand and laid it upon her other breast. Immediately her tenseness disappeared, and though her mouth stayed on his she became passive. He understood and moved his hand to her bare shoulder, then let her go. She smiled at him in a way that made his head swim more than the kiss had done.

When he didn't speak, she said: 'Yes, all right, then, but I still think it's a dirty trick. What do you suggest?'

Dixon felt like a man interrupted at his investiture with the Order of Merit to be told that a six-figure cheque from a football pool awaits him in the lobby. 'There's a very nice hotel in the town where we could have dinner,' he said.

'No, I don't think we'd better arrange anything for an evening, if you don't mind.'

'Why not?'

'I don't think we'd better, not just for the moment. We'd be bound to start drinking, and I . . .'

'What's the matter with drinking?'

'Nothing, but don't let's do any drinking together for the time being. Please.'

'All right, then. What about a tea?'

'Yes, a tea'd be fine. When?'

'Would Monday do?'

'No, I can't on Monday; Bertrand's having some people over he wants me to meet. What about Tuesday?'

'Fine. Four o'clock be right for time?' He explained how to get to the hotel where they were to meet, and had hardly finished when the unmistakable and growing sound of a car became audible. 'My God, here they are,' he said, instinctively whispering again.

'What are you going to do?'

'I'll wait until they've started coming in the front door, and then nip out by the window. You close it after me.'

'Right.'

The car began moving along the front of the house. 'You've got all that about where to meet?' he asked.

'Don't you worry, I'll be there. Four o'clock.'

They went over to the window and stood there with their arms round each other while the car's engine, after a terrible rattling roar, died away, and footsteps receded.

'Thanks for a lovely evening, Christine.'

'Good-night, Jim.' She pressed herself to him and they kissed for a moment; then she broke away with 'Wait a minute' and rushed over to where her bag lay on a chair.

'What's all this?'

She came back and thrust a pound note at him. 'For the taxi.'

'Don't be ridiculous, I . . .'

'Come on, don't argue; they'll be here in a second. It must have cost the earth.'

'But . . .'

She pushed the money into his outside breast-pocket, frowning, pursing her lips, and waggling her left hand to silence him in a gesture that reminded him of one of his aunts forcing sweets or an apple on him in his childhood. 'I've probably got more than you have,' she said. She propelled him to the window, which they reached just as Welch's voice, in its high-pitched, manic phase, became audible not so far away. 'Quick. See you on Tuesday. Good-night.'

He scuttled out and saw her blow a kiss into the darkness while she fastened the window; then the curtain fell back. The sky had cleared a little and there was enough light to see his way by. He moved off down towards the road, feeling more tired than he could remember ever feeling in his life before.

16

Dear Mr Johns, Dixon wrote, gripping his pencil like a breadknife. *This is just to let you no that I no what you are up to with yuong Marleen Richards, yuong Marleen is a desent girl and has got no tim for your sort, I no your sort. She is a desent girl and I wo'nt have you filing her head with a lot of art and music, she is to good for that, and I am going to mary her which is more than your sort ever do. So just you keep of her, Mr Johns this will be your olny warning. This is just a freindly letter and I am not threatenning you, but you just do as I say else me and some of my palls from the Works will be up your way and we sha'nt be coming along just to say How do you can bet. So just you wach out and lay of yuong Marleen if you no whats good for you. yours fathfully, Joe Higgins.*

He read it through, thinking how admirably consistent were the style and orthography. Both derived, in large part, from the essays of some of his less proficient pupils. He could hardly hope, even so, to deceive Johns for long, especially since Johns had almost certainly got no further with Marlene Richards, a typist in his office, than staring palely at her across it. But the letter would at any rate give him a turn and his dig-mates a few moments' amusement when it was opened, according to his habit, at the breakfast-table and read over cornflakes. Dixon wrote *To: – Mr Johns* and the address of the digs on a cheap envelope not specially bought for the purpose, sealed the letter up in it, and then, griming his finger on the floor, drew a heavy smudge across the flap. Finally he stuck a stamp on, slobbering on it for further verisimilitude. He'd post the letter on his way down to the pub for a lunch-time drink, but before that he must write up some of his notes for the Merrie England lecture. Before that in turn he must review his financial position, see if he could somehow restore it from complete impossibility to its usual level of merely imminent disaster, and before that again he must meditate, just for a couple of minutes, on the incredible finale to the Summer Ball the previous evening and on Christine.

He found himself unable to think coherently about, hardly able even to remember, what they'd said to each other at the Welches', nor could he now evoke what it had been like kissing her more clearly than that he'd enjoyed it. He was already so excited about Tuesday afternoon that he had to get up and walk about his bedroom. The great thing was to convince himself utterly that she wouldn't turn up, then whatever happened would be something extra. The trouble was that he could imagine exactly how she'd look coming across the hotel lounge towards him. Then he found he could visualize her face quite clearly, and looked inattentively out over the back garden of the lodging-house, which lay in thick, beating sunshine. He realized that when it wasn't set in that rather chilly life-mask, her face sometimes touched upon other sorts of face by a kind of physiognomical allusion. Some of the other sorts of face were very remote from her own. There was the permanent grin of an acrobat, or partner in an apache-dance routine; the sun-dazzle of some Honourable trollop photographed motor-boating on the Riviera; the sulky mindless glare theoretically detectable on the face of a pin-up; the frown of a plethoric and not very nice little girl. At any rate they were all female faces. He coughed loudly on recalling that Margaret had more than once reminded him facially of a man with an unintelligible accent and Service glasses whom he'd known by sight in the R.A.F. and had never seen doing anything except sweeping out the N.A.A.F.I. and wiping his nose on his sleeve.

To drive this thought away he opened the cupboard that contained his smoking engines and accessories – monuments, some of them costly, to economy. As long as he could remember he'd never been able to smoke as much as he wanted to. This armoury of devices had been assembled as each fresh way of seeming to smoke as much as he wanted to had come to his notice: the desiccated packet of cheap cigarette-tobacco, the cherry-wood pipe, the red packet of cigarette-papers, the packet of pipe-cleaners, the leather cigarette-machine, the quadripartite pipe-tool, the crumbling packet of cheap pipe-tobacco, the packet of cotton-wool filter-tips (new process), the nickel cigarette-machine, the clay pipe, the briar pipe, the blue packet of cigarette-papers, the packet of herbal smoking-mixture (guaranteed free from nicotine or other harmful substances. Why?), the rusting tin of expensive pipe-tobacco, the packet of chalk pipe-filters. Dixon took a cigarette from the packet in his pocket and lit it.

On the floor of the cupboard were the empty beer-flagons which represented his only sure method of saving money. There were nine of these, but two of them belonged to an impossibly distant pub; he'd bought them to drink in the bus on the way back from the Toynbee Society dinner in February. He'd hoped, by their aid, to efface the memory of a traumatically embarrassing speech Margaret had made at the dinner, but, sitting next to him throughout the journey back, she'd vetoed his project on disciplinary grounds (there'd been a lot of students in the bus, most of them drinking beer from flagons). He shivered at this memory, tried to drive it away by totting up the exchange value of the other seven bottles. Two and eight altogether; much less than he'd counted on. He decided not to review his financial position, and was just getting out his Merrie England notes when there was a knock at his door and Margaret came in. She was wearing the green Paisley frock and the quasi-velvet shoes.

'Hallo, Margaret,' he said with a heartiness which originated, he realized, in a guilty conscience. But why had he got a guilty conscience? Leaving her with Gore-Urquhart at the Ball had been 'tactful', hadn't it?

She looked at him with her air of not being quite sure who he was which had more than once entirely, and unaided, discomposed him. 'Oh, hallo,' she said.

'How are you?' he asked, keeping up the gimcrack friendliness. 'Have a seat.' He pushed forward the immense crippled armchair, of Pall Mall smoking-room size and design, that took up almost half the space left unoccupied by the bed. 'Cigarette?' He took out his packet to show that this was a sincere offer.

Still looking at him, she shook her head slowly, like a doctor indicating that there is no hope. Her face had a yellowish tinge, and her nostrils seemed pinched. She remained standing and not saying anything.

'Well, how are things?' Dixon said, tugging a smile on to his mouth.

She shook her head again, a little more slowly, and sat down on the arm of the chair, which creaked sharply. Dixon threw his pyjamas on to his bed and sat down on a cane-bottomed chair with his back to the window. 'Do you hate me, James?' she said.

Dixon wanted to rush at her and tip her backwards in the chair, to make a deafening rude noise in her face, to push a bead up her nose. 'How do you mean?' he asked.

It took her a quarter of an hour to make clear how she meant. She talked fast and fluently, moving about a lot on the chair-arm, her legs kicking straight as if hammered on the knee, her head jerking to restore invisible strands of hair, her thumbs bending and straightening. Why had he deserted her at the Ball like that? or rather, since she and he and everyone else knew why, what did he think he was up to? or rather, again, how could he do this to her? In exchange for such information on these and allied problems as he could give, she offered the news that all three Welches were 'out for his blood' and that Christine had referred slightingly to him at breakfast that morning. No mention of Gore-Urquhart was made, beyond a parenthetical attack on Dixon's 'rudeness' in leaving the dance without saying good-night to him. Dixon knew from experience that to counter-attack Margaret was invariably mistaken, but he was too angry to bother about that. When he was sure that she was going to say no more about Gore-Urquhart, he said, his heart pounding a little: 'I don't see why you're kicking up all this fuss. You looked as if you were doing all right for yourself when I left.'

'What the hell do you mean by that?'

'You were all over that Gore-Itchbag character, hadn't got time to say a single word to me, had you? If you didn't do yourself any good it wasn't for want of trying. I've never seen such an exhibition in my life . . .' His voice tailed off; he couldn't synthesize enough of the required righteous indignation.

She stared at him wide-eyed. 'But you can't mean . . . ?'

'Oh yes I bloody well can; of course I can mean.'

'James . . . you don't know . . . what you're talking about,' she said, slowly and painfully, like a foreigner reading out of a phrase-book. 'Really, I'm so surprised; I just . . . don't know what to say.' She began to tremble. 'I talk to a man, just for a few minutes, that's all it was . . . and now you start accusing me of making up to him. That's what you mean. Isn't that what you mean?' Her voice quavered grotesquely.

'That's what I mean all right,' Dixon said, trying to squeeze anger into his tone. 'It's no use denying it.' He could only manage to sound a little nettled and out of sorts.

'Do you really think I was trying to make up to him?'

'Well, it looked very much like it, you must admit.'

Going so close to Dixon that he flinched, she began looking out of the window. He couldn't see her face without craning his neck, so he took her seat on the arm of the Pall Mall armchair. She stayed there so long without moving that he began to hope she'd forgotten all about him; in a few moments he might be able to slip silently out to the pub. Then she began to speak, sounding quite calm. 'I'm afraid there's an awful lot you don't understand, James. I used to think you understood me, but now . . . You see, when you say a thing like that, I don't mind it being, er, offensive and all that, because I know you feel bad about this, at least I hope you do, for my own sake, and so I don't mind you . . . trying to lash out at me. What makes me feel so, so unhappy, is the awful gulf it shows that there is between us. It makes me say to myself, Oh, it's no good, he just doesn't know me at all, never has done, either. You see that, don't you?'

Dixon didn't make a face; he was afraid she might see it reflected in the window-pane. 'Yes,' he said.

'I don't want to go into it all, James, it's such a small, petty, trivial thing, but I suppose I'd better a little.' She sighed. 'Can't you distinguish between . . . ? No, obviously you can't. I'll just tell you this, just this one thing, and see whether that'll satisfy you.' She turned and faced him, then said less calmly than before: 'After you'd gone last night, I didn't spend a single moment with Gore-Urquhart. He was with Carol Goldsmith. I spent the whole of the rest of the time with Bertrand, thank you very much.' Her voice went up. 'And you can guess what sort of a . . .'

'Well, hard luck,' Dixon broke in before he should have time to relent. A grandiose disgust for the whole proceedings had filled him; not merely for this one hand, but for the whole game of poker, of non-strip poker, that he and Margaret were playing. Biting his lips, he vowed to himself that this time he'd take whatever she might have to deal out. He remembered Carol's phrase about not throwing Margaret any lifebelts. Well, he'd thrown his last one. He would not waste any more time trying to conciliate her, more because he knew it was a waste of time than because his powers of conciliation were at an end, though they were pretty well at an end as well. 'Look here, Margaret,' he said. 'I've no desire to hurt your feelings unnecessarily, as you know perfectly well, whatever you may say. But for your own sake, as well as mine, you must get some things straight. I know you've had a very hard time recently, and you know I know that as well. But it won't do you any good to go on thinking what you evidently do think about me and how we stand. It'll only make things worse. What I want to say is, you must stop depending on me emotionally like this. I agree I was probably in the wrong over the dance business, but right or wrong won't make any difference to this. I'll stick up for you and I'll chat to you and I'll sympathize, but I've had enough of being forced into a false position. Get it into your head that I've quite lost whatever interest I may have had in you as a woman, as someone to make love to, or go to bed with – no, you can have your turn in a minute. This time you're going to hear me out. As I said, the sex business is all finished, if it ever got started. I'm not blaming anyone; I just want to tell you you must count me out as far as anything like that's concerned. That's how things are. And I can't say I'm sorry because you can't say you're sorry for what you can't do anything about, and I can't do anything about this and neither can you. That's all.'

'You don't think she'd have you, do you? A shabby little provincial bore like you,' Margaret burst out as soon as he'd stopped speaking. 'Or has she had you already? Perhaps she just wanted a . . .'

'Don't be fantastic, Margaret. Come off the stage for a moment, do.'

There was a pause; then she came waveringly forward, put her hands on his shoulders, and seemed to collapse, or be dragging him, on to the bed. Unregarded, her spectacles fell off. She was making a curious noise, a steady, repeated, low-pitched moan that sounded as if it came from the pit of her stomach, as if she'd been sick over and over again and still wanted to be sick. Dixon half-helped, half-lifted her on to the bed. Now and then she gave a quiet, almost skittish little scream. Her face was pushed hard against his chest. Dixon didn't know whether she was fainting, or having a fit of hysterics, or simply breaking down and crying. Whatever it was he didn't know how to deal with it. When she felt that she was sitting on the bed next to him she threw herself forward so that her face was on his thigh. In a moment he felt moisture creeping through to his skin. He tried to lift her, but she was immovably heavy; her shoulders were shaking more rapidly than seemed to him normal even in a condition of this kind. Then she raised herself, tense but still trembling, and began a series of high-pitched, inward screams which alternated with the deep moans. Both were quite loud. Her hair was in her eyes, her lips were drawn back, and her teeth chattered. Her face was wet, with saliva as well as tears. At last, as he began speaking her name, she threw herself violently backwards and sideways on to the bed. While she lay there with her arms spread out, writhing, she screamed half a dozen times, very loudly, then went on more quietly, moaning with every outward breath. Dixon seized her wrists and shouted: 'Margaret. Margaret.' She looked at him with dilated eyes and began struggling, trying to free herself from him. Two lots of footsteps were now approaching outside, one ascending the stairs, the other descending. The door opened and Bill Atkinson came in, followed by Miss Cutler. Dixon looked up at them.

'Hysterics, eh?' Atkinson said, and slapped Margaret several times on the face, very hard, Dixon thought. He pushed Dixon out of the way and sat down on the bed, gripping Margaret by the shoulders and shaking her vigorously. 'There's some whisky up in my cupboard. Go and get it.'

Dixon ran out and up the stairs. The only thought that presented itself to him at all clearly was one of mild surprise that the fictional or cinematic treatment of hysterics should be based so firmly on what was evidently the right treatment. He found the whisky; his hand was shaking so much that he nearly dropped the bottle. He uncorked it and took a quick swig, trying not to cough. Down in his room again, he found everything much quieter. Miss Cutler, who'd been watching Atkinson and Margaret, gave Dixon a glance, not of suspicion or reproach, but of reassurance; she said nothing. As he felt at the moment, this made him want to cry. Atkinson looked up without taking the bottle. 'Get a glass or a cup.' He got a cup from the cupboard, poured some of the whisky into it, and gave it to Atkinson. Miss Cutler, as much in awe of him as ever, stood at Dixon's side and watched Margaret being given some whisky.

Atkinson heaved her up into a half-sitting position. Her moans had stopped and she was trembling less violently. Her face was red from Atkinson's blows. When he put the cup to her mouth it rattled once or twice on her teeth and her breathing was audible. With eerie predictability she choked and coughed, swallowed some, coughed again, swallowed some more. Quite soon she stopped trembling altogether and began to look round at them. 'Sorry about that,' she said faintly.

'That's all right, girlie,' Atkinson said. 'Like a fag?'

'Yes please.'

'Forward, Jim.'

Miss Cutler smiled at them all, mouthed something, and went quietly out. Dixon lit cigarettes for the three of them and Margaret sat up on the edge of the bed; Atkinson still kept his arm round her. 'Were you the one that slapped my face?' she asked him.

'That's right, girlie. It did you a power of good. How do you feel now?'

'A lot better, thanks. A bit hazy, but otherwise all right.'

'Good. Don't you try to move around for a bit. Here, put your feet up and have a rest.'

'There's really no need . . .'

He pulled her feet up on to the bed and took off her shoes, then stood looking down at her. 'You stay there for ten minutes at least. I'll leave you to the care of brother Jim now. Have some more whisky when you've finished that, but don't let Jim get at it. I promised his mother not to let him drink himself to death.' He turned his Tartar's face on Dixon. 'All right, old man?'

'Yes thanks, Bill. It's been very good of you.'

'All right, girlie?'

'Thank you so much, Mr Atkinson; you've been wonderful. I just can't thank you enough.'

'That's all right, girlie.' He nodded to them and went out.

'I'm sorry about all that, James,' she said as soon as the door was shut.

'It was my fault.'

'No, you always say that. This time I'm not going to let you. I just couldn't take what you said, that's all. I thought to myself, I can't bear it, I must stop him, and then I simply lost control of myself. Nothing more to it than that. And it was all so silly and childish, because you were absolutely right, saying what you did. Much better to clear the air like that. I just behaved like a perfect idiot.'

'There's no point in reproaching yourself. You couldn't help it.'

'No, but I ought to have been able to. Do sit down, James; you're getting on my nerves, prowling around like that.'

Dixon pulled the cane-bottomed chair to beside the bed. When he was settled and looking at Margaret, he was reminded of how he'd sat at her side, just like this, when he visited her in hospital after her suicide attempt. But she'd looked different then, thinner and weaker, with her hair drawn back to the nape of her neck; and, in a way, less distressing than she looked now. The sight of her smudged lipstick, her damp nose, her disordered, stiff hair filled him with a profound and tranquil depression. 'I'd better come back to the Welches' with you,' he said.

'My dear, I wouldn't hear of it. You'd better keep clear of that place as long as you can.'

'I don't care about any of that. And in any case I needn't come in. I'll just come back on the bus with you.'

'Don't be so ridiculous, James. It's absolutely unnecessary. I'm perfectly all right now. At least I will be when I've had another go at nice Mr Atkinson's whisky. Would you be an angel and pour me some?'

While he complied, Dixon thought with relief that he needn't go back on the bus with her. By now he could always tell what Margaret wanted, whatever she might say, and it was clear that this refusal of services was genuine. It wasn't that he didn't feel concern for her; he felt a lot, so much that the load was intolerable – intolerable, too, was the way in which to feel concern had now come, for him, to confuse itself utterly with the feeling of guilt. He gave her the cup, not looking at her; he said nothing, not for the familiar reason of not being able to say what he wanted to say, but because he could think of nothing to say.

'I'll just drink this and finish my cigarette, and then I'll be off. There's a bus at twenty to; it'll get me in nicely. Would you get me an ashtray, James?'

He brought her a copper one which bore the representation, in high-relief, of a small antique warship and the caption 'H.M. Torpedo-Boat Destroyer *Ribble*'. She dropped ash on to it, then sat

168

up on the edge of the bed and, taking cosmetics from her handbag, began making up her face. Looking into her compact-mirror, she said conversationally: 'It's strange that it should end like this, isn't it? In such a very undignified fashion.' When he still said nothing, she went on, moving her mouth about now and then to put lipstick on it: 'But then it hasn't been very dignified all the way through, has it? It's just been me flying off the handle in one way and another, and you rather reluctantly trying to get me to grow up. No, that's not fair to you.' She worked lipstick over her mouth, then peered into the mirror again. 'You did all a man could do, and more than most would, believe me. You've got nothing to reproach yourself with. Really, I don't know how you stuck it. I'm afraid none of it's been much fun for you. Just as well you decided to call it quits.' She snapped the compact shut and put it into her handbag.

'You know I'm fond of you, Margaret,' Dixon said. 'It's just that it wouldn't work, that's all.'

'I know, James. Don't you worry about anything. I shall be all right.'

'You must always come to me if anything goes wrong. That I can do anything about.'

She smiled slightly at his reservation. 'Of course I will,' she said as if she were soothing him.

He raised his head and looked at her. Under the powder, her cheeks were still slightly mottled where the redness was fading, but with her glasses back on the slight puffiness round her eyes was scarcely noticeable. That she'd only recently finished being hysterical seemed incredible to him, as did the thought that he could ever have said to her anything important enough to make her hysterical. As he watched her, she put out her cigarette on H.M.S. *Ribble* and stood up, brushing the ash from her dress. 'That just about takes care of everything, I think,' she said lightly. 'Well, good-bye, James.'

Dixon smiled uncertainly. What a pity it was, he thought, that she wasn't better-looking, that she didn't read the articles in the three-halfpenny Press that told you which colour lipstick went with which natural colouring. With twenty per cent more of what she lacked in these ways, she'd never have run into any of her appalling difficulties: the vices and morbidities bred of loneliness would have remained safely dormant until old age. 'Are you sure you're all right?' he asked her.

'Stop worrying about me; I'm perfectly all right. Now I must be off, or I shall miss my bus, and that'll make me late for lunch, and you know what Mrs Neddy is about meal-times. Well, I dare say we shall run into each other before very long. Good-bye.'

'Good-bye, Margaret. See you soon.'

She went out without replying.

Dixon put his own cigarette out, jabbing at *Ribble*'s bridge in a feeble rage he couldn't find any source for. He tried to tell himself that when he'd got over his own feelings of shock, he'd begin to be glad at having told Margaret what he'd been wanting to tell her for so long, but it wasn't convincing. He thought of his appointment with Christine the next day but one, and regarded it entirely without pleasure. Some part of what had happened in the last half-hour had spoilt all that, though he didn't know which part. Somewhere his path to Christine was blocked; it was all going to go wrong in some way he couldn't foresee. It wasn't that Margaret herself would take a hand in the matter and upset things by somehow alerting Bertrand and the senior Welches; it wasn't that he might be forced to withdraw his recent declarations to Margaret. It was something less unlikely than the first, harder to fight than the second, and much vaguer than either. It was just that everything seemed to be spoilt.

He began abstractedly brushing his hair in front of his small unframed mirror. He refused to think directly about Margaret's fit of hysterics. Soon enough, he knew, it would take its place with those three or four memories which could make him actually twist about in his chair or bed with remorse, fear, or embarrassment. It would probably supplant the present top-of-the-list item, the time he'd been pushed out in front of the curtain after a school concert to make the audience sing the National Anthem. He could hear his own voice now, saying in those flat tones, heavy with insincerity: 'And now . . . I want you all . . . to join with me, if you will . . . in singing . . .' And then he'd led off in a key that must have been exactly half an octave above or below the proper one. Switching every few notes, like everybody else, from one octave to the other, half a beat in front of or behind everybody else, he'd gone through the whole thing. Cheers, applause, and laughter had followed him when he ducked his burning face back through the curtains. He looked at his face now in the mirror: it looked back at him, humourless and self-pitying.

He picked up Atkinson's whisky-bottle and went to the door, intending to suggest a couple of pints of beer at the pub round the corner; then he turned back and picked up the letter to Johns. There seemed no point in not posting it.

17

Dixon plunged down the lodging-house stairs at eight-fifteen the next morning, not so much so as to be sure of being there while Johns read his letter as because he wanted, or rather had got, to spend a long morning in writing up his Merrie England lecture. He didn't like having to breakfast so early. There was something about Miss Cutler's cornflakes, her pallid fried eggs or bright red bacon, her explosive toast, her diuretic coffee which, much better than bearable at nine o'clock, his usual breakfast-time, seemed at eight-fifteen to summon from all the recesses of his frame every lingering vestige of crapulent headache, every relic of past nauseas, every echo of noises in the head. This retrospective vertigo collared him this morning as roughly as always. The three pints of bitter he'd drunk last night with Bill Atkinson and Beesley might, by means of some garbaged alley through the space-time continuum, have been preceded by a bottle of British sherry and followed by half a dozen breakfast-cups of red biddy. Holding his hands over his eyes, he circled the table like one trying to evade the smoke from a bonfire, then sat down heavily and saturated a plate of cornflakes with bluish milk. He was alone in the room.

Avoiding thinking about Margaret, and for some reason not wanting to think about Christine, he found his thoughts turning towards his lecture. Early the previous evening he'd tried working his notes for it up into a script. The first page of notes had yielded a page and three lines of script. At that rate he'd be able to talk for eleven and a half minutes as his notes now stood. Some sort of pabulum for a further forty-eight and a half minutes was evidently required, with perhaps a minute off for being introduced to the audience, another minute for water-drinking, coughing, and page-turning, and nothing at all for applause or curtain-calls. Where was he going to find this supplementary pabulum? The only answer to this question seemed to be Yes, that's right, where? Ah, wait a minute; he'd get Barclay to find him a book on medieval music. Twenty minutes at least on that, with an apology for 'having let my interest run away with me'. Welch would absolutely eat that. He blew bubbles for a moment with the milk in his spoon at the thought of having to transcribe so many hateful facts, then cheered up at the thought of being able to do himself so much good without having to think at all. 'It may perhaps be thought,' he muttered to himself, 'that the character of an age, a nation, a class, would be but poorly revealed in anything so apparently divorced from ordinary habits of thought as its music, as its musical culture.' He leant forward impressively over the cruet. 'Nothing could be further from the truth.'

At that moment Beesley entered, rubbing his hands in the way he had. 'Hallo, Jim,' he said. 'Post here yet?'

'No, not yet. Is he coming?'

'He's finished in the bathroom. Shouldn't be long now.'

'Good. What about Bill?'

'He was up before me; I heard him trampling the floor. Wait a minute; I think this must be him.'

While Beesley sat down and started on his cornflakes, Atkinson came slowly into the room. As so often, especially in the mornings, his demeanour seemed to imply that he was unacquainted with the other two and had, at the moment, no intention of striking up any sort of relation with them. This morning he looked more than ever like Genghis Khan meditating a purge of his captains. He halted contemptuously at his chair, clicking his tongue and sighing histrionically like one kept waiting in a shop. His dark, mysterious eyes ran round the walls, making leisured halts at each photograph, summing up adversely Miss Cutler's nephew in the uniform of a Pay Corps lance-corporal, Miss Cutler's cousin's two little girls, Miss Cutler's former employer's country house with a gig at the portico, Miss Cutler vehemently dressed as a bridesmaid in the fashions of the First World War. He was perhaps engaged in whittling down the huge volume of abuse evoked by these sights into four tiny toxic gouts of hatred, one for each photograph. Still silent, however, he took his place at the table, his large hairy hands idle and palm-upwards on the cloth. He never ate cereals.

While Miss Cutler was in the room dispensing vermilion bacon, the day's post could be heard arriving. Beesley nodded significantly at Dixon and went out into the hall. When he came back he nodded again, more significantly. Dixon felt none of the pleasurable excitement he'd expected; even when, a couple of minutes later, Johns came silently in holding his letter, he was still almost unmoved. Why was this? Merrie England? Yes, and other things too, but never mind about them. He tried to fasten his attention on the letter, which Johns was now opening and unfolding. Beesley, his mouth full of food, had stopped chewing; Atkinson, outwardly unconcerned, was watching Johns through his thick lashes. Johns began reading. The silence was intense.

Johns put his spoon down carefully. There seemed to be something subtly wrong about his hair. His usual lard-like pallor, though diversified this morning by several inflamed patches (the consequence, no doubt, of shaving with a blade far too blunt for anybody with a normal attitude towards money), was too extreme to allow of any further whitening in consequence of emotions like alarm or fury. Soon, however, he raised his eyes, not, of course, to the level of the others' faces, but much nearer it than usual. Once Dixon even fancied he caught Johns's glance for a moment or two. The man was evidently stirred in some way; he was twisting about with a sort of arch, self-deprecatory motion. After reading the letter through once or twice, be stuffed it quickly back in its envelope and shoved it into his breast-pocket. Looking up again and finding the others still watching him, he picked up his spoon so hurriedly that it spattered milk over his navy-blue cardigan. A bursting sound came from Beesley.

'What's the matter, sonny boy?' Atkinson asked Johns, clearly and very slowly. 'Had a bit of bad news?'

'No.'

'Because I shouldn't like to feel that you'd had a bit of bad news. It would spoil my day. Are you sure you haven't had a bit of bad news?'

'Nothing at all.'

'Haven't you had a bit of bad news?'

'No.'

'Oh. Well, be sure to let me know if you ever do. I might be able to give you some advice. Mightn't I?'

Atkinson lit a cigarette. 'Not much of a talker, are you?' he asked Johns. 'Is he?' he asked the other two.

'No,' they said.

Atkinson nodded and went out. From the passage they heard his rare laugh; without any definite point of change, it led to a fit of coughing which gradually receded up the stairs.

Johns began on his bacon. 'It isn't funny,' he said, suddenly and surprisingly. 'It isn't funny at all.'

Dixon caught a glimpse of Beesley's flushed, delighted face. 'What isn't?' he asked.

'You know what, Dixon. Two can play at that game. You'll see.' With a shaking, wristless hand he poured himself some coffee.

The encounter ended with no more said. With a last hostile glance in the direction of Dixon's tie, Johns hurried out. His work on the College staff's superannuation policies and National Health cards began at nine o'clock. As he went, Dixon saw that there was something funny about the back of his head.

Beesley leaned over. 'All right, eh, Jim?'

'Not too bad.'

'Did you notice how much he said? An absolute bloody flood of eloquence. It's what I've always maintained: he never says a word unless he feels he's being threatened in some way. Hey, I haven't told you. Did you notice how queer his hair looked?'

'Now you mention it, I did think it looked a bit odd.'

Beesley began eating toast and marmalade. Chewing angrily, he went on: 'He's bought himself a pair of hair-clippers. I found them in the bathroom yesterday. Cuts his own hair now, you see.

Too sodding mean to pay out his one-and-six, that's what it is. My God.'

This, then, was why, from the back, Johns appeared to be wearing a blatant toupee which had slipped over slightly to one side, and why, from the front, his face appeared to be surmounted by a curious helmet. Dixon was silent, thinking that Johns had at last done something he rather respected.

'What's up, Jim? You don't look too happy.'

'I'm all right.'

'Still worrying about the lecture? Look, I've got those notes on The Age of Chaucer I promised you. They're not very exciting, but there'll be a few things you can probably use. I'll stick them in your room.'

Dixon cheered up again; if he could dare to wait long enough, he might be able to construct the rest of his lecture entirely out of others' efforts. 'Thanks, Alfred,' he said; 'that'll be fine.'

'Going up to College at all?'

'Yes, I want to see Barclay.'

'Barclay? I shouldn't have thought you'd have much to say to him.'

'I want to pick his brains on medieval music.'

'Ah, got you now. Going up straight away, are you?'

'In a few minutes.'

'Grand, I'll go up with you.'

It was a warm day, but overcast. As they strolled up College Road, Beesley began talking about the examination results in his Department. The visit of the External Examiner at the end of the week would settle a number of doubtful cases, but the main outlines of the results were already clear. The position was the same in Dixon's own Department, so that there was something to discuss.

'One thing I like about Fred Karno,' Beesley said, 'though it's about the only thing when I come to think of it: he'll never try to push anyone through that he doesn't really think's worth it. No Firsts this year for us, four Thirds, and forty-five per cent of the first-year people failed; that's the way to deal with 'em. Fred's about the only prof. in the place who's resisting all this outside pressure to chuck Firsts around like teaching diplomas and push every bugger who can write his name through the Pass courses. What's Neddy's angle on the business? Or hasn't he got round to getting one yet?'

'That's right. He leaves most of it to Cecil Goldsmith, and that means everyone gets through. Cecil's a tender-hearted chap, you know.'

'Tender-headed, you mean. It's the same everywhere you look; not only this place, but all the provincial universities are going the same way. Not London, I suppose, and not the Scottish ones. But my God, go to most places and try and get someone turfed out merely because he's too stupid to pass his exams – it'd be easier to sack a prof. That's the trouble with having so many people here on Education Authority grants, you see.'

'How do you mean? The students have got to get their money from somewhere.'

'Well, you know, Jim. You can see the Authorities' point in a way. "We pay for John Smith to enter College here and now you tell us, after seven years, that he'll never get a degree. You're wasting our money." If we institute an entrance exam to keep out the ones who can't read or write, the entry goes down by half, and half of us lose our jobs. And then the other demand: "We want two hundred teachers this year and we mean to have them." All right, we'll lower the pass mark to twenty per cent and give you the quantity you want, but for God's sake don't start complaining in two years' time that your schools are full of teachers who couldn't pass the General Certificate themselves, let alone teach anyone else to pass it. It's a wonderful position, isn't it?'

Dixon agreed rather than disagreed with Beesley, but he didn't feel interested enough to say so. It was one of those days when he felt quite convinced of his impending expulsion from academic life. What would he do afterwards? Teach in a school? Oh dear no.

Go to London and get a job in an office. What job? Whose office? Shut up.

They entered the main building in silence, went into the Common Room, and moved over to their pigeon-holes. Dixon took out of his a reminder that he hadn't yet paid his Common Room subscription for the year and a postcard, addressed to *Jas Dickson Esq BA*, informing him of the publication of some flatulent work on textile trades in the time of the Tudors. These he dropped into the wastepaper-basket with the maximum of dispatch. Beesley was looking through a newly-arrived issue of the journal of university affairs to which he subscribed, muttering to himself. There was nobody else in the room. Before rousing himself to find Barclay, Dixon, feeling he could do with a sit-down at the start of such a day, dropped into an armchair and yawned.

In a moment or two Beesley came over, holding his journal open. 'Something that'll interest you here, Jim. "New appointments. Dr L. S. Caton to the Chair of History of Commerce, University of Tucumán, Argentina." Isn't that the chap you sent your article to?'

'Christ, let me have a look.'

'You'd better get through to him a bit sharpish, before he escapes on the banana-boat. Looks as if his new review'll be packing up, unless he thinks he can edit it from there.'

'Oh God, this looks pretty bad.'

'I should get through to him on the blower if I were you.'

'Oh God. Yes, I will. Well, thanks for pointing it out to me, Alfred. I'd better find Barclay before he gets a job out there too.'

A prey to vague but powerful misgiving, Dixon hurried out and over to the Music School, where, to his surprise, Barclay proved to be present, available, cooperative, and in possession of just the sort of book Dixon wanted. Feeling a little less disturbed, Dixon went round with it to the library and obtained, with almost sinister promptitude, a book on medieval costume and furniture. In the revolving door on the way out, his movement was abruptly checked by the intervention of somebody outside trying to revolve the door in the opposite, and (according to several large, well-designed notices) wrong, direction. It was Welch, looking suspiciously about him, stepping back with a frown as Dixon went on pushing and emerged by his side.

'Good morning, Professor.'

Welch recognized him almost at once. 'Dixon,' he said.

'Yes, Professor?' Dixon had forgotten until now Margaret's report that Welch, in common with the other members of his family, was 'out for his blood'. How would Welch manifest his pursuit of that entity?

'I was wondering about the library,' Welch said, rocking to and fro on his heels. He was looking more than usually wild-eyed and dishevelled this morning. There was a small golden emblem on his tie resembling some heraldic device or other, but proving on closer scrutiny to be congealed egg-yolk. Substantial traces of the same nutritive were to be seen round his mouth, which was now ajar.

'Oh yes?' Dixon asked, hoping to encourage Welch to indicate what point, within the framework of ideas connected with the library, could be taken as the focus of his wonderment.

'Do you think you could go there?'

Dixon began to feel definitely alarmed. Had Welch's long-heralded derangement finally come to pass? Or was this a bitterly sarcastic way of alluding to Dixon's own disinclination to approach any possible arena of academic work? Badly rattled now, he stole a glance over his shoulder to make sure that they were, in fact, standing within two paces of the library entrance. 'I expect so' seemed the safest sort of reply.

'You're not overburdened with work just now?'

'Just now?' Dixon bleated. 'I don't think I . . .'

'I was thinking of your lecture for Wednesday. I suppose most of it's complete by now?'

Dixon shifted the two books he had under his arm, in case Welch might be able to see their titles. 'Oh yes,' he said wildly. 'Professor. Yes.'

'I haven't got time to go to the library, you see,' Welch said in the tone of one removing the last trivial obstacle in the way of complete understanding. 'I've got to go in here,' he added, pointing towards the library.

Dixon nodded slowly. 'Oh, you've got to go in here,' he said.

'Yes, one or two points have come up in the examination answers. I want to check them up before the External Examiner's meeting tomorrow. You'll be all right for that, I take it? Five o'clock in my room.'

Christine was meeting Dixon at four o'clock the next day. Even with a taxi he could only have three-quarters of an hour with her. He wanted to bundle Welch into the revolving door and whirl him round in it till lunch-time. He said: 'I'll be there.'

'Good. Well, you can see that I shan't be able to spend any time pottering about looking things up in the library.'

'Oh, quite.'

'It's good of you to do this for me, Dixon. Now, as regards what I want from the library: it's all down here.' By degrees, he drew a sheaf of papers from his breast pocket and unfolded them. 'It's all quite self-explanatory, you'll find. The reference is down in nearly every case, I think . . . yes. Oh, there are a few here, yes, without . . . just long shots, really. I don't suppose there's much of value, if anything, but you might just look through the subject indexes. If there aren't any, then you'll just have to use your own . . . your own . . . The chapter titles will probably help you there. This one, for instance, you see. Just see if there's anything relevant. I shouldn't think there would be from the date. But you never know your luck, do you?' He scrutinized Dixon's face, seeking confirmation.

'No, you don't.'

'No, you don't. I remember being held up for weeks once over a thing I was doing, just because of one missing fact. It seems that in the autumn of 1663 . . . no, the summer . . .'

Dixon now had some of the basic facts clear. He was being asked to fill certain gaps in Welch's knowledge of the history of peasant arts and crafts in the county, and these papers, written in Welch's pointlessly neat and clear hand or typed by him with hilarious inaccuracy, would enable him, Dixon, to perform his task without all that much confusion, though not without some loss of time and integrity. Still, he daren't refuse; this sort of task might easily, to Welch, seem a more important test of ability than the merit of the Merrie England lecture. So much was obvious; but what was all this business about the library? When Welch's silence indicated the end, or possibly the abandonment, of the anecdote, Dixon asked: 'Will they have all this information here, sir? I mean, some of these pamphlets must be pretty rare. I should have thought the Record Office would have . . .'

Welch's expression was slowly adapting itself to incredulous rage. In a high, petulant tone he said: 'No, of course they won't have the information here, Dixon. I can't imagine any one thinking they would. That's why I'm asking you to go down to the library for it. I know for a fact they've got ninety per cent of the stuff I want. I'd go myself, but as I took the trouble to explain, I'm tied up here. And I must have the information by tonight, because I'm giving the talk tomorrow evening after Professor Fortescue gets . . . goes . . . goes back. Now do you see?'

Dixon did: Welch had all the time been talking about the public library in the city, and, since this was clear to him, naturally hadn't thought of the confusion he might cause by talking about 'the library' within five feet of a totally different building known in the area as 'the library'. 'Oh, of course, Professor; I'm sorry,' he said, having been well schooled in giving apologies at the very times when he ought to be demanding them.

'All right, Dixon. Well, I won't hold you up now; I expect you'll want to get started if you're to finish by five. You'd better come up to my room afterwards and show me what you've got. It's very kind of you to offer to help; I appreciate it very much.'

Dixon dropped the papers between the pages of Barclay's book and turned away, only to start violently and look back as a loud thundering noise broke out behind him. Welch, his hair flapping, was straining like a packed-down rugby forward to push the revolving door in the wrong direction. Dixon stood and watched, allowing his mandrill face full play. After a time Welch, somehow divining his error, began pulling instead at the now-jammed door, changing his semblance to that of anchor in a losing tug-o'-war team. With a sudden bursting click the door yielded and Welch overbalanced backwards, hitting his head on the panel behind him. Dixon went away, beginning to whistle his Welch tune in a solemn, almost liturgical tempo. He felt that it was things like this that kept him going.

18

'Well, that's really splendid, Dixon,' Welch said seven hours later. 'You've filled in all the gaps in a most . . . a most . . . Really quite admirable.' He gloated over his notes for a moment, then suddenly added: 'What are you doing now?' with an effect of suspicion.

In point of fact, Dixon had got his hands behind his back now and was gesturing with them. 'I was just . . .' he stammered.

'I was wondering if you were doing anything this evening. I thought you might like to come over and have a meal with us.'

After a day of doing Welch's work, there was plenty for Dixon to do that evening in connexion with his lecture, but it was obvious that he couldn't afford to turn down this offer, so he said unhesitatingly: 'Well, thank you very much, Professor. That's very kind of you.'

Welch nodded as if pleased, and gathered up the papers to put them into his 'bag'. 'I think this ought to go down very well tomorrow night,' he said, turning on Dixon his sexual maniac's smile.

'I'm sure it will. Who's the talk being delivered to?'

'The Antiquarian and Historical Society. I'm surprised you haven't seen the posters.' He picked up his 'bag' and put his fawn fishing-hat on his head. 'Come along, then. We'll go down in my car.'

'That'll be nice.'

'I must say they're a marvellously keen lot,' Welch said passionately as they went downstairs. 'A very good audience to talk to. Attentive and . . . keen, and plenty of questions to fire at you afterwards. Of course, you get mainly town people there, but we always get some of the better students along. Young Michie, for instance. A good lad, that. Have you managed to get him interested in your special subject at all?'

Reflecting that Michie was lying ominously low these days, Dixon said: 'Yes, he seems quite set on it,' and hoped that Welch would take due heed of this testimony to his power to 'interest' such a good lad.

Welch went on as before: 'A very good lad, he is. Very keen. Always turns up to the Antiquarians. I've had one or two chats with him, as a matter of fact. I think we've really got quite a lot in common.'

Dixon doubted whether Welch and Michie had much in common beyond a similar view of his own capacities, but, judging that Welch's professional ethics would prevent him from instancing that, asked with a show of curiosity: 'In what way?'

'Well, we both have this interest in the English tradition, as you might call it. His is more philosophical, I suppose, and mine more what you could sum up as cultural, but we've got quite a lot in common. I was thinking the other day, by the way, that it's remarkable how my own interests have turned more and more towards this English tradition in the last few years. Whereas my wife's are . . . I always sum her up as a Western European first and an Englishwoman second. With her, you see, with her sort of Continental way of looking at things, almost Gallic you might say she is in some things, well, the things that are so important to me, the English social and cultural scene, with a kind of backward-looking bias in a sense, popular crafts and so on, traditional pastimes and that, well, to her that's an aspect in a way, you see, just an aspect – a very interesting aspect, of course, but no more than an aspect,' and here he hesitated as if choosing the accurate term, 'a sort of aspect of the development of Western European culture, you might say. You can see it most clearly, really, in her attitude towards the Welfare State, and it's a great advantage to be able to view that problem in what you might describe as a wider perspective. She argues, you see, that if people have everything done for them . . .'

Dixon, having long ago summed up Mrs Welch on his own account, allowed Welch to go on about her political views, her attitude towards 'so-called freedom in education', her advocacy of retributive punishment, her fondness for reading what English-women wrote about how Parisians thought and felt. His own thoughts and feelings, all the time they were getting into the car and driving off, were busy on the subject of Margaret. He didn't know how he was to face meeting her; this reflection, which had been occupying him for most of the day at the Public Library, had become much more urgent now that he'd have to face meeting her very shortly. He'd also presumably have to face meeting Bertrand and Mrs Welch, but these encounters must in comparison be much less appalling. There'd be Christine as well; he didn't really want to see her either, not because of anything to do with her personally, but because she formed a portion of his worry about Margaret. He'd have to do something to show Margaret she wasn't entirely alone; he wouldn't, he mustn't let himself, get back on the old footing with her, but he must somehow reassure her of his continued support. How was he going to do that?

In search of some distraction, he looked out of the window at his left just as Welch slowed to a walking pace at a road junction. Standing on the pavement was a big fat man whom Dixon recognized as his barber. Dixon felt a deep respect for this man because of his impressive exterior, his rumbling bass voice, and his unsur-passable stock of information about the Royal Family. At that moment two rather pretty girls stopped at a pillar-box a few yards away. The barber, his hands clasped behind his back, turned and stared at them. An unmistakable look of furtive lust came over his face; then, like a courtly shopwalker, he moved slowly towards the two girls. Welch now accelerated again and Dixon, a good deal shaken, hurriedly switched his attention to the other side of the road, where a cricket match was being played and the bowler was just running up to bowl. The batsman, another big fat man, swiped at the ball, missed it, and was violently hit by it in the stomach. Dixon had time to see him double up and the wicket-keeper begin to run forward before a tall hedge hid the scene.

Uncertain whether this pair of *vignettes* was designed to illustrate the swiftness of divine retribution or its tendency to mistake its target, Dixon was quite sure that he felt in some way overwhelmed, so much so that he listened to what Welch was saying. He was saying 'Most impressive', and for a second Dixon felt like picking up the spanner he could see in the dashboard pocket and hitting him on the back of the neck with it. He knew the sort of thing Welch found impressive.

The rest of the journey passed uneventfully. Welch's driving seemed to have improved slightly; at any rate, the only death Dixon felt himself threatened by was death from exposure to boredom. Even this danger receded for a couple of minutes while Welch disclosed a few facts about the recent history of the effeminate writing Michel, a character always waiting in the wings of Dixon's life but apparently destined never to enter its stage. This Michel, as indefatigably Gallic as his mother, had been cooking for himself in his small London flat, and had in the last few days made himself ill by stuffing himself with filthy foreign food of his own preparation, in particular, Dixon gathered, spaghetti and dishes cooked in olive oil. This seemed fit punishment for one so devoted to coagulated flour-and-water and peasants' butter-substitute, washed down, no doubt, by 'real' black coffee of high viscosity. Anyway, Michel was evidently coming down in a day or two to recuperate on his parents' English fare. Dixon turned his head to laugh out of the window at this last stroke. This time he experienced nothing worse than a small rage at the thought of a little louse like that having a flat in London. Why hadn't he himself had parents whose money so far exceeded their sense as to install their son in London? The very thought of it was a torment. If he'd had that chance, things would be very different for him now. For a moment he thought he couldn't think what things; then he found he could conceive the things exactly, and exactly how they'd differ from the things he'd got, too.

Welch went on talking, his own face the perfect audience for his talk, laughing at its jokes, reflecting its puzzlement or earnestness, responding with tightened lips and narrowed eyes to its more important points. He went on talking even while he drove up the sandy path into the yard next to his house, grazed the shattered water-tap, nosed into the garage entrance, and, with a single frightful bound, brought the car to rest within a couple of inches of the inner wall. Then he got out.

Casting about for means to leave the car, Dixon rejected the six-inch corridor left to him between the door and the side-wall nearest him, and, after some bad-tempered leg-play with the gear- and brake-levers, slid across the front seat to the other door. As he did this, something seemed to pluck at the seat of his trousers. When he'd emerged into the giddy heat of the garage, he felt behind him and found he could comfortably insert his first two fingers into a rent in the material. A glance at the driver's seat showed the tip of what must have been a broken spring just emerging from the upholstery. He began slowly to follow Welch, his heart starting to pound and mist breaking out on his spectacles. He allowed a terrible grimace to dawn on his features, forcing his chin down as far as possible and trying to bring his nose up between his eyes. When this was nearing completion, he took off his glasses to rub them clear. His sight was good enough without their aid for him to observe that four witnesses of his actions were posted at the long window some yards away; they were (left to right) Christine, Bertrand, Mrs Welch, and Margaret. He quickly restored his nose to its normal position and began pensively fondling his dropped chin, in the hope of seeming assailed by imbecilic doubt; then, unable to think up any gesture or expression of greeting comprehensive enough to include all the members of such a quartet, pursued Welch's retreating figure round the corner of the house.

What was he going to do about his trousers? Which would be worst: mending them himself, which would involve finding, or more likely re-buying, the required materials, having them repaired at a shop, which meant remembering to ask someone where such a shop could be found, remembering to take the trousers to it and remembering to fetch and pay for them, or asking Miss Cutler to do them? Would the last be quickest? Yes; but it might carry with it the penalty of watching the operation and being talked to by Miss Cutler during it and for an incalculable time after it. Apart from a pair belonging to a suit much too dark for anything but interviews and funerals, his only other trousers were so stained with food and beer that they would, if worn on the stage to indicate squalor and penury, be considered ridiculously overdone. Welch should do the repairs. It was his horrible car, wasn't it? Why hadn't he torn his own vile trousers on the barbed seat? Perhaps he would soon. Or perhaps he had already without noticing.

Passing under the thatched barbette over the front door, Dixon averted his eyes from a picture Welch had recently bought and talked about and which now hung in the hall. The work of some kindergarten oaf, it recalled in its technique the sort of drawing found in male lavatories, though its subject, an assortment of barrel-bodied animals debouching from the Ark, was of narrower appeal. On the other side was a high shelf with an array of copper and china utensils on it. Among them was Dixon's special Toby jug, and, sneering, he now fixed this with his eye. He hated that Toby jug, with its open black hat, its blurred, startled face, its spindle-limbs coalesced with its torso, more strenuously than any other inanimate occupant of this house, not excepting Welch's recorder. Its expression proved that it knew what he thought of it, and it could tell nobody. He put a thumb on each of his temples, waggled his hands at it, rolled his eyes, mouthed jeers and imprecations. A third Welch property now manifested itself, a young ginger cat called Id. It was the only survivor of a litter of three; the other two Mrs Welch had christened Ego and Super-Ego. Trying his best not to think of this, Dixon bent and tickled Id under the ear. He admired it for never allowing either of the senior Welches to pick it up. 'Scratch 'em,' he whispered to it; 'pee on the carpets.' It began to purr loudly.

As soon as Dixon had joined the company within, the leisurely tempo of his day jerked abruptly into frenzy. Welch wheeled towards him; Christine, more apple-cheeked even than he remembered her, was grinning at him in the background; Mrs Welch and Bertrand moved in his direction; Margaret turned her back. Welch said energetically: 'Oh, Faulkner.'

Dixon's nose twitched his glasses up. 'Yes, Professor.'

'At least, Dixon.' He hesitated, then went on with unprecedented fluency: 'I'm afraid there's been a bit of a mix-up, Dixon. I'd forgotten that we'd all promised to go to the theatre this evening with the Goldsmiths. We shall have to dine early, so I shall just have time to change and freshen up and drive us into town. There'll be room for you if you want a lift, you see. I'm sorry about it, of course, but I shall have to rush off now. We must have you over another time.'

Before he was out of the room, Mrs Welch moved up like an actress dead on her cue. Bertrand was at her side. Rather red in the face, she said: 'Oh, Mr Dixon, I've been wondering when I should see you again. I've one or two points I want to take up with you. First of all, I'd like you to explain, if you can, just what happened to the sheet and blankets on your bed when you were our guest here recently.' While Dixon was still trying to moisten his mouth enough to speak, she added: 'I'm waiting for an answer, Mr Dixon.' The Englishwoman in her seemed, for the moment, to have forged well ahead of the Western European.

Dixon noticed that Christine and Margaret had moved down the room together, talking quietly. 'I don't quite know what . . .' he mumbled. 'I didn't see . . .' How could he have forgotten what she'd said over the phone on the occasion of the Beesley-*Evening Post* impersonation? It hadn't crossed his mind once in the meantime.

'Am I to understand that you deny having had anything to do with the matter? If so, the only other possible culprit's my maid, in which case I shall have to . . .'

'No,' Dixon broke in, 'I don't deny it. Please, Mrs Welch, I'm desperately sorry about it all. I know I should have come to you and told you about it, but I'd done so much damage I was afraid to. It was silly, I hoped you somehow wouldn't find out, but I really knew you would, of course. Will you send me the bill for what it costs you to replace it? Blankets as well, I mean. I must make it good.' Thank God they still didn't know about the table.

'Of course you must, Mr Dixon. Before we discuss that, though, I want to hear how the damage was caused. Exactly what happened, please?'

'I know I've behaved very badly, Mrs Welch, but please don't ask me to explain that. I've apologized and promised to pay for the damage; won't you let me keep the explanation to myself? It's nothing very terrible, I can assure you of that.'

'Then why do you refuse to say what it is?'

'I don't refuse; I'm only asking you to spare me a lot of embarrassment that wouldn't help you at all.'

Bertrand now joined in. Putting his shaggy face on one side, he brought it nearer, saying: 'We can put up with that, Dixon. It won't hurt us to put up with your embarrassment. It'll be some kind of small return for the way you've behaved.'

His mother put a hand on his arm. 'No, don't interfere, darling. It won't do any good. Mr Dixon is used to being talked to like that, I'm sure. We can leave this; it doesn't alter the main facts of the situation. I want to get on to the next thing. I'm now fairly firmly convinced, Mr Dixon, that it was you who rang me up recently and pretended, in fact you lied when I asked you, pretended both to myself and to my son to be a newspaper reporter. It was you, wasn't it? It'll be much better if you admit it, you know. I haven't mentioned any of this to my husband, because I don't want to worry him, but I warn you that unless I get a satisfactory . . .'

Like a criminal who, having begun to confess, sees no reason for not going on, Dixon was about to admit it, but remembered in time that this would incriminate Christine. (How much, if anything, had Bertrand got out of her?) 'You're quite wrong there, Mrs Welch. I can't imagine why you should think any such thing. Your husband'll tell you I haven't been away once this term.'

'Haven't been away? I don't see how that affects matters.'

'Well, simply that I couldn't have been here and in London at the same time, could I?'

Restraining Bertrand, Mrs Welch said in puzzlement: 'What's that got to do with it?'

'How could I have phoned through from London if I was here all the time? I take it it was a London call?'

Bertrand looked questioningly at his mother. She shook her head and said quietly, hardly moving her mouth: 'No, it was a local call all right. Whoever it was spoke right away. You always get the operator first if it's a London call.'

'I told you you were wrong,' Bertrand said peevishly. 'I told you old David West was behind all this. Damn it, Christine was certain it was him on the phone to her, calling himself Atkinson. It was some pal of his who spoke to us, not . . .' His eye fell on Dixon and he stopped speaking.

Dixon was savouring his defensive triumph. He'd remember the advantages of pretending misunderstanding in this situation. And it was now clear, too, that Bertrand had got nothing out of Christine. 'Has that cleared things up at all?' he asked the others politely.

Mrs Welch began to go red again. 'I think I'll just go and see how your father's getting on, darling,' she said. 'There are one or two things I want him to . . .' Leaving the sentence in the air, she went out.

Bertrand moved a pace closer. 'We'll forget all about that business,' he said generously. 'Now, I've been wanting us to have a little get-together for quite some time, old boy. Ever since that Ball affair, in fact. Now look here: here's a question for you, and I don't mind telling you I mean to get a straight answer. What precisely was your game the other evening when you induced Christine to skip out of the dance with you? A straight answer, mind.'

This must all have been clearly audible to Christine, who now came down the room with Margaret. Both girls avoided Dixon's eye while they went out, leaving him alone with Bertrand. When the door was shut, Dixon said: 'I can't give any sort of answer, straight or crooked, to a meaningless question. What do you mean, what was my game? I wasn't playing any sort of game.'

'You know what I mean as well as I do. What were you up to?'

'You'd better ask Christine that.'

'We'll leave her out of this, if you don't mind.'

'Why should I mind?' Dixon, in spite of the thought of how Mrs Welch's bill would gobble up his bank-balance, suddenly began to exult. The preliminary manoeuvrings, the cold war between himself and Bertrand, were over at least. This was the whiff of grapeshot.

'Don't be funny, Dixon. Just tell me what was going on, will you? Or I shall have to try something a little more forcible.'

'Don't you be funny, either. What do you want to know?'

Bertrand clenched his fist; then, when Dixon took off his glasses and squared his shoulders, unclenched it again. Dixon put his glasses back on. 'I want to know . . .' Bertrand said, then hesitated.

'What my game was? We've been into that.'

'Shut up. What did you intend doing with Christine, that's what I want to know.'

'I intended doing exactly what I did do. I intended to go away from that place with Christine, to bring her back here in a taxi, and finally to return to my digs in the same taxi. That's what I did do.'

'Well, I'm not having that, do you understand?'

'It's too late not to have it. You've had it already.'

'Now just you get this straight in your head, Dixon. I've had enough of your merry little quips. Christine is my girl and she stays my girl, got mam?'

'If you mean do I follow your line of thought, I do.'

'That's splendid. Well, if I find you playing this sort of trick again, or any sort of bloody clever trick, I'll break your horrible neck for you and get you dismissed from your job as well. Understand?'

'Yes, I understand all right, but you're wrong if you think I'll let you break my neck for me, and if you think they chuck people out of academic jobs for taking their professors' sons' girl-friends home in taxis, then you're even more wrong, if possible.'

Bertrand's reply reassured Dixon that Bertrand hadn't so far found out from his father about Dixon's present standing in the eyes of College authority. The reply was: 'Don't think you can defy me and get away with it, Dixon. People never do.'

'People are beginning to, Welch. You must realize that it's up to Christine whether she sees any more of me. If you feel you must threaten someone, go and threaten her.'

Bertrand suddenly yelled out in a near-falsetto bay: 'I've had about enough of you, you little bastard. I won't stand any more of it, do you hear? To think of a lousy little philistine like you coming and monkeying about in my affairs, it's enough to . . . Get out and stay out, before you get hurt. Leave my girl alone, you're wasting your time, you're wasting her time, you're wasting my time. What the hell do you mean by buggering about like this? You're big enough and old enough and ugly enough to know better.'

Dixon was saved from replying by the sudden re-entry of Christine and Margaret. The scene broke up: Christine, who seemed to be trying to flash Dixon a message he couldn't read, took Bertrand by the arm and led him, still loudly protesting, out of the room; Margaret silently offered Dixon a cigarette, which he took. Neither spoke while they sat down side by side on a couch, nor for some moments afterwards. Dixon found himself trembling a good deal. He looked at Margaret and an intolerable weight fell upon him.

He knew now what he'd been trying to conceal from himself ever since the previous morning, what the row with Bertrand had made him temporarily disbelieve: he and Christine would not, after all, be able to eat tea together the following afternoon. If he was going to eat that meal with any female apart from Miss Cutler, it would be not Christine, but Margaret. He remembered a character in a modern novel Beesley had lent him who was always feeling pity moving in him like sickness, or some such jargon. The parallel was apt: he felt very ill.

'That was about the dance business, was it?' Margaret asked.

'Yes. He seemed to resent it all rather.'

'I'm not surprised. What was he shouting?'

'He was trying to persuade me to keep off the grass.'

'As far as she's concerned?'

'That's right.'

'Are you going to?'

'Eh?'

'Are you going to keep off the grass?'

'Yes.'

'Why, James?'

'Because of you.'

He'd been expecting a demonstration of some strong feeling or other here, but she only said 'I think that's rather silly of you' in a neutral tone that wasn't ostentatiously neutral, but simply neutral.

'What makes you say that?'

'I thought we got all that settled yesterday. I don't see the point of starting the whole thing over again.'

'It can't be helped. We'd have started it again some time; it might just as well be now.'

'Don't be ridiculous. You'd have much more fun with her than you ever had with me.'

'That's as may be. The point is that I've got to stick to you.' He said this without bitterness, nor did he feel any.

There was a short silence before she replied: 'I don't hold with these renunciations. You're throwing her away for a scruple. That's the action of a fool.'

This time, a minute or more went by before either spoke. Dixon felt that his role in this conversation, as indeed in the whole of his relations with Margaret, had been directed by something outside himself and yet not directly present in her. He felt more than ever before that what he said and did arose not out of any willing on his part, nor even out of boredom, but out of a kind of sense of situation. And where did that sense come from if, as it seemed, he took no share in willing it? With disquiet, he found that words were forming in his mind, words which, because he could think of no others, he'd very soon hear himself uttering. He got up, thinking that he might go to the window and somehow derive alternative speech from what he saw out of it, but before reaching it he turned and said: 'It isn't a matter of scruples; it's a matter of seeing what you've got to do.'

She said clearly: 'You're faking this up because you're frightened of me.'

He looked at her closely for the first time since she'd come back into the room. She was sitting there with her feet drawn up on the couch and her arms round her knees; her expression was one of intentness. She might have been discussing some academic point on which she was both informed and interested. He noticed that she was wearing much less make-up than usual. 'Not after yesterday,' he said. Again he wasn't conscious of having decided what to say.

'I don't know what you mean.'

'Never mind. Stop objecting like this. The whole thing's perfectly straightforward.'

'Not as far as I'm concerned, James. I can't understand you at all.'

'Yes you can.' He went and sat beside her again. 'Let's go to the pictures tonight. You can get out of the theatre. Carol won't mind, I know.'

'I wasn't going, anyway.'

'That's all right, then.'

He reached out and took her hand: she made no movement. There was another pause, during which they heard someone run heavily downstairs into the hall. Margaret glanced at him for a moment, then turned her head away. In a parched sort of voice, she said: 'All right, I'll come to the pictures.'

'Good.' Dixon felt glad it was over. 'I'll go and find Neddy and book a seat in the car. He can get six in all right. You go up and get ready.'

They went out into the hall, where Welch, now wearing a blue serge suit of startlingly extravagant cut, was to be seen admiring his picture. When Margaret said 'I shan't be a minute' and went up the stairs, Dixon reflected that their conversation, whatever its other peculiarities, had reflected an honesty on both sides that their relations had never shown before. That was something, anyway.

Welch's mouth opened at his approach, no doubt in preparation for some pronouncement beginning 'The point about child art, of course', but Dixon got in first by explaining that Margaret would also, if convenient, like a seat in the car. After a very brief visitation from his wondering frown, Welch nodded and walked with Dixon to the front door, which he opened. They went out on to the step. A light breeze was blowing and the sun shone through a thin tissue of cloud. The heat had gone out of the day.

'I'll just go and bring the car round,' Welch said. 'I'd quite forgotten we were going out, you see, or I wouldn't have garaged it. I shan't be a minute.'

He went off. As he did so, somebody else's step could be heard on the stairs. Dixon turned round and saw Christine coming towards him wearing a little black bolero, but otherwise dressed exactly as he'd seen her on the arty week-end. Perhaps these were the only ordinary clothes she had, in which case he oughtn't to have let her give him that pound for the taxi. She smiled at him and joined him on the step. 'I hope you didn't have too bad a time with Bertrand,' she said.

'Bertrand? Oh . . . no, it was all right.'

'I managed to calm him down after a bit.'

He watched her; she stood with her legs apart and looked very sturdy and confident. The breeze blew a small lock of fair hair the wrong way, half-across the parting. She screwed up her eyes slightly as she faced the sun. It was as if she were about to do something dangerous, important, and simple which she knew she could have a creditable shot at whether she succeeded or not. A feeling of grief that was also a feeling of exasperation settled upon Dixon. He looked away over the fields beyond the nearby hedge to where a line of osiers marked the bed of a small stream. A crowd of rooks, perhaps a couple of hundred, flew towards the house, then, directly above the stream, swerved aside along its course.

'About this tea tomorrow,' Dixon said, half-turning back to Christine.

'Yes?' she said, looking a little nervous. 'What about it?' As she said this, Welch started up his car at the side of the house. She added: 'You needn't worry. I'll be there all right.' Before he could reply she glanced over her shoulder into the hall and shook her finger at him, frowning.

Bertrand came out on to the step, glancing from one of them to the other. He was wearing a blue beret, which had much the same effect on Dixon as Welch senior's fishing-hat. If such headgear was a protection, what was it a protection against? If it wasn't a protection, what was it? What was it for? What was it for?

As if divining what he wanted to ask, Christine again frowned at him, then at Bertrand. 'Now whatever you two think of each other,' she said, 'for goodness' sake pull yourselves together, both of you, and behave decently in front of Mr and Mrs Welch. I thought you'd both gone off your heads just now.'

'I was only telling him where he . . .' Bertrand began.

'Well, you're not going to tell him anything now,' she turned to Dixon, 'and you're not going to tell him anything. If you start quarrelling in the car I'll jump out.'

They stood apart from each other for a few moments, while Dixon's regret concentrated on the fact that to abandon the pursuit of Christine meant imposing a cease-fire in the Bertrand campaign. Then Welch's car, with its owner at the wheel, came bouncing round the corner and the three of them moved towards it. Mrs Welch, accompanied by Margaret, came out of the house, shut the front door, and joined them, not looking at Dixon. A rather undignified scramble for places now ensued, ending with Dixon in occupation of the middle of the triple front seat with Margaret on his left. Behind them sat Mrs Welch, Christine, and Bertrand. Dixon thought the arrangement prettily symmetrical. Breathing noisily, Welch snatched his foot off the clutch-pedal, and, in the kangaroo mode to which it must by now be accustomed, the car started on its journey.

19

Dixon looked at the telephone where it stood on a black plush cloth in the middle of a bamboo table situated in Miss Cutler's drawing-room. He felt like an alcoholic surveying a bottle of gin; only by using it could he obtain the relief he wanted, but its side-effects, as recent experience had proved, were likely to be deleterious. He must cancel the tea-date with Christine, now only six hours ahead. To do that he must take the chance of Mrs Welch answering the phone. This, in other circumstances a certain deter-rent, he'd decided to risk in preference to keeping the date and telling Christine to her face that their little adventure was at an end. The thought of such a meeting being their last was not to be endured. He sat down by the phone, gave the number, and in a few seconds heard Mrs Welch's voice. It didn't discompose him, but before saying anything he made his lascar's face in order to draw off his anger. Did Mrs Welch spend all her time sitting, had she perhaps had a bed made up, within arm's length of the phone in case he might ring up?

'Trying to connect you,' he fluted as he'd planned. 'Hallo, who is that?'

Mrs Welch mentioned her number.

'Speak up, London,' he went on; 'you're through.' Then he jammed his teeth together, opened his mouth laterally as far as he could, and said in a growling over-cultured bass: 'Hallaher, halla-her,' following this with a whinnying 'You're through, London' and, in the bass voice 'Hallaher, have yaw a Miss Kellerhen steng with yaw, plizz?' He made a rushing noise with his mouth which he thought imitated line disturbances.

'Who's that speaking, please?'

Dixon rocked to and fro as if in grief, bringing his mouth up to the phone and back again as he spoke: 'Hallaher, hallaher. Forteskyah hyah.'

'I'm sorry, I didn't quite catch . . .'

'Forteskyaw . . . Farteskyaw . . .'

'Who is that speaking? It sounds like . . .'

'Hallaher . . . Is thet yaw, Miss Kellerhen?'

'Is that you, Mr . . . ?'

'Farteskyah,' Dixon bawled desperately, muffling his mouth with his hand and trying not to cough.

'That's Mr Dixon, isn't it? What are you trying to . . . ?'

'Hallaher . . .'

'Kindly stop this . . . ridiculous, this . . .'

'Three minutes up,' he neighed, slobbering. 'Finish off, please, time's up.' He added a last throat-peeling 'Hallaher', the phone at the full length of his arm, and fell silent. This was a rout.

'If you're still there, Mr Dixon,' Mrs Welch said after a moment, in a voice sharpened to excoriation by the intervening few miles of line, 'I'd like to tell you that if you make one more attempt to interfere in my son's or my affairs, then I shall have to ask my husband to take the matter up with you from a disciplinary point of view, and also that other matter of the . . .'

Dixon rang off. 'Sheet,' he said. Trembling, he reached for his cigarettes; in the last few days he'd given up all attempt to ration himself. He'd have to keep his date now; a telegram would be too curt. And Mrs Welch would probably station herself so as to intercept it anyway. As he was lighting his cigarette, the bell of the phone went off within two feet of his head; he started violently and began coughing, then took up the phone. Who could this be? An oboist for Johns, most likely, or perhaps a clarinettist. He said 'Hallo.'

A voice he realized with relief was quite strange to him said: 'Oh, have you a Mr Dixon living there, please?'

'Speaking.'

'Oh, Mr Dixon, I'm so glad I've got to you. Your University gave me the number. My name's Catchpole; I expect you've heard of me from Margaret Peel.'

Dixon grew tense. 'Yes, I have,' he said noncommittally. It wasn't the sort of voice he'd have expected Catchpole to have; it was quiet, polite, and apparently diffident.

'I rang up because I thought you might be able to give some news of Margaret. I've been away recently, and I haven't managed to get to hear anything of her since I got back. How is she these days, do you know?'

'Why don't you get hold of her and ask her yourself? Or perhaps you've tried that and she won't speak to you. Well, I can understand that.' Dixon began to tremble again.

'I think there must be some mistake about . . .'

'I've got her address, but I don't see why I should give it to you, of all people.'

'Mr Dixon, I can't understand why you're taking that tone. All I want to know is how Margaret is. There can't be anything objectionable about that, can there?'

'I warn you that if you're thinking of making a comeback with her, you're wasting your time, see?'

'I don't know what you mean by that. Are you sure you haven't got me confused with someone else?'

'Your name's Catchpole, isn't it?'

'Yes. Please . . .'

'Well, I know who you are all right, then. And all about you.'

'Please give me a hearing, Mr Dixon.' The voice at the other end shook slightly. 'I just wanted to know whether Margaret is all right or not. Won't you even tell me that?'

Dixon calmed down at this appeal. 'All right, I will. She's in quite good health physically. Mentally, she's about as well as can be expected.'

'Thanks very much. I'm glad to hear that. Do you mind if I ask you one more question?'

'What is it?'

'Why were you so angry with me a moment ago when I asked you about her?'

'That's pretty obvious, isn't it?'

'Not to me, I'm afraid. I think we're talking rather at cross-purposes, aren't we? I can't think of any reason why you should have a grudge against me. No real reason, that is.'

It sounded remarkably sincere. 'Well, I can,' Dixon said, unable to keep the puzzlement out of his voice.

'There's some kind of mix-up here, I can see that. I'd like to meet you some time, if I may, and try to straighten things out. We can't do it over the phone. What about it?'

Dixon hesitated. 'All right. What do you suggest?'

They arranged to meet for a pre-lunch drink in a pub at the foot of College Road the next day but one, Thursday. When Catchpole had rung off, Dixon sat for some minutes smoking. It was worrying, but then most of the things that had happened to him recently were that, and a good deal more besides. Anyway, he'd turn up and see what was what. Keep quiet about it to Margaret, of course. With a sigh he referred to the pocket diary for 1943 in which he wrote down telephone numbers, pulled the phone towards him again, and gave a London number. In a little while he said: 'Is Dr Caton there, please?'

There was another brief delay, then a rich confident voice came clearly over the line: 'This is Caton.'

Dixon gave his name and that of his College.

For some reason, the richness and confidence of the other voice waned sharply. 'What do you want?' it asked snappishly.

'I read about your appointment, Dr Caton – incidentally may I offer my congratulations? – and I was wondering what was going to happen to that article of mine you were good enough to accept for your journal. Can you tell me when it'll come out?'

'Ah, now, Mr Dickerson, things are very difficult these days, you know.' The voice was confident again, as if reciting a saying-lesson it knew it knew. 'There's quite a lot of stuff waiting to go in, as you can imagine. You really mustn't expect your article – which I liked very much, I may say – to go in in five minutes, you know.'

'I appreciate that, Dr Caton; I can quite understand there must be a long queue. I was just wondering if you could give me some sort of tentative date, that's all.'

'I wish you knew how difficult things are here, Mr Dickerson. Setting up our kind of stuff in type is a job which only an exceptionally highly-skilled compositor can tackle. Have you ever thought what slow work it must be getting even half a page of footnotes set up?'

'No, but I can quite see it must be a very complicated matter. All I wanted to know, actually, is a rough idea of when you think you could manage to get my article out.'

'Well, as to that, Mr Dickerson, things aren't by any means as simple as they may look to you. You probably know Hardy of Trinity; I've had a thing of his at the printers for weeks now, and two or three times a day, or even more, I get them coming through on the phone with some query or other. Very often, of course, I just have to refer them to him, when it's a question of a foreign document or something of that kind. I know chaps in your position think an editor's job's all beer and skittles; it's very far from being that, believe me.'

'I'm sure it must be most exacting, Dr Caton, and of course I wouldn't dream of trying to pin you down to anything definite, but it's rather important to me to have some estimate of when you'll be able to publish my article.'

'I can't start making promises to have your article out next week,' the voice said in a nettled tone, as if Dixon had been stupidly insisting on this one point, 'with things as difficult as they are. Surely you must see that. You don't seem to realize the amount of planning that goes into each number, especially a first number. It's not like drawing up a railway timetable, what? what?' he finished, loudly and suspiciously.

Dixon wondered if, without knowing it, he'd allowed an imprecation to pass his lips. A hollow, metallic tapping had begun on the line, like galvanized iron being hammered in a cathedral. In a louder voice he said: 'I'm sure it isn't, and I'm quite resigned to the delay. But to be quite frank, Dr Caton, I want rather urgently to improve my standing in the Department here, and if I could just quote you, if you could give me a . . .'

'I'm sorry to hear of your difficulties, Mr Dickinson, but I'm afraid things are too difficult here for me to be very seriously concerned about your difficulties. There are plenty of people in your position, you know; I don't know what I should do if they all started demanding promises from me in this fashion.'

'But Dr Caton, I haven't been asking you for a promise. All I want is an estimate, and even the vaguest estimate would help me – "the second half of next year" for example. You won't be committing yourself in the least by just giving me an estimate.' There was a silence which Dixon interpreted as one of maturing rage. 'Could I have your permission to say "the second half of next year" when I'm asked?'

Though Dixon waited for ten seconds or more, nothing answered him except the metallic tapping, which had increased in volume and pace.

'Things are very difficult, things are very difficult, things are very difficult,' Dixon gabbled into the phone, then mentioned a few difficult things which occurred to him as suitable tasks for Dr Caton to have a go at. Still devising variations of this theme, he went out muttering to himself, wagging his head and shoulders like a puppet. A rival to Welch had appeared in the field of evasion-technique, verbal division, and in the physical division of the same field this chap had Welch whacked at the start: self-removal to South America was the traditional climax of an evasive career. Up in his room, Dixon filled his lungs to their utmost and groaned for half a minute or more without drawing breath. He got out the notes for his lecture and went on working them up into a script.

Five hours later, he had what he estimated as forty-four minutes' worth of lecture. It seemed by then as if there were no facts anywhere in the universe, in his own brain or anyone else's or just lying about loose, which could possibly be brought within his present scope. And even so, he'd been travelling for a large part of his forty-four minutes along the knife-edge dividing the conceivably-just-about-relevant from the irreducibly, immitigably irrelevant. The fifteen minutes needed to top the thing up to the fifty-nine minutes he'd set himself would have to be occupied by a presumably rather extensive conclusion, and he didn't want to write one of those. Something on the lines of 'Finally, thank God for the twentieth century' would satisfy him, but it wouldn't satisfy Welch. Then he seized his pencil again, gave a happy laugh, and wrote: 'This survey, brief as it is, would have no purpose if left as a mere' – he crossed out 'mere' – 'historical record. There are valuable lessons here for us, living in an age of prefabricated amusements as we do. One wonders how one of the men or women I have tried to describe would react to such typically modern phenomena as the cinema, the radio, the television. What would he think, accustomed as he was (had been? would have been? is?) to making his own music (must look at Welch at this point), of a society where people like himself are regarded as oddities, where to play an instrument himself, oneself, instead of paying others to do so, to sing a madrigal instead of a cheap dance-lyric, is to incur the dreaded title of "crank", where . . .'

He stopped writing and ran out into the bathroom. He started washing with frenzied speed. He'd left it just late enough; with luck he'd have time to get ready and rush along to the hotel for tea with Christine, but no time to think about tea with Christine. Nevertheless, for all the energy of his movements, he began to feel a little queasy with apprehension.

He arrived at the hotel two minutes late. On turning into the lounge where tea was served, he felt a pang of fear, or whatever emotion it was, kicking at his diaphragm when he saw Christine already sitting waiting for him. He'd counted on a few minutes' grace to think of things to say to her; if it had been Margaret, he'd have had them and more.

She smiled as he approached. 'Hallo, Jim.'

He was feeling physically very nervous. 'Hallo' he said with a half-cough. Fighting off temptations to see that his tie was straight, his pocket-flaps not tucked in, his flies buttoned, he sat down cautiously in front of her. Today she wore a jacket of the same material as her plum-coloured skirt, and these and the white blouse all seemed newly ironed. She looked unmanningly pretty, so much so that Dixon's head began to spin with the effort of thinking of something to say, something different from what he'd come on purpose to say.

'How are you?' she asked.

'All right, thanks; I've been working. You managed to get away without any fuss, I hope?'

'I don't know about without any fuss.'

'Oh, I'm sorry to hear that. What happened?'

'I think Bertrand was rather suspicious. I told him there were one or two things I wanted to do in town. I didn't mention anything in particular, because I thought that would have looked a bit . . .'

'Quite. And how did he take that?'

'Not too well. He came back with a lot of things about me being my own mistress, and I was to do what I wanted to do, and wasn't to feel I was tied in any way. It made me feel rather mean.'

'I can understand that all right.'

She leant forward and put her elbows on the low circular table between them. 'You see, Jim, in a way I think it was rather a bad thing my coming to meet you at all. But I'd said I would and so I had to come. And, of course, I still wanted to, just as much as I did when you asked me. But I've been thinking it all over, and I've decided . . . Look, shall we have our tea first, and then talk about it?'

'No, tell me now, whatever it is you want to say.'

'All right, then. It's this, Jim: I think I was a bit carried away by one thing and another then, when you asked me to come today, I mean. I think I wouldn't have said I'd come if I'd had time to think what I was doing. I'd still have wanted to come just as much, though. I'm sorry to have got on to this straight away, we've hardly had time to say hallo to each other, but you can see what I'm leading up to, can't you?'

Dixon didn't reflect that this attitude would make his task an easy one. He said in a flat voice: 'You mean you don't want to go on with this?'

'I don't really see how we could go on with it, do you? I wish I'd left all this till later, but it's been rather on my mind. You see, you're sort of stuck up here, aren't you? Or do you get to London fairly often?'

'No, I hardly ever go there.'

'Well then, the only chance we'd have to see each other would be when Bertrand asked me to come and stay with his parents, like now, and I wouldn't feel right about sneaking off to see you the whole time. And in any case . . .' She stopped and made a facial movement which caused Dixon to turn round in his chair.

A youthful waiter had approached, his footfalls silenced by the carpet, and was now shifting from one foot to the other close by, breathing through his mouth. Dixon thought he'd never seen a human frame radiating so much insolence without recourse to speech, gesture, or any contortion of the features. This figure swung a silver tray in an attempt at careless grace, and was looking past Dixon at Christine. When Dixon said 'Tea for two, please' the waiter smiled faintly at her, as if in lofty but sincere commiseration, then swung aside, allowing the tray to rebound from his kneecap as he walked off.

'Sorry; what were you saying?' Dixon said.

'It's just that I am, oh, tied up with Bertrand, that's all. It's not so much a question of having obligations towards him or anything like that. I just don't want to behave foolishly. Not that I think there's anything foolish about coming to see you. Oh, I just don't seem to be able to put it in any way that sounds at all sensible.' Little by little and intermittently, she was adopting her 'dignant' tone and physical attitude. 'I'm afraid all I can ask you to do is try to understand. I know that's what people always say, and I don't feel I understand very well myself, so how I can expect you to I don't know, but there it is.'

'You're going back on what you said about being rather fed-up with Bertrand, then?'

'No, all that's still quite true. What I'm trying to do now is take the rough with the smooth. The rough parts are still as rough as they were when we talked about it in the taxi. But I must make an effort; I mustn't walk out of things just when I feel like it, I can't go about expecting people to behave as I want them to the whole time. There's bound to be a certain amount of up and down in a relationship like the one I'm having with Bertrand. It's no use getting in a paddy about that, it's got to be accepted, even if I don't want to accept it. The trouble is I've got to push you around while I'm doing it.'

'Don't worry about that,' Dixon said. 'You must do as you think best.'

'Whatever I do can't be very satisfactory,' she said. 'I feel I've been very stupid the whole way through.' Though her pose was now complete, Dixon barely noticed it. 'What I want to stop you thinking is that I was being frivolous about, you know, letting you kiss me and saying I'd come today, and all that. And I meant everything I said; I wouldn't have said it otherwise. And I don't want you to think that I was doing it just for fun or that I've decided since I don't like you enough, or anything like that. It's not like that and you're not to think it is.'

'That's all right, Christine. You can forget about that part of it. Oh . . . here we are.'

The waiter reappeared at Dixon's side with a loaded tray. This he half-lowered, half-dropped to within an inch of the table; then, with an offensive exaggeration of care, he laid it soundlessly to rest. Straightening up, he gave another smile, this time at Dixon, paused, as if to emphasize his non-intention of setting out any of the tea-things, and moved off counterfeiting a heavy limp.

Christine began moving crockery about and pouring tea. When she gave him his cup she said: 'I'm sorry, Jim. I didn't want to be like this about it. Have a sandwich?'

'No thanks, I don't want anything to eat.'

She nodded and began eating with every appearance of appetite. Dixon was interested by this conventional absence of conventional sensitivity; for almost the first time in his life a woman was behaving in a way alleged to be typical of women. 'After all,' she said, 'you've got your commitments with Margaret, haven't you?'

He sighed rather tremulously; although the worst part of the encounter was theoretically over, without yet having had on him the numbing effect he knew it soon would have, he still felt nervous. 'Yes,' he replied. 'That was what I was going to tell you about this afternoon, only you got in first. I came here to tell you that I thought we shouldn't see any more of each other from my own point of view, because of my business with Margaret.'

'I see.' She began eating another sandwich.

'Things have all rather come to a head in the last few days, as a matter of fact. Since the Ball, really.'

She looked at him quickly. 'There was a row over that, was there?'

'Well, yes, I suppose you could say that. A good deal more than a row, actually.'

'There you are, you see. I was causing all sorts of trouble by sneaking off with you like that.'

'Don't be silly, Christine,' Dixon said irritably. 'You're talking as if you were the one who initiated everything. If anybody was responsible for all sorts of trouble, as you call it, it was me. Not that I think I'm much to blame for anything, any more than you were. It was all perfectly natural. All this self-reproach strikes me as a bit forced.'

'I'm sorry; I must have put it badly. I wasn't forcing anything as far as I knew.'

'No, I don't suppose you were for a moment. I didn't mean to sound hot under the collar. The Margaret business has been getting me down rather.'

'How bad was it? What did she say to you?'

'Oh, she said all sorts of things. There wasn't much she could have said she didn't say.'

'You make it sound pretty formidable. What actually went on?'

Dixon sighed again and drank some tea. 'It's all so . . . complicated. I don't want to bore you with it.'

'You won't bore me. I'd like to hear, if you feel you want to tell me. It's your turn, after all.'

The grin she gave with this remark nearly put Dixon right off his stroke. Was she really finding this funny? 'That's right,' he said heavily. 'Well, there's a lot of past history that's all mixed up with it, you see. She's a decent girl really, and I like her a lot, at least I would if she'd only let me. But I've got tied up with her without really meaning to, though I know that sounds ridiculous. When I first met her, last October some time, she was going round with a fellow called Catchpole . . .' He gave a compressed, but otherwise only slightly edited, account of his past relations with Margaret, finishing with their visit to the pictures the previous evening. He gave a cigarette to Christine, who'd eaten all the food the waiter had brought, took one himself, and said: 'So now it's all more or less on again, though I shouldn't like to have to explain just what it is that's more or less on again, and on's a bit vague too. I don't think she knows quite how interested I've been in you, by the way, and I don't imagine she'd thank me for telling her.'

Christine avoided his eyes, puffing amateurishly at her cigarette. She asked in a disinterested tone: 'How do you think she seemed when you left her?'

'Just the same as she'd been all the evening, quite quiet and apparently sensible. Oh, I know that sounds pretty offensive; I don't quite mean that, I mean she . . . well, she wasn't so excitable, there wasn't any of the nervous tension about her that there usually is.'

'Do you think she'll go on being like that, now that she feels things are more settled?'

'Well, I must admit I have been beginning to hope . . .' Now that the hope was voiced, it seemed ludicrously naïve. 'Oh, I don't know. It doesn't make much difference anyway.'

'You sound pretty miserable about the whole business.'

'Do I? It hasn't been easy, certainly.'

'No, and it's not going to get any easier, is it?' When Dixon, irritated by this question, said nothing, she went on, tapping ash into a saucer: 'I don't suppose you want me to say this, but you must realize it yourself, I should think. I don't see how either of you can be very happy with the other one.'

Dixon tried to suppress his irritation. 'No, I don't suppose we can, but there's nothing to be done about it. It's just that we can't split up, that's all.'

'Well, what are you going to do, then? Are you going to get engaged to her or anything?'

It was the same curiosity as she'd shown some weeks ago about his drinking habits. 'I don't know,' he said coldly, trying not to think about getting engaged to Margaret. 'I suppose it's possible, if things carry on as they are for a time.'

She didn't seem to notice his unfriendly tone. Shifting in her seat, she glanced round the room, then said didactically: 'Well, it looks as if we're both taken care of, doesn't it? It's just as well.'

The authoritative vapidity of this reacted with Dixon's general feeling of peevish regret and made him begin to talk fast. 'Yes, there's not really much to choose between us when you look into it. You're keeping up your little affair with Bertrand because you think that on the whole it's safer to do that, in spite of the risks attached to that kind of thing, than to chance your arm with me. You know the snags about him, but you don't know what snags there might be about me. And I'm sticking to Margaret because I haven't got the guts to turn her loose and let her look after herself, so I do that instead of doing what I want to do, because I'm afraid to. It's just a sort of stodgy, stingy caution that's the matter with us; you can't even call it looking after number one.' He looked at her with faint contempt, and was hurt to see the same feeling in the way she looked at him. 'That's all there is to it; and the worst of it is I shall go on doing exactly what I was going to do in the first place. It just shows how little it helps you to know where you stand.' For some reason, this last remark brought into his mind the thought that a few words from him could dispose of Christine's attachment to Bertrand; he'd only to tell her what Carol had told him. But she probably knew, perhaps she was so devoted to Bertrand that she wouldn't break with him even over a thing like that, would rather have half of him than nothing at all. And, anyway, what would she think of him if he came out with it at this point? No, he might as well forget about that. It seemed there'd never be a valid opportunity to make that disclosure to anyone, which was cruelly unfair, considering how loyally he'd kept his mouth shut and how long he'd waited for the right moment.

Christine had bowed her head – how well-brushed her hair was – over the saucer where she was stubbing out her cigarette. 'I think you're making a bit of a fuss, more than you need, don't you? Nothing's happened between us to speak of, has it?' She still kept her face down.

'Agreed, but that's not the way to judge . . .'

She met his eyes now, her face flushed, and this silenced him. 'I think it's silly to talk the way you were talking,' she said, with a faint cockney intonation about her voice that he'd half-noticed before. 'You seemed to think you'd proved something by saying all that. Of course that's what we're doing; you talk as if that's all we're doing. Don't you think people ever do things because they want to do them, because they want to do what's for the best? I don't see how it helps to call trying to do the right thing caution and lack of guts. Doing what you know you've got to do's horrible sometimes, but that doesn't mean to say it isn't worth doing. There was something you said, it made me think you've got the idea I sleep with Bertrand. You can't know much about women if you think that. No wonder you're having a rough time if that's the sort of thing you think. You're the sort of man who'd never be happy whatever you did. I think I'll go now, Jim; there's not much point in . . .'

'No, don't go,' Dixon said in agitation. Things were happening much too fast for him. 'Don't be angry. Stay a little longer.'

'I'm not angry. I'm just fed-up with it all.'

'So am I.'

'Four shillings,' the waiter said at Dixon's side. His voice, heard now for the first time, suggested that he had a half-eaten sweet at the back of his throat.

Dixon searched his pockets and gave him two half-crowns. He was glad of the interruption, which allowed him time to recover something of his emotional balance. When they were alone, he said: 'Are we ever going to see each other again, then?'

'Once more, anyway. I'm coming to your lecture, and to the sherry-party at the Principal's before it.'

'Oh, God, Christine, you don't want to come to that, you'll be bored stiff. How have you let yourself in for that?'

'Uncle Julius has been asked by the Principal, and it seems he said he'd come in a weak moment, and now he insists on me coming to keep him company.'

'Rather queer.'

'He said he was looking forward to meeting you again.'

'Why the hell did he say that? I've hardly said two words to the man.'

'Well, that's what he said. Don't ask me what he meant.'

'I shall see you at a distance, then, anyway. Good thing, really.'

Christine suddenly said in a different voice: 'No it isn't a good thing really. How can it be? It'll be wonderful fun, won't it? Standing there chatting away to Bertrand and Uncle Julius and the rest of them like a good little girl. Oh yes, I shall be having a fine time, thanks very much. It's all so . . . It's intolerable.' She stood up and so did Dixon, who could find nothing to say. 'That's about enough of that. This time I really am going. Thank you for the tea.'

'Give me your address, Christine.'

She looked at him scornfully, her brown eyes dilated under the dark eyebrows. 'That'll do no good at all. What on earth would be the point?'

'It would make me feel we hadn't seen the last of each other.'

'Well, there's no point in feeling that, is there?' She went quickly past him and out of the room without looking back.

Dixon sat down again and smoked another cigarette with an

almost-cold half-cup of tea. He wouldn't have thought it possible that a man who'd done so exactly what he'd set out to do could feel so violent a sense of failure and general uselessness. He reflected for a moment that if Christine looked like Margaret and Margaret looked like Christine his spirits would now be very much higher. But that was to speculate about nonentities: Margaret with Christine's face and body could never have turned into Margaret. All that could logically be said was that Christine was lucky to look so nice. It was luck you needed all along; with just a little more luck he'd have been able to switch his life on to a momentarily adjoining track, a track destined to swing aside at once away from his own. He gave a start and jumped up; it must be nearly time for the examiners' meeting. Averting his attention from the thought that Margaret would be there, he went out, then came back again and approached the waiter, who was leaning against the wall. 'Can I have my change, please?'

'Change?'

'Yes, change. Can I have it, please?'

'Five shillings you give me.'

'Yes. The bill was four shillings. I want a shilling back.'

'Wasn't that for my tip?'

'It might have been, but it isn't now. Give it to me.'

'The whole shilling?'

'Yes. All of it. Now. Give it to me.'

The waiter made no attempt to produce any money. In his half-choked voice he said: 'Most people give me a tip.'

'Most people would have kicked your arse for you by now. If you don't give me my change in the next five seconds I shall call the Manager.'

Four seconds later Dixon was on the way out of the hotel into the sunlight, his shilling in his pocket.

20

'What, finally, is the practical application of all this? Can anything be done to halt, or even to hinder, the process I have described? I say to you that something can be done by each one of us here tonight. Each of us can resolve to do something, every day, to resist the application of manufactured standards, to protest against ugly articles of furniture and table-ware, to speak out against sham architecture, to resist the importation into more and more public places of loudspeakers relaying the Light Programme, to say one word against the Yellow Press, against the best-seller, against the theatre-organ, to say one word for the instinctive culture of the integrated village-type community. In that way we shall be saying a word, however small in its individual effect, for our native tradition, for our common heritage, in short, for what we once had and may, some day, have again – Merrie England.'

With a long, jabbering belch, Dixon got up from the chair where he'd been writing this and did his ape imitation all round the room. With one arm bent at the elbow so that the fingers brushed the armpit, the other crooked in the air so that the inside of the forearm lay across the top of his head, he wove with bent knees and hunched, rocking shoulders across to the bed, upon which he jumped up and down a few times, gibbering to himself. A knock at his door was followed so quickly by the entry of Bertrand that he only had time to stop gibbering and straighten his body.

Bertrand, who was wearing his blue beret, looked at him. 'What are you doing up there?'

'I like it up here, thanks. Any objection?'

'Come down and stop clowning. I've got a few things to say to you, and you'd better listen.' He seemed in a controlled rage, and was breathing heavily, though this might well have been the result of running up two flights of stairs.

Dixon jumped lightly down to the floor; he, too, was panting a little. 'What do you want to say?'

'Just this. The last time I saw you, I told you to stay away from Christine. I now discover you haven't done so. What have you got to say about that, to start with?'

'What do you mean, I haven't stayed away from her?'

'Don't try that on with me, Dixon. I know all about your surreptitious little cup of tea with her on the sly yesterday. I'm on to you all right.'

'Oh, she told you about that, did she?'

Bertrand tightened his lips behind the beard, which looked as if it could do with a comb-out. 'No no, of course she didn't,' he said violently. 'If you knew her at all, you'd know she didn't do things like that. She's not like you. If you really want to know – and I hope it'll give you a kick – it was one of your so-called pals in this house who told my mother about it. You ought to enjoy thinking about that. Everybody hates you, Dixon, and my God I can see why. Anyway, the point is I want an explanation of your conduct.'

'Oh dear,' Dixon said with a smile, 'I'm afraid that's rather a tall order. Explain my conduct; now that is asking something. I can't think of anybody who'd be quite equal to that task.' He was watching Bertrand closely, filing away the news of this latest blow from Johns – who else could it be? – for later pondering and appropriate action.

'Cut it out,' Bertrand said, flushing. 'I gave you a straight warning to leave Christine alone. When I say that sort of thing I expect people to have the sense to do as I say. Why haven't you? Eh?'

Bertrand's rage, and the mere fact of his visit here, combined nicely with their superfluousness, in view of Dixon's having already given up his interest in Christine for other reasons and so abandoning the Bertrand campaign. But he'd be a fool not to keep that to himself for a bit and enjoy himself with a spot of sniping. 'I didn't want to,' he said.

There was a pause, during which Bertrand twice seemed on the point of uttering a long inarticulate bay. His unusual eyes looked like polished glass. Then, in a quieter voice than before, he said: 'Look here, Dixon, you don't seem quite to appreciate what you've got yourself into. Allow me to explain.' He sat down on the arm of the Pall Mall chair and removed his beret, which went rather oddly with the dark suit, white collar, and vine-patterned tie he wore. Dixon sat down on the bed, which whimpered softly beneath him.

'This business between Christine and myself,' Bertrand said, fiddling with his beard, 'is a serious business, unquestionably. We've known each other for some considerable period of time. And we're not in it just for a spot of the old slap and tickle, do you follow. I don't want to get married yet awhile, but it's distinctly on the cards that I might marry Christine in a couple of years or so. What I mean is, it's a long-term affair, quite definitely. Now, Christine's very young, younger even than her age. She's not used to having individuals abducting her from dances and inviting her to off-the-record tea-parties in hotels and all the rest of it. In the circumstances, it's only natural she should feel flattered by it, enjoy the excitement of it, and so on, for a time. But only for a time, Dixon. Very soon she's going to start feeling guilty about it and wishing she'd never agreed to meet you at all. And that's where the trouble's going to start; being the sort of girl she is, she's going to feel bad about getting rid of you, and about doing things behind my back – she doesn't know I know about this yet – and about the whole shooting-match. Well, I want to prevent all that, for the very adequate reason that it's not going to help me at all. I've had quite a time straightening her out already; I don't want to have to start all over again. So what I want to say to you is, keep off the grass, that's all. You're causing nothing but trouble by behaving as you are. You won't do yourself any good, and you'll only hurt Christine and inconvenience me. She's got a few days more down here, and it would be silly to spoil them for all concerned. Does that make sense, now?'

Dixon had lit a cigarette to hide the effect on him of this account of Christine's motives; it was more penetrating than he'd have expected from Bertrand. 'Yes, it makes sense all right, up to a point,' he said in what he hoped was a casual tone. 'Except for the part about straightening Christine out, of course, which is mere wishful drooling. Never mind that, though; it all obviously makes very good sense to you. None of it does to me, though. You don't seem to realize that it's all only all right if your first assumptions are right.'

'I'm telling you that they're right, my lad,' Bertrand said loudly. 'That's what I'm telling you.'

'Yes, I noticed that. But don't expect me to make your assumptions. It's my turn to tell you something now. The serious, long-term part of this business isn't anything to do with you and Christine. Oh no, it's to do with me and Christine. What's happening isn't me unnecessarily distracting her from you. It's you unnecessarily distracting her from me – just for the moment. It won't go on much longer. How's that for sense, now?'

Bertrand rose to his feet again and faced Dixon with his legs slightly apart. He spoke in a level tone, but his teeth were clenched. 'Just get this straight in your so-called mind. When I see something I want, I go for it. I don't allow people of your sort to stand in my way. That's what you're leaving out of account. I'm having Christine because it's my right. Do you understand that? If I'm after something, I don't care what I do to make sure that I get it. That's the only law I abide by; it's the only way to get things in this world. The trouble with you, Dixon, is that you're simply not up to my weight. If you want a fight, pick someone your own size, then you might stand a chance. With me you just haven't a hope in hell.'

Dixon moved a pace nearer. 'You're getting a bit too old for that to work any more, Welch,' he said quickly. 'People aren't going to skip out of your path indefinitely. You think that just because you're tall and can put paint on canvas you're a sort of demigod. It wouldn't be so bad if you really were. But you're not: you're a twister and a snob and a bully and a fool. You think you're sensitive, but you're not: your sensitivity only works for things that people do to you. Touchy and vain, yes, but not sensitive.' He paused, but Bertrand was only staring at him, making no attempt to interrupt. Dixon went on: 'You've got the idea that you're a great lover, but that's wrong too: you're so afraid of me, who's nothing more than a louse according to you, that you have to march in here and tell me to keep off the grass like a heavy husband. And you're so dishonest that you can tell me how important Christine is to you without it entering your head that you're carrying on with some other chap's wife all the time. It's not just that that I object to; it's the way you never seem to reflect how insincere . . .'

'What the bloody hell are you talking about?' Bertrand's breath was whistling through his nose. He clenched his fists.

'Your spot of the old slap and tickle with Carol Goldsmith. That's what I'm talking about.'

'I don't know what you're talking . . .'

'Oh, my dear fellow, don't start denying it. Why bother, anyway? Surely it's just one of the things you have because it's your right, isn't it?'

'If you ever tell this tale to Christine, I'll break your neck into so many . . .'

'It's all right, I'm not the sort to do that,' Dixon said with a grin. 'I'm not like you. I can take Christine away from you without that, you Byronic tail-chaser.'

'All right, you've got it coming,' Bertrand bayed furiously. 'I warned you.' He came and stood over Dixon. 'Come on, stand up, you dirty little bar-fly, you nasty little jumped-up turd.'

'What are we going to do, dance?'

'I'll give you dance, I'll make you dance, don't you worry. Just stand up, if you're not afraid to. If you think I'm going to sit back and take this from you, you're mistaken; I don't happen to be that type, you sam.'

'I'm not Sam, you fool,' Dixon shrieked; this was the worst taunt of all. He took off his glasses and put them in his top jacket pocket.

They faced each other on the floral rug, feet apart and elbows crooked in uncertain attitudes, as if about to begin some ritual of which neither had learnt the cues. 'I'll show you,' Bertrand chimed, and jabbed at Dixon's face. Dixon stepped aside, but his feet slipped and before he could recover Bertrand's fist had landed with some force high up on his right cheekbone. A little shaken, but undismayed, Dixon stood still and, while Bertrand was still off his balance after delivering his blow, hit him very hard indeed on the larger and more convoluted of his ears. Bertrand fell down, making a lot of noise in doing so and dislodging a china figurine from the mantelpiece. It exploded on the tiles of the hearth, emphasizing the silence which fell. Dixon stepped forward, rubbing his knuckles. The impact had hurt them rather. After some seconds, Bertrand began moving about on the floor, but made no attempt to get up. It was clear that Dixon had won this round, and, it then seemed, the whole Bertrand match. He put his glasses on again, feeling good; Bertrand caught his eye with a look of embarrassed recognition. The bloody old towser-faced boot-faced totem-pole on a crap reservation, Dixon thought. 'You bloody old towser-faced boot-faced totem-pole on a crap reservation,' he said.

As if discreetly applauding this terminology, a quiet knocking came at the door. 'Come in,' Dixon said with reflex promptness.

Michie entered. 'Good afternoon, Mr Dixon,' he said, then added politely 'Good afternoon' to the still-prostrate Bertrand, who at this stimulus struggled to his feet. 'I seem to have come at an inconvenient time.'

'Not at all,' Dixon said smoothly. 'Mr Welch is just going.'

Bertrand shook his head, not in contradiction, but apparently to clear it, which interested Dixon. He moved host-like to the door with the departing Bertrand, who went out in silence.

'Good-bye,' Dixon said, then turned to Michie. 'And what can I do for you, Mr Michie?'

Michie's expression, though as usual unreadable, was a new one to Dixon. 'I've come about the special subject,' he said.

'Oh yes. Do sit down.'

'I won't, thanks; I must be on my way in a moment. I just dropped in to tell you that I've been into the matter quite thoroughly with Miss O'Shaughnessy, Miss McCorquodale, and Miss ap Rhys Williams, and we've all finally made up our minds.'

'Good. What conclusion did you come to?'

'Well, I'm sorry to say that all three of the ladies have decided that the thing's rather too formidable for them. Miss McCorquodale's decided to do Mr Goldsmith's Documents, and Miss O'Shaughnessy and Miss ap Rhys Williams are going to do the Professor's subject.'

This announcement pained Dixon: he wanted the three pretty girls to have conquered their objections and opted for his subject because he was so nice and so attractive. He said: 'Oh, well that's rather a pity. What about you, Mr Michie?'

'I've decided that your subject attracts me a good deal, and so I'd like to be put down officially for it, if I may.'

'I see. So I shall just have you.'

'Yes. Just me.'

There was a silence. Dixon scratched his chin. 'Well, I'm sure we shall have some fun with it.'

'I'm sure, too. Well, thank you very much; I'm sorry I barged in like that.'

'Not at all; it was a great help. See you next term, then, Mr Michie.'

'I'm coming to your lecture tonight, of course.'

'What on earth are you going to do that for?'

'The subject interests me, naturally. I think it must interest quite a lot of other people, too.'

'Oh? How do you mean?'

'Everybody I've mentioned it to says they're coming. You should have a very good house, I think.'

'That's a comfort, I must say. Well, I hope you enjoy it.'

'I'm pretty sure I shall. Thanks again. Good luck for tonight.'

'I'll need it. Cheero.'

When Michie had gone, Dixon reflected with some complacency

that he hadn't called him 'sir' once. But how horrible next term was going to be. On the other hand, he was beginning to feel more and more positively that there wasn't going to be a next term as far as he was concerned. Not a University term, anyway.

He fingered his chin again. He'd better shave before he did anything else. After that he'd run up and see if Atkinson was in. His company, and perhaps some of his whisky, were just what Dixon felt he could do with before starting the evening.

21

'I hope it isn't too painful, Dixon,' the Principal said.

Dixon's hand went up involuntarily to his black eye. 'Oh no, sir,' he replied in a light tone. 'I'm surprised it's come up at all, really. It was quite a light knock; didn't even break the skin.'

'On the corner of the wash-hand basin, you said?' another voice asked.

'That's right, Mr Gore-Urquhart. One of these silly things one does occasionally. I dropped my razor, bent down for it, and – bang; there I was reeling about like a heavyweight.'

Gore-Urquhart nodded slowly. 'Most unfortunate,' he said. He looked Dixon up and down from under his heavy brow, and his lips twitched into a pout and back again two or three times. 'If I'd been asked, now,' he went on, 'I'd have said he'd got himself into a fight, eh, Principal?'

The Principal, a small ventricose man with a polished, rosy bald head, gave one of his laughs. These strongly recalled the peals of horrid mirth so often audible in films about murders in castles, and had been known, in the Principal's first few weeks at the College just after the war, to silence the conversations of an entire Common Room. Now, however, nobody even turned his head, and only Gore-Urquhart looked a little uneasy.

The fourth member of the quartet spoke up. 'Well, I hope it won't interfere with your reading from your . . . from your . . .' he said.

'Oh no, Professor,' Dixon said. 'I guarantee I could read that script blindfold, I've been through it so many times.'

Welch nodded. 'It's a good plan,' he said. 'I remember when I first began lecturing, I was silly enough just to write the stuff down and not bother about . . .'

'Have you got anything new to tell us, Dixon?' the Principal asked.

'New, sir? Well, in this sort of . . .'

'I mean it's a subject that's been fairly well worked over, isn't it? I don't know whether it's possible to get a new slant on it these days, but personally I should have thought . . .'

Welch thrust in with 'It's hardly a question, sir, of . . .'

A remarkable duet ensued, the Principal and Welch both going on talking without pause, the one raising his voice in pitch, the other in volume, giving between them the impression of some ambitious verse-speaking effect. Dixon found that he and Gore-Urquhart were staring at each other, while the room began to grow quiet except for the voices of the two contestants. Finally the Principal broke free, and, like an orchestra that has launched a soloist on his cadenza, Welch abruptly fell silent. 'Worth restating in every generation or not,' the Principal concluded.

There now appeared a diversion in the shape of the porter Maconochie with a tray of glasses of sherry. Dixon willed his hand to stay at his side until his three seniors had helped themselves, then let it bear the fullest remaining glass to his lips. The Registrar, who controlled the liquor supply on such occasions, was notorious for cutting it off altogether after the first couple of rounds, except from the Principal and whoever might be talking to him. Dixon knew he couldn't hope to stay in this group much longer and was determined to make the most of it. He felt slightly ill in an indefinable way, but swallowed half his new glassful at one go; it slid warmly down to join the previous three sherries and the half-dozen measures of Bill Atkinson's whisky. In a sense, but only in a sense, he was beginning not to worry about the lecture, which was to start in twenty minutes' time, at six-thirty.

He looked round the crowded Common Room, which seemed to contain everybody he knew or had ever known, apart from his parents. Mrs Welch was a few feet away talking to Johns, for whose presence in this room, normally inadmissible, she must be in some indirect way to blame. Beyond them were Bertrand and Christine, not saying a great deal to each other. Right over by the window Barclay, the Music Professor, was talking earnestly to the Professor of English, no doubt urging on him the necessity of voting for Dixon's removal when the College Council met at the end of the following week. In the other direction the Goldsmiths were laughing at something Beesley had said to them. Elsewhere were figures Dixon barely recognized: economists, medicals, geographers, social scientists, lawyers, engineers, mathematicians, philosophers, readers in Germanic and comparative philology, lektors, lecteurs, lectrices. He felt like going round and notifying each person individually of his preference that they should leave. There were several he'd never seen in his life before, who might be anything from Emeritus Professors of Egyptology to interior decorators waiting to start measuring up for new carpets. One large group was made up of local worthies: a couple of aldermen with their wives, a fashionable clergyman, a knighted physician, all of whom were members of the College Council, and at the edge of the group, Dixon saw with a start, the local composer he'd seen at Welch's arty week-end. He looked round distractedly, but in vain, for the amateur violinist.

After a moment the Principal moved over to the local worthies and addressed some remark to the fashionable clergyman that was received with general laughter, except by the knighted physician, who stared coldly from face to face. Almost at the same time a signal from Mrs Welch drew Welch away and left Dixon with Gore-Urquhart, who now said: 'How long have you been in this game, then, Dixon?'

'Getting on for nine months now. They took me on last autumn.'

'I've a notion you're not too happy in it; am I right?'

'Yes, I think you are right, on the whole.'

'Where's the trouble? In you or in it?'

'Oh, both, I should say. They waste my time and I waste theirs.'

'Mm, I see. It's a waste of time teaching history, is it?'

Dixon resolved not to mind what he said to this man. 'No. Well taught and sensibly taught, history could do people a hell of a lot of good. But in practice it doesn't work out like that. Things get in the way. I don't quite see who's to blame for it. Bad teaching's the main thing. Not bad students, I mean.'

Gore-Urquhart nodded, then shot a quick glance at him. 'This lecture of yours tonight, now. Whose idea was it?'

'Professor Welch's. I could hardly refuse, of course. If it goes well it'll improve my standing here.'

'You're ambitious?'

'No. I've done badly here since I got the job. This lecture might help to save me getting the sack.'

'Here, laddie,' Gore-Urquhart said, and snatched two glasses of sherry from Maconochie's tray as he went towards the group that now included the Principal. Dixon thought perhaps he oughtn't to drink any more – he was already beginning to feel a little splendid – but took the glass that was held out to him and drank from it. 'Why have you come here tonight?' he asked.

'I've evaded your Principal so many times recently that I felt I had to come to this.'

'I can't see why you bother, you know. You're not dependent on the Principal. You're only letting yourself in for a lot of boredom.'

When Gore-Urquhart looked at him again, Dixon had a moment's trouble disposing of a slight spin of the head, caused by the other's out-of-focus face. 'I let myself in for several hours' boredom every day, Dixon. A couple more won't break my back.'

'Why do you stand it?'

'I want to influence people so they'll do what I think it's important they should do. I can't get 'em to do that unless I let 'em bore me first, you understand. Then just as they're delighting in having got me punch-drunk with talk I come back at 'em and make 'em do what I've got lined up for 'em.'

'I wish I could do that,' Dixon said enviously. 'When I'm punch-drunk with talk, which is what I am most of the time, that's when they come at me and make me do what they want me to do.' Apprehension and drink combined to break through another bulkhead in his mind and he went on eagerly: 'I'm the boredom-detector. I'm a finely-tuned instrument. If only I could get hold of a millionaire I'd be worth a bag of money to him. He could send me on ahead into dinners and cocktail-parties and night-clubs, just for five minutes, and then by looking at me he'd be able to read off the boredom-coefficient of any gathering. Like a canary down a mine; same idea. Then he'd know whether it was worth going in himself or not. He could send me in among the Rotarians and the stage crowd and the golfers and the arty types talking about statements of profiles rather than volumes and the musical . . .' He stopped, aware that Gore-Urquhart's large smooth face had tilted over to one side and was being held towards his own. 'Sorry,' he muttered, 'I forgot . . .'

Gore-Urquhart looked him up and down and then covered one eye with a hand, afterwards drawing a finger down the side of his face and smiling slightly. Though it wasn't a smile of ordinary amusement, it wasn't unfriendly either. 'I recognize a fellow sufferer,' he said. Then his manner changed: 'What school did you go to, Dixon, if I may ask you?'

'Local grammar school.'

Gore-Urquhart nodded. The fashionable clergyman and one of the aldermen now came over, filled glasses in their hands, and drew him off to join their group round the Principal. Dixon couldn't help admiring the way in which, without saying or doing anything specific, they established so effortlessly that he himself wasn't expected to accompany them. Then, as he watched incuriously, he saw Gore-Urquhart fall slightly behind his two companions and look across to where the Goldsmiths were standing. Cecil and Beesley were deep in talk and didn't notice Carol catching Gore-Urquhart's eye. An almost imperceptible and quite indecipherable glance passed between them. This puzzled Dixon, of course, and in some way troubled him, but, deciding to ponder about it later, if ever, he drained his glass and went up to Christine and Bertrand. 'Hallo, you two,' he cried gaily. 'Where have you been hiding?'

Christine flashed a look at Bertrand that made him not say

whatever he'd been going to say, and said herself: 'I'd no idea this was going to be such a grand affair. Half the big-wigs in the city must be here.'

'I'd like us to go over to your uncle now, Christine,' Bertrand said. 'There are one or two things I want to discuss with him, if you remember.'

'In a minute, Bertrand; there's plenty of time,' Christine said 'dignantly'.

'No no, there isn't plenty of time; the thing's due to start in about ten minutes, and that isn't plenty of time for what I want to talk about.'

Dixon had noticed that Bertrand always said 'No no' instead of 'No', combining at small outlay a simultaneous lowering and raising of the eyebrows in verbal form. He wished he wouldn't do that. Past Bertrand's head, he could see Carol beginning to edge away from Cecil and Margaret – he noticed her for the first time – in his own direction. Quoting from a film he'd once seen, he said to Christine: 'Better do as he says, lady, otherwise he's liable to kick your teeth in.'

'Run away and play, Dixon.'

'Bertrand, how can you be so rude?'

'Me be so rude? I like that. Me be so rude. What about him? Who the hell does he think he is? Telling you to . . .'

Christine had gone red. 'Have you forgotten what I told you before we came?'

'Look, Christine, I didn't come here to talk to this . . . this fellow, nor about him, I may say. I came here simply and solely to get hold of your uncle, and it's now . . .'

'Why, hallo, Bertie dear,' Carol said behind him. 'I want you. Come over here, will you?'

Bertrand had performed a start of surprise and half-turn in one movement. 'Hallo, Carol, but I was just . . .'

'I shan't keep you a minute,' Carol said, and gripped his arm. 'I'll return him in good condition,' she added over her shoulder to Christine.

'Well . . . hallo, Christine,' Dixon said.

'Oh, hallo.'

'This really is the last time, isn't it?'

'Yes, that's right.'

He felt petulant and self-pitying. 'You don't seem to mind as much as I do.'

She looked at him for a moment, then abruptly turned her head aside, as if he were showing her a photograph in a book of forensic medicine. 'I've done all my minding,' she said. 'I'm not going to do any more now. Neither will you if you've got any sense.'

'I can't help minding,' he said. 'Minding isn't a thing you can do anything about. I can't help going on with it.'

'What's the matter with your eye?'

'Bertrand and I had a fight this afternoon.'

'A fight? He didn't say anything to me about it. What were you fighting about? A fight?'

'He told me to keep off the grass where you were concerned, and I said I wouldn't, so we started fighting.'

'But we agreed . . . You haven't changed your mind about . . . ?'

'No. I just wasn't going to let him tell me what to do, that's all.'

'But fancy having a fight.' She seemed to be repressing a laugh. 'You lost, by the look of you.'

He didn't like that, and remembered her tendency to grin during the hotel tea. 'Not at all. Take a look at Bertrand's ear before you start deciding who won and who lost.'

'Which one?'

'The right. But there probably won't be much to see. The damage was mostly internal, I should think.'

'Did you knock him over?'

'Oh yes, right over. He stayed down for a bit, too.'

'My God.' She stared at him, her full, dry lips slightly apart. A pang of helpless desire made Dixon feel heavy and immovable, as if he were being talked to by Welch. Then he felt that never had he been reminded so clearly of his first meeting with her as in the last couple of minutes, and glared at her.

At this moment of silence, Bertrand suddenly reappeared from behind the wife of one of the aldermen with a quick shuffling movement, rather like a left-arm bowler coming into a batsman's view round the umpire. His face was red; he was obviously almost beside himself with rage, either in its pure form or compounded with some other emotion. Carol followed him, looking inquisitive.

'That's enough of that,' Bertrand said, his voice a choking bay. 'This is just how I expected things to bam.' He caught hold of Christine's arm and pulled her away with some violence. Before moving off, he said to Dixon: 'Right, my lad. This is the finish for you. You'd better start looking for another job. I mean that.' Christine gave Dixon a brief, startled glance over her shoulder as she was virtually frog-marched towards the group that contained her uncle. Carol too looked at Dixon, a speculative look. Then she followed the other two. A loud homicidal-maniac laugh came from the Principal.

Dixon experienced a return of the ill feeling he'd had some minutes before. Then he found his thoughts being blindly swept along by panic. Bertrand must mean what he said; whatever it was that went on in Welch's head, the facts his son had to reveal must surely have a significant influence – and even if they didn't, there were his wife's contributions to add to the scale, that was if she hadn't added them already on her own initiative. Dixon realized he'd been wrong in thinking that the Bertrand-campaign was over and won; the last shot had still to be fired, and he was in the open and unarmed. What he'd warned himself of at the outset had really happened; he'd let himself be carried away, the joy of battle really had robbed him of his discretion and prudence. He was helpless; above all, helpless to prevent that bearded slob from standing there with his hand on Christine's arm, confident, proprietary, victorious. She stood by her boy-friend in an awkward, uncomfortable attitude, even an ungraceful one, but for Dixon's money there could be no more beautiful way for a woman to stand.

'Taking your last look, eh, James?'

At this sudden appearance of Margaret on his blind side, Dixon felt like a man fighting a policeman who sees another approaching on a horse. It dazed him. 'What?' he said.

'You'd better have a good look at her, hadn't you? You won't get another chance.'

'No, I don't suppose I . . .'

'Unless of course you've fixed it to run up to London every so often, just to keep in touch.'

Dixon stared into her face, genuinely surprised, surprised too that Margaret could, at this stage, do anything to surprise him. 'What do you mean?' he asked dully.

'No use pretending, is there? Doesn't take much imagination to see what you're thinking.' The tip of her nose wiggled slightly as she talked, in the way it always did. She stood with her feet apart and her arms crossed on her breast, as Dixon had seen her many times, making small-talk in this room or one of the little teaching-rooms upstairs. She didn't look at all strained, or excited, or ill-at-ease, or annoyed.

Dixon heaved a sigh of weariness before plunging in with the kind of protests and excuses laid down for him by the conventions of this particular pursuit. As he talked, he reflected how easily, by what deft sleight-of-hand, he'd been deprived of his one moral advantage in recent dealings with Margaret: his uninfluenced deci-sion to take no more active interest in Christine. It was a bit rough to be reproached for hankering after what he'd voluntarily turned down. His spirits were so low that he wanted to lie down and pant like a dog: jobless, Christineless, and now grand-slammed in the Margaret game.

With no conclusion reached, their conversation was brought to an end by the drift of the Principal's group towards the door. Gore-Urquhart was apparently deep in talk with Bertrand and Christine. Welch called: 'Ready, Dixon?' With Mrs Welch at his side, he more than ever resembled an old boxer, given to a bit of poaching now and then, standing with his ex-kitchenmaid wife.

'See you in the Hall, Professor,' Dixon called back; then, with a word to Margaret, he hurried out and into the Staff Cloakroom.

Stage-fright was upon him now; his hands were cold and damp, his legs felt like flaccid rubber tubes filled with fine sand, he had difficulty in controlling his breathing. While he was using the lavatory, he began making his Evelyn Waugh face, then abandoned it in favour of one more savage than any he normally used. Gripping his tongue between his teeth, he made his cheeks expand into little hemispherical balloons; he forced his upper lip downwards into an idiotic pout; he protruded his chin like the blade of a shovel. Throughout, he alternately dilated and crossed his eyes. Turning away, he found himself confronted by Gore-Urquhart, allowed his face to collapse, and said: 'Oh, hallo.'

'Hallo, Dixon,' Gore-Urquhart said, walking on past him.

Dixon went to the mirror above the wash-basin and examined his eye. It looked a good many shades brighter than he'd remembered it. In the circumstances, any attempt at smartness of clothes or hair seemed beside the point. He took from a shelf the stolen R.A.F. file that contained his lecture-script and was about to leave when Gore-Urquhart called: 'Hold on a minute, Dixon, will you?'

Dixon stopped and turned. Gore-Urquhart approached and stood gazing at him intently, as if planning a funny sketch of him, in charcoal, perhaps, or ink-wash, to be begun as soon as the lecture was over. After a moment, he said: 'Are you maybe feeling a little nervous, laddie?'

'Very nervous.'

Gore-Urquhart nodded and produced a slim but substantial flask from his ill-fitting clothes. 'Have a swig.'

'Thanks.' Deciding not to bother about coughing, Dixon took a good pull at what was evidently neat Scotch whisky – more evidently than any drink he'd ever had. He coughed wildly.

'Ah, it's good stuff, that. Have another swig.'

'Thanks.' Dixon did exactly as before, then, gasping and wiping his mouth on his sleeve, gave the flask back. 'I'm very grateful for that.'

'It'll do you a power of good. Out of my sherry-cask. Well, we'd best get along if we don't want to keep them waiting.'

The last stragglers were still leaving the Common Room and moving up the stairs. At the stairhead a little group was waiting: the Goldsmiths, Bertrand, Christine, Welch, Beesley, and the other lecturers in the History Department.

'We may as well go up the front, sir,' Bertrand said.

They began moving into the Hall, which was disconcertingly full. The front row of the gallery held an unbroken line of students. There was a loud mixture of conversations.

'Well, give it to them, Jim,' Carol said.

'All the best, old boy,' Cecil said.

'Best of luck, Jim,' Beesley said. They all moved away into their seats.

'Here you go then, laddie,' Gore-Urquhart said in an undertone. 'No need to worry; to hell with all this.' He gripped Dixon's arm and withdrew.

Aware that a shuffling for places was going on behind him, Dixon followed Welch on to the platform. The principal and the fatter of the two aldermen were already there. Dixon found that he felt rather drunk.

22

Welch uttered the preludial blaring sound, cognate with his son's bay, with which he was accustomed to call for silence at the start of a lecture; Dixon had heard students imitating it. A hush gradually fell. 'We are here tonight,' he informed the audience, 'to listen to a lecture.'

While Welch talked, his body swaying to and fro, its upper half more strongly illuminated by the reading-lamp above the lectern, Dixon, so as not to have to listen to what was said, looked furtively round the Hall. It was certainly very full; a few rows at the back were thinly inhabited, but those nearer the front were packed, chiefly with members of Staff and their families and with local people of various degrees of eminence. The gallery, as far as Dixon could see, was also packed; some people were standing up by the rear wall. Dropping his eyes to the nearer seats, Dixon picked out the thinner of the two aldermen, the local composer, and the fashionable clergyman; the titled physician had presumably come for the sherry only. Before he could look further, Dixon's vague recurrent feeling of illness identified itself as a feeling of faintness; a wave of heat spread from the small of his back and seemed to become established in his scalp. On the point of groaning involuntarily, he tried to will himself into feeling all right; only the nervousness, he told himself. And the drink, of course.

When Welch said '. . . Mr Dixon' and sat down, Dixon stood up. His knees began shaking violently, as if in caricature of stage-fright. A loud thunder of applause started up, chiefly, it seemed, from the gallery. Dixon could hear heavily-shod feet being stamped. With some difficulty, he took up his stand at the lectern, ran his eye over his first sentence, and raised his head. The applause died away slightly, enough for sounds of laughter to be heard through it; then it gathered force again, soon reaching a higher level than before, especially as regards the feet-stamping. The part of the audience in the gallery had had its first clear view of Dixon's black eye.

Several heads were being turned in the first few rows, and the Principal, Dixon saw, was staring irritably at the area of disturbance. In his own general unease, Dixon, who could never understand afterwards how he came to do it, produced an excellent imitation of Welch's preludial blaring sound. The uproar, passing the point where it could still be regarded as legitimate applause, grew louder. The Principal rose slowly to his feet. The uproar died down, though not to complete silence. After a pause, the Principal nodded to Dixon and sat down again.

Dixon's blood rushed in his ears, as if he were about to sneeze. How could he stand up here in front of them all and try to talk? What further animal noises would come out of his mouth if he did? He smoothed the edge of his script and began.

When he'd spoken about half a dozen sentences, Dixon realized that something was still very wrong. The murmuring in the gallery had grown a little louder. Then he realized what it was that was so wrong: he'd gone on using Welch's manner of address. In an effort to make his script sound spontaneous, he'd inserted an 'of course' here, a 'you see' there, an 'as you might call it' somewhere else; nothing so firmly recalled Welch as that sort of thing. Further, in a partly unconscious attempt to make the stuff sound right, *i.e.* acceptable to Welch, he'd brought in a number of favourite Welch tags: 'integration of the social consciousness', 'identification of work with craft', and so on. And now, as this flashed into his labouring mind, he began to trip up on one or two phrases, to hesitate, and to repeat words, even to lose his place once so that a ten-second pause supervened. The mounting murmur from the gallery indicated that these effects were not passing unappreciated. Sweating and flushing, he struggled on a little further, hearing Welch's intonation clinging tightly round his voice, powerless for the moment to strip it away. A surge of drunkenness across his brain informed him of the arrival there of the advance-guard of Gore-Urquhart's whisky – or was it only that last sherry? And how hot it was. He stopped speaking, poised his mouth for a tone as different from Welch's as possible, and started off afresh. Everything seemed all right for the moment.

As he talked, he began glancing round the front rows. He saw Gore-Urquhart sitting next to Bertrand, who had his mother on his other side. Christine sat on the far side of her uncle, with Carol next to her, then Cecil, then Beesley. Margaret was at the other end, next to Mrs Welch, but with her glasses catching the light so that he couldn't see whether she was looking at him or not. He noticed that Christine was whispering something to Carol, and seemed slightly agitated. So that this shouldn't put him off, he looked further afield, trying to pick out Bill Atkinson. Yes, there he was, by the central aisle about half-way back. Over the whisky-bottle an hour and a half earlier, Atkinson had insisted, not only on coming to the lecture, but on announcing his intention of pretending to faint should Dixon, finding things getting out of hand in any way, scratch both his ears simultaneously. 'It'll be a good faint,' Atkinson had said in his arrogant voice. 'It'll create a diversion all right. Don't you worry.' Recalling this now, Dixon had to fight down a burst of laughter. At the same moment, a disturbance nearer the platform attracted his attention: Christine and Carol were pushing past Cecil and Beesley with the clear intention of leaving the Hall; Bertrand was leaning over and stage-whispering to them; Gore-Urquhart, half-risen, looked concerned. Flustered, Dixon stopped talking again; then, when the two women had gained the aisle and were making for the door, went on, sooner than he should have done, in a blurred, halting mumble that suggested the extremity of drunkenness. Shifting nervously on his feet, he half-tripped against the base of the lectern and swayed perilously forward. A hum of voices began again from the gallery. Dixon had a fleeting impression of the thinner alderman and his wife exchanging a glance of disapproving comment. He stopped speaking.

When he recovered himself, he found that he'd once more lost his place in mid-sentence. Biting his lip, he resolved not to run off the rails again. He cleared his throat, found his place, and went on in a clipped tone, emphasizing all the consonants and keeping his voice well up at the end of each phase. At any rate, he thought, they'll hear every word now. As he went on, he was for the second time conscious of something being very wrong. It was some moments before he realized that he was now imitating the Principal.

He looked up; there seemed to be a lot of movement in the gallery. Something heavy crashed to the floor up there. Maconochie, who'd been standing near the doors, went out, presumably to ascend and restore order. Voices were now starting up in the body of the Hall; the fashionable clergyman said something in a rumbling undertone; Dixon saw Beesley twisting about in his seat. 'What's the matter with you, Dixon?' Welch hissed.

'Sorry, sir . . . bit nervous . . . all right in a minute . . .'

It was a close evening; Dixon felt intolerably hot. With a shaking hand he poured himself a glass of water from the carafe before him and drank feverishly. A comment, loud but indistinct, was shouted from the gallery. Dixon felt he was going to burst into tears. Should he throw a faint? It would be easy enough. No; everybody would assume he'd succumbed to alcohol. He made a last effort to pull himself together and, the pause now having lasted nearly half a minute, began again, but not in his normal voice. He seemed to have forgotten how to speak ordinarily. This time he chose an exaggerated northern accent as the least likely to give offence or to resemble anybody else's voice. After the first salvo of laughs from the gallery, things quietened down, perhaps under Maconochie's influence, and for a few minutes everything went smoothly. He was now getting on for half-way through.

While he read, things began slowly to go wrong for the third time, but not, as before, with what he was saying or how he was saying it. These things had to do with the inside of his head. A feeling, not so much of drunkenness, but of immense depression and fatigue, was taking almost tangible shape there. While he spoke one sentence, sadness at the thought of Christine seemed to be trying to grip his tongue at the root and reduce him to an elegiac silence; while he spoke another, cries of irritated horror fumbled for admission at his larynx so as to make public what he felt about the Margaret situation; while he spoke the next, anger and fear threatened to twist his mouth, tongue, and lips into the right position for a hysterical denunciation of Bertrand, Mrs Welch, the Principal, the Registrar, the College Council, the College. He began to lose all consciousness of the audience before him; the only member of it he cared about had left and was presumably not going to come back. Well, if this was going to be his last public appearance here, he'd see to it that people didn't forget it in a hurry. He'd do some good, however small, to some of those present, however few. No more imitations, they frightened him too much, but he could suggest by his intonation, very subtly of course, what he thought of his subject and the worth of the statements he was making.

Gradually, but not as gradually as it seemed to some parts of his brain, he began to infuse his tones with a sarcastic, wounding bitterness. Nobody outside a madhouse, he tried to imply, could take seriously a single phrase of this conjectural, nugatory, deluded, tedious rubbish. Within quite a short time he was contriving to sound like an unusually fanatical Nazi trooper in charge of a book-burning reading out to the crowd excerpts from a pamphlet written by a pacifist, Jewish, literate Communist. A growing mutter, half-amused, half-indignant, arose about him, but he closed his ears to it and read on. Almost unconsciously he began to adopt an unnameable foreign accent and to read faster and faster, his head spinning. As if in a dream he heard Welch stirring, then whispering, then talking at his side. He began punctuating his discourse with smothered snorts of derision. He read on, spitting out the syllables like curses, leaving mispronunciations, omissions, spoonerisms uncorrected, turning over the pages of his script like a score-reader following a *presto* movement, raising his voice higher and higher. At last he found his final paragraph confronting him, stopped, and looked at his audience.

Below him, the local worthies were staring at him with frozen astonishment and protest. Of the Staff contingent, the senior members looked up with similar expressions, the junior wouldn't look up at all. The only person in the main body of the Hall who was actually producing sounds was Gore-Urquhart, and the sounds he was producing were of loud skirling laughter. Shouts, whistles, and applause came from the gallery. Dixon raised his hand for silence, but the noise continued. It was too much; he felt faint again, and put his hands over his ears. Through all the noise a louder noise became audible, something between a groan and a bellow. Half-way down the Hall Bill Atkinson, unable at that distance, or unwilling, to distinguish between the scratching and the covering of ears, collapsed full length in the aisle. The Principal rose to his feet, opening and shutting his mouth, but without any quietening effect. He bent and began urgently whispering with the alderman at his side. The people near Atkinson started trying to lift him up, but in vain. Welch began calling Dixon's name. A stream of students entered and made towards the recumbent Atkinson. There were perhaps twenty or thirty of them. Shouting directions and advice to one another, they picked him up and bore him through the doors. Dixon came round in front of the lectern and the uproar died away. 'That'll do, Dixon,' the Principal said loudly, signalling to Welch, but too late.

'What, finally, is the practical application of all this?' Dixon said in his normal voice. He felt he was in the grip of some vertigo, hearing himself talking without consciously willing any words. 'Listen and I'll tell you. The point about Merrie England is that it was about the most un-Merrie period in our history. It's only the home-made pottery crowd, the organic husbandry crowd, the recorder-playing crowd, the Esperanto . . .' He paused and swayed; the heat, the drink, the nervousness, the guilt at last joined forces in him. His head seemed to be swelling and growing lighter at the same time; his body felt as if it were being ground out into its

238

constituent granules; his ears hummed and the sides, top, and bottom of his vision were becoming invaded by a smoky, greasy darkness. Chairs scraped at either side of him; a hand caught at his shoulder and made him stumble. With Welch's arm round his shoulders he sank to his knees, half-hearing the Principal's voice saying above a tumult: '. . . from finishing his lecture through sudden indisposition. I'm sure you'll all . . .'

I've done it now, he managed to think. And without even telling them . . . He drew air into his lungs; if he could push it out again he'd be all right, but he couldn't, and everything faded out in a great roar of wordless voices.

23

'That's all it was,' Beesley said the next morning. 'Quite understandable. But it was that whisky he gave you that really finished you, wasn't it?'

'Yes, I suppose I should have been all right without that. I can't tell Welch that, though.'

'No, of course you can't, Jim. But you can plead nervousness and the heat and so on. After all, you did pass out.'

'They'll never forgive me for wrecking a public lecture, though. And nervousness wouldn't make me imitate Neddy and the Principal, would it?'

They went in through the College gates. Three students hanging about there fell silent and nudged each other as Dixon passed. Beesley said: 'I don't know. You could try it, couldn't you? You've got nothing to lose.'

'No, you're right there, Alfred. Oh, it doesn't matter. I've had it anyway. There's the Christine business too. Welch'll know about that by now.'

'You mustn't be so gloomy. I don't think Welch would take any notice of what Bertram or whatever his bloody name is says to him. It's nothing to do with him what you do to his son's girl-friend, is it?'

'There's the Margaret angle, you see. There's no doubt he'd look at it as letting her down. Which it was, of course, however you look at it.'

Beesley glanced at him without replying; then, as they went into the Common Room, said: 'Don't let it get you down, Jim. See you coffee-time?'

'Yes,' Dixon said absently. His stomach turned over as he recognized Welch's handwriting on a note in his pigeon-hole. He went out and upstairs reading it. Welch felt he ought to let him know, unofficially, that when the Council met next week he would be unable to recommend Dixon's retention on the Staff. He advised Dixon, also unofficially, to wind up his affairs in the district and leave as soon as possible. He would furnish what testimonials he could for any application Dixon might make for a new job, provided it were outside the city. He himself was sorry Dixon had got to leave, because he'd enjoyed working with him. There was a ps. telling Dixon he needn't worry about 'the matter of the bedclothes'; for his part, Welch was prepared to 'consider it settled'. Well, that was decent of him; Dixon felt a slight stab of conscience at having rather let Welch down over the lecture, and a less slight one at having spent so much of his time and energy in hating Welch.

He went into the room he shared with Cecil Goldsmith and stood at the window. The sultriness of the previous few days had passed without thunder and the sky promised hours of sunshine. Alterations were being made to the Physics Laboratory; a lorry had drawn up by the wall, bricks and cement were being unloaded, and the sound of hammering could be heard. He could easily get a schoolteaching job; his old headmaster had told him at Christmas that a senior history post in the school wouldn't be filled until September. He'd write to him and say he'd decided he wasn't cut out for University teaching. But he wouldn't write today, not today.

What was he going to do today? He wandered from the window and picked up a fat and luxurious periodical that lay on Goldsmith's table, the journal of some Italian historical society. Something on the cover caught his eye and he turned to the relevant page. He'd never learnt any Italian, but the name at the head of this article, L. S. Caton, presented no difficulty, nor, after a minute or two, did the general drift of the text, which was concerned with shipbuilding techniques in Western Europe in the later fifteenth century and their influence on something or other. There could be no doubt about it; this article was either a close paraphrase or a translation of Dixon's own original article. At a loss for faces, he drew in his breath to swear, then cackled hysterically instead. So that was how people got chairs, was it? Chairs of that sort, anyway. Oh well, it didn't matter now. But what a cunning old . . . That reminded him. One of the things he'd got to do today was to see Johns and abuse, or even assault, him for his latest piece of treachery. He went out and down the stairs.

Reconstruction of the crime had been easy; by consulting Beesley and Atkinson, Dixon had deduced that Johns must have overheard the other two discussing the Christine tea-date and had taken the first opportunity of passing the news on to his friend and patroness. He could have done this, and so he must have done this; at any rate, Dixon had virtually Bertrand's word for it that Johns was the informer, however he got hold of the information. Hatred lit him up briefly like a neon sign as he tapped at the door of Johns's office and went in.

There was nobody there. Dixon advanced to the desk, where a lot of insurance policies lay. He pondered for a moment; had he done anything to deserve Johns's two betrayals? The decorations added to the face of the composer on the periodical? A harmless joke. The letter from Joe Higgins? A transparent piece of horseplay. Dixon nodded to himself and, clutching up a handful of the insurance policies, stuffed them into his pocket and left.

A few moments later he was descending cautiously into the boiler-house. There seemed to be nobody about. Coal-dust cracked under his feet as he nosed about among the boilers, looking for one in action. There must be one to heat the water for the various cloakrooms. Here it was, smoking vigorously. He picked up some sort of tool from the floor in front of it and shoved the lid aside. The policies burned very quickly and thoroughly; there wouldn't be any sort of trace. He put the lid back and ran up the stairs. Nobody saw him emerge.

What was he going to do now? He'd come up to College with, he realized, nothing very clear in mind, chiefly out of a reluctance to leave Beesley's company. Now he'd got the sack, however, he didn't want to wait about till coffee-time, when moreover he might run into Welch or the Principal. There was really no reason why he should ever come up here again, unless to remove his belongings. Well, that was clearly the next job, and it could be done in one go, because he'd never brought anything to College beyond two or three reference-books and some lecture-notes. He went back up to his room and started getting these together. Working in his home town, he reflected, would mean seeing less of Margaret, but not enough less, because her home and his were only fifteen miles apart. As experience had already proved, that was a reasonable, or not sufficiently unreasonable, journey to make for an evening together at least once a week during vacation-time. And three months of vacation lay just ahead.

On the way out of College, he found himself being approached by a man he didn't quite recognize, but about whose appearance there was something familiar. This man said: 'That was a very good lecture you gave us last night.'

'Michie,' Dixon said. 'You've shaved off your moustache.'

'That's right. Eileen O'Shaughnessy said she was browned-off with it, so I said farewell to it this morning.'

'Good advice, Michie. A great improvement.'

'Thanks. I hope you're fully recovered from your fainting fit or whatever it was?'

'Oh yes, thanks. No permanent injuries.'

'Good. We all enjoyed your lecture.'

'I'm very glad to hear it.'

'It went down like a bomb.'

'I know.'

'Pity you didn't manage to finish it.'

'Yes.'

'Still, we got the main drift.' Michie paused while a group of strangers went by, deluded visitors to the College's Open Week. He went on: 'I say . . . don't mind me asking this, do you? but some of us wondered if you weren't slightly . . . you know . . .'

'Drunk? Yes, I suppose I was, rather.'

'Been a row about it, I suppose? Or haven't they had time to get round to it yet?'

'Oh yes, they've had time.'

'Bad row, was it?'

'Well, yes, as these things go. I've got the push.'

'What?' Michie looked sympathetic, but neither surprised nor indignant. 'That's quick work. Well, I'm really sorry about that. Just over the lecture?'

'No. There'd been one or two other little departmental difficulties before, as you probably know.'

Michie was silent for a moment, then said: 'Some of us'll miss you, you know.'

'That's nice. I shall miss some of you.'

'I'm going home tomorrow, so I'll say good-bye now. I passed all right, I suppose? You can tell me now, can't you? I shan't hear till next week otherwise.'

'Oh yes, all your crowd are through. Drew failed, though. Is he a friend of yours?'

'No, thank God. Very satisfactory, that. Well, good-bye. I suppose I shall be doing Neddy's special subject after all next year.'

'Looks like it, doesn't it?' Dixon put his effects under his left arm and shook hands. 'All the best, then.'

'Same to you.'

Dixon went off down College Road, forgetting to take a last look at the College buildings until too late. He felt almost free of care, which, considering the circumstances, he thought rather impressive of him. He'd go home that afternoon; he'd have gone anyway in a couple of days. He'd come back next week to pick up the last of his stuff, see Margaret, and so on. See Margaret. 'Ooooeeeeyaaa,' he called out to himself, thinking of it. 'Waaaeeeoooghgh.' With his home so near hers, leaving this place wouldn't seem like a move on, but a drift to one side. That was really the worst of it.

He remembered now that this was the day he was to see Catchpole at lunch-time. What could the fellow want? No use wondering about that; the important thing was how to kill time until then. Back at his digs, he bathed his eye, which was beginning

244

to fade a little, though its new colour promised to be just as disfiguring and a good deal less wholesome. A conversation with Miss Cutler about rations and laundry followed; then he had a shave and a bath. While he was in the water, he heard the phone ring, and in a few moments Miss Cutler tapped at the door. 'Are you there, Mr Dixon?'

'Yes, what is it, Miss Cutler?'

'A gentleman on the telephone for you.'

'Who is it?'

'I'm afraid I didn't get the name.'

'Was it Catchpole?'

'Pardon? No, I don't think so. It was longer, somehow.'

'Oh, all right, Miss Cutler. Would you ask him for his number and say I'll ring him in about ten minutes?'

'Right you are, Mr Dixon.'

Dixon dried himself, wondering who this could be. Bertrand with more threats? He hoped so. Johns, having intuited the fate of his insurance policies? Possibly. The Principal, summoning him to an extraordinary meeting of the College Council? No, no, not that.

While he dressed, he thought how nice it was to have nothing he must do. There were compensations for ceasing to be a lecturer, especially that of ceasing to lecture. He put on an old polo sweater to signify his severance of connexions with the academic world. The trousers he wore were the ones he'd torn on the seat of Welch's car; they'd been expertly repaired by Miss Cutler. By the phone he found a pencilled slip in her girlish hand. Though she'd again found the name beyond her, she'd got the number, which, he saw with some surprise, referred to a small village some miles away, in the opposite direction to the Welches'. He didn't know he knew anyone there. A woman's voice answered his call.

'Hallo,' he said, thinking he could write a thesis on the use of the phone in non-business life.

The woman's voice announced her number.

'Have you got a man there?' he asked, feeling a little baffled.

'A man? Who's that speaking?' The tone was hostile.

'My name's Dixon.'

'Oh yes, Mr Dixon, of course. One moment, please.'

There was a brief pause, then a man's voice, the mouth too close to the microphone, said: 'Hallo. That you, Dixon?'

'Yes, speaking. Who's that?'

'Gore-Urquhart here. Got the sack, have you?'

'What?'

'I said, got the sack?'

'Yes.'

'Good. Then I won't have to break a confidence by telling you so. Well, what are your plans, Dixon?'

'I was thinking of going in for schoolteaching.'

'Are you right set on it?'

'No, not really.'

'Good. I've got a job for you. Five hundred a year. You'll have to start at once, on Monday. It'll mean living in London. You accept?'

Dixon found he could not only breathe, but talk. 'What job is it?'

'Sort of private secretarial work. Not much correspondence, though; a young woman does most of that. It'll be mainly meeting people or telling people I can't meet them. We'll go into the details on Monday morning. Ten o'clock at my house in London. Take down the address.' He gave it, then asked: 'Are you all right, now?'

'Yes, I'm fine, thanks. I went to bed as soon as I . . .'

'No, I wasn't inquiring after your health, man. Have you got all the details? You'll be there on Monday?'

'Yes, of course, and thank you very much, Mr . . .'

'Right, then, I'll see you . . .'

'Just a minute, Mr Gore-Urquhart. Shall I be working with Bertrand Welch?'

'Whatever gave you that idea?'

'Nothing; I just gathered he was after a job with you.'

'That's the job you've got. I knew young Welch was no good as soon as I set eyes on him. Like his pictures. It's a great pity he's managed to get my niece tied up with him, a great pity. No use saying anything to her, though. Obstinate as a mule. Worse than her mother. However. I think you'll do the job all right, Dixon. It's not that you've got the qualifications, for this or any other work, but there are plenty who have. You haven't got the disqualifications, though, and that's much rarer. Any more questions?'

'No, that's all, thank you, I . . .'

'Ten o'clock Monday.' He rang off.

Dixon rose slowly from the bamboo table. What noise could he make to express his frenzy of hilarious awe? He drew in his breath for a growl of happiness, but was recalled to everyday affairs by a single hasty chime from the legged clock on the mantelpiece. It was twelve-thirty, the time he was supposed to be meeting Catchpole to discuss Margaret. Should he go? Living in London would make the Margaret problem less important – or rather less immediate. His curiosity triumphed.

Leaving the house, he dwelt with exaltation on Gore-Urquhart's summary of the merit of Bertrand's pictures. He knew he couldn't have been wrong about that. Then his walk lost its spring as he realized that Bertrand, jobless and talentless as he was, still had Christine.

24

Catchpole, already there when Dixon arrived, turned out to be a tall, thin young man in his early twenties who looked like an intellectual trying to pass himself off as a bank-clerk. He got Dixon a drink, apologized to him for taking up his time, and, after a few more preliminaries, said: 'I think the best thing I can do is give you the true facts of this business. Do you agree with that?'

'Yes, all right, but what guarantee have I got that they are the true facts?'

'None, of course. Except that if you know Margaret you can't fail to recognize their plausibility. And before I start, by the way, would you mind enlarging a little on what you said over the phone about her present state of health?'

Dixon did this, managing to hint as he talked at how matters stood between himself and Margaret. Catchpole listened in silence with his eyes on the table, frowning slightly and playing with a couple of dead matches. His hair was long and untidy. At the end he said: 'Thanks very much. That clears things up quite a bit. I'll give you my side of the story now. Firstly, contrary to what Margaret seems to have told you, she and I were never lovers in either the emotional or what I might call the technical sense. That's news to you, I take it?'

'Yes,' Dixon said. He felt curiously frightened, as if Catchpole were trying to pick a quarrel with him.

'I thought it might be. Well, having met her at a political function, I found myself, without quite knowing how, going about with her, taking her to the theatre and to concerts, and all that kind of thing. Quite soon I realized that she was one of these people – they're usually women – who feed on emotional tension. We began to have rows about nothing, and I mean that quite literally.

I was much too wary, of course, to start any kind of sexual relationship with her, but she soon started behaving as if I had. I was perpetually being accused of hurting her, ignoring her, trying to humiliate her in front of other women, and all that kind of thing. Have you had any experiences of that sort with her?'

'Yes,' Dixon said. 'Go on.'

'I can see that you and I have more in common than we thought at first. However, after a particularly senseless row about some remark I'd made when introducing her to my sister, I decided I didn't want any more of that kind of thing. I told her so. There was the most shattering scene.' Catchpole combed his hair back with his fingers and shifted in his seat. 'I'd got the afternoon off and we were out shopping, I remember, and she started shouting at me in the street. It was really dreadful. I felt I couldn't stand another minute of it, so finally, to keep her quiet, I agreed to go round and see her that evening about ten o'clock. When the time came, I couldn't face going. A couple of days later, when I found out about her . . . attempted suicide, I realized that that was the very evening I'd been supposed to go and see her. It gave me a bit of a shock when I realized I could have prevented the whole thing if I'd taken the trouble to put in an appearance.'

'Wait a minute,' Dixon said with a dry mouth. 'She asked me to go round that evening as well. She told me afterwards that you'd come and told her . . .'

Catchpole brushed this aside. 'Are you quite sure? Are you sure it was that evening?'

'Absolutely. I can remember the whole thing quite clearly. As a matter of fact, we'd just been buying the sleeping pills when she asked me to come round, the ones she must have used in the evening. That's how I remember. Why, what's up?'

'She bought some sleeping pills while she was with you?'

'Yes, that's right.'

'When was this?'

'That she bought them? Oh, about midday I suppose. Why?'

Catchpole said slowly: 'But she bought a bottle of pills while she was with me in the afternoon.'

They looked at each other in silence. 'I imagine she forged a prescription,' Dixon said finally.

'We were both supposed to be there, then, and see what we'd driven her to,' Catchpole said bitterly. 'I knew she was neurotic, but not as neurotic as that.'

'It was lucky for her the chap in the room underneath came up to complain about her wireless.'

'She wouldn't have taken a risk like that. No, this pretty well confirms what I've always thought. Margaret had no intention of committing suicide, then or at any other time. She must have taken some of the pills before we were due to arrive – not enough to kill her of course – and waited for us to rush in and wring our hands and see to her and reproach ourselves. I don't think there can be any doubt of that. She was never in any danger of dying at all.'

'But there's no proof of that,' Dixon said. 'You're just assuming that.'

'Don't you think I'm right? Knowing what you must know about her?'

'I don't know what to think, honestly.'

'But can't you see . . . ? Isn't it logical enough for you? It's the only explanation that fits. Look, try to remember; did she say anything about how many pills she took, what the fatal dose was, anything like that?'

'No, I don't think so. I just remember her saying she was holding on to the empty bottle all the time she . . .'

'The empty bottle. There were two bottles. That's it. I'm satisfied now. I was right.'

'Have another drink,' Dixon said. He felt he must get away from Catchpole for a moment, but while he was standing at the bar he found he couldn't think, all he could do was to try vainly to get his thoughts into order. He hadn't yet recovered from the ordinary basic surprise at finding that a stranger knew very well someone he knew very well; one intimacy, he felt, ought to rule out any others. And as for Catchpole's theory . . . he couldn't believe it. Could he believe it? It didn't seem the kind of theory to which belief or disbelief could be attached.

As soon as he'd rejoined him with the drinks, Catchpole said: 'You're not still unconvinced, I hope?' He swayed about in his chair with a kind of unstable exultation. 'The empty bottle. But there were two bottles, and she only used one. How do I know? Do you imagine she'd have failed to tell you she'd used two if she had used two? No, she forgot to tell a lie there. She thought it wouldn't matter. She couldn't predict my getting hold of you in this fashion. I can't blame her for that: even the best planner can't think of everything. She'd have checked up, of course, that she'd be in no danger with one bottle. Perhaps two bottles wouldn't have killed her, either, but she wasn't taking any risks.' He picked up his drink and put half of it down. 'Well, I'm extremely grateful to you for doing this for me. I'm completely free of her now. No more worrying about how she is, thank God. That's worth a great deal.' He gazed at Dixon with his hair falling over his brow. 'And you're free of her too, I hope.'

'You didn't ever mention the question of marriage to her, did you?'

'No, I wasn't fool enough for that. She told you I did, I suppose?'

'Yes. And you didn't go off to Wales with a girl around that time either?'

'Unfortunately not. I went to Wales, yes, but that was for my firm. They don't provide their representatives with girls to go away with, more's the pity.' He finished his drink and stood up, his manner quietening. 'I hope I've removed your suspicions of me. I've been very glad to meet you, and I'd like to thank you for what you've done.' He leaned forward over Dixon and lowered his voice further. 'Don't try to help her any more; it's too dangerous for you. I know what I'm talking about. She doesn't need any help either, you know, really. The best of luck to you. Good-bye.'

They shook hands and Catchpole strode out, his tie flapping. Dixon finished his drink and left a couple of minutes later. He strolled back to the digs through the lunch-time crowds. All the facts seemed to fit, but Margaret had fixed herself too firmly in his life and his emotions to be pushed out of them by a mere recital of facts. Failing some other purgative agent than facts, he could foresee himself coming to disbelieve this lot altogether.

Miss Cutler provided lunch, for those who asked for it, at one o'clock. He'd planned to take advantage of this and catch a train home just after two. Entering the dining-room, he encountered Bill Atkinson sitting at the table reading a new number of the wrestling periodical to which he subscribed. He looked up at Dixon and, as sometimes happened, addressed a remark to him. 'Just had your popsy through on the blower,' he said.

'Oh God. What did she want?'

'Don't say "Oh God".' He frowned threateningly. 'I don't mean the one that gets me down, the one that's always chucking dummies, I mean the other one, the one you say belongs to the bearded sportsman.'

'Christine?'

'Yes. Christine,' Atkinson said, contriving to make the name sound like a term of abuse.

'What did she want, Bill? This might be important.'

Atkinson turned to the front page of his journal, where two Laocoöns were interlocked. He indicated that the conversation was still in existence by saying: 'Wait a minute.' After reading attentively something he'd written in the margin, he added in a wounding tone: 'I didn't get all of it, but the main thing is her train goes at one-fifty.'

'What, today? I heard she wasn't going for a few days yet.'

'I can't help what you heard. I'm telling you what I heard. She said she had some news for you that she couldn't tell me over the old phone, and that if you wanted to see her again you could see her off on this one-fifty caper. It was up to you, she said. She seemed a bit set on the idea that it was up to you, but don't ask me what she meant by it, because she didn't let on. She did say she'd "understand" if you didn't come. Don't ask me to translate

252

that, either.' He added that the train referred to was leaving, not from the main city station, but from the smaller one near Welch's house. Some trains not originating from the city stopped at this station on their way towards London.

'I'd better get moving, then,' Dixon said, making calculations.

'You had. I'll tell the bag you won't be wanting your lunch. Go and get on that bus.' Atkinson lowered his face towards his paper.

Dixon ran out into the street. He felt as if he'd been hurrying all his life. Why wasn't she getting a train from the city station? There was an excellent one to London at three-twenty, he knew. What was her news? At any rate, he had some for her; two lots, in fact. Did her unexpected departure mean that she and Bertrand had had another row? A bus was due to turn up College Road between one-ten and one-fifteen. It was that now. The next was at one thirty-five or so. Hopeless. He ran faster. No, she wouldn't have left just because of a row. He'd stake anything on her not being the type to take a revenge of that sort for a thing of that sort. Oh, hell, her news was probably just that 'Uncle Julius' was going to offer him a job. She wouldn't have counted on his having heard so quickly. Would she have asked him to come all this way just to tell him that? Or was it all just an excuse for seeing him again? But why should she want to do that?

He suddenly bounded aside into the road, where, some yards away, a large taxi-like car was waiting in a side-street to insert itself in the further stream of traffic. Dixon cut through the nearer stream, bawling 'Taxi. Taxi.' Just what he wanted. In a moment he was able to make for the far pavement, but the taxi simultaneously drove out into the main road and began to gather speed away from him. 'Taxi. Taxi.' He was nearly there when the face of the Principal's wife, wearing a hat like a biretta, appeared at the back window, frowning at him from what had looked like an empty rear compartment. The taxi was clearly not a taxi, but the Principal's car. Was the Principal in it too? Dixon veered away through an open gate into someone's front garden, where he knelt for a minute behind the hedge. Was it really so important for him to meet Christine at the station? Wouldn't he be able to get in touch with her afterwards through 'Uncle Julius'? Had he still got the piece of paper with her phone number on it?

A rapping on glass made him turn round. An old lady and a big parrot were glaring at him from a ground-floor window. He bowed deeply, then remembered his bus and ran out on to the pavement. A couple of hundred yards away a bus was coming slowly up the hill from the city. It was too far off for him to be able to read its destination screen, and in any case his exertions had misted his glasses over. But it must be the one and he must get it. He sensed, as far as he could sense anything at the moment, that something would go badly wrong if he failed to turn up at the station, that something he wanted would be withdrawn. He began running even faster, so that people began to skip out of his way and look at him with wondering resentment. The bus, unable for the moment to begin its turn into College Road, was halted in mid-traffic and was, he could now see, his bus. He ran steadily towards the corner of College Road, but the bus began moving again and reached it before him. When he next saw the bus, it was halted about fifty yards away up College Road, and someone had just got on.

Dixon broke into a frenzied, lung-igniting sprint, while the conductor watched him immobile from the platform. When he was half-way to the bus, this official rang the bell, the driver let in the clutch, and the wheels began to turn. Dixon found he was even better at running than he'd thought, but when the gap between man and bus had narrowed to perhaps five yards, it began to widen rapidly. Dixon stopped running and favoured the conductor, who was still watching unemotionally, with the best-known obscene gesture. At once the conductor rang the bell again and the bus stopped abruptly. Dixon hesitated for a moment, then trotted lightly up to the bus and boarded it with some diffidence. He found himself unwilling to meet the eye of the conductor, who now said admiringly 'Well run, wacker' and rang the bell for the third time.

Dixon gasped out a question about the bus's time of arrival at the station, which was where it terminated its run, got a civil but evasive answer, spent a few moments beating down the stares of the nearby passengers, and climbed effortfully to the top deck. There he made his rebounding way to the front seat and collapsed into it without being able to afford the breath to groan. He began swallowing the thick burning substance that filled his mouth and throat, panted energetically for a time, and tremulously took out his packet of small cigarettes and his matches. After reading the joke on the back of the matchbox a few times and laughing at it, he lit a cigarette; this was the only action he could take for the moment. He looked out of the window; the road unfolded itself in front of him, and he couldn't help feeling some sort of exhilaration, especially at the brightness of the landscape under the sun. Beyond the lines of green-tiled semi-detached villas open fields were already appearing, and through some trees he could see a gleam of water.

Christine had said that she'd 'understand' if he failed to turn up to see her off. What did that mean? Did it mean that she 'understood' that his commitments with Margaret would have decided him not to come? Or had it some vaguely unwelcome overtone, implying that she'd 'understand' that the whole thing between them now appeared to him as a romantic mistake, Margaret or no Margaret? He couldn't allow Christine to escape him today; if she did he might not see her again at all. Not at all; that was a disagreeable phrase. Suddenly his face altered, seeming to become all nose and glasses; the bus had moved up behind a lorry slowly drawing along an elaborate trailer, which had a notice on it recommending caution and saying how many feet long it was. A smaller notice adduced further grounds for caution in the elliptic form: *Air brakes*. Lorry, trailer, and bus began moving, at a steady twelve miles an hour, round what gave firm promise of being a long series of bends. With difficulty Dixon snatched his gaze from the back of the trailer and, to fortify himself, began thinking about what Catchpole had said to him about Margaret.

He realized at once that his mind had been made up as soon as he decided to make this journey. For the first time he really felt that it was no use trying to save those who fundamentally would rather not be saved. To go on trying would not merely be to yield to pity and sentimentality, but wrong and, to pursue it to its conclusion, inhuman. It was all very bad luck on Margaret, and probably derived, as he'd thought before, from the anterior bad luck of being sexually unattractive. Christine's more normal, *i.e.* less unworkable, character no doubt resulted, in part at any rate, from having been lucky with her face and figure. But that was simply that. To write things down as luck wasn't the same as writing them off as non-existent or in some way beneath consideration. Christine was still nicer and prettier than Margaret, and all the deductions that could be drawn from that fact should be drawn: there was no end to the ways in which nice things are nicer than nasty ones. It had been luck, too, that had freed him from pity's adhesive plaster; if Catch-pole had been a different sort of man, he, Dixon, would still be wrapped up as firmly as ever. And now he badly needed another dose of luck. If it came, he might yet prove to be of use to somebody.

The conductor now appeared and negotiated with Dixon about his ticket. When this was over, he said: 'One forty-three we're due at the station. I looked it up.'

'Oh. Shall we be on time, do you think?'

'Couldn't say, I'm sorry. Not if we keep crawling behind this Raf contraption we shan't, I shouldn't think. Train to catch?'

'Well, I want to see someone who's getting the one-fifty.'

'Shouldn't build on it if I were you.' He lingered, no doubt to examine Dixon's black eye.

'Thanks,' Dixon said dismissively.

They entered a long stretch of straight road, with a slight dip in the middle so that every yard of its empty surface was visible. Far ahead an emaciated brown hand appeared from the lorry's cab and made a writhing, beckoning movement. The driver of the bus ignored this invitation in favour of drawing to a gradual halt by a bus-stop outside a row of thatched cottages. The foreshortened bulks of two old women dressed in black waited until the bus was quenched of all motion before clutching each other and edging with sidelong caution out of Dixon's view towards the platform. In a moment he heard their voices crying unintelligibly to the conductor, then activity seemed to cease. At least five seconds passed; Dixon stirred elaborately at his post, then twisted himself about looking for anything that might have had a share in causing this caesura in his journey. He could detect nothing of this kind. Was the driver slumped in his seat, the victim of syncope, or had he suddenly got an idea for a poem? For a moment longer the pose prolonged itself; then the picture of sleepy rustic calm was modified by the fairly sudden emergence from a cottage some yards beyond of a third woman in a lilac costume. She looked keenly towards the bus and identified it without any obvious difficulty, then approached with a kind of bowed shuffle that suggested the movements of a serviceman towards the pay-table. This image was considerably reinforced by her hat, which resembled a Guardsman's peaked cap that had been strenuously run over and then dyed cerise. Indeed, it was possible that the old bitch – a metallic noise came from the back of Dixon's throat when he saw her smile of self-admiration at having caught her bus – had actually found what was to become her hat lying in the road outside her nasty little cottage after a military exercise, the legacy of some skylarking lout in the carrier platoon, from whose head it had fallen under the tracks and wheels of an entire battalion.

The bus nosed its prudential way on to the crown of the road, and the gap between it and the lorry began to diminish. Dixon found that his whole being had become centred in the matter of the bus's progress; he couldn't be bothered any longer to wonder what Christine would say to him if he got there in time, nor what he'd do if he didn't. He just sat there on the dusty cushions, galvanized by the pitchings of the bus into the appearance of seismic laughter, sweating stealthily in the heat and the apprehension – thank God he hadn't been drinking – stretching his face in a fresh direction at each overtaking car, each bend, each motiveless circumspection of the driver.

The bus was now resolutely secured again behind the trailer, which soon began to reduce speed even further. Before Dixon could cry out, before he'd time to guess what was to happen, the lorry and trailer had moved off to the side into a lay-by and the bus was travelling on alone. Now was the time, he thought with reviving hope, for the driver to start making up some of the time he must have lost. The driver, however, was clearly unable to assent to this diagnosis. Dixon lit another small cigarette, jabbing with the match at the sandpaper as if it were the driver's eye. He had, of course, no idea of the time, but estimated that they must, by now, have covered five of the eight or so miles to their destination. Just then the bus rounded a corner and slowed abruptly, then stopped. Making a lot of noise, a farm tractor was laboriously pulling, at right angles across the road, something that looked like the springs of a giant's bed, caked in places with earth and decked with ribbon-like grasses. Dixon thought he really would have to run downstairs and knife the drivers of both vehicles; what next? what next? What actually would be next: a masked hold-up, a smash, floods, a burst tyre, an electric storm with falling trees and meteorites, a diversion, a low-level attack by Communist aircraft, sheep, the driver stung by a hornet? He'd choose the last of these, if consulted. Hawking its gears, the bus crept on, while every few yards troupes of old men waited to make their quivering way aboard.

As the traffic thickened slightly towards the town, the driver added to his hypertrophied caution a psychopathic devotion to the interests of other road-users; the sight of anything between a removal-van and a junior bicycle halved his speed to four miles an hour and sent his hand, Dixon guessed, flapping in a slow-motion St Vitus' dance of beckonings and wavings-on. Learners practised reversing across his path; gossiping knots of loungers parted leisurely at the touch of his reluctant bonnet; toddlers reeled to retrieve toys from under his just-revolving wheels. Dixon's head switched angrily to and fro in vain search for a clock; the inhabitants of this mental, moral, and physical backwater, devoting as they had done for years their few waking moments to the pursuit of offences against chastity, were too poor, and were also too mean . . . Dixon, seeing the hulk of the railway station thirty yards off, returned painfully to reality and rattled along the aisle to the stairs. Before the bus had reached the station stop he plunged down, out, across the road, and into the booking-hall. The clock over the ticket-office pointed to one forty-seven. At once the minute hand stepped one pace onward. Dixon flung himself at the barrier. A hard-faced man confronted him.

'Which platform for London, please?'

The man looked at him appraisingly, as if trying to gauge in advance his fitness to hear a more than usually improper joke. 'Bit early, aren't you?'

'Eh?'

'Next to London's eight-seventeen.'

'Eight-seventeen?'

'No restaurant car.'

'What about the one-fifty?'

'No one-fifty. Haven't got it mixed up with the one-forty, by any chance?'

Dixon swallowed. 'I think I must have done,' he said. 'Thanks.'

'Sorry, George.'

Nodding mechanically, Dixon turned away. Bill Atkinson must have made a mistake in taking down Christine's message. But it wasn't like Atkinson to make mistakes of that sort. Perhaps it had been Christine who'd made the mistake. It didn't really matter. He walked slowly to the entrance and stood looking out from the shadows at the little sunlit square. He still had his job. And it wouldn't be very difficult to get in touch with Christine. It was only that he felt it would be too late when he did. But, anyway, he'd met her and talked to her a few times. Thank God for that.

As he watched, wondering what to do next, he caught sight of a car with a damaged wing moving uncertainly round a Post Office van. Something about this car held Dixon's attention. It began to crawl towards him, roaring like a bulldozer. The roar was cut off by a spine-tingling snort of cogs and the car froze in its tracks. A tallish blonde girl wearing a wine-coloured costume and carrying a mackintosh and a large suitcase got out and began hurrying towards the spot where Dixon stood.

Dixon skipped out of sight behind a pillar, as best he could under the impact of what must surely be a lesion of the diaphragm. How could he, of all people, have ignored the importance of Welch's car-driving habits?

25

Another frenzy of mechanical rage outside told him that Welch
was still at the wheel. Good; perhaps he was under orders to return
without delay. Dixon had no feelings or thoughts beyond the
immediate situation. He heard Christine's steps approaching and
tried to press himself back into the pillar. Her feet took a few paces
on the boards of the entrance-hall; she came into view four or five
feet away, turned her head, and saw him at once. Her face broke
into a smile of what seemed to him pure affection. 'You got my
message, then,' she said. She looked ridiculously pretty.

'Come here, Christine, quickly.' He drew her into the shelter
of his pillar. 'Just a minute.'

She stared about her and then at him. 'But we ought to be
running up on to the platform. My train's nearly due.'

'Your train's gone. You'll have to wait for the next. At least the
next.'

'That clock says I've got one more minute. I can just . . .'

'No, it's gone, I tell you. It went at one-forty.'

'It couldn't have done.'

'It could and did. I asked the man.'

'But Mr Welch said it went at one-fifty.'

'Oh, he did, did he? That explains everything. He was wrong
about that, you see.'

'Are you sure? Why are we hiding? Are we hiding?'

Ignoring her, his hand unnoticed on her arm, Dixon leant carefully past her. Welch was now broadside-on across the main exit
from the square. 'Right, well we'll just give the bloody old fool
time to get clear, and then we'll go and have a drink.' He would
begin with an octuple whisky. 'You've had lunch, I suppose?'

'Yes, but I could hardly eat a thing.'

'Not like you, that. Well, I haven't had any, so we'll have some together. I know a hotel not far from here. I used to go there with Margaret in the old days.'

They left Christine's case in the luggage-office and walked out into the square. 'A good thing old Welch didn't insist on putting you on the train,' Dixon said.

'Yes . . . Actually I was the one who insisted.'

'I don't blame you.' Dixon's physical discomfort grew steadily at the thought of Christine's 'news', now nearing revelation. He wanted to bet himself it would be bad so that he might stand a chance of its being good. His head, and an inaccessible part of his back, itched.

'I wanted to get away as quickly as I could from the whole bunch of them. I couldn't bear any of them for another moment. A fresh one arrived last night.'

'A fresh one?'

'Yes. Mitchell or some such name.'

'Oh, I know. You mean Michel.'

'Do I? I picked the first train I could get.'

'What's happened? That you wanted to tell me.' He tried to force his spirits down, to expect nothing but unexpected and very nasty nastiness.

She looked at him, and he again noticed that the whites of her eyes were a very light blue. 'I've finished with Bertrand.' She spoke as if of a household detergent that had proved unsatisfactory.

'Why? For good?'

'Yes. Do you want to hear about it?'

'Come on.'

'You remember me and Carol Goldsmith leaving your lecture in the middle yesterday?'

Dixon understood, and felt breathless. 'I know. She told you something, didn't she? I know what she told you.'

They stopped walking involuntarily. Dixon put out his tongue at an old woman who was staring at them. Christine said: 'You knew about Bertrand and her all the time, didn't you? I knew you did.' She looked as if she were going to laugh.

'Yes. What made her tell you?'

'Why didn't you tell me?'

'I couldn't. It wouldn't have done me any good. What made Carol tell you?'

'She hated him for taking her for granted. I didn't mind what he'd done before he started going about with me, but it was wrong of him to try to keep us both on a string, Carol and me. She said he asked her to come away with him the night we all went to the theatre. He was quite sure she would. She said she began by hating me and then she saw the way he was treating me, things like the way he behaved at the sherry thing. Then she saw he was the one to blame, not me.'

She stood with her shoulders a little hunched, saying all this quickly and with embarrassment, her back to a shop-window full of brassières, corsets, and suspender-belts. The lowered blind shadowed her face as she looked almost slyly at him, possibly to see whether she'd said enough to satisfy his curiosity.

'A bit noble of her, wasn't it? Bertrand won't look at her after this.'

'Oh, she doesn't want him to. I gather . . .'

'Well?'

'I sort of gathered from what she said that there's someone else in the background now. I don't know who.'

Dixon was pretty sure he did; the last thread was untangled. He took Christine's arm and walked off with her. 'That's enough,' he said.

'There's a lot more about what he told her about . . .'

'Later.' A leer of happiness suffused Dixon's face. He said: 'I think you might like to hear this. I am going to have nothing more to do with Margaret. Something's come up – never mind what for now – which means I needn't bother with her any more.'

'What, you mean you're absolutely : . . ?'

'I'll tell you all about it later, I promise. Don't let's think about it now.'

'All right. But it is genuine, isn't it?'

'Of course, perfectly genuine.'

'Well then, in that case . . .'

'That's right. Tell me: what are you going to do this afternoon?'

'I suppose I shall have to go back to London, shan't I?'

'Do you mind if I come with you?'

'What's all this?' She pulled at his arm until he looked at her. 'What's going on? There's something else, isn't there? What is it?'

'I've got to find somewhere to live.'

'Why? I thought you lived somewhere in this part of the world.'

'Didn't Uncle Julius tell you about my new job?'

'For goodness' sake tell me about this properly, Jim. Don't tease me.'

While he explained, he pronounced the names to himself: Bayswater, Knightsbridge, Notting Hill Gate, Pimlico, Belgrave Square, Wapping, Chelsea. No, not Chelsea.

'I knew he had something up that sleeve of his,' Christine was saying. 'I didn't know that'd be it, though. I hope you'll be able to put up with him. Couldn't be better, could it? I say, there won't be any difficulty about you leaving your job with the University here, will there?'

'No, I don't think so.'

'What job is it, by the way? The one he's given you?'

'The one Bertrand thought he was going to get.'

Christine began laughing noisily and blushing at the same time. Dixon laughed too. He thought what a pity it was that all his faces were designed to express rage or loathing. Now that something had happened which really deserved a face, he'd none to celebrate it with. As a kind of token, he made his Sex Life in Ancient Roman face. Then he noticed something ahead of them and slowed in his walk. He nudged Christine. 'What's the matter?' she asked.

'See that car?' It was Welch's, parked slightly nearer one kerb than the other, outside a teashop with green linen curtains and copper pots on the window-sills. 'What's it doing there?'

'He's picking up Bertrand and the others, I suppose. Bertrand said he wasn't going to have lunch in the same house with me after what I said to him. Hurry up, Jim, before they come out.'

Just as they drew level with the shop-window, the door opened and a crowd of Welches came out and blocked the pavement. One of them was clearly the effeminate writing Michel, on stage at last just as the curtain was about to ring down. He was a tall pale young man with long pale hair protruding from under a pale corduroy cap. Sensing the approach of passers-by, the whole group, with the natural exception of Welch himself, began automatically shifting about out of the way. Dixon squeezed Christine's arm encouragingly and walked up to them. 'Excuse me,' he said in a fruity comic-butler voice.

On Mrs Welch's face appeared an expression of imminent vomiting; Dixon inclined his head indulgently to her. (He remembered something in a book about success making people humble, tolerant, and kind.) The incident was almost closed when he saw that not only were Welch and Bertrand both present, but Welch's fishing-hat and Bertrand's beret were there too. The beret, however, was on Welch's head, the fishing-hat on Bertrand's. In these guises, and standing rigid with popping eyes, as both were, they had a look of being Gide and Lytton Strachey, represented in waxwork form by a 'prentice hand. Dixon drew in breath to denounce them both, then blew it all out again in a howl of laughter. His steps faltered; his body sagged as if he'd been knifed. With Christine tugging at his arm he halted in the middle of the group, slowly doubling up like a man with the stitch, his spectacles misting over with the exertion of it, his mouth stuck ajar in a rictus of agony. 'You're . . .' he said. 'He's . . .'

The Welches withdrew and began getting into their car. Moaning, Dixon allowed Christine to lead him away up the street. The whinnying and clanging of Welch's self-starter began behind them, growing fainter and fainter as they walked on until it was altogether overlaid by the other noises of the town and by their own voices.

read more 🄟

PENGUIN ESSENTIALS

The Penguin Essentials are some of the twentieth-century's most important books. When they were first published they changed the way we thought about literature and about life. And they have remained vital reading ever since. These new, stylish editions remind readers that once upon a time each book in the Essentials series was the only book worth being seen with.

Lucky Jim by Kingsley Amis

Junky by William S. Burroughs

In Cold Blood by Truman Capote

Heart of Darkness by Joseph Conrad

The Diary of a Nobody by George and Weedon Grossmith

The Thin Man by Dashiell Hammett

Three Men in a Boat by Jerome K. Jerome

Dubliners by James Joyce

The Periodic Table by Primo Levi

The Prime of Miss Jean Brodie by Muriel Spark

Mrs Dalloway by Virginia Woolf